FLORENCE NIGHTINGALE:
A LIGHT IN DARKEST CRIMEA

ALSO BY WENDY LOUISE BARDSLEY

FICTION

The Other Concerto

Jupiter & Passage to Osiris

Branwell Bronte's Creation

The Passions of Mary Wollstonecraft

William Wordworth: A Conflict of Love

The Troubled Mind of Mary Shelley

NON-FICTION

Introducing Information Technology

ADULT POETRY

Amphitheatre

Steel Wings

Solving Atlantis

Selected Poems

CHILDREN'S POETRY

The Imaginator

ANTHOLOGIES

An Enduring Flame: The Bronte Story in Poetry and Photographs

Poetry In The Parks: The National Parks of England and
Wales in Poetry and Photographs

Co-author: Journeys, Poetry and Literacy for the
National Curriculum Key St 3/4

Florence Nightingale:
A Light in Darkest Crimea

Wendy Louise Bardsley

methuen

FLORENCE NIGHTINGALE:
A LIGHT IN DARKEST CRIMEA

First published by Methuen in 2022

1

Methuen
Orchard House
Railway Street
Slingsby
York YO62 4AN

A CIP catalogue record for this book is available from
the British Library

ISBN: 978 0 413 77868 0

Typeset by SX Composing DTP, Rayleigh, Essex
Printed and bound in Great Britain by Clays Ltd, Elcograf S.p.A.

www.methuen.co.uk

For Serving Soldiers Everywhere.

CHAPTER I

10, South Street, Mayfair 1881

A MEETING OF MINDS

"The world is put back by the death of every one who has to sacrifice the development of his or her peculiar gifts to conventionality."

(Florence Nightingale.)

Florence Nightingale had left Crimea a long time ago and was now living in Mayfair, weak and tired. As for the future, she could not think about that. But she hadn't finished her work, her knowledge and experience were being used to help the suffering and infirm. There was much to write about and teach. She considered what she had learned in her time at Scutari hospital. - Let there be good, clean hospitals for the sick and dying, the best care possible delivered through sheer hard work and undaunted effort. All that was vital! And the statistics shown through her charts and graphs had helped answer complicated questions that might otherwise be dwelt upon endlessly without resolution. But she must always take to her bed. Her whole body was in pain, and it would not leave her. She lived with the pain, just like the soldiers who had suffered serious injuries or lost their limbs in war, or sometimes even their minds.

At 10, South Street, in London, her home since the age of 45, she felt still and remote from what mattered. The energy had left her limbs and there were days when the over-familiar room seemed to close on her like a vice ready to crush her. At such times she would breathe in deeply, raise herself up and write, or else bend her head in prayer: *"My soul is weary with sorrow: strengthen me according to thy word."*

The people of Westminster knew Florence Nightingale was ill, but "The Lady with the Lamp" liked her privacy and people left her alone. Settled in London's West End, she was eager as ever to answer her calling and continued to do so, but now she answered it through writing instead of nursing and spread what she knew through publication and statistical analysis, enriched by her knowledge and what she could offer the world, and there was great satisfaction in that. What did ordinary citizens understand about the sick and dying in wartime, she asked herself, the dreadful wounds inflicted on soldiers, the wretched music of a reluctant soul as it left the body before entering the eternal silence? Soldiers were brave and offered their lives to their country, but need they suffer as they did when they were wounded? More than that, need they *die*? Questions. Questions. There was so much to do. Perhaps her knowledge of statistics and their use would help bring forth the reforms she urgently longed for. Facts must be shown for what they were and believed in for only then could they be trusted.

She had loathed the constant unnecessary deaths at Scutari. Many of them were not suffered on the battlefield, but occurred instead in hospitals through unhealthy conditions and poor sanitation. Sick men might be as needful as little children when seriously wounded and would reach for a nurse's hand in the worst of their pain. A touch, a word, could help them find peace in their broken, desolate state. And what joy there was in their faces when good nourishing soup was put into their mouths. Some days she felt the world was a dark savage wilderness, lost and unloved, at such times she would take to her bed and ask for God's forgiveness for her anger.

Her room on South Street was spacious and airy, and when she felt strong she could look through her window to watch people passing on warm sunny days or in cold wet weather like today at the end of November. People were alighting from carriages, talking and laughing, hurrying on with their lives, far from the blood and horror of war, still alive in her memory, where countless numbers of men, sick and bloody from Crimea, had been carried ashore to the barracks hospital moaning with pain. And she and her nurses had entered that screaming darkness, away from the comforts they had known, the accustomed love they had enjoyed at home with their families. A cold chill ran through her. Words could never describe how it was, the break with sanity at the sound of surgeons sawing off limbs of previously able-bodied men with nothing to alleviate their pain, the very sounds of hell coming from their throats. They were fine, dedicated soldiers, men who had fought on the battlefields of Balaclava, Inkerman and others, many of them were young and had never known life without war. Scutari hospital had been desperately overcrowded and the beds were so close it was hard for a nurse to walk between them, but she and her nurses had assisted the wounded again and again in their pain. Decent food in their stomachs, freshly washed pillows and sheets, their wounds cleaned and bandaged, brought them some relief. It was a terrible, sometimes nauseating business, but nursing had been her calling and she felt that calling in her bones. Tired and sick, she'd returned to England attempting to fight her illness, but her limbs hurt too often and there were days she could scarcely take a breath. Here in Mayfair, visitors came and went, but she could not endure much company. Her work in Scutari had drained her and however she tried she could not replenish her strength and constantly needed to rest. Was there nothing left of her spirit, she asked herself, other than what she could find to give to her pen?

Elizabeth Butler sat on the chaise longue waiting, quiet, dignified and content. 'Thank you for letting me see it,' said Florence, turning to look at her at last, and then to the painting, large and grand against the wall. 'You are kind.' Florence's eyes searched the soldiers in the picture, bloody bandages falling from their wounds, their bodies bent and broken as they waited with their companions. The painting depicted soldiers from the Grenadier Guards in the time of the Crimean War struggling to stand for the roll call with their regiment. 'Sheer honesty,' Florence whispered, finding her chair and sitting down slowly. 'Truth can make us ashamed.' The painting she gazed at was indeed truthful. War paintings rarely were, as more often, they were painted by men celebrating victory. She grimaced at the sight and sighed. 'Hardly what the government wants to see,' she murmured. 'You are brave to paint it.'

'Yes,' Elizabeth said, sighing. 'Though one needs to challenge the norm now and again, don't you think?' She smiled, thoughtful.

'Without doubt,' said Florence. 'Your work is certainly challenging.'

For a moment or two they both sat looking at the painting. Yes, thought Florence, the painting belonged to truth, bitter, cruel truth that had to be shown.

Elizabeth spoke again. 'Ruskin thought women couldn't paint, you know, until he saw my pictures.' She smiled triumphantly. 'You do wonder why women pretend they can't do things. When I think of Lady Byron's power with mathematics, I am astonished. How fulfilled she was, despite the pain of her husband's betrayals.' She laughed quietly and braced herself. 'But Ruskin had a shock when I exhibited *Quatre Bras*. He said in his Academy Notes, "It is Amazon's work this, no doubt of it and the first fine Pre-Raphaelite picture of battle we have had . . ."'

4

'Yes,' said Florence. 'And *The Roll Call* too is a wonderful picture. Thank you for bringing it. I admire your talent, oh, and Lady Byron's also. She was clever enough to break out of the nonsense that imprisoned her.' Florence moved about in her chair, trying to find a more comfortable position. 'I am not too well, as you know,' she said frowning. She spoke softly, reverently, and narrowed her eyes, looking at the painting. It was as if she could smell the paint, as if she could hear the voices of the men, as if she could feel their weariness. Then came the tears. She wiped them away with her handkerchief. The men in the painting were *saved*, yielding themselves now to glory or pity. Who was to choose? *The Roll Call*. The names. Oh, how the names mattered. And what of the men who didn't make it? – How did they die, and why? She blinked hard, her handkerchief close to her eyes. 'The painting hurts,' she said, 'I'm sorry.' She hated the illness that had taken her energy, the aching limbs and the constant need to lie down. There was something the matter with her body, but nobody knew what it was, even the best doctors were puzzled. She must rest, they said, just rest. But when she laid her head on her pillow, the ghosts of dead soldiers plagued her, the ones she felt she had failed. But she consoled herself with the thought of those she'd nursed back to health. Her care, her writings, her pleadings to the government for money had helped so many, and she had suffered scornful remarks and insults for the sake of her cause. But those who mattered had valued her devotion and much good had been achieved through her work. The thought of that gave respite. There was much to consider. '*"For he shall give his angels charge over thee: to keep thee in all thy ways . . ."*' she murmured. How she hoped it was true!

Elizabeth Butler smiled. 'Psalm 91,' she said softly. 'I believe you are fond of the psalms.' Her hands were clasped, she was interested and intent.

'Yes,' Florence said sitting up. 'Some of them I know by heart. I find them comforting.' She closed her eyes, suddenly conscious of the shadows gathering in the room. She loved the dusk in November, the soft unearthly light that came up close and embraced her. She thought about soldiers in battle, staggering, reeling, terror in their hearts while she was safe in Mayfair. She could never forget.

Her visitor was in no hurry, a highly accomplished painter; Elizabeth Butler was used to taking her time, eager to capture the precise look and emotion. The two women had settled easily into one another's company. Florence Nightingale was past middle age, whilst her guest was young and vibrant, slender and graceful, her posture strong and upright in her well-boned corset, her hair piled high and her pale blue satin dress gleaming in the last of the sunlight. She did not wear a bustle, bustles were often ridiculed in journals nowadays, but it was doubtful her guest would have worn one anyway, bustles could be most uncomfortable. Elizabeth Butler was beautiful. Florence didn't think she could ever have called herself beautiful. She'd always been popular with men at her father's parties and people said she was attractive. She liked to think she was attractive, but what did it matter, wasn't the mind more important than the body? As far as intellect was concerned, her own mind was busy and inventive and she was far better educated than most of the women of her class. Her father had taught her history, languages, literature and philosophy as well as mathematics, inspiring her to study statistics. She had always liked analysing data; it gave her a sense of order and allowed her to see things plainly. And wasn't statistical analysis a kind of proof of the way things really were, and therefore encouraged a responsible attitude to life? She and her older sister Parthenope had travelled Europe with their father, enjoying the company of many interesting people. There had been some wonderful times. Even so, she'd seen a good deal of hardship and sickness on their travels. And at the age of 16, living at Embley Park, one of her father's estates, she'd experienced a kind of epiphany. She could never have explained it in words and argued with her family that the overwhelming feeling she'd had was a call to service from God. 'You are a fine painter,' she said to Elizabeth, admiringly, "Lady Butler" now, since her marriage to Sir William Butler, a distinguished officer in the British Army. Her guest sat quietly, her voluminous blue silk skirt flowing about her. Florence felt plain by comparison in her simple grey dress as if she were mere dark rain against a beam of sunshine. She saw that Elizabeth was aware of her penetrating gaze, so she smiled and looked downwards. 'When did you discover your gift?' she asked. Such accomplished talent must have been worked at since childhood, she thought.

Elizabeth Butler was a modest sort of woman and understood her privileged position in society. Yes, she had drawn and painted since childhood, she said, and could not deny her important connections for they had aided her talent immensely. And money had been most important. She pitied the poor, she said, for they too would want to use their talent but were forced to work for their bread.

'The world loses so much brilliance and sagacity through poverty,' Florence added quietly. 'It is as if we rob the sky of its stars. Who knows what writers there might have been, what artists, indeed what great mathematicians, women, as well as men.'

'You have fired up the hearts of a great many women with your strength,' Elizabeth exclaimed. 'You have shown us what women can do.' Florence was much admired by the military, Elizabeth said, and it was sad that the work had made her ill. 'My husband said it was rotten luck that you had to be confined to your room with this tiring illness.' She threw out her soft white hands and took on her husband's tone. "She has suffered unbearable experiences," he said, "and who did she have to comfort her? I don't know how she could stand it. You, my dear, have me if you are ever unhappy."' Elizabeth smiled. 'My husband is good and kind and he sends you his best regards.' William Butler had been born into a family of Tipperary gentry, she said, who were loyal to the British crown. He had seen the effects of the terrible famine as a child and determined he would always be fair.

'The painting is very moving,' sighed Florence. She shook her head in amazement. 'How on earth did you do it?'

'Talent, of course.' Elizabeth gave a breathless pause. 'And dedication. As a very young child I had a passion for drawing and painting. And I knew that nothing would stop me. Watercolours are good for the beauty of nature, but oil gives an added power and reality I think.'

The maid came in to light the candles. 'I am not yet old,' Florence said quietly. 'And yet whenever the maid lights the candles, I feel as if the next world calls me. I can feel it tugging my spirit. But what can I do for the dead!' She laughed softly. 'I can only assist the living.'

Elizabeth smiled, thoughtful.

Florence continued. 'Connections are vital, that is undeniable. How can we achieve our potential if we do not have connections? And even then there are always obstacles for women. However . . .' For a moment she gazed at space. 'I have to say that women have never really helped me, you know, apart from my nurses that is; only men have assisted me.' She straightened her sleeves and frowned as if her thoughts disturbed her. 'Women can be quite irritating. You, my dear, are rather special. I am glad you are here. And you are *brave*. Oh yes, it is brave to paint as you do, and it is brave to be married. You might well have lost your soul getting married, never have painted a thing. I did not want to be married. I had offers . . .' She leant forward and whispered, 'I too have been *desired*.'

Elizabeth nodded thoughtfully. 'We owe a lot to our fathers,' she said, talking in the modest voice of her youth, unfitted to the woman who could paint such powerful pictures. 'Mine encouraged me to draw and has constantly supported my art.'

'I too was encouraged by my father,' said Florence, recalling the countless hours he had given of his time. 'He taught me so much, and he would often recite from the poets at night time – Coleridge, Wordsworth, many others. I would lie down to sleep with their marvellous verse in my mind. We have both been privileged. Your connections have helped you paint, mine enabled me to gather a team of nurses and train them to care for the sick. I needed to fight, you see, for there is always a fight for a woman with a mission. And there is always a need for money. – Provisions, clothes, food, medicines, such things must be bought.' Florence met Elizabeth's gaze and gave her a serious look. 'Oh yes. And people have been most generous. *The Times* has been extremely helpful.' She nodded slowly, noting how well her visitor understood. 'My health will improve, I'm sure. I am bound to fall ill sometimes.' She smiled and adjusted the clip in her thinning grey hair. 'Some days I think I am ancient, as if I've lived many different lives over and over . . .'

'And perhaps you have,' said Elizabeth in a low soft voice.

'Who knows?' Florence said lightly. She was grateful for her visitor's company, glad of her visit. The sense of two special people talking together lent a mystical grace to the room.

'I have so wanted to meet you,' Elizabeth told her happily. 'It's a privilege to show you *The Roll Call*. It belongs to Queen Victoria of course, and is now very precious. She paid me a handsome sum.'

'I know!' said Florence, smiling, astonished. 'How wonderful that she should buy it! The Queen is a good woman; she has been kind to me as well. Very kind indeed. The men will no doubt be eager to return her painting, so I had better have a long last look.

'Yes,' she smiled, bending forward. 'That painting has made me very happy today.' She stared at it one last time.

Lady Butler's attendants waited in an adjoining room.

'You have worked so hard,' Elizabeth said, looking at Florence earnestly.

'At Scutari?' said Florence, meeting her gaze.

'Everywhere,' Elizabeth answered, throwing out her hands. 'But Scutari especially, of course.'

Florence nodded. She knew full well how hard she had worked; harder perhaps than she should. But her nature was such as to always go the extra mile.

'My husband brought me. He often speaks of you,' Elizabeth told her, glancing outside through the window. The day was darkening.

'And where has he gone?' Florence would like to have met him, but only Elizabeth and her escorts had arrived with the painting.

'He went to see one of his officers who lost an arm in battle.' She shook her head sadly. 'Some time ago now, but the pain persists in his mind. His sleep is tormented and he can scarcely get through the day.'

'Yes,' Florence replied. 'Your husband has given much service. He is a fine officer.' Her manner was thoughtful and assured with the self-containment of a nurse. She talked again of Elizabeth Butler's work. '*The Defence of Rorke's Drift* I am told, is also splendid,' she said. 'I must see it sometime. How could you know how it was?' She shook her head and frowned. 'One hundred and fifty soldiers against four thousand Zulu warriors, yet we see it as a British victory.' She breathed in deeply. 'But our soldiers were certainly courageous. The Zulus saw bravery and left. Soldiers know bravery when they see it.' Florence gave a little shrug. 'And here am I, sleeping in a comfortable bed and living in affluence but suffering and death constantly creep through my veins.'

Lady Butler was silent, leaving them time for thought. Florence had darkness in her soul no lamp could ever light up. She recalled Crimea, the sound of the winds roaring from the Black Sea, the wailing, the howling, as if it were the home of wolves. 'The Crimea,' she whispered. 'It seems like a long time ago.' She was safe in Mayfair but so many wars continued. There were things she could never speak of, terrible to even think of, and she still had a great deal to do, but time, money, health and politics were persistent stumbling blocks to progress. 'Those who lose limbs in war are never the same as before,' she sighed. 'Amputation is terrible.'

'My husband is quite heroic,' said Elizabeth firmly. 'He steadfastly stays by his men if he can, but he will lose himself in silence for hours sometimes when he's at home. I have no idea what is happening in his mind and I dare not ask.' She nodded slowly and smiled, still glowing from the pleasure of her reception. They had eaten good food and the eminent, much loved nurse had poured out the tea. It had been a magical meeting.

'And do you have children?' Florence asked her.

'I do.' Elizabeth said happily.

'That is good,' Florence said wistfully. 'Children were not in my gift. I like to see children playing. Play is quite extraordinary isn't it? We *live* when we are young, as if past, present and future abide in us at once . . . such precious sacred days.' She stared ahead abstractedly. 'But it does not do to look back, we must always look forward. I am not at all sure though where we think we are going.' She murmured a verse from Shakespeare;

> *"'Life's but a walking shadow, a poor player,*
> *That struts and frets his hour upon the stage,*
> *And then is heard no more."'*

Elizabeth, bending in closer frowned slightly, trying to hide the surprise she felt hearing Florence Nightingale speaking so gently, this woman who had lived with dying soldiers, written letters to their relatives dictated from their last dying breath, this woman who had walked through hell. Elizabeth Butler felt humbled. She saw that Miss Nightingale's hands were red and worn. She'd reportedly knelt down with her nurses to scrub filthy hospital floors ensuring spotless sanitation. Florence Nightingale's hands stayed still today as she talked, until she plunged one into the deep pocket of her dress as if searching for something she'd lost. 'I imagine wounded soldiers reaching for your hand,' Elizabeth said smiling, 'your palms, resting on the temples of delirious men, delirious with pain and fear.' But Florence was known to be fearless. Elizabeth's eyes were filled with admiration. 'Were you afraid at Scutari?' she whispered.

'Oh yes,' said Florence.

'I can imagine . . .' Elizabeth sighed.

'What we fear most is loss of hope,' said Florence, frowning at the thought. 'I have fought that demon to the death.' She bent her head and lowered her voice. 'It is hard to conceive of the true horrors of war.'

Elizabeth waited some moments, then spoke from the depths of her thoughts. 'I wonder how I could depict a demon on the battlefield,' she said strangely, 'while soldiers charge with their weaponry, the nostrils of their horses flaring with terror.'

'War is a demon in itself,' said Florence. 'The men are seized by madness, how else could they ever sustain it? The warrior ethic – valour, fortitude, glory, ah, it is madness.'

Elizabeth waited.

'The torture of the body is one thing,' Florence continued, 'but who can know what tortures the soul must endure in the midst of battle.' She gave Elizabeth a long and curious look. 'Perhaps paint can help us see it?' She gazed again at the painting. '*The Roll Call* is truly magnificent. It shows such loss, such despair. Hardly what the government wants to see for its Empire.'

Elizabeth's voice trembled slightly as she spoke. 'I never painted for the glory of war, but to portray its pathos and heroism,' she said emotionally. 'For the soldiers are indeed heroes. They do as instructed, and must.'

Florence listened intently. 'Heroes?' she murmured. Her thoughts were complex. 'Statistics help us find order in the chaos,' she said earnestly. 'If there is order to be found, that is . . . Perhaps order can be knocked into shape . . . The numbers might be neat and precise, but chaos remains . . .'

Elizabeth nodded in agreement.

'You too are a hero,' said Florence, 'to fight as you did to have your work in the Royal Academy. Men will attempt to judge us as less than they.' She laughed quietly. 'According to some, we women are less courageous, less talented, less worthy. But women themselves let it happen. My father tried to stop me from nursing. It wasn't a fit occupation for a woman of my class, he said, it was dangerous, even indecent, in fact my parents thought I should never work at all.' A brief triumphant look crossed her face. 'Well, I did what I wanted, didn't I!'

Again they were thoughtful.

'My husband believes in my art,' said Elizabeth happily. 'And for that I am grateful. I love him and to have him believe in me is vital.'

'Of course,' smiled Florence. 'How could he not? You are a highly accomplished artist.' She removed her hand from her pocket and reached for some drawings Elizabeth had brought for her to see. 'Your talent for sketching horses is quite remarkable. You know the workings of their minds, it must hurt to feel their emotions like that, and to show it in their every feature.'

'Yes,' Elizabeth said quietly. 'I have always loved horses. I loved them as a girl, and still do. It is sad to see them at the mercy of men who must ride them so savagely, wielding a lance or a gun. – Oh, the *lancers* . . .' She shivered as she spoke.

Florence returned her hand to her pocket. Elizabeth's eyes followed. 'Pockets can be comforting,' she said, with a curious look.

'Ah, you miss nothing,' Florence murmured, smiling. She lowered her voice to a whisper. 'I have a secret, you see.'

'Am I to know what it is?' asked Elizabeth. Her bright blue eyes widened with interest.

'Perhaps,' Florence said playfully. 'I have a little guilt about it, though.'

'Then I want to know all the more!' said Elizabeth.

'It is the spirit of an owl,' said Florence, half closing her eyes.

Elizabeth looked at her, waiting. *'A spirit?'*

'It gives me strength as Athena did during her lifetime.'

'"Athena?" – The ancient goddess of wisdom and warfare?' Elizabeth added quickly. Again she waited. Florence Nightingale was full of mysteries.

'Yes, that's what I called her. Athena is long since dead. I do not have her by me just now, but a trusted taxidermist preserved her, my maid will tell you where to go if you want to see her. She was just an owlet when I found her, such a soft, warm little creature. Some boys were attacking her. I made a rescue and put her in my pocket. At home I fed her and took care of her for several years.' She laughed quietly, briefly. 'She had quite a temper too. One or two people who approached me too closely got nasty pecks; she was very jealous and wanted me all to herself. But I did not think it through, you see. I was preparing to leave for Scutari and I put her in the attic where I thought she could fly about, but she did not like it, and pined away. She needed to be loved, of course, not just fed.

All things need to be loved, for what is life without love?' She cast her eyes across her guest. '*You* have been loved.'

'I have, and he loves me still.' Lady Butler straightened. 'And I love him in return. We are blessed.'

Florence sighed, remembering how she too had been loved by someone special, and how she had longed for his arms. When feelings had overwhelmed her and she thought of Richard she had cast the thoughts from her mind. Now she felt a tight knot in her stomach for her beloved had married. But a man cannot wait for ever. And her work was essentially for ever. 'Richard was very much loved, but somehow I lost him.'

'"Richard?"' Elizabeth Butler waited.

'Richard Monckton Milnes, a clever and serious man, heavily involved with politics and elected to parliament, something of a literary man too. He made friends with Tennyson and others at Cambridge.' Florence watched Elizabeth searchingly. Her own self-revelation surprised her. She was divulging secrets. The painting and talk had roused her deeply. She felt drawn to this woman who understood so much about the naked emotions of humanity. 'Richard wanted to marry me,' she said softly. 'I might have been married like you, had children, but I chose to commit the whole of my energies to nursing.'

'It is admirable,' Elizabeth said sighing. 'I have been fortunate. I've had a lot of help with the children and my husband is very sensitive to my needs.'

'You were called to paint, and you have painted wonderful pictures. *The Roll Call* has made you famous.'

Elizabeth smiled. 'It has. I was reminded of Byron, who awoke to find himself famous after *Childe Harold's Pilgrimage* sold out in only three days!'

Florence spoke wistfully. 'I hope for so much,' she said, her voice small and appealing.

Elizabeth gazed at Florence intensely. 'And what do you hope for?' she asked, cautiously. She did not want to offend her.

Florence looked away deep in thought. 'Oh, so many things . . . Things that exist beyond the numbers. Statistics are one thing, real life is another. I search for the weaknesses where worms break through and devour what might otherwise be sound. But life is fickle; it does not keep its promises.'

Elizabeth gazed in wonder at Nightingale. Her hair was grey but her brow was yet unlined and fervour still gleamed in her eyes. '*"Promises?"*' Elizabeth said curiously. 'We promise things to ourselves also but life creates its own disorder.'

'Indeed it does. But we hope, we must always hope.' Florence spoke assuredly. 'Destiny is no ordinary path. Do we choose to follow it, or does it draw us towards it?'

'We *feel* it,' Elizabeth said, fascinated by Nightingale's talk.

'Oh we do,' said Florence taking a breath. 'Something happens inside us and calls us. Or that is how it was for me. I was only a girl but I knew the call of my destiny.' Florence Nightingale had rarely taken to her bed, but she did so now on the advice of her doctors and had allowed herself respite. She had given her life, her love, her work, her mind, and of course, her ferocious dedication. Again, she picked up the drawings and looked at them again. 'Such wonderful horses,' she said earnestly. 'You capture their every mood.'

For a few moments Elizabeth glowed with pride.

'All great art aspires to love,' Florence murmured. 'You are full of vigour, eager to seal in oil the honesty that speaks in your soul; it is indeed a calling, for I see it in your eyes.' The drawings were exquisite and would seem to leap off the page. Florence went through them again. 'You know the bone and sinews of a horse so precisely. It is quite extraordinary.' Florence thought of the afterlife of men on the battlefield and imagined their ghosts after death, treading between the dead and wounded and the fallen horses. What did dead men look like when the battle for everything or nothing was over, no more screaming, no more shrieking, no more longing, what did their faces express when there was nothing more to hope or fight for? Could Elizabeth Butler conceive of that, could anyone ever *paint* it? She herself had worked to keep soldiers alive, trying to alleviate their sufferings, both mental and physical. Yet she owned there were times when death was preferable to what lay ahead when a man was severely wounded. Then it seemed love and compassion was all that was left of deliverance. But how could death be preferable to life? She breathed in deeply, it was always there on the edge of her thought, the fact that men might want to waste themselves for a cause, a woman, a country. She'd experienced them begging to die so often in the worst of their pain and there were times she had held it dear and had found herself thankful when the last breath left their body. She had held the hands of soldiers almost blasted to pieces, ragged remains of the proud men they had been. And she had made herself bear it, she had gone into that place of horror they were forced to inhabit when they knew their lives were ending. And she and her nurses had cared for them lovingly.

The room had darkened and the maid entered again, lighting more candles. 'The carriage has arrived Miss Nightingale,' she said, giving her a brief curtsey. 'The escort is here for M'lady.'

Elizabeth Butler rose to her feet. Loud footsteps were heard in the hall. Men walked in through the shadows.

Soon Florence was alone once more in the silence. She touched the necklace beneath her collar and a flood of warmth went through her, feelings she might indulge in now, safe in the distance of time. *How she had loved him* . . . But that was then . . .

17

CHAPTER 2

Lea Hurst, Derbyshire 1834
A GIRL APART

William Shore, Florence Nightingale's father, was the son of a Sheffield banker. At 21 years of age in 1815, the year in which Wellington defeated Napoleon at the battle of Waterloo, William inherited the Derbyshire estate of Lea Hurst from Peter Nightingale, his mother's uncle. Peter Nightingale had made himself a fortune from lead mining in Derbyshire, lead being highly effective as a serviceable commodity. Used in the roofs of public buildings and houses, by the 17th century lead was becoming as important a product as wool. Leaded windows, made from various lengths and shapes of glass bound within thin strips of lead, were increasingly popular, and due to its water proofing qualities lead had a role in many aspects of life, including the storage of water. There were though people who claimed they could taste the lead in their drinks and that it entered their blood and made them ill, or could even kill them. Others took issue with the mines and lamented that men had lost their lives in there from heavy falling stones and collapsing walls. Oh, it was true. People gathered in groups and said so. Why, some had been buried alive! But men needed work and the mining carried on despite controversies. By the time William Nightingale, Florence Nightingale's grandfather, took over, Derbyshire mining however, was in decline due to worked-out veins, production costs and cheaper foreign imports.

But the mining of lead had made Peter Nightingale rich, and in turn William Shore, Florence's father, who owing to the terms of the will had taken on Nightingale's name and the family coat of arms. When he was 23 and she 29, Peter Nightingale had married Frances Smith, daughter of William Smith, a Whig Member of Parliament and known to be a fervent abolitionist, whose powerful outbursts of feeling might well have led to the cautious demeanour of Florence's mother, Frances, and which now suffused through Parthenope their eldest daughter, though not so much the younger Florence who did whatever she wanted and spoke as the spirit moved her.

By the year 1825, Florence's father had taken his family to live at Lea Hurst, a manor on the Lea Hurst estate in Derbyshire, originally a 17th century farmhouse but now a grandiose home. The house had 15 bedrooms and exquisite gardens overlooking the Derwent Valley with its swathes of woodland and splendid craggy terrain. William had enjoyed a gentleman's education at Trinity College, Cambridge, and was also known to be a wise and considerate man. The wind and sun had place in his features for he was often out riding or walking, the glow in his skin equal to his glowing energy. The thing to do, he said, was always to keep pace with important matters and never waste time, and could a man not turn a bad thing into a good one with a little more effort? He clung to his beliefs with passion and people were drawn to his warmth.

Derbyshire was a colourful and lovely county with plateaus of limestone, flanked by sparkling grit stone, its weather was moody and the land varied from bleak moorland in winter to flower rich meadows in summer. Little cottages were dotted all over and William encouraged his daughters to visit the poor and take them food and kind words. They might take a couple of loaves and a bag of apples, or even an apple pie from the kitchen. They might also tender condolences for bereavements and listen to their tales of woe, offering assistance as they could. Florence liked to take care of their injuries and took pains to bandage their wounds, though her mother thought she was all too serious and far too wonderfully good, for some of the poor might not be as righteous as they seemed.

William Nightingale was known to be something of a scholar who read literature, languages, history, mathematics and philosophy, and he also had progressive ideas on women's education, which in England had only of late offered similar educational advantages for girls as it did for boys. William taught his daughters extensively and his daughters responded, while his interest in politics could draw him into good-humoured argument or downright battle. He had stood for parliament and supported the Reform Bill, delivering his thoughts and feelings emphatically at dinner parties, often attended by well known public figures, the dining room filled with excitable chatter as loud as a flock of jackdaws. He loathed all forms of corruption and voiced his opinions with vigour. But somehow he'd lost the election and had vowed he would never stand again.

Calls for reform had echoed unsuccessfully down the years, and due in the main to public pressure the Reform Bill at last went through in 1832, giving seats in the House of Commons to cities that were heavily populated and had come into being in the time of the Industrial Revolution whilst removing seats from boroughs with small electorates where wealthy patrons held power. But many complained that the bill showed a strange wisdom, for only qualifying men had a vote, and a voter was defined as male, therefore denying women a say in the way their country was governed.

It would not do, and resentful females gathered in groups to voice their opinions, took tea on their lawns expressing their feelings in less than respectable terms, bringing to mind events like the march of the women in France at the time of the French Revolution, when mobs of market women ransacked the city armoury for weapons and marched to the Palace of Versailles taking their anger to the monarch Louis XVI and his Queen Marie Antoinette. Women in England could not voice their anger and it found its outlet instead in their bodies so that they feigned to faint with emotion, or might even be called hysterical and be placed in an asylum. A woman must be calm and serene no matter what raged in her mind. But many developed a strange hostility towards what they saw as enslavement and became hard and cold towards others, some were filled with indifference others with anger.

William Shore, now named William Nightingale, had also acquired the beautiful Embley Park estate in Hampshire, an estate considered as one of the best in the country for shooting and fishing, and in 1829 he was made High Sheriff of Hampshire. Embley House, a lovely Elizabethan mansion, stood north-west of the park with views south-westwards looking towards the New Forest. South-east was a large landscape of expansive woodland with all manner of trees and vegetation. Large and grand, the red brick house shone and sparkled in the sunlight. This was their winter home and William had bought it with the intention of making changes, for his wife had felt the need for more space and more bedrooms, to embrace their growing social circle. And was it not right and proper for a man to make his wife content and provide the best home he could for her and his daughters, Florence stubborn and intent, and Parthenope always *comme il faut*. Ah, easy compliant Parthenope!

Just then they were all at Lea Hurst, their Derbyshire home for the summer, and the girls were preparing for bed in the bedroom.

Their mother had given a party and it was well past midnight. All was quiet downstairs; guests were sleeping in their rooms or had left and were on their way home. It had been an excellent evening filled with dancing and laughter, though Florence had gone to the drawing room at times to escape the noise and think.

'Parthe, will you brush out my hair?' asked Florence, handing her sister the brush. 'The way you do it is so soothing.' Her voice came softly through the night. Parthenope held up the dark heavy locks and brushed them down Florence's shoulders. The two sisters were as one just then and spoke openly. They would joke, make suggestions, even chastise with a freedom of thought and language they might never dare use elsewhere.

'I believe the poor die mainly from poverty,' said Florence sympathetically. She frowned at her sister through the mirror. Parthe stood back, thoughtful. 'No, seriously,' Florence persisted, 'it's obvious, you know. I do believe Papa thinks the same. They get ill, they starve, and they are often cold in the winter. We, who have plenty have no idea how it is.' Her voice rose with emotion. 'You can hear the Derbyshire winds in December, forever moaning and complaining, as if they would enter our homes and wreak havoc if they could. Those cottages are sometimes so chilly.'

'That's true,' said Parthe unhappily and suddenly thoughtful. She went to sit on her bed. 'Did Papa really say the poor die mainly from poverty though? He never said it to me. I haven't given it much thought.'

'But it's true, Parthe. We don't need Papa to tell us something like that, do we? Anyway, I doubt you talk with him like I do.' Florence sighed. Familiar frustrations stirred in her mind. For a moment or two they were silent.

'Fifteen bedrooms,' murmured Parthe. 'And yet we are made to share.' She looked at Florence curiously.

'Just so those chattering people can stay overnight,' Florence said irritably. 'The men talk only of parliament and war and the women talk only of dresses and jewellery and who is about to be married.'

'Oh dear,' said Parthe. 'If you didn't do so much thinking, Flo, you might feel happier. It's only social conversation, you know. You must stay within the rules of etiquette at parties. Mama says you embarrass her sometimes.' She bit her lip and frowned.

'"Embarrass her?"' Florence said, confused. 'All because I say what I think? I won't talk nonsense Parthe.' She settled into her chair and stared at herself through the dressing table mirror.

'Well, don't talk at all,' Parthe said, yawning. 'It would be better for Mama's nerves. You are always complaining.'

Florence frowned. There was so much tension in the air. She knew she disappointed her family. She had said things that evening that were best left unsaid, but she had laughed with the guests and tried to be pleasant, she'd tried so hard, while her heart of hearts held many unanswered questions. Were such questions never to be answered, never even to be asked? 'How do you stop yourself thinking?' she murmured. 'You would have to be dead for that.' She shrugged her shoulders and went to her bed.

'I saw you talking with Richard,' said Parthe. 'Richard Monckton Milnes has an excellent mind and intends to write lots of books. I talked with him tonight. He's at Trinity College, Cambridge. And he knows his poetry too and recites it beautifully. But he will, of course, he has an excellent group of friends. He is even friends with Tennyson . . . And I do think him very handsome. He was the best looking man of the evening.' Parthenope was thoughtful, staring out at the moon. On clear summer evenings they would leave the curtains undrawn and gaze at the stars. 'Anyway, I shall be married in a few years' time. Papa has said so.'

'So Papa has decided has he? And who will you marry?' Florence plumped up her pillow and got into bed.

For a moment or two they were silent. 'See, you don't even know who Papa expects you to marry,' said Florence. 'It's ridiculous. Women are seen as 'creatures', creatures to service children and men. I won't be anyone's creature.'

'Well, I certainly won't be marrying Richard,' sighed Parthe. 'Oh no, *you* are to marry Richard. Mama says he's madly in love with you.'

'But I'm only fourteen,' Florence said tensely, biting her lip. Richard was certainly attractive, and she'd danced with him a lot that evening, but she was still in her girlhood whilst he was a grown man.

'But everyone says how lovely you are, Flo, and your manner and deportment are those of a young lady. I am one year older than you, yet I somehow feel younger. You are something apart, Flo. And Papa looks at you with pride. You are prettier than I am, too,' Parthe sighed and slipped beneath the bedclothes.

'Oh Parthe, the terrible hopelessness of our lives!' moaned Florence. 'Must we choose husbands now, while we are children?'

'Mama wants us to be safe, have a secure place in society as the wives of successful men, mothers of children who will thrive and flourish, that's what it is.'

'Wives? Mothers? But what about *us*? What about our selves, our own longings?' said Florence. 'Not just for love, but for *fulfilment*.'

'Fulfilment will come from our children and our duties,' came Parthe's muted reply. 'Mama is fulfilled is she not?'

'If Mama wants grand houses and money, with all the accoutrements of a high class lifestyle then perhaps she's fulfilled. But I don't want that for me. Papa understands me best I think. I won't be married to anyone, not ever. I want to do something useful like men do.'

'Oh yes, like going to war and killing people?' Parthenope said sleepily. 'Women spend their lives trying to put things right that men do wrong.'

'There you are,' Florence said flatly. 'You give yourself away.'

'But it's complicated isn't it. We won the battle of Waterloo, you see? I suppose the war was worth it.'

'I doubt the dead soldiers would say so,' Florence said softly. 'Papa said the battle might have been lost, if the Prussians hadn't come when they did. Wellington said, "Give me night, or give me Blucher." He often says it.'

'"Blucher?"'

'The Prussian General. Did Papa not tell you? Or did you not listen? It was the Prussians arriving to help Wellington that helped win the war against Napoleon. The man who brought the potatoes yesterday said just one of those dreadful musket balls could shatter every bone and muscle of a man's leg in an instant.' Florence's voice wavered as she spoke. 'Imagine struggling from the battlefield with one of your legs shattered. What pain, what suffering. Those soldiers are human beings, they hurt, they scream.'

'A very nice image to sleep with,' Parthenope murmured.

'But it happens Parthe. The noise of the battlefield can be heard somewhere right now.'

'Don't think about it Flo!' said Parthenope, clapping her hands to her ears. 'Imagine beauty instead – flowers, rivers, sunshine. Sara once said it was best to imagine good and beautiful things, for what you imagine somehow lives in your mind.'

'I doubt I learned much from our governess,' Florence said dejectedly. 'I rarely learn anything from women. They must always play a part and do not think for themselves. It affects their imagination. I learn best from Papa, who speaks from his heart. There is something real about men.'

'Oh Flo, you do make women sound foolish. It makes me sad to think of Sara dying in childbirth. But thankfully her son survived.'

'Perhaps it would have been better if she'd never got married in the first place,' said Florence, flatly. 'Then she wouldn't have had a baby and died. I can't see her husband thought it fair. He gained a son but lost a wife. I would hate it if Mama had died giving birth to me.' She puffed up her cheeks and blew out the thought. 'Papa would probably hate me.'

'I assure you he wouldn't,' said Parthe looking shocked. 'What a curious thing to say. And are you not sad about Sara?'

'She made her choice,' sighed Florence. 'People have a right to their choices. Others might suffer for our choices, but we make them. And they take us wherever they will.'

The moon shone in on their beds, finding Parthenope her eyes determinedly shut, her sister still talking energetically, her voice and manner imperative and urgent as ever.

'You are a bad influence, Flo. Mama thinks so too,' said Parthenope drowsily. 'She fears you will take me deep beneath the water and I do not swim as well as you do.'

Florence sighed with despair. 'Do you think Papa would rather we were boys?' she murmured. 'Daughters don't quite fit. I believe I might secretly be a boy, you know. I can feel him there inside me trying to escape . . . And yet . . .' She went on, talking sleepily. 'I have an urgent need to do something of value. I am going somewhere, Parthe. I know it.'

'I see. So where are you going?' Her sister yawned and turned over.

'I don't know until I get there,' Florence replied softly. She felt so alone with her thoughts, the black sheep of the family with wool that could not be dyed, an embarrassment with her errant ways. She would go out walking, as far as her eye could see, but alone, until she got lost and only came to her senses when she heard the sound of her father's horse behind her, followed by his angry words. She wanted and needed the loving connection with her family, but what was the price? The life they imagined she'd have was not what she wanted. But what did she want instead? If only she knew.

Suddenly wide awake, Parthenope turned to her. 'As as matter of fact I was most put out by something Mama said this evening to one of our guests. She told her that *my* main interests were drawing and poetry, whilst you, dear Flo, could apply yourself to matters of importance. I mean, as if I couldn't. And she didn't seem to mind that I was standing beside her listening. I was certainly put in my place. I never heard Mama say that before. It hurt me.'

'Dear Parthe,' Florence began, trying to right the indiscretion. 'I am simply *Florence*, named after Florence, the city I was born in, whereas you are the siren Parthenope, who drowned herself when Odysseus evaded the lure of the sirens' singing. You are named after the daughter of the god Achelous and the Muse Terpischore. Oh, a very poetic heritage. It is there in your drawings too. You have such an understanding of perspective, and your still life paintings are astounding.'

'Thank you, Flo. How kind of you to say so. I like to see nature as at peace with itself, though I know such thoughts are naive.' Having found a burst of energy Parthe went on. 'And I am named after Naples, the place of my birth, *Parthenope* in Ancient Greece. We were both born in Italy. Poor Mama, to have us so close together, I suspect we tired her endlessly.'

For a moment or two they were silent.

'. . . And what's more,' Florence added. 'I own that the freedom to be creative is most important, but there has to be order, Parthe. That is what you mean by peace I think. I do wish you'd return things to their rightful places, though. I am often missing my combs. If you do not return the combs to their proper place they will not be there when we need them.'

'You need to sleep,' said Parthenope. 'Breakfast will be busy.'

And indeed it was a busy breakfast. Florence went into the dining room in her slow observant way, smiling at people as she passed. Parthenope was up and conversing already in her usual animated manner. Florence found her seat by her sister and smiled again at the guests seated about them, her eyes busy and attentive. There was something unreal about it all, even less real than a dream. Her father stood in a corner, talking with a man from the War Office, though she didn't know who he was. 'I wonder who Papa is talking to?' she said. 'He looks like an interesting person. See how he gesticulates and talks so eagerly. I would like Papa to introduce me.'

'Not now, Flo. Not at breakfast.' Parthenope shook her head. 'They will all be leaving us soon, it's raining, there won't be any riding today. Papa is making last minute conversation, I suspect it's important.'

'Papa might leave this morning, and then he'll be gone for the week,' Florence protested quietly. She felt controlled and imprisoned. Could she never be a part of things, properly a part of things and talk as she wanted? 'Look,' she said. 'There's a blackbird on the window ledge. It is looking in on us I think. How free it is, and how lucky it is to have wings! – But why can't I speak to Papa?' she said irritably. 'What is it I can't be part of?'

'Men like to talk about parliamentary matters by themselves,' sighed her sister. 'They do not bother the women. They go to their clubs to discuss things, out of the way.'

Florence raised her eyebrows in annoyance. 'But women talk about wealth and fashion mainly.'

'Not all of them, Flo. Some of them play the piano and sing, and give time to their children too. Sadie paints beautiful pictures, Others go visiting the poor like we do.'

Florence sat watching them all. Everyone looked so happy. She was angry with herself for always feeling discontented.

'Richard isn't here,' Parthe said flatly. 'I'd hoped he might stay.'

'I didn't expect it,' said Florence, also disappointed. 'And we danced together three times. I am fond of him, Parthe. He is handsome and clever. But I know I am only a child. – Though I won't be a child much longer. I intend to crack through this shell and break out. Just watch me. All in good time.'

'Talking of shells, won't you eat some eggs?' Parthe passed her two poached eggs on a small china plate.

Florence looked out through the window, the blackbird had gone.

Just then a clatter of footsteps was heard in the hall. Mr Nightingale opened the door quickly, looking alarmed. Seeing the maid standing before them distraught, the breakfast gathering looked up. She was grasping the sleeve of a dishevelled young girl who looked about ten years old. 'I've got her!' said the maid, gritting her teeth. 'I think you should hear her story Mr Nightingale.' She lowered her voice to a whisper. 'She dares to suggest you are wealthy because you've killed people in the mines, and you cruelly set traps for the poor who creep into the woods to pinch a rabbit.'

The girl stood weeping profusely.

Nightingale glanced about and straightened his silk cravat. His guests, out of good manners, talked on. 'And so I am a murderer am I. Tell me now, what is this all about?' He gazed at the girl and frowned.

The maid went on. 'Her brother was caught in a rope trap and fell down a hole; he twisted his ankle and has well near twisted his foot off! She says he could lose it.'

'What, lose his foot? My goodness,' said Mr Nightingale looking incredulous.

'You are only a junior housemaid,' said Mrs Nightingale coming across. 'Were you not told that you should never interrupt breakfast, especially when we have guests.'

The maid gave a brief curtsey and looked at the girl. 'I'm sorry Ma'am. It's her, you see. She wanted to see Mr Nightingale. I had to tell him. Her brother might lose his foot and her mother has five children.'

'You should have knocked on the door quietly and waited,' said Mrs Nightingale.

'But why?' said Florence, rising from her chair. 'We might not have heard her and the girl has something to say. She is quite out of breath from running.'

'Hush,' warned Parthenope, pulling on her sister's dress. 'Flo, sit down!'

The guests spoke quietly to each other and carried on eating.

'I think your father can deal with it Flo,' said her mother, smiling at her husband. The girl's dark hair was tangled about her shoulders and tears streamed down her face.

'My brother thinks you'll put him in prison, Mr Nightingale,' said the girl, trembling. 'I've come to beg your pardon.'

'Did somebody send you?' William Nightingale looked at her quizzically.

'No, sir, I came to save my brother. He's in such terrible pain and his foot's all blue. I ran all the way.'

'So what do you want me to do?' asked Nightingale, glancing outside. The gardens were silent. 'Is he bleeding?'

The girl dried her tears on her sleeve. 'Not as you could see it, but my Ma says his foot must be bleedin' inside cos it's swollen real bad.'

William Nightingale breathed in deeply and straightened. 'And he fell down some hole, did he? I shall speak to the gamekeeper. Now tell me the truth, for it seems your brother was poaching?'

The girl stared at the floor. 'He got us a rabbit Mr Nightingale. It were only a small un. There's a lot of us to feed, y'see.' She put her hand to her brow. 'I'm flummoxed now. We haven't got much. That's why my brother went poachin'.'

'So he *was* poaching?' Nightingale sighed, thoughtful. 'He got himself a rabbit and suffered for it.'

'Not so much as the rabbit did, sir. Ma stripped its fur, an' it's now in the pot.'

Frances Nightingale stood perplexed. 'You are bound to keep the rabbit, of course, it is your dinner.'

'And it's in the cooking pot,' said Nightingale, frowning. 'Now, do stop crying girl. No-one will go to prison.'

'But what about my brother's foot?' she said, still sobbing.

The maid shook her head and looked downwards.

Florence passed them and went down the hall. She returned with a box of bandages and ointments. The great mirror on the wall reflected the faces of twelve spellbound guests, a deeply embarrassed Frances, a shaking Parthenope, a confused William Nightingale, and Florence, who was preparing to leave.

'Florence, you are wearing your cloak,' said her father. 'And you have brought a medicine box and a bag. Now where do you think you are going?'

'You must not go to the cottage!' Mrs Nightingale cried, stepping forward. 'I forbid it. I shall arrange for the priest to visit them. He'll know what to do. Her brother has been stealing. He must learn.'

'That's a little provocative Frances,' her husband said quietly. 'I doubt the countryside will miss the odd rabbit. I can sort it out myself.'

'The man is in pain,' Florence said firmly. 'He will need attention.' She turned to her mother. 'Please tell the doctor, Mama. I am sure he will know the cottage.' She reached across the table and filled her bag with food. The guests looked on in amazement. The child stood watching, calmer now than before. Florence took hold of her hand and they left the house, making towards the woodland.

CHAPTER 3

Lea Hurst 1849
THE ROOTS OF SELF

During the following years the Nightingales grew increasingly familiar with the environs of Lea Hurst and Embley Park. They learned about its people, and its people learned about them. William Nightingale and his wife were popular and enjoyed giving parties. Their daughters were kind and pleasant, and could talk with all levels of society from the humble villagers to the aristocratic Members of Parliament who came to dine at the house. The girls learned languages, philosophy and history and could quote from the works of great poets and novelists. They were though quite different in nature. Parthenope often silent and serene, sat drawing and painting pictures, while Florence had a passion for numbers and had insisted on learning mathematics along with her other studies. Life was all about questions, she said. A perverse will had its way with the world, constantly rewarding the rich and disabling the poor. There were days she felt sick at heart over what she read in the papers and many of the questions she put to her father would leave him staring into space. She had put it to Lord

Palmerston, the Foreign Secretary, at a dinner party once; that women might take care of the soldiers in military hospitals better than men, for women were natural carers. Not always, people would argue, but probably in the main. Gin was too easily come by, someone had whispered, and women nurses were often heavy drinkers and as easy to get hold of as the gin. Florence had looked at her father, who had bent his head avoiding the conversation. She'd been robbed of her case just then, but she'd held it safe in her heart waiting for a better time. Tout en temps utile!' But her mind was made up. Her life would be about nursing. A silence like death fell about the table however if it was mentioned.

On a three months stay at The Protestant Deaconess Institute, in Kaiserwerth, Germany, Florence had first experienced ward work and had learned about hospital discipline. And encouraged by Sidney Herbert, Minister for War, she had taken charge of the Harley Street Home for Sick Governesses, which had badly needed new management, and she'd shown her expertise, surprising herself and others. Now she was eager to put her ideas into practice elsewhere. But she could not make herself heard and it left her in torment. It wasn't a question of why women of her class were so restricted, it was a simple, immovable fact. There were days she grew angry and withdrew from her family, the people she loved. She knew she had a mission vital for the good of humanity, but she could not free it, she could not let it fly. When she read of the failings in the military hospitals her heart beat hard with purpose, and her energies felt bound within her. But good things were happening in the world as well, things her father's guests liked to talk about, someone had taken the first successful photo of the moon – oh the moon, the moon, that place of romantic resourcefulness, far away from the horror of war and the continuing madness of mankind.

★ ★ ★

Time moved on, men came to talk with Florence's father and flirt with the Nightingale sisters. It was the year 1849 and Princess Alexandrina Victoria of Kent had become Queen of England in 1837. Florence was now 29, and Richard Monckton Milnes, now 40, would often ride over to see her. Frances Nightingale, Florence's mother, would see him sometimes from an upstairs window cantering over the hills and would hurry downstairs to tell the family where he was heading. An excellent writer and poet and a wealthy, personable fellow, Richard delighted Frances Nightingale. He was the son of Robert Pemberton Milnes, of Fryston Hall, West Yorkshire, and the Honourable Henriette, daughter of Robert Monckton-Arundell, 4th Viscount Galway. Richard had entered Trinity College, Cambridge in 1827, and had joined The Apostles Club there, an animated literary group that included Tennyson and others. Monckton Milnes was known to be something of a poet and had published two volumes of verse. Amongst other notable works, he had also written *The Life and Letters of Keats*, published in 1848, one of the first accounts of Keats's correspondence in his tragically brief life and read with great interest. After he'd gained his M.A., Monckton Milnes studied further at Bonn University in Germany and also travelled through Italy and Greece, publishing vibrant accounts of his excursions. In 1837 he'd been elected to parliament as Conservative candidate for Pontefract with a special interest in reformatory schools, and it seemed like a good idea to the grand ladies who met him that the dashing Monckton Milnes should also become a member of their family, for they each had a lovely daughter sure to capture his heart. Though it appeared his heart was set on Florence Nightingale, the girl with the heavy dark hair and piercing hypnotic eyes, undoubtedly a beauty, but perhaps a little too thin? Richard liked to write poetry, and was drawn to poetry in general. Some said his work, though thoughtful and graceful, lacked the heightened emotion needed to rise to greatness. But Florence Nightingale, that day, as they stood beneath a tree in the grounds of Lea Hurst, found his heightened emotion most alluring as he recited a poem by Shelley;

> *"'The fountains mingle with the river*
> *And the rivers with the ocean,*
> *The winds of heaven mix for ever*
> *With a sweet emotion;*
> *Nothing in the world is single,*
> *All things by a law divine*
> *In one another's being mingle—*
> *Why not I with thine?*
> *See the mountains kiss high heaven,*
> *And the waves clasp one another;*
> *No sister-flower would be forgiven*
> *If it disdain'd its brother;*
> *And the sunlight clasps the earth,*
> *And the moonbeams kiss the sea—*
> *What is all this sweet work worth*
> *If thou kiss not me?'"*

A kiss! Did he want to kiss her? What, there, in the grounds of her home where everyone could see from the window? How she would like him to kiss her, but the thought confused her. She turned from him quickly. Usually self-controlled, just then he was nervous. Florence knew he had come to talk about marriage. She turned back, and his eager needful eyes met her own. Oh, she would have him for her own, she would marry him, have his children! She would, she would. But only in imagination. Richard's instinct, she reflected, was always for the good of others never for himself. And she loved him. She had always loved him. How she would like to steal that smile from his lips and replace it with a kiss. But she could not. She could not abandon what she saw as her divine purpose.

Drops of rain fell through the branches of the tree where they sheltered; they would have to return to the house. But first she needed to speak. She must tell him why she couldn't get married, how it had been when she'd made her decision to nurse, in the grounds of Embley Park on that sunlit autumn day. She believed she had heard a voice, she said, different from any other and quite beyond words, something deep in her soul. – 'Grandmother Shore would pray with such passion in her room,' she told him earnestly. 'I would stop to listen by her door. Her prayers were so beautiful and I too would pray, knowing I must help the sick and dying, those in pain and misery. When I heard the voice, I knew I was called.' He stood there quiet and pensive while she spoke her important words, bravely, proudly and with certainty. The silver Derbyshire sky had started to darken. She talked on quickly, determined. 'And I would like to help prepare them for heaven if I must.'

'But my dear Florence,' he protested. 'It is surely impossible. How will you do it?' He breathed in deeply, awaiting her answer, holding back from her intensity.

'I shall nurse,' she said, into the deep sadness of his eyes. 'I know God wants me to nurse.'

'I take it you've told your parents,' he said softly, with a hint of annoyance. 'About hearing the voice of God, I mean?' He frowned, concerned and gazed at the sky.

She shrugged. 'You think I'm selfish, don't you. You think I don't care about my family. I do, I really do. – Oh, look at me Richard. Don't look at the sky!'

He looked at her again. 'That's not what I think at all, and please don't think for me Flo. I can think for myself. But you need to know how your parents feel about this. It is quite irregular, you know.'

The day was darkening. Drops of rain continued to fall through the branches of the tree where they sheltered. She saw that his thick brown hair was wet, some of it sticking to his face. 'I have told them,' she said firmly. 'But it wasn't easy.' And she told him about their conversation in the drawing room, her mother's horrified face, the tears and disapproval; her sister's inflamed words, her father gazing through the window dumbfounded. But she'd stayed resigned. Her family must know her for who she was and accept her. She didn't want their cold indifference. She didn't want their anger. And she did not want to embarrass them. She wanted their love and encouragement, though as yet it wasn't forthcoming. Richard looked at her sadly. For a moment or two they were silent as she gazed at the splendid man before her leant against the tree, he appeared quite broken by her words.

'Florence . . .' he murmured. 'What about me?'

She watched his face. 'What do you want?' she asked, as he moved towards her. She could not bear to reject the warmth of his love. But she had gone as far as she could.

'I want *you,*' he said, his voice cracking with emotion. 'Just you. I can't live without you, Flo.'

'You want my love, and you have it,' she said firmly. 'But I cannot marry you, Richard. I shall never get married.'

He stamped about on the grass. 'You are in love with an idea,' he said irritably. 'You reject me for God who would have you instead of me!'

'Perhaps you want more than I can give?' she murmured.

He continued regardless. 'I have waited so long,' he said wearily. 'You reject me for some . . . some visionary thing, some light through the trees, some whisper on the breeze. Some . . .'

'Stop it!' she said, frowning. 'Do not say such things. I won't listen. Richard, I beg you. I love you and I shall never love anyone else. But I have something important to do.'

He sighed. 'You will always have something important to do. That is your nature,' he said, smiling tenderly. Then he turned to look at the woodland, a wind was up and the trees had started to wave. 'You have much to be thankful for Florence. But you are obviously not content.' He spoke in a very low voice. 'Sir Harry is often here . . . and I know he would like to marry you. Parthe has told me.'

She looked downwards confused. 'Sir Harry Verney is married. I know that his wife is dying, but I shall never marry anyone Richard. How many times must I tell you? How could you think such a thing? I always tell you the truth.' She looked at him hurt and disappointed. She was a good daughter, a good sister, she fulfilled all her duties, but she could not yield to expectations that made her feel lost. '"*Content*" she whispered. 'How can I be content when there is so much suffering and pain in the world, so much war?'

'But you can't solve the problems of the world,' he said sighing. 'Even politicians live in hell over that.'

'I can help,' she said defensively.

'And you can be happy sometimes. It is allowed.' He looked at her directly and held her gaze. 'I have seen you happy Florence. We have danced together often. Those times, when I held you and you laughed, I wanted no more than that moment. And that love has stayed in my heart.' He put his hand in his pocket and drew out a small box, and in cupped hands held it before her. 'Will you have it?' he asked earnestly. 'I bought it in London . . . Flo, you have the prettiest neck . . .'

'What is it?' she asked taking the box curiously. For a moment or two they were silent as she drew out a thin gold necklace. 'It's beautiful!' she gasped, fingering the delicate chain. 'See how it glistens, even in the late afternoon! – But Richard, you know I don't care for jewellery.'

'See it as my heart,' he said softly. 'Please accept it.'

'Oh yes, yes!' she murmured. 'And with searching wonder she placed it around her neck.

'Here, let me fasten it,' he said, quickly moving towards her and lifting her hair.

'Let it be our secret,' she whispered. 'The years ahead are unknown but this necklace will help guide my way.'

'Dear Florence, I could offer you such joy if you'd let me,' he said, clasping his hands intently.

'We must give the slip to the rain!' she said quickly, linking his arm. 'Come, let's run or I fear we'll be soaked.' They made their way down the pathways back to the house, the scent of the pending evening rising from the grass as they went, the thin patter of rain falling through the trees and the sound of distant streams dancing careless down the hillsides.

CHAPTER 4

Embley Park 1854

Sidney Herbert, Secretary of State for War in the British Government, had spoken with his fellow ministers in the Cabinet that week regarding certain thoughts he'd had about Miss Florence Nightingale's valorous aspirations, and to his relief he'd received their assurance that were she to undertake the formidable task of taking a batch of nurses to Scutari hospital, as she so urgently desired, she'd have the total support of the government.

He had found it rather difficult though to see how her work at Kaiserwerth could in any way compare with what would be required at Scutari. But William Russell, *The Times* correspondent, had made a pressing and serious appeal about the wretchedness of army hospitals in Crimea, and the general public, concerned for the sons of England, had flooded his office with letters, for by 1854, no fewer than 18,000 soldiers had been admitted into military hospitals at Scutari and in the Crimea. Nursing had developed a bad reputation which meant the War Office had been disinclined to hire nurses, for many had been seen to be desperate for the money and had no idea about nursing. Help for the wounded soldiers in the Crimea usually came from male orderlies. Florence Nightingale was a capable nurse, without doubt, and an excellent administrator too, but Scutari hospital? The place had been described as "a hell hole". Sidney Herbert could hardly believe what he was writing when he'd written the letter to request her support, and he'd made himself a copy so he might read it again later on.

After he'd saddled his horse for Embley Park, he sat for a moment to read through the letter once more in his garden. Now what had he said . . . *"There is but one person in England that I know of who would be capable of organising and superintending such a scheme . . . "* Well, of course, it was true. *"And . . . My question simply is this. Would you listen to the request to go out and supervise the whole thing?"* The words sent a chill down his spine. Florence was so slender, and she didn't look particularly strong. Was she really capable of taking on such a task? He carried on reading. *"You would, of course, have plenary authority over all the nurses, and I think I could secure you the fullest assistance and co-operation from the medical staff, and you would also have an unlimited power of drawing on the government for the success of your mission".* Oh that he could keep his word! *"I do not say one word to press you,"* the letter continued, *"yet I must not conceal from you that upon your decision will depend the ultimate success or failure of the plan."* And he'd gone on to say, *"There is one point which I have hardly a right to touch upon, but I trust you will pardon me. If you were inclined to undertake the great work, would Mr and Mrs Nightingale consent?"*

I do not expect they will agree in the least, thought Herbert, but William and Frances must be advised of all this and he hoped Florence had discussed it with them for they had every right to take an interest in her welfare. He ended his letter by meekly assuring her that he knew she would come to a wise and right decision. And *"God grant it may be one in accordance with my hopes – Believe me, dear Miss Nightingale, ever yours, SIDNEY HERBERT."*

Well, he had written it and he had sent it, what's more it had been a startling discovery to find that she had written to him already to offer her services. Their letters had crossed in the post. *"It is not in the stars to hold our destiny but in ourselves,"* he murmured, lifting his eyes to the sky. Life was full of mysteries. Well, that was that, now he must ride to her home and suffer the wrath of her father, who was bound to be against the idea and send him off on his way. What father would want his daughter to work at Scutari? Sydney was nervous; this powerful, determined woman had had her way, and here he was supporting her in what some had called "madness".

The fragrant scent of narcissi reached him through the open window as he sat in the parlour at Embley Park. He bent towards Florence, seated opposite, 'Quite so, my dear, I do believe you are right,' he said, nodding his head at her words A friend of the family, he understood Florence's fervour, and though she wanted the impossible her strong and certain gaze suggested she talked a lot of sense. 'The hospitals there are in a terrible state,' he said. 'But we did not realise how many men would be injured, let alone how many would die. We were totally unprepared and must somehow try to improve things.'

It was mid afternoon. Herbert's horse, tethered at the front of the house, had been fed and watered and now rested. With a little quiet laugh Herbert said he truly believed the creature had been reading his thoughts on the way, for the Crimean war was an ever-present concern and he always had it in mind. The sound of his horse's hooves on the way to Embley House had resonated in his mind with his own intense preoccupations. Herbert had entered the House of Commons in 1832 as Conservative member for Wiltshire. As Secretary of State for War it was now his duty to attend to the matters of the devilish Crimean war between the Russians, the British, the French and the Ottoman Turks. It had started in 1853 and was part of a long-standing contest between major European powers for influence over the declining Ottoman Empire. *Money! Power! Territory!* Who should have it, to whom did it belong, and why? And the Mediterranean Sea? Russia wanted to get into that by way of the Black Sea, for was it not a passage to British India? Oh yes, a most significant water. Sidney Herbert's mind was awhirl. He was expected to accomplish things often contrary to reason, while reason was the order of the day. So many documents to read, so much talking in parliament, so many minds to deal with, he must constantly rack his brains and try to stay sane.

'Your concerns, dear Florence, are most relevant,' he said kindly. 'You know my thoughts on this issue. The theatre of war is vicious and cruel, and oh, what suffering it brings. The discordant Middle East factions and their political problems are complex. There are too many differing opinions and far too many unknowns.' He lowered his voice. 'And there are far too many injured and dead as well.' Sidney Herbert speculated this way and that, talked, wrote letters, gave speeches and walked his gardens, but little cheered him and he was forced to maintain the British stiff upper lip and to behave in a gentlemanly manner when he wanted to swear to high heaven. He took out his pocket watch and looked at the time. 'I must leave very soon,' he said frowning. 'I have to be in London tomorrow.' For a moment or two they were thoughtful. 'We can't let Turkey be overthrown by Russia . . .' he murmured, as if to himself. 'The Russian desire to move towards the south is disturbing. We know what they're up to.'

'The hospitals for our soldiers are dreadful,' said Florence. 'The reports in *The Times* are disturbing. I can't bear to think of those wounded men dying from inadequate nursing.'

'Rightly so, dear Florence, rightly so,' said Herbert stroking his chin. 'You have summed it up precisely in your letter. The mounting carnage is vile. Wounded men are dying who might otherwise be healed and live.'

Bright spring flowers were poking their heads through the rich Hampshire soil in the grounds of Embley Park; tulips, daffodils and other wonderful blooms claimed place in the gardens. The trees by the window were heavy with blossom and Sidney Herbert must constantly blow his nose, for he had something of a problem with allergies, he said, at this time of year.

'Poor Sidney,' sighed Florence, as he blew his nose yet again. 'The blossoms are causing you discomfort.'

'It is hardly a war-cry, my dear,' he smiled. 'It is just a natural process, though my nose does not like it.'

'I believe ginger tea can be helpful,' Florence said smiling hopefully. 'Ginger for everything!' She looked across at the window. 'I could close the window, of course. But Mama likes the scent of flowers in the drawing room and this is her territory, you see.'

'Ah, *territory*,' Herbert said, sitting back sighing heavily. 'How people fight over territory, even in houses!'

Florence looked away, thoughtful. 'I think it is a good idea to let fresh air in the house, however. Whenever I enter the homes of the cottagers I always suggest they should open the windows and admit the fresh air.' She frowned, concerned.

Herbert sneezed again. Florence gave him a worried look and made to rise.

'No, no, my dear, leave the window. I am quite alright. I have far more serious concerns than the occasional sneeze. I must deliver an important speech to parliament tomorrow. I do hope Palmerston and Aberdeen do not oppose me; I am all the time watching their faces. If only we might agree on policies more quickly.'

The sound of piano playing came from a distant room. Parthe was playing Mozart. Herbert and Florence however were absorbed in their own concerns. Florence handed him his tea, then offered him a slice of cake. She liked and admired Herbert. He was sensible, courteous and charming and a good manager of men in general, but she wasn't surprised by his words. Her father often lost patience with parliamentary affairs and would sometimes slam down his paper on reading the news.

'Lord Palmerston and Aberdeen might argue for ages,' said Herbert.

'Well, if the Chancellor and the Prime Minister cannot agree, how do you make any progress?' She looked at him earnestly.

'Ah, terribly slowly sometimes. Chancellor Gladstone, is popular with the working classes, largely because of his policy of equal opportunity. He is a man of causes; he is intent just now on rescuing poor young women from prostitution, he wants to rehabilitate these fallen young creatures somehow by finding them suitable employment or even husbands.' Herbert continued with a sigh. 'Oh, indeed he should be sad if he heard some of the gossip.'

Florence lowered her voice. 'I doubt he would care about gossip. If a cause is strong enough what does it matter if others do not understand? We must do as we feel inclined.'

For a moment or two there was a perfect stillness in the room. They were both thoughtful.

'So much drill with our soldiers,' she murmured. 'I watched them when I visited London with father. The men move in unison as if they were toys.' She gazed at Herbert, absorbed in her thoughts. 'I fear that war is a sort of game.'

'We have a fine army,' said Herbert with a nod. 'They are well disciplined.' He braced himself and stared at her curiously. '"A game", you say, oh no, we must protect ourselves from the enemy. The soldiers must be ready to fight.'

'But they are not taught how to scream quietly,' said Florence. 'We are well away from the battlefields and do not hear them of course.' For a few moments they were silent. The sound of the piano came louder. Florence spoke again. 'You talk of discipline Sidney. But I hear that Cardigan can be rather cruel with the soldiers. A soldier must not fall from his horse in training or he might suffer a cruel lashing. And I am led to believe he can be mean to his officers too if they do not behave like gentlemen, whilst the soldiers are often called "scum".' She sat calmly, drinking her tea. Such words had to be said. She continued. 'My father was angry when he read about what happened to The Light Brigade. Who gave the orders? Did Lucan understand when he gave command to Cardigan? Did Nolan need to die, along with so many young soldiers? She hung her head; her eyes were dark just then, dark with confusion and pain. Lifting her face, she saw that Herbert looked preoccupied. 'I'm sorry if my boldness disturbs you,' she said, lowering her voice.

'No, no, your own cause is strong,' he said, breathing in deeply and changing his position on the chair. 'As to that, you know where I stand; it is all in my letter.'

'Of course, and I am eager to get to work. The months I spent in Kaiserwerth at the Deaconess Institute have made me more determined than ever. I have learned so much and want to put my learning into practice.'

He met her eyes and spoke quietly. 'To take nurses to the Crimea is certainly a grand idea, but are you really sure you want to do it? Those hospitals are hellish places. They are filthy and full of vermin. And you do not know if the nurses would be able to take it. It's a long way to go to find yourself coming back when you have seen the horror of the place.'

Florence was thoughtful. Herbert spoke again, slowly and deeply serious. 'It would certainly be a brave endeavour and hazardous too.' He straightened his cravat and frowned. 'But tell me, Florence, what are your spiritual inclinations regarding religion, for the nurses may vary in their stance.'

Florence raised her eyebrows; the question went right to her heart. Religion could make things difficult; she had thought about it a lot, especially when it came to nurses. How should nurses behave, how should they pray, and to whom? She answered steadily, carefully choosing her words. 'As regards the ways of the spirit, I think we must proceed with reason, personal inclinations are important for we all come to God in our own way.'

'Quite right, quite right,' Herbert said solemnly. 'Reason is most important.' He looked away abstracted as if wondering what to say next.

Florence knew how difficult his work was and often felt sympathetic when he talked with her father over dinner. He had a soft and gentle voice, not at all what might be expected considering his impassioned speeches.

'My wife sends her love,' he said, quietly. 'She enjoys your letters. Elizabeth admires you.'

'I must go to see her,' said Florence. His eyes were warm and embracing. She felt she knew him, had always known him, and could always relax in his company.

'My wife has faith in your purpose. She believes in you, Florence.'

Florence smiled. 'Elizabeth has been most supportive. She sends me beautiful words.'

He glanced about the room. 'I am to ask you about your owl,' he said playfully.

Florence laughed quietly. 'Oh, you mean Athena? She is very bad tempered at present. I must always have her beside me or she objects and makes dreadful sounds.' She looked across at the caged owl nearby. 'She knows you are here and I think she likes you. She will hear the tone of our voices.'

'Is that so?' Herbert gave her a look of dramatic surprise. 'She likes me, does she? I'm glad. I am short on popularity at present.'

'She listens carefully. I think she fears you might take me away or something.'

He laughed quietly. 'Well, certainly *something* Florence. For I cannot speak with you without something demands my attention.' He clapped his hands lightly.

'I'm sorry,' she said, looking downwards.

'No, no. There is always something to bother me. I tend to put bothers in my pocket like you did with that owlet, though parliamentary matters grow heavier by the day and make outrageous demands.'

'Does our talk make your pocket heavy?' She smiled concernedly.

Herbert's voice fell low. 'Our talk has been good.' He shook his finger before her. 'I have one or two ideas. That's all I can tell you just now, but I'll write.'

There was the sound of the door softly opening.

'Sidney!' cried Frances Nightingale, smiling widely. 'I see you have taken tea. And did you have a slice of cake? It was only baked yesterday.'

'Sidney has eaten quite a large piece, Mama,' said Florence. 'It is very good cake.' What she really wanted to say would only cause her mother anxiety. 'We were talking about Athena. I told Sidney how difficult she'd been for us today.'

'Oh yes,' said Frances, 'She bit the finger of the maid and all because she took her to the kitchen away from Florence. She can be such a bad bird; her beak and talons are sharp. She must always be close to Florence.'

'But an owl is a wild creature,' said Herbert, looking confused. 'She is strong and full grown. It is quite some time since Florence found her at the Parthenon. Why not let her go free?'

'The ways of the woods would confuse her,' said Florence quickly. 'I fear she would die within an hour.'

'And so she is imprisoned,' murmured Herbert, frowning deeply. He braced himself. 'Ah, let us not talk of the ways of the woods. I have enough problems with the ways of the world for now. Though I doubt there is very much difference.'

'The poor little bird was rescued,' said Frances. 'Those boys would have killed her. How wicked they were to throw stones at a tiny owlet.'

'Well, they didn't do it for long,' said Florence, anger in her voice. 'I saved her. And I believe she knows it. We underestimate animals.'

'You are quite right, Florence,' said her mother. 'And we underestimate insects too. The maid said the spider in the kitchen knows when she's there and hides until she has gone.'

Florence looked at Herbert with thoughtful, curious eyes. There was sensitivity in him she was glad of.

'Your owl would find that spider in seconds and eat it!' laughed Herbert.

'I doubt she would have the skill,' Florence said frowning. 'She has never experienced hunting. I feed her myself.' She breathed in deeply. 'You must be careful though, she will not eat food from anyone other than her mistress.'

'So what do you feed her?' Herbert asked curiously. He rose from his seat and went across to the bird, still and silent in her cage.

'Oh, little pieces of fish or rabbit . . . anything,' said Florence. 'She eats whatever I give her.'

'William is away on business,' said Frances, 'or he would surely have enjoyed your company, Sidney. I'm sorry he's missed you.' She glanced at her daughter and frowned. 'It was most important however that Florence should talk with you today, though her father and I were not apprised of your visit.' She sighed, half annoyed.

Florence braced herself and smiled at Herbert wryly, this was one of those moments when she and her mother might quarrel. Herbert eyed her knowingly. He spoke quickly.

'To tell the truth we have exchanged some important letters and I wanted to come to Hampshire. – I wasn't sure when I could make it. – My wife is not very well so could not join me. – I thought I would make the journey today, though I have little time nowadays and have urgent matters pending. – I am to see someone else nearby, and so . . .'

Frances shook her head and smiled. 'Dear Sidney, don't be embarrassed. I am fully aware of Florence's ambition. I may not have her mathematical skills but it isn't too difficult to put two and two together. You are no doubt aware that I do not approve of this nursing idea, but I know you indulge it. Her father does not, of course.'

Florence sighed at the tone in her mother's voice. Herbert stood slowly and reached for his hat. 'I rather expected he wouldn't like it,' said Herbert. I must talk with him soon. Forgive me, Frances,' he said, frowning. 'Please excuse me. I must make good speed to Wiltshire.'

Just then through the window they saw that a figure came walking fast down the path. Slender and strong, her fair hair flying about her, Florence saw it was Amelia, a young woman who lived in the woods with her family. She had befriended their maid and often came to the house. They all three watched as she made her way to the door. She looked worried.

'It's Amelia,' Frances said to Florence. 'She hopes to be one of our maids, but your father isn't happy with her history . . .'

'But Mama, it is all hearsay. They are a poor family. You know of their hardships.' She turned to Herbert who listened in silence.

'Amelia came to us once as a child. Her brother had stolen a rabbit and she feared Papa might have him put into prison. The boy had broken his ankle. He is a grown man now and in the army.'

Herbert pursed his lips. 'Poaching,' he muttered. 'Ah yes, trespassing on land owned by the rich while hoping to catch a rabbit for dinner, and all the while countries steal land from each other, killing men in their thousands.' He sighed and stared at the floor.

Florence continued boldly. 'A lot of young girls are made to work on the streets Mama, to help feed their families. Prostitution is rife. Something should be done.'

Frances Nightingale straightened her hair, embarrassed, and took to watching a flight of birds through the window.

'Absolutely,' sighed Herbert. 'Gladstone has a lot to say about that. He has invested much time assisting prostitutes. I believe he will even stop his coach to talk with them sometimes. Most of them are simple girls who have never known anything but poverty.'

The young woman talked in the hall with the housemaid, but their voices were almost inaudible.

Sidney Herbert donned his hat and bade them farewell. Frances went to find Amelia, and took her to the kitchen, while Florence saw Herbert to the porch where they arranged to meet again in London. He turned to look at her as he set his horse to depart, and she met his eyes with confidence. He nodded assuredly. They were on the same side.

CHAPTER 5

A Fearsome Vision

William Nightingale sat pondering over the articles in his newspaper. Florence sat writing at the table. With a lively fire burning in the grate the parlour at Lea Hurst was warm and restful that late October morning.

'The world is going insane,' Nightingale murmured. The weather was chilly and he and Florence were dressed in their winter woollies. They weren't expecting any visitors that day, Parthe was somewhere else in the house and Frances was in the kitchen chastising the maid, who, it seemed, let Amelia into the house too often, to gossip, to complain and to despair.

'Quite right, father,' said Florence, looking up from her work. 'The world is losing its wits, if it ever had any to start with.'

'Are you writing to Sidney?' he asked, turning another page of *The Times*.

'Of course,' she answered, in an equally casual tone. 'As you can imagine, we have much to say to each other.'

'Well, I have said my piece most forcefully. I can do no more.'

'And how do I appear in your words?' he said, sighing. He lowered his voice to a serious tone. 'You must not relate our conversations to Sidney, my dear. You know that, don't you? What I say to my family is private.'

'Papa,' she said crossly, putting down her pen. 'I am no fool. I know exactly what to say. What's more I know Sidney Herbert very well. He is a fine Minister for War. He must make such weighty decisions I wonder his head isn't spinning.'

'Ah, so much achieved yet so much lost.' William Nightingale said, raising his shoulders and dropping them slowly. 'I trust you are sensible Florence. Of course you are. I share a correspondence with Sidney myself but it is very different from yours. Should the two collide there might just be a bit of warfare.'

'I hope not Papa,' Florence said straightening. Two birds flitted about on the lawn. She watched them. 'Whatever do those birds eat?' she murmured, screwing up her eyes to look, 'once they have finished the berries. And how cold they must be when the leaves have gone from the trees and they must perch on the bare branches.'

'Cold? – Birds?' said her father, following the line of her eye.

'Yes, Papa, the birds must be cold in winter.'

'Oh, I doubt it. Anyway, a lot of them they fly to other countries in winter, my dear.' He coughed, irritated. 'I taught you that in your infancy.'

'But how do they know how to get there?' she said, staring at the thin blue sunlight beaming through the branches of the trees and entering the parlour in what seemed like long straight lines. Time passed quickly, she thought, it was now late autumn and the grounds of Lea Hurst were still and silent as if resting. The family would soon take leave of Derbyshire and return to Hampshire for the winter. Though Florence had other ideas as to where her future might lead.

Her father continued. 'The regular movement of birds from one part of the world to another and back is a miracle. How they get back astounds me!'

'Home is precious . . .' she said wistfully, glancing about at the familiar furniture, the wall hangings and pictures, and her father's well-worn shoes. One of the laces hung loose. He liked his shoes and would wear them until they were well near falling off before buying another pair.

'Those birds always have their coats on,' he smiled, 'whatever the season.'

She looked again at her writing. She was anxious. Her father was right; it was another letter to Sidney Herbert. She was in deeply serious mode and had much to say. She wrote on quickly then sat back.

'Yes, birds have their coats Papa. They are not as cold as the soldiers in the Crimea in winter. And soldiers don't always get their pay, you know. And those who have died don't always get their money sent home to their widows. Amelia has told us. It isn't right. Her brother should receive his pay, or is it not a kind of theft?'

Her father put aside his paper. 'Are you writing about that in your letter?'

'Yes. And rightly so, I shall get it posted straight away.' She spoke assertively. For a moment or two they were silent. 'Amelia tells us a lot,' she said finally, coming to warm her hands by the fire. 'Bare facts and all. That is what I want, truthful, bare facts.'

'Amelia is too fond of talking,' her father said, grimacing. 'And her facts might not be so truthful as you think. She is a very imaginative woman.'

'She is a cottager father and speaks freely. And she is brave. I shall never forget how she burst in here when she was all but ten years old to deliver us the woeful tale of her brother's plight in the woodland.'

'*Plight*'? My dear he was poaching. Those traps can be nasty and

I'm sorry about his foot. It is still a little twisted apparently. Yes, very unpleasant. But nothing like as bad as she said. The gamekeeper has changed things now, or so he tells me.'

Florence gave her father a glance of disapproval. 'They are poor,' she said firmly. 'I have found Amelia to be a person of integrity and I trust she tells me the truth. She does not *imagine* their poverty, it is all too real.' Florence took a seat on the chaise longue and continued to talk earnestly. 'Her brother's pay is vital to the family resources, which are very meagre. We made out a list of their needs last week at the cottage. They scarcely have enough to eat since the death of her father and often have only firelight for lighting when the days grow shorter. Candles are very expensive. We are lucky Papa and able to afford the best, those that do not smoke or smell.' She put her hand to her brow tiredly and for a moment or two there was silence. 'Are you quite comfortable, Papa?' she asked, bending to stir ashes from the hearth into the ash pan.

'Of course, my dear,' he replied, though he was thoughtful and subdued. Florence continued. 'Amelia told me her grandfather benefitted greatly from the invention of safety lamps when he worked in our mines.'

Nightingale frowned. 'Did she? Well, I'm sure he did. Upon my soul it's a dark place to be down the mines. But you have to be careful, methane is quick to ignite. It's a beggar that methane.'

Florence drew a breath, she did not often have her father to herself like this to talk with and she had much to say. 'Her brother should get his pay,' she said assertively, again stressing her point. 'A soldier's pay is relied on; many of the soldiers are penniless and abused.' She talked on quickly, emotional. 'A lot of those officers bought their status, you know, they haven't been promoted, it came because of their standing in society. – Oh, father, don't look at me like that, you know what I say is true. The way the officers speak of the soldiers is appalling. And I have heard that only the officers get anaesthetic for amputations. I think . . .'

William Nightingale waved his hand. 'You think too much, my dear. Sidney will get it sorted, I'm sure.' He sighed irritably. 'When men are at war things are never straightforward. If only they were.'

'They need to be better organised, and should keep proper accounts,' Florence said flatly. 'It's important, Papa, good communications and proper, thorough accounts.'

'Ah yes, that is the top and bottom of it,' her father said gravely. 'Proper accounts. Heaven knows where this Crimean war is going.' He pointed to a page of *The Times*, open on a low table. 'I should think you'll have read about The Light Brigade? Lord Cardigan will never live it down.'

'Yes,' she said gravely. 'It's absurd. To charge into artillery like that is suicidal.' She read the piece another time . . .

The Times/1854/News/*The Charge of the Light Brigade*
by William Howard Russell

". . . I shall proceed to describe, to the best of my power, what occurred under my own eyes, and to state the facts which I have heard from men whose veracity is unimpeachable, reserving to myself the right of private judgement in making public and in surpressing the details of what occurred on this memorable day . . .

[After losing ground to a British force half its size, the Russians retreated to the heights above Sebastopol, a port town on the Black sea].

At 11:00 our Light Cavalry Brigade rushed to the front . . . The Russians opened on them with guns from the redoubts on the right, with volleys of musketry and rifles.

They swept proudly past, glittering in the morning sun in all the pride and splendor of war. We could hardly believe the evidence of our senses. Surely that handful of men were not going to charge an army in position? Alas! It was but too true—their desperate valour knew no bounds, and far indeed was it removed from its so-called better part – discretion . . ."

'Bad management, bad planning,' she said sighing. 'It seems they thought the Russians might steal the artillery guns from the Turkish positions. Mixed messages brought on an awful frontal assault. The men in command didn't communicate properly. How ridiculous. – I hear they are often having arguments. Personal feelings shouldn't be involved Papa, when it comes to war.'

'Not at all, Florence, you are right. And it's true they don't get on. Cardigan is Lucan's brother in law and I believe they hate each other. And so The Light Brigade went down because of a faulty command.' Her father spoke in a horrified tone. 'Absolute mayhem!'

Frances Nightingale entered the room. 'You asked me to join you with your father, Florence?' she said, looking from one to the other. Her eyes were tired and the sound of her thin voice lingered in the still room. She adjusted her shawl and stood for a moment staring at the fire.

'Sit down my dear. Sit down,' said her husband, patting the seat of the chair beside him.

At that moment all three of them seemed quite lost. Florence perceived that the daughter her mother had known and loved had changed dramatically and it disturbed her to see that her mother didn't understand her. She was a good mother and wife and had lots of friends, in whom she no doubt confided and who often gave Florence dark looks. There were strange moments of silence when friends came to dinner. Florence was difficult. Parthe was good and sensible. Parthe would get married, have children. Florence would turn her back on her suitors and go her own way, with furious purpose too. "God help Frances Nightingale," some of them whispered. "Whoever would want such a daughter?" Florence knew these things from the maid, who always kept track of gossip and reported back. The tone in her mother's voice just then implied she was deeply upset. Florence spoke shakily, 'I wanted to reassure you, Mama,' she said softly. She smiled at her parents warmly. 'Both of you . . .' She saw that her father's eyes had narrowed concernedly. Taking a breath, she continued. 'Sidney and I have discussed this thoroughly and you'll be pleased to know he supports me. All will be well.'

Frances Nightingale glanced at her husband. 'And it seems your father also supports you, at last,' she said coolly and formally.

Florence exchanged a sorry look with her father. Her mother hadn't been party to a lot of their talks. But it wasn't out of secrecy, it was more by way of discretion, for the path Florence had trod with Herbert had been rocky, and could hardly be considered 'ladylike.' There was no ladylike way to talk about war.

William Nightingale took hold of his wife's hand. 'Dearest Fanny, Florence is determined to nurse, all that is left for us now is to help her do it the best way she can. If it can properly be done, that is. I have promised her an allowance which will help her feed and clothe herself and buy whatever she needs.'

'A proper pair of conspirators,' Frances Nightingale whispered, drawing a breath.

'I intend to do it Mama,' Florence said flatly. 'I shall choose a team of nurses and go to the Scutari hospital where we are needed. You know my feelings about it.'

'I am not as foolish as you think,' Frances Nightingale said assertively. 'I know about Scutari hospital. People have told me and I have read about it too. Shall I tell you what it is like?' She straightened. 'You think I am stupid don't you, refined out of all intelligence. Well, I am not. I simply choose not to talk about things like Flo does. She is sometimes extremely vulgar and cannot hold her tongue!'

'Enough, I think, my dear,' said William, his hands clasped tight with emotion. He could not bear it when his family argued. He got up, went to the window and looked out.

The door opened again. Parthe came in quickly.

'What a miserable bunch you are,' she said frowning. 'Just look at you. And poor Sir Harry is about to lose his wife. She is very sick Mama.'

'I know, I know,' said Frances Nightingale bracing herself. 'What did he come for?'

'I am making a drawing of him, Mama. He thinks it is very good. It's an excellent likeness. I am rather proud of it actually.'

'I am sure your portrait will cheer him,' said her father. 'Come to the fire, my dear. He didn't come to see *me* now, did he? Though I know what he's after.'

'So what is he after?' said Parthe, adjusting the folds of her dress.

William glanced at each of the women. They were waiting. 'Well, he knows that his wife will die very soon. He's a very busy man with a large family of children. What do you think?'

Parthe looked down at her silk-slippered feet and straightened her hair. 'Papa, what are you suggesting?' she said quietly.

'Oh, you know what Papa is suggesting, Parthe. Need you ask?' said Florence.

'You think he is looking for another wife, don't you?' said Frances, scowling at her husband.

'But he loves Eliza dearly,' Parthe protested. 'He has always been devoted to his family. He's a highly respected Member of Parliament with an illustrious military career. Poor Eliza is dying, that is true, but . . . '

'Men always need wives,' said Florence, folding her arms and staring at the fire.

'But it is you he adores, Florence,' said Parthe, sharply. 'And you know it. He comes to see me because I draw things. Florence wants to talk and I want to draw.'

'Drawing is very much safer,' said her mother, pulling herself together. 'Sir Harry is still quite handsome,' she added, looking her daughters up and down. 'And he's very learned too. I believe he speaks several languages and has considerable wealth as well.'

They were all four silent for a moment. Then Frances rang for the maid.

'I should like you to bring us a pot of strong tea,' said Frances, 'and a few slices of cake.'

'Oh – that we should sit eating cake whilst men are dying in Crimea,' murmured Florence.

'Ah, to the devil with all that for today,' said William Nightingale. 'I rather prefer the chocolate sponge to the plain one,' he said to the maid. 'Bring us some of that.'

'Of course, sir,' said the maid, giving him a brief curtsey. He laid more logs on the fire.

'I do think – I really do think it is most unnecessary to be so unfeeling Papa,' said Parthe.

'So when was I so unfeeling?' he said, looking surprised.

'What you said, or implied about Sir Harry.'

'Oh that. Well, it's the way things go isn't it.'

Parthe looked at him straight. 'I find his company interesting Papa. We enjoy being together. Now what can be wrong with that?'

'Nothing,' said Frances. 'What matters is that people are happy.'

'Thank you,' said Parthe, reassured like a child.

Florence stared through the window. Her thoughts were in the Crimea, far, far away. She had made a pledge with her soul and was face to face with her destiny.

CHAPTER 6

Heartfelt Contemplations

W illiam Nightingale sat by himself that morning in his study, trying to think everything through. He was quite out of sorts. Had Florence lost her way? Had he been a bad father? What did it mean to have his daughter defy the norms for women of her class and in such a profound way? And how could he console his dear wife, Fanny, for she certainly needed consoling. She had always imagined Florence would be married with children, living in a stately house with a good and worthy husband and nothing to spoil her joy. But wounded soldiers, amputations, blood and warfare? And wouldn't dear Florence miss the flowers in their gardens, the lovely hollyhocks, dahlias, nasturtiums and such, and the hills where she liked to ride her horse? He shook his head in dismay. The dark, cold reality of Crimea entered his veins like sharp particles of ice. The future he feared for his daughter was close as skin and he couldn't avoid it. Why, oh why, did she want to be a nurse, and of all things go to Crimea? She knew how it was, she had read the reports in *The Times,* and she'd been privy to conversations around their dinner table, often in the company of leading politicians and reliable authorities. Everyone knew what was happening with that war; William Russell had made sure of that, his reports in *The Times,* were frightening. Florence had also seen the fearsome paintings of war hanging on the walls of the grand houses they'd visited, at home and in other countries, and he'd watched her contemplate them closely. Was his dear daughter to be carried away by some harpy, some ugly winged creature half woman half bird, and taken to live in a bottomless pit of misery? She believed she'd had a calling from God. But might it be something else? And did that bird she talked to have a sort of connection. It didn't bear thinking about. But think about it, he must. Florence would have her way just as she'd done since childhood. And just as she'd given all she had to her learning, she would give all she had to her decisions. Perhaps he hadn't been a strong enough father, or might he have been a bit too forceful? He'd asked a lot when it came to her learning, from both of his daughters actually. But Parthe would conform and not give him anything to worry about. Florence though . . . She would not marry Richard that much was clear, grand fellow though he was. And the man had almost wept when he'd been rejected, he would never find another woman like her, he'd said, not ever. – "Is there somebody else?" he'd challenged. "Tell me why she won't have me. For heaven's sake Nightingale, surely bandaging wounded soldiers in that filthy Scutari hospital isn't preferable to becoming my wife?" Then he'd buried his face in his hands, murmuring miserably. "I do wish Russell wouldn't send us those damned dispatches," he'd groaned. "He's persuaded her, you know, all that begging for women to go to that god-forsaken place!"

William Nightingale had stared at Richard perplexed. He had tried his best to reason with his daughter, but to no avail, he'd said. Florence was Florence. She was charming in her persistence and Richard undoubtedly loved her. But William had seen how he'd suffered. Richard was clever and accomplished; he'd travelled widely and after visiting Greece had published *Memorials of a Tour in some Parts of Greece* describing his experiences there, and very good writing it was. And he was certainly humane and warm hearted, everyone said so. A Conservative Member of Parliament with extensive sympathies, he'd championed the abolition of slavery and was able to consider all manner of opinion, even visiting France in 1848 to see how things were developing there since the wave of revolutions in Europe and the overthrow of the French king, Louis Philippe. Richard knew the ways of the world. He had a bright, quick smile and ready laughter and would seize on an issue and argue it out till the end. But his sympathies with continental liberalism, which he'd made well known on returning to England were challenging when monarchies were fearful and he was wont to give opinions too freely. Poets were a bit like that, he decided. But he was certainly a caring sort of fellow. What's more he was well-to-do. He could offer Florence a more than comfortable lifestyle. His daughter would do well if she married Monckton Milnes and it would get her out of the clutches of that wretched harpy! William Nightingale stared at the ceiling and couldn't help feeling that something had passed away; the die was cast and Florence had chosen her path.

The 19th century Industrial Revolution had brought about enormous changes and the literary greats had immortalised them in poetry, novels, plays and journalism. Life in England was intensely busy and in 1851, the Great Exhibition, a fabulous spectacle conceived of and organised by Prince Albert and Queen Victoria, was presented in London in an enormous glass and iron structure called "The Crystal Palace". The vast display of exhibits, mainly from Britain or the

British Empire, included pottery, ironwork, furniture, perfumes and a considerable number of firearms. The show was attended by a multitude of people, transport being available to all with the advent of railways, and millions of people passed through the exhibition from May to October. Times were changing rapidly and novelists like Charles Dickens had brought into focus the cruel inequalities between classes in Victorian England, while Charlotte Brontë in *Jane Eyre* showed how women might assert themselves and never lose self-respect however they were pushed to the boundaries of their own principles. Women had very few rights in the 19th century once they were married, and everything they owned became the property of their husband. Divorce was rare, though men could divorce their wives if their wives committed adultery or did not conform to their needs. It was commonly thought wrong for a woman to find work outside the home, though they often worked for the aristocracy as cooks or maids, and industries like textiles relied heavily on women's labour. A few middle class women worked before marriage, but once they were married their earnings belonged to their husbands. Florence thought a lot on such issues as she prepared to depart for Crimea. What was a woman, how should she be, and could she not simply be herself? She reflected on how hard she had studied and learned, but she'd made the extra leap of wanting to put her efforts into practice. It was certainly important to know things, she reasoned, but wasn't it important to do something useful with that learning for the benefit of others?

The Nightingale and Gaskell families, living in the north of England, were both of Unitarian persuasion and were warmly acquainted. In October that year, Elizabeth Gaskell, well-known for her novel, *Mary Barton*, a tale of Manchester life, was at Lea Hurst finishing *North and South*; a social novel which she hoped to publish very soon. She sat just now at the table in the Lea Hurst drawing room, writing vigorously. There was a sense of urgency in the air, as if a whole era of life was changing fast and time was of the essence. Florence sat by the fire, repairing a fraying edge on one of her shawls, which she intended to take to Scutari. Both women were lost in thought. Florence glanced up abstractedly then put down her sewing and went across the room to look at Elizabeth's work; it was exciting to know she was coming to the end of her novel. But Florence found that the pages of the novel were laid on a chair and instead Elizabeth was writing a letter.

'You frown, my dear,' Elizabeth said, seeing that Florence looked on. 'Does the letter disturb you?' She gazed at her searchingly. 'You know how I am, I write as I see and feel.' It was an awkward moment; she was describing Florence's appearance.

'It's rude of me to snoop,' Florence said. 'I thought you were writing your novel and wanted to look.' She straightened, embarrassed.

Elizabeth breathed in deeply. 'I hope you don't mind if I write about you, Flo. I wouldn't want to offend you.' She spoke quietly and frowned. 'I am quite inconsiderate sometimes.'

'You say that my eyes are grey?' Florence said, smiling. 'Are they really? She looked at Elizabeth self-consciously. 'Why do you study me so hard?'

Elizabeth Gaskell looked attractive and grand in her black silk dress, certain of herself and totally fearless with her pen. She was kind and warm and the family enjoyed her company. It was wrong to make her feel ill at ease. But she scribbled things down constantly; it was all quite mysterious.

Elizabeth passed her the page. 'See what I've written,' she said. 'No, please look. It's a letter to a friend; she wants to know what you look like. People admire you.' She sighed as Florence stepped away. 'I intended to show you anyway. I have much more to write and would like to send it off this week. But do please read it,

Florence. I'll feel better about it then. From the bottom of my heart, I do not wish to upset you.' Elizabeth gazed at her directly. 'Yes, I do believe your eyes are grey, for that is how I see them, but sometimes they appear pale blue when you stand by the window. Oh dear, I cannot help but observe such things, forgive me.'

Florence took the paper from her hand, and read through the words, curious as to how she was depicted. Parthe had often drawn likenesses, though she did not see herself like that. How was she portrayed in words?

"Florence is tall, very slight and willowy in figure; thick shortish rich brown hair very delicate complexion grey eyes which are generally pensive and drooping, but when they choose can be the merriest eyes I ever saw; and perfect teeth making her smile the sweetest I ever saw. Put a long piece of soft net . . . round this beautiful shaped head, so as to form a soft white framework for the full oval of her face . . . and dress her up in black glace silk up to the long round white throat – and a black lace shawl on and you may get near an idea of her perfect grace and lovely appearance. She is like a saint."

'"Like a saint?"' laughed Florence. 'You really are far too generous. You do not mean it, of course.'

'But I do,' said Elizabeth, leaning back in her chair and looking at Florence straight. 'You are a sort of holy creature. And you tread so softly, your footsteps are almost silent.'

'And do saints have silent footsteps?' Florence said wryly, handing back the page.

'Well, ghosts are silent, are they not?' Elizabeth said, smiling.

Florence feigned a shiver. 'A noisy ghost would disturb me,' she answered quietly. She rubbed her arms then went to stir the fire. 'I have serious work ahead of me,' she told her gravely.

'Of course' said Elizabeth. 'But you say so little about it.'

'It's difficult,' Florence said softly. 'Nothing must hinder my purpose. We've had awful arguments here. You speak of ghosts. Why, they have all been frightened away.'

Elizabeth tidied her papers. 'I do not come to pry, dear Florence. I am here as a sort of goodbye, and for inspiration for my work of course. What better inspiration could I have than to be here at Lea Hurst in Derbyshire with your wonderful family?'

'You are going back to Manchester tomorrow,' said Florence. 'I've been so inattentive, I'm sorry.' She looked around the room wistfully taking in the furniture and décor as if she were breathing them in. 'I too must leave. I don't know how long I shall be gone.'

For a moment or two they were silent.

'Do you hear from Charles Dickens?' asked Florence. She poked the logs into flame.

'I do, but we are prone to argue. Not that I mind. I enjoy a good argument. I met him first at a celebration dinner for *David Copperfield*. Even then we squabbled, if I remember. It was nonsense really. He is a man of immense energy and it does not do to cross him.'

'He very much admired *Mary Barton*.'

'He did. *But North and South* is quite different, it is long and complex and I do not see how it can lend itself to serialisation. That is what he wants, you see, he likes to serialise.'

'Parthe tells me he calls you his "Scheherazade". He says, you could never write too much for him, and you have never written half enough.' Florence looked at her and waited.

Elizabeth laughed quietly. 'Does he say so?'

'Your Cranford stories are loved by all,' said Florence, looking at her straight, 'even by the likes of Charlotte Brontë and Ruskin. But you will know about that, I'm sure.'

'I am glad,' said Elizabeth. She slipped her pages of work in a bag and smiled thoughtfully. 'I write to entertain and instruct. It is the real life for me.'

'I understand absolutely,' said Florence. She put out her hand. 'Shall we take a walk in the gardens? I would like to do that once more before I leave for Scutari. Let us walk about and talk. Perhaps you will tell me what you've been writing today, apart from writing about me, that is, which must have been a terrible bore.'

Elizabeth laughed and reached for her shawl, within minutes the room was silent.

Elizabeth Gaskell left next day with hurried goodbyes. There hadn't been a lot of togetherness during her stay, the time had been punctuated by bouts of heavy silences, and sadness pervaded the air. Parthe had kept to herself or had gone to play the piano. No-one wanted Florence to leave for Scutari and the presence of anyone else in the house was a strain. Whenever Florence looked at her parents she met with the same anxious faces, and every morning at breakfast she was confronted by Parthe's tear-stained cheeks. They quarrelled furiously. Parthe claimed Florence would finally make their mother ill with worry, and that what she wanted to do was ridiculous. Worse than that, she would probably die. Florence decided all three were unutterably weak in that they could not accept her resolve. She felt very alone with her thoughts, unable to talk about how it might be, how instead of something terrible it might be something wonderful, allowing her to answer her calling in a dignified and satisfying way. In the back of her mind, however, she could hear the guns of Crimea, the cries of pain from the soldiers, and the sound of thunder and lightning as the winter weather set about its dark cold business.

Just now she sat alone with her owl in the parlour. William Russell, the war reporter, had said November was the wettest month in Crimea and it was often foggy and cold. December brought rain, snow and thunder. I shall either survive or die, she told herself stoically. And that is the end of it. She'd been advised to pack warm clothing. January and February were much the same, though March was usually drier and the wind more gentle, at least there was that to look forward to, she thought, but men had to fight in cold wet weather with wind in their faces, she reflected, and how could they know who they charged at with their sabres in the fog? She had been reading poetry to her owl and saw that the bird had fluffed up its feathers which it often did when fearful. It had probably heard the tension in her voice she thought, or a change in tone. It was very sensitive to her person. She was its mother.

'Why so frightened?' she laughed. She leant towards its cage. 'That is my poetry voice; you silly, surely you know it by now. Now listen again, my precious, it's a very important poem. We can only imagine how awful it was for those soldiers. They must always do as commanded whatever their private feelings. That is the way of the military.'

She settled herself in a chair, holding the page of poetry before her. 'It is a poem written by an excellent poet named Tennyson. He is one of our finest poets, dear owl. Now, do not hide in your feathers like that, you must hear it again and be good. The Light Brigade was destroyed, you must feel the words of the poet, men and horses went down, so many men, so many horses. It was terrible. Tennyson tells an extremely moving tale.' She waved a finger at the owl, which was something Athena responded to. Her feathers went down and she straightened her head as if listening. 'That's better,' said Florence. 'Good bird.'

There was an irritable tone however to her voice as she spoke. It was a rainy day, the same sort of rain that would fall on the soldiers in Crimea. Today she was glad to be alone; her thoughts were complex and heavy. 'There are things I must tell you,' she said, with a deep intake of breath. 'You can come out to play when I've finished, but you must hear the poem through, you have only heard the beginning. I shall have to leave you very soon, for I am off to assist the sick and dying in a hospital at Scutari. It is a place far away and I cannot take you, my dear. I must help the soldiers, you see, so many soldiers, such awful conditions, such misery . . .' She frowned and shivered. 'The hospital is riddled with vermin and the soldiers die from disease as much as from wounds. You are wise, dear owl, but men and war you will not understand, and thank goodness you don't.' She continued with the poem, this time speaking more softly;

> *'"Half a league, half a league,*
> *Half a league onward,*
> *All in the valley of Death*
> *Rode the six hundred.*
> *"Forward, the Light Brigade!*
> *Charge for the guns!" he said.*
> *Into the valley of Death*
> *Rode the six hundred.*
>
> *"Forward, the Light Brigade!"*
> *Was there a man dismayed?*
> *Not though the soldier knew*
> *Someone had blundered.*
> *Their's not to make reply,*
> *Their's not to reason why,*
> *Their's but to do and die.*
> *Into the valley of Death*
> *Rode the six hundred.*

Cannon to right of them,
Cannon to left of them,
Cannon in front of them
Volleyed and thundered;
Stormed at with shot and shell,
Boldly they rode and well,
Into the jaws of Death,
Into the mouth of Hell
Rode the six hundred."'

And she recited the poem to the end. 'But why did it go so badly?' she said quietly, putting down the page and covering her face with her hands. A brief gust of wind came through a gap in the door and she tightened her shawl around her shoulders. Her father had brought a carpenter in to fix it, but the wood changed shape with the weather. There were days when it was hard to open, other days the wind whispered through as if bringing melancholy memories. You had to put up with it, her father had said; the wood was stubborn and would always go its own way. Florence went across and pushed some rolled up paper in the gap. 'There now, that should do it,' she murmured. 'At least for now. Life is a difficult journey. You, dear bird, might have suffered like one of those soldiers at Scutari if I hadn't been there to make a rescue. Your parents would have been thankful. There you were under the walls of the Acropolis hiding away in a corner.' She shook her finger in disapproval. 'But your parents did not care for you enough. They left you. I am your mother, my dear. All the way from Athens you stayed in my pocket, sweet little creature and what a greedy appetite you had! I have fed you and loved you. Well! Well! I hope you love me in return. And you mustn't be unhappy, I won't stay away for good, and you'll be safe with Mama and Parthe. They love you the same as I do.'

She sat for a moment staring through the window, looking at the rain. Sidney Herbert had invited her to London where she intended to choose her nurses. She hoped to take about forty and had advertised widely. The pay would be around eighteen shillings a week, the conditions were bound to be bad, but the abundance of replies was encouraging. There had been widespread talk about the terrible conditions at Scutari hospital and the deaths of so many men; the Crimean war stirred everyone's emotions as they sat at home with their families. Writing to Sidney Herbert, Florence had insisted her nurses be responsible, kind and energetic. She did not mind what religion they were, but she hoped they'd be virtuous. Nursing had suffered a poor reputation for drunkenness and debauchery. With effort all that could be changed. There were many good nurses, but their work was often obscured by the bad practices of others, and cheap gin was too easily available. William Howard Russell, writing for *The Times*, had told terrible tales of bungling and neglect at the hospital. Florence had read them over and over and her heart was prepared for action and change. Russell was a fine reporter and though it could be gruesome reading, he was trusted to always tell the truth.

She opened the door of the birdcage and in one light movement, the owl hopped on to her finger. Then she reached for a small piece of fish from a plate on the low table before her. 'Now, my precious, I must feed you,' she told her. 'Gently now, gently, your beak is so hard and sharp, nothing would war with you, my treasure!' The bird fed quickly and quietly from her palm. 'Crimea is so far away,' she murmured. 'How shall I get there?' She could read the distance on a map, but what about the actual journey?

CHAPTER 7

Towards Crimea

The Crimean peninsula in Eastern Europe where the fierce war was raging was encompassed by the Black Sea and the smaller sea of Asov towards the northeast. The Black Sea was a busy and profitable waterway on the crossroads of the ancient world, and a highly prized route towards Constantinople and the Mediterranean. In 1853, the Turkish Ottoman Empire had warred with Russia over issues concerning the holy places in Jerusalem and the Russian resolve to have protection over the sultan's Orthodox subjects. Turkey's allies, Britain, France and Sardinia fought also against Russian expansionism, attempting to weaken its power by attacking the Russian naval base at Sebastopol on the southern shores of the peninsula, the home of the Tsar's Black Sea Fleet which threatened the Mediterranean. A vicious battle had ensued reported in *The Times* by William Russell, their correspondent, who claimed British wounded soldiers were being neglected and that the French allies looked after their own much better. It was angry, even furious reporting, demanding immediate action. – There were "… *hospitals for the sick, bread and biscuit bakeries, wagon trains for carrying stores and* baggage, *every necessary and every comfort . . . In every respect the French can teach us a lesson in these matters. While our sick men have not a mattress to lie down upon, and are literally without blankets, the French are well provided for. We have no medical comforts . . . "* And Russell went on, and on, sparing not an ounce of emotion, informing his readers of the truth, that the English soldiers had awful unappetising food, no rice or sugar, no potatoes, no tea, not even a substitute. In fact the situation was hopeless! The camps were dirty and the men were down with dysentery and cholera before you could say Jack Robinson. Then came the rats. There were rats everywhere! Russell also reported that when the wounded were taken away, he could not see an English ambulance anywhere, and the men were put to sea on jolting uncomfortable vessels, whilst the French were provided with *"covered hospital vans, to hold ten or twelve men, drawn by fine mules, and their wounded were sent in much greater comfort than our poor fellows, so far as I saw."* He noted also that the French had nurses, women who'd been trained for the work. And in utter desperation he'd made an appeal in *The Times* pleading urgently; *"Are there no devoted women amongst us able and willing to go forth to minister to the sick and suffering soldiers of the East in the hospitals of Scutari? Are none of the daughters of England, at this extreme hour of need, ready for such a work of mercy?"* English voices had risen in anger and disgust. Both women and men were appalled and ashamed that the army had come to this. Something had to be done!

Florence Nightingale, living luxuriously in a grand house for the summer and another grand house for the winter, had felt the injustice keenly and was determined to offer her support. It seemed that she and Sidney Herbert at the War Office thought along common lines. It was a question of gathering a team of capable nurses to take to Crimea where they would tend the wounded soldiers at Scutari hospital. The nurses would need to be strong and sturdy, claimed the government, able to suffer the anguish of wounded men, even those who were dying.

How many dead, how many wounded, Florence pondered as she sat making notes that morning at Embley Park. How did the soldiers' wages get to their families? It had to be documented carefully. A man could not brutally die in war with no-one to care for him, or hopefully see he got better. It could not be. And his earnings must be sent to his home straight away. It would not do to see humans made into machines. She warmed her hands by the fire then made more notes briskly. She was alert with ideas. That day, she'd been up at dawn. There was packing to do, letters to write, final arrangements to be made. She gazed at the trees through the window, watching the light as it crept through the branches, always the same every day, always reliable. 'I too shall be reliable,' she murmured. 'I too shall bring light.'

The British military hospital in Scutari was opposite Constantinople, and across the Bosphorus strait, a narrow waterway linking the Black Sea and the Sea of Marmara. William Howard Russell's reports had stirred the hearts of the nation. Whoever would believe it? Scutari barracks hospital didn't even have basic supplies. And the military commanders – did they know what they were doing or were they all numbskulls? Where was the planning, the energy, the authority? The futile charge of the Light Brigade that autumn had made the public mistrustful and angry.

Florence bent to her notes. Thirty eight nurses would accompany her; some of the nurses would be nuns . . . How would she manage nuns? It wouldn't be easy.

'And Sidney has authorised this?' said a voice from over her shoulder.

'Ah, there you are, Papa, you came in quietly, I was preoccupied. Yes, he has. I showed you his letter and you have talked about it with him – or more precisely you have tried to hinder my plans.' She drew a breath and took on a softer tone of voice. 'You were surprised to learn that Sidney Herbert, the Minister for War had actually asked for my assistance weren't you. Well then, what about that? Florence Nightingale, your daughter, has quite an elemental energy. She has actually exchanged letters with the Minister for War.'

William Nightingale straightened and clasped his hands behind his back in an almost military fashion. 'Indeed you have, my dear, and you'll pursue your purpose till the end, regardless of your mother's health.' He lifted his shoulders and sighed.

'I have said all I can to Mama,' Florence said quietly. 'She must trust that all will be well. I shall offer the strength of my spirit to the wounded soldiers, and I sincerely hope that what I do with my nurses will help the soldiers live on. I shall consider it a privilege to assist and give succour in that filthy inhuman place.' She rose from her seat and poked at the fire, her eyes glassy and thoughtful. 'I shall work, Papa, and work well. And I shall write. You will know how everything is going. Please don't distress yourself. It is all planned out.'

'My dear Flo,' her father said, taking a seat. 'Matters . . . especially when it comes to war . . . have a hard job going to plan. Sidney knows this as well as anyone. Accounts can never be precise. It's impossible. It seems our commanders get it wrong sometimes. Heaven help us.'

'And heaven will, Papa. I realise how hard it will be, how impossible it seems. And I shall harness all the strength I can find. My work will bring its rewards.'

'Will it?' her father said softly. He stood and paced the floor. 'Who is to pay these nurses?' He stopped and faced her suddenly.

'The hospital nurses will be paid by the government, but the religious nurses go unpaid, except for expenses that come from their order.'

'And are these women practised nurses?' He gazed at her quizzically.

'Some of them are, but the others will learn. I shall teach them. Nursing comes naturally to people who care; to help and attend to the sick is second nature to those with compassion. Mrs Clarke, our housekeeper will also join us, as I'm sure you will know. She is quite industrious and her skills will be immensely useful.'

'Yes, yes, I know about that,' her father said, biting his lip. 'Your mother told me yesterday. Mrs Clarke, however, did not consult me about this. Now, that was wrong, my dear. What goes on behind my back astounds me.'

'But Papa, you are often away. Must we send you messages with the birds? Mrs Clarke is strong as an ox and won't stand any nonsense from the officers, who we shall no doubt have to take on. What's more she understands my moods. I shall need her.'

Her father shook his head. 'Nobody tells me anything! – Oh, Florence, Florence, how can I let you to do it?' William Nightingale raised his fists to the ceiling.

Florence looked at him fixedly. 'Don't upset yourself Papa, please.'

Her father sat down, then put his hand in his pocket and drew out a small piece of cloth. Florence watched and frowned. 'What is it?' she asked. She moved in closer to look.

'Something from a garment,' he said solemnly. 'Amelia brought it earlier. She told the maid to let you have it.' He passed it across.

Florence examined it carefully, turning it over in her fingers. 'It's military,' she said, curiously.

Her father looked on. 'Indeed. Amelia says it comes from Crimea. It's a piece of her brother's uniform.'

Florence gazed at it concernedly. 'He insisted on going, though his foot has never been right since he caught it in the trap in the woods. He limps quite badly. I was surprised he had joined the army, or even that it was allowed. – Oh, Papa, please don't say he's been killed.'

William gazed outside and screwed up his eyes as if thinking deeply. 'They're not sure; it did not come with a letter, only a note to say it was a piece of his uniform, nothing more.'

'He sent this remnant to England?'

'Yes, Amelia thinks it's for you.'

'But surely she wants this precious piece of cloth for herself?' Florence shook her head confounded.

'Not so, apparently, she insists you should have it. Your name was written on the note.'

'Do the soldiers know of my intentions?' Florence stared at her father, waiting.

'I should think so. I suppose they will read the papers, and there is word of mouth of course. You are talked about. Those boys find strength on the battlefield, but lying wounded in Scutari hospital is bound to be lonely and gruesome to say the least.'

'See Papa, you feel it just as I do. You must be strong enough to give me your blessing.'

For a moment or two they were silent. William Nightingale looked at his daughter perplexed.

Florence gazed at the piece of cloth in her fingers. 'I shall keep it safe and speak of it next time I see her. I hope she visits us again very soon for I shall have to leave England shortly.'

'And you will not take her with you?'

Florence shook her head. 'No, Papa, she is with child.'

'I thought so,' her father said, nodding slowly. 'And who is the father?'

Florence turned aside and straightened her papers. 'He is someone who worked on the land with her brother.'

William Nightingale sighed. 'And how is she to cope financially? Your mother thought about finding her some work with our maid. But I haven't asked about that, there is so much whispering going on it is just like the buzzing of bees.'

'There is nothing amiss, Papa. Not really. Amelia is strong and good. She is learning fast about the world and how to grapple with life. The child will be well taken care of, its father loves her. He has gone to fight in the war with her brother. Her younger brothers work for us now as woodcutters and gardeners.'

'Do they? That's good. My goodness Flo, you do keep up with things don't you.' He smiled and folded his arms.

'Well, that's better Papa, now you are smiling. Your other look disturbs me. In any case where we are going would never have suited her; she needs to be with her mother and the others. We have no idea what awaits us.'

'You will meet with savagery, my dear, absolute savagery. War is an uncivilised business. But I have tried to warn you. Oh, what worries you will bring to your family!'

'Civilisation is very tenuous,' Florence murmured.

For a moment or two they were thoughtful. She gazed at her father fondly. 'Don't be depressed,' she pleaded. 'I could never be happy just playing a piano or painting. Painting pictures and drawing are wonderful pastimes Papa, but they are not for me. Parthe paints well and enjoys it, but I am quite different, you see, I need to do something useful to benefit mankind. You do understand?'

'Only too well,' he murmured. He gazed about the room as if it were losing an important irreplaceable energy. And it was.

★ ★ ★

Later that day, after lunch, Richard Monckton Milnes came riding over on his horse. Having returned to the parlour, Florence carried on packing. His heavy footsteps in the hall caused her to stop. He was at the door already.

He stood quite still as the maid let him in then he gave a slight bow and smiled. Florence gazed at him surprised; she thought he looked ill and grey, as if he'd lost sleep. 'Have you eaten?' she asked. 'You look pale.'

'Yes,' he said, quietly, 'but food gives me little pleasure, it is not what I need.'

For a moment or two they were silent. He took off his hat and put it down on a chair, then sat down slowly. 'The picture out there, on the wall . . . It is a copy of *La Belle Rosine*, a lovely painting by Wiertz, a captivating image.'

'Yes, it is an excellent copy,' she said looking away. 'Parthe is most talented.' Her heart was heavy with love, and it troubled her to have Richard call on her now when she thought they had dealt with their sadness.

'Indeed she is. And she has captured the artist's passion.' He continued to hold her with his eyes.

Florence looked downwards. 'The painting is famous. You will have seen it. And you'll have seen Parthe's copy before, many many times, why do you speak of it now?'

'It's beautiful,' he murmured. 'It moves me.'

'I do not care for it myself,' she said shakily, tears in her eyes. 'The woman faces a skeleton and what's more, she is naked. Is it right to stand naked for so long and have every detail of your body scrutinised like that?'

Richard changed his position on the chair. His mood was intense. 'The painting has given a lot of people much pleasure,' he said quietly. 'Artistic appreciation is often a matter of opinion, of course. I imagine it comes from feelings deep in the soul.'

'My sister is very soulful,' Florence said archly.

Richard drew a breath and continued. 'It shows the artist's interest in life and death. Such matters are on my mind, you see?' He sighed. 'Yes, Parthe must surely be a very passionate woman.'

'But she weeps at the least misfortune,' Florence said quietly, 'and will not allow her feelings to reach her tongue. That is, unless they're hysterical.'

Richard bit his lip, still holding her with his gaze. 'Not nice, my dear.'

'No, you are right. She is my sister and it's wrong to be mean.'

'You are jealous.'

'Really, but why?'

'Because I said she was passionate.'

'Ah, but you tricked me. You tricked me into jealousy.'

'And so you see, you are not quite perfect, my dear. You can be tricked into feeling emotional.' He clicked his fingers in the air. 'And oh so easily.'

'Why have you come?' she asked looking vexed.

He ran his fingers through his hair then straightened his frockcoat. 'I hoped I might stop you from leaving,' he said flatly. 'I live in hope, you see.'

They were both silent a moment.

'You make it so difficult,' she protested. She paced the floor, her arms folded, her eyes fixed downwards. 'We have discussed it so many times.' She could feel the tears rising in her throat. Her words were scarcely audible.

'And you know how I feel too. But that doesn't matter, does it.' He talked on softly of the times they had spent together walking the woods, dancing at parties, talking about important and silly matters. He reminded her of the way she kicked leaves in the autumn, then didn't do it any more, more serious thoughts taking precedence.

He had loved her girlish ways. 'Where has it gone,' he asked painfully, 'that wonderful girlish spirit?'

'When I was a child, I spoke as a child, I understood as a child, I thought as a child; but when I became a woman, I put away childish things.' She stopped and looked at him painfully. She loved this man, but she felt he didn't understand her. Not properly. She was filled just then with the loneliness of her calling. The cold of winter and the hardness of her resolve came to her fixedly as hard as the rocky Scutari terrain she must travel to where the army hospital was based.

'I did not come to be preached at!' he said, loudly. 'This is your art isn't it; it is all about you and your God. He has called you, of course. I am often told in the Commons that my voice should be louder.'

She rubbed her arms, hurting and anxious. 'Oh Richard, I hear you, I do. And I am very glad to see you. It warms my heart to have you with me. – Does Papa know you're here?'

He shook his head. 'No, just Parthe and the maid. Parthe knows of my pain. She feels, you see, she *feels*. I love you Flo. I am quite wretched. Do you ever think about that? – Ah, you and your caring!'

She stared at the fire. 'You will find another.'

'Another what?'

'Another woman to love.'

He sighed and blew out. 'Thank you, my dear. I will drink to that when next I'm in London with friends.'

'Are you bound for London?'

'Very soon, yes. But I cannot go until I know it is impossible to stop you hurtling into this madness.'

'You accept my intentions?'

'How can I not? It is there in the stars. I shall be there with countless others who will wave you away. They will say you are

83

mad. Oh yes, they will say you are mad. But mark my words; their hearts will be filled with admiration, whilst mine will be filled with suffering.'

She touched her neck. 'I shall always wear my necklace,' she told him softly.

'Oh, lucky, lucky necklace, if only it could be my lips!' His voice trembled as he spoke.

'It is my secret,' she said.

'Move your collar and let me look,' he said, rising and moving towards her.

She did as he asked and showed him the necklace, glistening against her skin.

'It's lovely,' he whispered. He stood back thoughtful. 'I am told Sir Harry Verney is a frequent visitor here.' He glanced about, frowning. 'Did he . . . Did he ever ask you to marry him?'

She smiled. 'Of course not.'

'He often speaks of you.'

'Does he?'

'Oh yes, whenever I see him. It is Florence this, and Florence that. I think he adores you. He's a very good soldier and a clever politician at that. But his wife is seriously ill.'

'Yes, I know.'

'He won't fall apart though, not Verney. He has quite a few children you know, but he won't come unstuck. If he can't have you he'll have Parthe. And he can't have you because you're about to go off to sea. So there we are. He will have your sister instead.'

'Will he? You sound quite certain.'

'I have seen them dancing together.'

'But Sir Harry is 18 years older than Parthe, it would . . .'

'I'm serious Flo, he is looking for another wife and he will marry Parthe.'

'And you?'

'I shall continue to grieve,'

'But I won't be away forever. The wars will come to an end, and then . . .'

'And then you will marry me?'

She bent her head confused. There were tears on her cheeks.

'You are entering dangerous territory Flo, in so many ways.'

'I know,' she said softly. 'And your love gives me strength.'

'And I cannot take it away and weaken you,' he murmured. 'It will always be with you. Your strength is my pain.'

For a moment or two they were silent. Her fingers touched the necklace on her neck.

'At least let me hold you for a minute before you leave me,' he said.

He moved towards her and took her in his arms and kissed her. It was a strong potent kiss, hard to break away from. It was such a perfect moment, something she would always remember. Richard reached for his hat. Within minutes he was riding away.

CHAPTER 8

1854 – The End Of The Old Life

'What's happened?' asked Florence. The maid stood huddled in the doorway of the parlour sobbing heavily.

'I don't know how to tell you, Miss Florence! Really I don't,' she wailed. Florence saw that Parthe was also weeping in the hall, otherwise the house was silent.

'But what is it?' Florence asked, rising quickly from her chair. There was a tone of repentance in their voices, as if they'd done something wrong. 'Tell me what's happened,' she persisted. 'Parthe, why on earth are you both crying?' She looked again at the maid.

'Oh, Miss Florence, oh no!' moaned the maid.

'It's too terrible Flo, it really is,' Parthe said softly from the hall. She joined them slowly. 'We found her, just now. She was ever so still.'

'We didn't know how to tell you,' the maid said, trying to calm down. She turned to Florence and braced herself, her hands clasped before her. 'I went to feed her, you see. I took her pieces of meat, just small, like you said, but . . .'

'But what?' Florence asked urgently? 'What are you saying? Do speak plainly. Is it about Athena?' She turned to her sister

86

irritably. 'Parthe, what's happened? You bring me this storm of feeling but do not explain it.'

Parthe sat down, sobbing. 'Oh, Flo, I'm so sorry. – I really don't know how it happened . . . The maid cut the pieces of meat up ever so tiny, just like before. The bird ate them readily last time, but this time . . .'

'This time, what?' Florence spoke louder, in earnest. 'Has she been sick?'

The maid covered her face with her hands, then threw them out in a hopeless, final movement. 'Oh Miss Florence, it's terrible.'

Florence looked at her straight. 'Where is my owl?'

The maid's long thin face flickered with guilt, but neither she nor Parthe answered. Florence looked from one to the other by turns; waiting, shocked by their obvious distress. The truth came to her, painfully.

Parthe braced herself and dried her tears on her hanky. 'We have left her in the attic. She would not eat. We tried to talk to her like you do, but she buried herself in her feathers and would not listen.'

The maid stepped forward. 'I let her out of the cage, like you said, and thought she would fly about, but she fell to the floor and lay there, perfectly still, oh ever so still, and her eyes wide open. I never saw her eyes so wide before. I'd been cutting up beef for the stew then I remembered to feed her. It was a little later than usual, but not as she'd notice. Or I didn't think so. I'm really sorry Miss Florence . . .' She glanced at Parthe, for support. 'Miss Parthe came to find me. But the bird . . .'

Florence advanced to the door.

'She is still in the attic Miss Florence, where you said we should put her,' said the maid, hurrying behind her. 'You said she might want to fly about but I think she got lonely. And she wouldn't eat her food. You see, she likes to be fed by you, Miss Florence.'

'It isn't just that,' Parthe said, following quickly. 'She sort of gave up. She thought you'd abandoned her Flo. It was a whole two days. She hadn't heard your voice or seen you. I didn't want to bother you about it, but the poor creature got depressed. You might have come to see her, Flo. Just once you know, to say hello. You've been so absorbed in this venture of yours that you've forgotten everything else.'

'You are quite right,' Florence called, hastening up the stairs. 'Let's hope I am not too late.' It was evident Parthe was wretched and annoyed. But what she had said was true. The endless writing and replying to letters, the travel arrangements for herself and her nurses, the getting together of uniforms, which must all be the same, except for those of the nuns and sisters who could wear their habits, had absorbed her. All three of them were rushing up the stairs frantically until arriving at the attic door. Florence went in first. The morning daylight streamed in through the little attic window, falling in a long white haze on the tiny bundle on the floor, illuminating the small white feathers bristling amidst the brown.

'Oh see how she is!' cried Parthe. 'I didn't dare touch her myself, but the maid thinks Athena is dead.'

'I think she is Miss Florence,' spluttered the maid. 'When I opened the door, there she was on the floor, so still, not even fluttering by the window, just lying there cold and . . .'

'Hush!' Parthe whispered, a sense of relief in her voice, at the sight of her sister's calm acceptance of the tragedy.

Florence got down and gathered the owl in her hands then stroked its head tenderly. 'The dear creature has left us,' she said shakily.

'Will she go to heaven?' asked the maid. Parthe stood beside her, thoughtful.

Florence sighed. She thought of the little bird, what it had meant to have her beside her while she read in the evenings, how wonderful it had been to see her grow, to hear her chirp and whistle, and occasionally screech, a sound from her dark antiquity, a screech deserving of the woods, where she had never flown. Sidney Herbert had been so right; perhaps she should have set her free. On second thoughts, perhaps not, for she would surely have been devoured out there in the cruel world of the wild. '"Heaven?"' she murmured. 'It would be nice to think everything that lives goes to heaven after death, but how can we know these things?'

'But can you imagine it Miss Florence, flies and insects everywhere, creatures wandering like they do in the jungle? Oh, I think they'd fight to the death. But what is the point of fighting in heaven where everything is said to be good. And they couldn't fight to the death Miss, could they, not when they're dead already. Oh, Miss Florence, where has Athena gone?'

'I do not know,' Florence said softly, holding the owl to her breast, the little bony body so light and easy in death. 'But the life of her has left us behind.' Florence's voice trembled. 'Poor little beastie, it was odd how much I loved you,' she murmured. She turned to Parthe, now recovering. 'We must get a taxidermist, Parthe, someone who can preserve her for us to look at and remember. Dear, sweet Athena. We must remember you, precious creature.'

'I shall ask Papa if he knows of someone who will do it,' said Parthe, turning immediately to the stairs. 'I believe he is in his study.'

A lot of people were out cheering on the morning of Florence's departure from London. Her parents and Parthe had followed in wonder amidst the sounds of hopeful encouragement. Several coaches awaited the nurses. 'Miss Nightingale!' people shouted. 'Good luck and have a safe journey!' Everyone knew that Florence

Nightingale, the slender, tender, forcible woman in the blue silk dress and grey bonnet had persuaded Sidney Herbert, Secretary of State for War, that she was perfectly capable of managing the team of nurses who now climbed into the coaches, proudly waved off by their families, and that the poor wounded soldiers would be taken care of at last.

Florence's family were filled with pride, but fearful. Even with all the calling and rejoicing they felt there was something at fault, and that somehow they were to blame for some terrible indiscretion, and they hated the fact that they could not be with her inwardly. But Florence's eyes were filled with gladness and hope.

Not so, however, the eyes of her lover standing nearby. Richard Monckton Milnes had been forced to let her go. Her will was beyond him. As she passed him, she captured his look and knew she would hold it in her heart. But she could not look at him again. She caught sight of her family, standing in silence, their faces grim and concerned. She braced herself and smiled. She felt strong. A new self surged in her now with urgent intensity and she pitied their fear. Smiles were what she needed now. She had such a long journey ahead. It would take them several weeks to reach Constantinople, a journey of over 2,000 miles. First they would travel by night boat to Calais, then through Paris and Lyons over land, after that by ship down the Rhône towards Avignon, and then they would travel by rail to the port of Marseilles before boarding the *Vectis*, the steam ship to Constantinople. A long, long way. It would be cold November weather when her party arrived at Scutari, and anything could happen on the way. Storms could be vile, and vessels were often overturned, sometimes lost with their passengers. Added to that she did not travel well on the sea and got seasick. She had packed away bags of gingerbread and candied ginger, which often helped ease it. The coachman pulled on the reins of his horses and signalled them to go. It was pouring with rain as the people went back to their homes, sweet English rain that she knew she would not feel again for quite some time.

CHAPTER 9

A Need For Special Courage

'If we could learn to love each other more then war would cease to exist,' one of the nuns lamented as they found their seats on the vessel. 'War is corrupted love. What else is it, if it is not that? It is created by jealousy and spite.'

'And greed,' murmured another. 'I believe war comes from greed. Greed will be the end of the world.' The nuns sat huddled together in their outfits, cold and deeply thoughtful. They affected an air of nonchalance and strength, but their feelings showed in their eyes. They were all anxious and one of them said the vessel seemed somehow forsaken.

'Miss Florence, are you comfortable?' Mrs Clarke asked her. The housekeeper from Florence's home was concerned for her mistress's health and safety. 'I'm instructed by your father to see you are at ease. And you mustn't forget to eat, for you do sometimes, you work and write and will often forget to eat.'

'I do. You are quite right Mrs Clarke,' Florence said smiling. Mrs Clarke was all-seeing and clever, wise as her little owl had been, with something of a similar spirit. 'I am fine Mrs Clarke,' Florence replied, 'now we are out of the wind. You have always been good to me and have certainly helped the nurses on our journey, but remember who is in charge of this mission. Do not try to take over.' She nodded at the middle-aged woman who looked at her now with a seriousness like never before. Could it possibly be that Mrs Clarke was afraid? The nurses had shown remarkable courage during the journey, they had battled horrendous winds and weather and the management of their things helped by the sailors, who did not know quite how to treat them. 'I have to be seen to lead Mrs Clarke. I do not want to feel desolate in this endeavour; I need you, of course, but my dear, you must allow me my adult strength.'

'Of course,' Mrs Clarke said, suddenly looking humbled and embarrassed and glancing around at the others. Some sat talking quietly together, others sat deep in thought.

'My father will not expect you to spy on me,' Florence continued, seeing she'd disturbed her highly regarded companion. Poor Mrs Clarke, she thought, a bundle of concerns and feelings. How she would wring her hands and bite her lip, and sometimes mutter, "Oh dear, oh dear" when matters got out of hand. Florence leant to her and smiled. 'I value your loyalty and affection, and we must always work as a team and be there for each other. A chain is only as strong as its weakest link.'

Those who listened looked at Florence with dark tired eyes. Florence knew that her nurses were exhausted from travelling, and she didn't want to think their silence suggested second thoughts. They were waiting on deck for a cabin, the wind had been harsh as they'd waited at Marseilles, the ship had suffered stormy weather and some of the cabins had been soaked, the sailors were busy putting things back in order. She'd been trying to assess the characters of the nurses and felt she'd identified those who would rise to the challenge and those who might cause her concern.

So far, so good. No-one had been taken ill and they'd accepted her authority irrefutably, which was vital. She had wondered about the nuns, who were a union of manner and countenance, she'd noted the captain's ways with his crew and their careful attention to his requests, and she'd learned. That is how it would be done. She would captain her ship in a firm, systematic manner.

She brushed some mud off her boots with her gloved hands. It was as well they were gloved, for they might have been frozen solid otherwise, the air was so cold. How dirty everywhere was, how damp! And how would they dry themselves off? Everything was soaked. The journey from England to Scutari reportedly took several weeks, all being well. They had come a long way and were weary. The fathomless distance over land and sea and the atrocious weather felt like a sort of death in itself, but she had stayed eager and intent and she would give as much as her heart and soul could muster to her team. The desire to lead was one thing, to do it was quite another. Oh, what a test! Just now it was a fight with the weather and the aggressive thunder itself sounded like a war cry, while the perilous sea was like a roaring riotous beast beating against the vessel time and again, made worse by the shouts of the sailors as they went about their work.

The *Vectis* was a heavy, strong ship, a mail boat, used to the sea, but the storms had been heavy and damaging. Florence was from a travelling family, and liked to take an interest in ships, fascinated by their construction and the way they could take on the sea like a warrior. Today though she had other concerns and must manage her charges, many of whom had never travelled at all and were obviously nervous. At times on their journey she had gazed at the moon, so alone in the still dark sky, and she'd thought of her favourite trees at Lea Hurst, thinking of their roots, bound in the earth and certain, their purpose to grow and blossom in tune with the seasons. There was a right time for everything, she thought, and this was her time.

'I'm sorry Miss Florence, but I really must remind you to eat,' Mrs Clarke said, anxiously. 'You have eaten so little today. I think you know what I'm saying.'

'Of course, Mrs Clarke,' said Florence, gazing around the ship. 'But the seasickness plagues me when I eat and it is always worse on deck. I'll eat when we go to our cabins. We ate very well in Marseilles. No-one will starve. I have lots of food packed away. One of the crew can bring the food to our cabins when the sailors have made them ready.'

'We'll eat if there's food to be had,' moaned Evie, one of the team; she was young and pretty and girlish. 'I should think a lot has been stolen. Some of the sailors were looking in our things. People are always stealing. I wouldn't trust the sailors one bit. Oh, why did I come, it's freezing, and that awful wind has bitten holes in my neck!'

'You will eat,' said Florence. 'I promise. We have plenty of food and the sailors are honest working men. I bought provisions in Marseilles, though the doctor at Scutari said everything we needed would be there on arrival. I thought it best however to be cautious and further provisions will be unloaded along with the medicines. Do not fear, Evie, you will not starve.' Florence glanced about, wondering how long they would be sailing. It was late afternoon and the last rays of the sun were fast disappearing in the sea.

'Oh Evie, do stop grumbling,' said another member of the group. 'And for goodness sake, put on your bonnet. We are quite sheltered just here, but we must cross the deck to the cabins and you will need to protect your head.' She picked up the bonnet from where Evie had placed it beside her on the bench. 'There now, do as I say,' the older woman insisted 'I know you would rather not wear it, but it will help keep your head warm, heat is lost mainly from the top of the head, and if you lose your bonnet, you won't be getting another, there won't be any bonnets at Scutari.'

'But I'm hungry,' Evie persisted. 'How long must we wait?'

'Your life will be very different from the life you have known in England,' Florence said flatly. 'I have tried to explain. None of us know what we'll find. We have to be prepared for anything. A nurse must not fail in her duty. Duty is all.'

'But we are certain to fail if we're hungry,' Evie said petulantly, tying the strings of her bonnet. 'My sister is very bossy,' she murmured sideways.

'Evie, do be quiet,' her sister said tiredly. 'You make us afraid. What's more you'll upset Miss Nightingale, and what is to happen then? – Look, you have let your uniform get soiled around the bottom, you were told to lift up your skirts when we went down the muddy pathways to the boat. Oh, Evie, you do cause bother. You only came because of me. You have followed me around since our childhood. Our mother should have kept you at home.'

'I shall be just as good a nurse as you are,' Evie retorted. 'I looked after little Bertie the whole of the summer when mother was taken ill and you were away in the city. Leave me alone!'

'The only boss you have here is Miss Nightingale,' Mrs Clarke said assertively. 'And you two will have to stop arguing, we have a difficult task ahead.'

'Arguing is fighting,' said Florence quietly. 'We must not fight. Think of the happiness in your soul, the things you love and remember, the people you care for, it will sustain you in your hour of need. You must conserve your energy and be kind. Let us be still and calm. Take the example of the nuns over there, silent as night. That is how you should be.'

'Silent as the grave,' murmured Evie. 'The captain said we wouldn't have to stay on deck very long once they'd prepared our cabins, yet we've been sitting here ages and are practically frozen.' For a minute or two they were silent. 'Why are they fighting Miss Florence?' asked Evie mournfully. Her voice came painfully on the wind. 'The soldiers I mean in Crimea?'

Florence felt slightly dazed with the movement of the ship and the threatening weather. One or two stars glimmered above them already. 'I rather fear it is for power,' said Florence sadly. 'Man craves power over others.'

'Indeed,' said one of the nuns. 'Those in power are often corrupt as well, and the more power they have, the more corrupt they may become.'

'But perhaps it is others who make them so,' another of the nuns said quietly. 'How easy it is to perpetuate badness, so much harder to be good.'

'I can't see it's good to shut yourself away though,' Evie said, still petulant. 'To my mind to simply hide away and say prayers is hardly practising goodness.'

'But *your* mind is yours,' said her sister. 'And it's as well you keep it to yourself, Evie.' She smiled at the nuns and apologised for her sister's loose tongue. 'The Sisters of Mercy will help us Evie. They will do their best with their work and their prayers, and you might be glad of those prayers yourself eventually. Oh, I do wish you hadn't joined us.' Her sister gathered her cape closer about her and carried on speaking quietly, though her words were scarcely audible.

'I can say prayers for myself if I want to,' said Evie, sighing loudly. 'But I don't say prayers very much. God is too busy to be bothered with me.'

One of the nuns sang softly.

Florence Nightingale and her nurses were a proud dignified group. The presence of the nuns however had alarmed the captain, for he was sometimes wont to use language not for the ears of women, he said, and certainly not those who were holy.

'You are so strong-willed Miss Florence,' Mrs Clarke said, sighing. 'You are just like one of those heroes from the past – Odysseus, Hercules, those sorts of people.'

Florence smiled in amusement. Yellow afternoon light lit Mrs Clarke's features making them smooth as glass, a sharp contrast next to the heaving sea. Mrs Clarke was a strange sort of person, Florence reflected, one minute powerful, the next timid and afraid. She wondered if she ought to have brought her, but an expert housekeeper and reliable companion, she'd decided to add her to the list. And Mrs Clarke, it seemed, had a subtle influence on others when they were stressed, for there were bound to be times of extreme anxiety when the mission might seem to be failing. As she looked at her now, she hoped she could rely on her strength, and prayed she could rely on her own.

'It will kill me!' Evie moaned again. 'Just as soon as we reach that deathly place I shall die. I know it!'

'It might be quite beautiful there,' one of the nuns said gently. 'I am told there are splendid mountains and on some days the sky is a wonderful azure blue.'

'Guns, cannons and sabres aren't beautiful,' whined Evie. 'Most of the time it's cold and wet and nobody cares about anybody. It's a game of death out there. Remember what it said in *The Times*. That reporter told us the truth. I want to go home.'

'Yes, William Russell spares nothing when it comes to the grisly details,' Mrs Clarke added with a shiver. 'But you enlisted, my dear. It is far too late to go back.'

'My mother told me the officers treat the ordinary soldiers like dirt. My brother writes to her and we can't believe how he's treated.' Evie whimpered. 'They call them terrible names, and when they die in battle, their uniforms and hats are trodden on – and sometimes their bodies are left to rot on the battlefield. There now, that's the truth of it, and worse!'

'It certainly is,' Mrs Clarke said quietly, bending her head. 'And Lord Cardigan, the chief commander, is far too fond of women I'm told and cares nothing for his wife.'

'Be careful of hearsay,' Florence said quietly. 'Matters can become exaggerated.'

'The man is surely hideous,' Mrs Clarke sneered, steadying herself in her seat. She, like Florence, felt nauseas when travelling by sea. 'Where are we?' she asked Florence, screwing up her eyes and looking out into the distance. The day was darkening.

'We are on our way to Scutari, Mrs Clarke. When we get off the boat we will be met by officers, who will take us up the cliffs to the hospital.'

'Up the cliffs?' said Evie fearfully. 'Must we climb cliffs?'

'The paths are well defined,' said Florence. 'They are trod each day by the soldiers and male orderlies at the hospital when they take the wounded from the ships after the battles.'

'The thought of wounded soldiers having to get up cliffs makes me shiver,' Mrs Clarke said, tightening the strings of her bonnet. 'In their hundreds too, poor souls. And I'll wager that hospital is just as foul as *The Times* man reports.'

'Are we to stay at the hospital?' asked Evie, looking at Florence earnestly. The ship was sailing more steadily now and the rain was abating, but it was still very cold and windy on deck.

'That is what I am told,' said Florence. 'I have given you all the details I can. So far as I know, we are to sleep in a large dormitory there. I presume they will have it ready.'

'And will it be warm?' Evie went on, shivering.

'Perhaps not,' said Florence flatly. 'But I hope you have packed warm clothing as advised.' Evie glanced at her sister. Her sister nodded. It would soon be night. The party was to sleep on the boat with only the sound of the sea for company and the sailors on deck, who were left to do their best in the bitter, uncertain weather. Florence had travelled a lot with her parents and her sister, and she thought the world a very strange place when travelling on a ship in the darkness. She did not like the eerie echoing voices of sailors heralding the loneliness of night. Her nurses had gathered together, the reality of their undertaking now taking shape in their minds. Florence trusted they would arrive at the hospital safely and felt the full weight in her mind of the mission that lay before her as daylight receded. She had talked with some of the crew, hearing their tales of shipwrecks and the loss of entire families. Would they actually get there, or might they instead meet with some terrible fate, even worse weather, or rocks beneath the water that would batter the ship and cause it to sink? She'd been told there were a great many rocks beneath the water approaching Scutari. She thought of her family at home, and wondered what they were thinking. At that moment, like a sudden spectre, a tall young man stood before them. 'Florence Nightingale?' he asked, giving her a slight bow.

'Yes,' she said curiously. The man wore a black woollen frock coat and a silk cravat; a gentleman's attire, and he held his hat beneath his arm. There was something strong and steady about him she liked. His eyes glistened in the fading light, warm and abiding.

'I am Benjamin Harrison, Miss Nightingale,' he said firmly, as if she might be expecting him. 'I feared I would miss you. I was told I could travel to Scutari with you.' He glanced around the group. 'It was a last minute arrangement, but I have found you and here I am!'

He looked to be in his thirties, she thought. His educated manner suggested he came from a good family background. 'Are you a reporter?' she asked, deeply curious and surprised.

'Oh no,' he said firmly. 'No, no, I could not do it.' He sighed loudly. 'And I do not know how William Russell is able to write like he does. I do admire him. He knows my father and visited us once. I was working in the library and he came to talk with me. He was very quick with his thoughts and most impressive. Whatever I asked, he gave answers, colourful, real, important answers. I do not write myself, for I am far more interested in reading. And the truth as Russell unfolds it is quite astonishing. I suppose I am a sort of librarian.'

'Ah, I see,' Florence said, looking him over. 'Fascinating work, I'm sure, but we are not going to a library Mr Harrison. We are going to a hospital for the sick and dying, a hospital that used to be a barracks. It is hardly a library. I understand your love of books however, for I know the feeling myself. It occurred to me, you know, that the wounded soldiers might like to read while convalescing, and I thought about providing a sort of library. Yes, I have thought about that, an excellent idea, though how to make it a reality might be difficult.'

'Not at all, Miss Nightingale.' Harrison's voice heightened with pleasure. 'It could work very well. And that is why I am here. I have brought a chest full of books, wonderful, well chosen books, which I am sure with a little persuasion I can encourage the soldiers to read. And if they cannot read, I shall teach them. And I can send for more from England. I can also assist as interpreter for I have studied the language of our allies, and I also speak Russian, which I'm sure will be helpful, considering.'

Florence looked at him curiously. He would surely be a valuable addition to her team. Benjamin Harrison was tall and dignified and it surprised her that Sidney Herbert hadn't mentioned him; a last minute arrangement indeed! Wet and tired he donned his hat and stepped back. 'Now, I shall depart to my cabin Miss Nightingale if

I may. I am told it is ready.' He glanced at the team of nurses awaiting shelter. – 'You there, sailor!' he called. A sailor came running. 'When will the cabins be ready for these ladies?'

'Not so long now, sir,' the sailor replied. 'We had to repair a porthole and needed to dry out the floors. There were a lot of cockroaches scuttlin' about, but I think we've killed 'em all off.' The sailor faced Florence and nodded with certainty. 'If ye see any Miss, just hit 'em wi' summat heavy.' He called to another of the sailors, who stood nearby with a lamp. The sailor said the cabins were ready and would the ladies be good enough to follow him.

Florence rose from her seat and went along with the others. But where had Mr Harrison gone, she wondered, glancing about searchingly. He had quite disappeared. It was good to know he was around. And a library for convalescing soldiers was such a gladdening thought. The nurses walked on quietly, it was time to dry themselves out, to eat and to sleep.

CHAPTER 10

Early November 1854
EMBLEY PARK

The Nightingale family, living just now at Embley Park in Hampshire, their winter residence, had been in a sort of suspense since Florence's departure. All manner of imagined catastrophes had plagued them; they should never have allowed her to go, they ought to have known better, what they had done was unforgiveable. It seemed to have happened as if in a kind of dream, Frances would say, she had hated the idea from the first, their daughter came from a wealthy family, she wanted for nothing and had nothing to prove. And no, she hadn't run away, why on earth would she want to do that? It was though a worrying time, and their dear adventurous daughter was causing them much anxiety, she was written about in the newspapers, gossiped about throughout London, some of Frances's friends stopped her in the city, saying how commendable it was that she'd supported her daughter's ambition. Others had turned their shoulder and caused her to hurry back home and sit by the window sobbing, until her husband came to seek her out, knowing somehow, for his own part, that Florence was in a private battle with herself that only she understood.

But a horseman had arrived that morning with a message. Now, at last, they could breathe! Florence was safe and well and had arrived in Constantinople! And there hadn't been any mishaps. Apart from a feeling of nausea on the *Vectis*, she was perfectly healthy and energetic, as were her nurses. How lucky they were, William said to his wife, to receive such speedy information. Modern times could be good. The government that year had a military Telegraph Detachment for the Army and a field electric telegraph was busy in operation. News from war correspondents came fast and frequent.

'Well, Frances,' said William, as he stood by the fire in the parlour, 'Sidney's message is such a relief isn't it. They are about to disembark from the *Vectis*. Isn't that grand, my dear. I'm so glad.'

Frances Nightingale smiled weakly. 'I'm glad dear Flo hasn't drowned, if that's what you mean, and that the ship wasn't set upon by pirates, but I can't say I'm glad about anything to do with Scutari. Just to think of it gives me palpitations, and Parthe is hardly soothed by that piece of paper.'

'*Pirates?*' William smiled. 'There are fleets all over the area watching for anything sinister. Do not fear. We should be thankful they have got there, my dear. Flo was determined, and she is about to answer that "calling" of hers. Parthe will have to grow used to the new situation, just like ourselves. There is much to worry about if we contemplate the horror of that place, but we must try to think of the advantages, the joy she will feel as she helps those soldiers recover. Think of the satisfaction she is going to experience.'

'I doubt Parthe will ever see it like that,' Frances said solemnly. 'She wanted her sister to be just like herself, get married, have children, do everything right and proper.'

'Ah yes,' said William, 'all that.' He took a seat beside her and pointed to a picture on the wall. 'Look at that painting, my dear.

It is a spring woodland, our very own woodland, painted by our own dear Parthe. That is how you should think, the cold winter will pass and there will be new life everywhere. Florence celebrates life. She will do much good at Scutari, I know it. Now then, my dear, if you are miserable, Parthe will be miserable too. You are setting a bad example.'

Frances sat quietly for a while looking pale. Then her features brightened. 'Sir Harry Verney brought his little dog today,' she said, laughing briefly. 'I saw him from my window upstairs. That dachshund he has, it jumped from his arms the minute he stopped his carriage, and ran up the steps to the maid. She feeds it scraps from the kitchen. It is such a happy little creature.'

'There now, that's better,' said William, relaxing with a sigh. 'Did Verney come to see Parthe?'

'Who else?' Frances cocked her head to one side. 'He didn't come to see me.'

William chuckled. 'Nor me.'

'Look,' she said, filled with sudden merriment and thrusting a brown suede glove into his hand. 'I have made an excellent repair; you can scarcely see where I've stitched it. Florence loved those opera gloves and they fasten so nicely up the wrist, such beautiful pearl buttons. I thought they'd be warm when she is wandering about at Scutari. She will need to wear gloves, you know. Her hands get so cold.'

'Yes, it's a splendid repair,' he said. 'But she'll have taken gloves, my dear. She's careful like that. And she'll have told the nurses to pack them as well. Oh yes, their hands will be cold.'

'They are opera gloves, William. They will remind her of wonderful times. And they are made from soft warm suede. She had left them out on her dressing table. I saw they had come unstitched you see and thought it a good idea to sew them and send them to Scutari.'

'I'm sure she'll be pleased,' William said, fingering the gloves fondly. 'Yes, a very good idea. We'll send them with our next letter. I wonder what she will think of Constantinople. That place has a remarkable history. It won't be lost on Florence. They called it "the New Rome" you know, at one time, it was a Christian city with magnificent architecture and enormous wealth, the capital city of the Roman Empire until the Turks swooped in and took it over. Oh, such wonderful architecture, though I've only seen it in pictures. Florence will enjoy the history of the place I'm sure.'

'If she gets any time for herself,' said Frances, taking a deep breath. 'Good heavens, she'll be so taken up with nursing those wounded soldiers, she won't have a minute to spare. And I hope she doesn't go wandering about. My dear, she hasn't gone on holiday! I am fully aware of the reality of it all, you need not coat it in sugar.'

Her husband looked at her and frowned. For a moment or two they felt weakened with deep concern, till they found their stronger selves and smiled. A ball was in order, Frances declared, to celebrate Florence's arrival at Constantinople. Yes, she would organise a ball. She could always escape from her worries when dancing, she said. It would be good for Parthe too.

'*Constantinople*,' William whispered. 'Florence has reached Constantinople.'

In 1453 Constantinople had been captured by the Sultan Mehmed II's armies after a crippling siege which lasted seven weeks. The capture of the city had allowed the Ottomans to enter mainland Europe and claim much of the Balkan Peninsula. William had read about it recently. He shook his head and frowned at the thought of warfare. The fight for territory was indeed a nasty business. That shrewd and brave young man, Sultan Mehmed II, aged just 21, had dared to muscle in on history and direct it his own way. He was surely a courageous warrior, but how much beauty had been destroyed, beauty that was lost forever? Florence, he told himself, staring at the flames in the fire, was far more interested in the beauty of the soul than the beauty of man made things. She had a deep love of nature, animals, the countryside and people. Beauty it seemed was of little worth if it wasn't enjoyed, and was it not human greed that destroyed it? Florence would say so. And Sidney would say so, too. He would lay his hand on his heart and proclaim that he hated war. But he did not say it in the Commons chambers nor in committees; a Minister for War must always be cautious with his tongue.

William went to stand by the window, looking out. There was a light mist over the woodland that day. It reminded him of gunfire. Since ancient times, cities and castles had defended themselves with ramparts and mighty walls, but gunpowder had arrived in the shape of cannons and bombards that shot stone projectiles at the walls of the enemy's forts, enabling troops to break in. By 1450 Constantinople had been exhausted, and by the 1700s it was crumbling. By a series of treaties it had lost its economic independence. Then came rebellions and more loss of territory. 'And now the Crimean war,' William murmured.

'What?' said his wife, looking up from her sewing as her husband picked up a book from the table by the fire. 'I leafed through that book yesterday. How awful those women were treated when that city was taken over. I could scarcely read on.'

'One hopes that men are more civilised now,' he said, assuming an air of wisdom.

'One hopes so but I doubt it,' sighed Frances.

William placed the book beneath his arm. 'I'll return it to the library,' he said, making for the door. 'Constantinople has an interesting history. I haven't looked at that book in ages.' Just then there was a perfect stillness about them. But he could hear the gunfire and fighting of Crimea in his mind, and imagined his daughter yielding herself up to her mission. And the sadness of her loneliness came to him like the strange sound of a lark singing in winter.

★ ★ ★

'Major, they're here! The officer cried, rushing into the Army Commander's office. 'Stays, big skirts and bonnets, nuns in both black and white habits, making their way up the cliffs, women, that's what they are, *women*!'

'Calm down, man. I'm expecting them,' said Major Duncan Menzies. He braced himself and sighed. 'So at last they've arrived.' He rubbed his face with his hands. 'We must stay composed. The barracks is full to the brim with wounded soldiers. I thought the stretchers would never stop coming, one war ends and another begins; that woman has no idea.' Duncan Menzies had many responsibilities. He hadn't a clue how to cope with an army of nurses but he wasn't about to let his officers know about that.

'Well, perhaps it isn't a good idea sir, to send letters saying we have everything we need when we don't. Even if we have, we can never get hold of our stocks, the Purveyor is so disorganised.'

Menzies raised his eyebrows. 'Oh, I know, they're calling me all sorts of names out there. – Now don't you go complaining to that woman. I've told you before. I won't have you bloody complaining. We're doing alright. And what's more, we don't need women coming in here interfering. Oh, she'll not come here and order me about in my office.'

'She might well, sir,' said the officer, straightening. 'I heard she won't stand any nonsense.'

'You what? Who does she think she is, dammit.' He rubbed his hands together hard and stared at the ceiling. 'Bloody nurses. All is in order. Or as much as can be expected, that is, under such conditions.' He lowered his voice. 'This wretched war was supposed to be over in a flash but it's endless. And we still have Inkerman to contend with. Another battle. There are bound to be a lot more casualties arriving from that.'

The officer shrugged. 'Thousands more wounded', he whispered. 'And fighting in heavy fog, they won't know who they are killing. I've heard the French have built huts for the wounded, and they're laid with beds in rows all clean and neat, with the names of the wounded soldiers over their beds. Oh, it's all very civilized. And they have huts full of medicines as well, and cooking huts where you can get some good hot soup.'

Menzies waved away his words. 'Yes, yes, I have heard it all before. Are you trying to embarrass me? Because it isn't a good idea, if you are.'

'I'm only saying what I've heard,' said the officer, stepping back.

'It seems you hear a lot,' said Menzies, looking the officer up and down.

The officer bit his lip and frowned.

'Women, ah yes – but what are they going to do?' Menzies gritted his teeth. 'I can't let them loose on those wards, there are men crying and groaning in there. We can well do without women in here!'

The officer shook his head. 'You'd best be a gentleman, sir,' he said quietly. 'Miss Nightingale has the weight of the War Office behind her. You haven't to argue with that lot. And Russell will be scribbling away somewhere. He loves telling the world how useless we are. He doesn't miss a thing.'

'Aye, I know,' sighed Menzies. 'I shall have to tidy up this office. I forget where I've put things. Now, get out of my way. I need to comb my hair, and I've a button missing on this tunic. That had better not get to the embassy over in Constantinople or I'll be for it. We must always look smart, mustn't we? I don't even know where that blasted button has gone.' He rummaged about on his desk. 'And look at this paperwork. I haven't even time to get my boots on some days. Go on now then, go and meet them. And if any of the sultan's troops are there as well, tell them not to drop their fezzes in the snow. If the red dye seeps into the snow, it will look like blood. Let's not frighten the poor ladies on their arrival.'

'They'll have worse than that to frighten them,' the officer said, turning on his heels and running out.

CHAPTER II

The Hard Earth Of Scutari

'**M**y feet are hurting,' moaned Evie as they climbed the cliff face. 'These rocks are sharp and my ankle's bleeding! Oh, why did I come?' She lifted her skirts to look at her injury, exposing her pretty petticoat, wet with clay and sludge.

'Please let me help you,' Benjamin Harrison said, close by. He smiled warmly, coming forward. 'Benjamin Harrison, at your service! You are a bird with a broken wing. I have seen you struggling. These rocks would be difficult to climb in the best of weathers, never mind snow.' He took out his clean white handkerchief and passed it across. 'You can tie it about your ankle it will help stop the bleeding. This snow will give over before long, it is only sleet.'

Evie, pale and obstinate, took the handkerchief quickly and pressed it against her injury, looking down at the cliffs. The rock face was awful, she said, it was horrible, she had hurt herself badly and would bleed to death, and what's more the barracks hospital high on the hill looked like an enormous prison.

Scutari hospital occupied all four sides of a huge quadrangle and was said to have corridors and galleries that seemed to go on forever.

Evie touched her ankle and sobbed, must they go right up there, she moaned. The hospital was opposite Constantinople and overlooking the Bosphorus strait, which she'd been led to believe was a dark and sinister river filled with ghosts of the dead.

'It's only a superficial graze,' said Benjamin looking at it concernedly. 'The bleeding is stopping already. I have cut myself worse on paper. But these rocks are certainly sharp and you have to be careful.' He glanced about the cliff, looking for somewhere dry where they might rest. 'There,' he said pointing. 'Why not stop for a moment. I can see Miss Nightingale and the others ahead. We can follow on at the back. There's a lot of luggage to fetch up the crags, it will take some time. The soldiers are doing well with those trunks and boxes, some of them will be as heavy as a ton of bricks.' They found a dry flat rock, and Benjamin unbuttoned his frock coat, suggesting Evie might like to sit down on it for a while.

Evie watched as he removed his coat and lay it on the snow covered rock. 'Oh, but I shall spoil it,' she said, taken aback. 'Put it back on, I beg you. This weather's so wintry. You're a good man to think of me though, and thank you.' She examined her injury. 'This bleeding will stop very soon,' she said, sighing. Benjamin lifted his coat from the ground and pushed his arms in the sleeves. It was now quite damp, but never mind. Evie held on to his arm and they went up the rocks together. 'You're ever so kind,' she said softly. 'And you've found a good path to walk on as well.'

Benjamin pressed his hat down on his brow and watched the ground as they went.

'What have you come for?' she asked him.

He straightened and gazed at the sky. 'Well, it isn't to join the fighting. I could never be a soldier. The whole business of soldiery astounds me. I am a man of books.'

'What sort of books?' She eyed him with interest.

He assisted her over the rocks carefully as they went. 'All kinds of books. I like to acquire knowledge. Books instruct us, don't you think?'

'I can't say I'm well instructed,' she said unhappily. 'My sister gets annoyed because I can't put my mind to reading.'

'And she can?'

'She enjoys reading and prides herself on it. She likes to read to our little brother at bedtime. I want to get better at reading.'

'I must speak to your sister sometime. I thought I might start a reading room for the soldiers who are convalescing, a sort of library. I'm sure they would like it.'

'But what if they can't read? Most of them come from very poor families. I heard a lot of them can't even write their names.'

He sighed sympathetically. 'Well, I shall try to teach them to read, and write too, if they want. Not if they are disinclined, of course. Some of the injuries they've suffered will mean they'll be here quite a while. I have simple volumes in the trunk as well as others more scholarly. All manner of soldiers get wounded in the military. War knows no rank when it comes to fighting to the death.'

'It's frightening,' Evie said shakily. 'I hope I can help them somehow. I don't know if I can do it.'

'Do what?' He looked at her curiously.

'Whatever we have to do? I am fussing about a grazed ankle; those men in the hospital will have terrible wounds, won't they?'

They were both suddenly serious. Benjamin Harrison too, had been brought to heel by the reality of what he'd heard and seen. How many wounded soldiers would be at the hospital? Probably thousands! And he had only brought fifty books.

Three Turkish soldiers passed them carrying boxes, spattering snow as they went. Benjamin brushed it off his clothes. 'We still have quite a way to go,' he murmured, screwing up his eyes to see ahead. 'Where is your luggage?'

'My sister has it up there with Miss Nightingale and the others. One of the soldiers is carrying it.'

'And what's happening with your little brother?' he asked. 'The one you mentioned before.'

'He's at home with my mother and my two young brothers in Dorset. Our auntie lives with us now. We used to have a farm till my father got killed when lightning struck a tree in the wood and it fell and knocked him over. My mother and my aunt do their best to look after the family.'

'Goodness, your poor father. And your poor mother, too. What made you come to Crimea with your sister?'

'It was excitement I think.' Her eyes glistened as she spoke. 'I thought of the sea and the mountains . . . When we went to London and talked about it, it seemed so different from what we were used to. I thought I might like to be a nurse. And they were paying us too. I had never been paid for anything before. All those shillings each week! Miss Nightingale though, kept saying, "Are you sure? Are you sure?" and I really thought I was . . .'

'And now you are sorry?'

'Well, it isn't what I expected. It's very different from London. And I lied.'

He turned to her and frowned. 'How have you lied?'

'Well, I never did any nursing in the whole of my life, except when I nursed my brother through pneumonia. My sister was working as a maid in the city and I had to help mother. My brother might have died. The doctor said I'd saved his life. So I thought I might save some lives if I came with my sister and we could send some money to mother as well. The boys are growing up and help her with the chores and the animals. I have an older brother fighting somewhere out here. My little brother is safe and well because of me. I am very capable when it comes to dealing with sickness. The doctor said I was "most adept". My mother keeps saying it.'

'I am very impressed,' Benjamin said smiling. 'And your sister is a trained nurse? Miss Nightingale requested trained nurses.'

'My sister has had lots of experience. I don't know half of what she does though. She'll work very hard. And she's a better person than me.'

'Why do you say so?' He looked at her and frowned. 'Do not be so hard on yourself. Our self is either our friend or our enemy. Don't give in before you start, just do as Miss Nightingale tells you. You too, will do well.'

'I shall try,' she murmured. 'I'm only seventeen. I'll get better.' She gazed up at the hospital. 'Oh it's so big!' she exclaimed, 'and is it filled with wounded soldiers?'

'I'm afraid it is. I don't think the way is as steep as it looks. Yes, it's enormous isn't it. It used to be an army barracks. It isn't really equipped to be an infirmary. Miss Nightingale has brought all manner of things along with her, medical supplies, food and such, as much as she could manage. And it's all been paid for by her family. It's generous of her father to support her like that.'

'Yes, I hear she is very rich.'

'Her family is rich. But I'm told they are very generous. Her father has said she must ask for whatever she needs and he will see that the government provides it. He is a friend of Sidney Herbert, the Minister for War. It's a strange title to have, but I'm sure Sidney Herbert is a competent minister and fights his own wars very well.'

'A good friend to have,' said Evie. 'And what about you, what will you do at the hospital?' She stopped for a moment and looked at him quizzically. 'Will the wounded soldiers really want to read? They are going to be very sick. There have been such a lot of battles. Terrible things have been happening.'

'I have one or two ideas,' he smiled.

'You will have to see if Miss Nightingale agrees with them though,' Evie cautioned. 'She is quite bossy. I don't think the nuns like her keep bossing them about. I heard them talking.'

For a moment or two they climbed in silence.

'Oh look!' she cried. 'See the graveyards! And men are digging out the earth, how awful to think that so many men have died.'

'You will make an excellent nurse, Evie,' he said at last. 'I'm certain. Yes, I think you will attack it with a savage excitement. You have energy, you see, vital energy that will be used to help heal the wounded. It's new, you know, the business of *proper* nursing. Miss Nightingale has been trained to do things properly and she will show you how nursing is done. The work has been left to elderly people before, or else those who are drunk and simpleminded. Better they didn't nurse at all!'

'I know,' Evie said quietly and thoughtfully. 'I have heard bad things about nurses. But you only hear the bad things. I'm sure there are good nurses too, but goodness is rarely spoken of unless you are a nun or something. I also heard there are very few doctors at Scutari, and sometimes a man must have his leg sawn off with nothing to ease his pain, nothing at all. Can you imagine? And there is little in the way of medication.' She shivered at the thought.

'I understand there are plenty of medical supplies,' Benjamin replied thoughtfully, 'but the ships that transport them have been taken over for despatching the troops. This war is worse than a pestilence.' His long dark shadow spread across the ground before them, as if it were reaching ahead. It was now late afternoon. 'Evie, you wanted to join Miss Nightingale's nurses, and now you are here at Scutari. And there is much to be done. I have read of terrible conditions. *The Times* spares nothing. We haven't done as well for our soldiers as the French, but we intend to do better, and must.

Our soldiers must exercise both mind and body as they recuperate. I have knowledge of exercise techniques and I hear Miss Nightingale believes in them. It does not do to let repairing bodies stay still.'

'Are you trained to deal with the wounded?' she asked as they carried on climbing.

For a moment or two they were silent.

'No, I am not,' he said finally. 'But I have done some study and am a quick learner. I won't be just turning the pages of books. I have lots of ideas and hope to be of use to Miss Nightingale.' He nodded for certainty and smiled. 'I intend to find books that are helpful.'

'You are very kind-hearted and have a lot of feeling for others,' she said, reaching for his hand. 'We must all assist the injured soldiers best we can.' Her voice echoed in the thin cold air as the great barracks hospital was suddenly there before them. 'See!' she cried. 'We have reached it!'

'Evie, thank goodness!' called her sister as Evie and her new-found friend joined the others. 'Thank you Mr Harrison. I was so concerned for her safety. It's getting dark and that climb was so slippery. Mrs Clarke was searching for you, Evie. You went on a different path. Why did you stray?'

'I am the one to blame,' said Benjamin. 'Evie followed me then somehow got lost. Bright low sun can be rather blinding. I was a little lost myself actually. But we found you eventually.'

'Thank goodness, you did,' said Florence coming forward. 'Please stay with the party, Evie. Thank you for being so helpful, Mr Harrison. I thought we might need to send soldiers out searching.' She watched him knock snow off his boots, then adjust his hat. It would be good to have books for the soldiers, she thought. Already she was planning ahead.

'You mustn't wander off like a child, Evie,' Mrs Clarke scolded, looking both annoyed and relieved. 'I couldn't see you. Not anywhere. You ought to have kept with the others. You have put us to a lot of bother. Two of the others went back down the cliff to look for you. We are a team, Evie, a team!'

'Scutari is a dangerous place,' said Florence. 'But now you are here and safe. You must be careful who you speak to, and always keep up with the others.' Florence stared at the young woman before her who appeared to be very distressed, holding her skirts above her boots, a blood stained handkerchief tied about her ankle. 'You have hurt yourself?' she said frowning.

'It isn't important,' Evie said, embarrassed, 'I know I'm a nuisance, but I intend to get better, Miss Nightingale. I really do. I have talked with Mr Harrison and he has told me things I have never thought about before.' She smiled at him and he smiled back warmly.

'You have done well, Mr Harrison,' said Florence. 'I can see you will be most helpful.' She turned her attention back to Evie. 'If we do not work as a team, Evie, I cannot see how our work can ever be accomplished.' She gazed up at the barracks. It was far far bigger than she'd imagined. As they approached, she saw that a quadrangle, previously used for special parades and ceremonies was a mess of foul-smelling refuse and running with rats. The rats made one of the nurses scream as she stepped across a heap of waste and its tail touched her legs, the stench made some of them gag as they made their way towards the doors, but they soon resumed their stoic demeanour as the officers led them inside.

Florence found the sound of their footsteps strangely eerie as they made their way down the long stony corridor. It felt good to have her nurses together in the building though. They were here at last and she could now contemplate whatever might lie ahead. The nurses would stand or fall, she thought, by their skills, patience and compassion. There was nothing else for it; they must do what had to be done! And they would do it well. She glanced backwards pleased with their self-possession and felt she had chosen wisely. They were proud, strong women, and had made the journey with courage. As she watched them march down the corridor, they might have been soldiers themselves for they were so determined. She gazed about the building in wonder. The hospital was three storeys high with a multitude of windows and space enough to accommodate a great many active soldiers, powerful, healthy men, however, not men who were sick and dying.

The corridor was cold and draughty. In shadowy corners were the splendid busts of earlier commanders the military liked to remember, and other markers commemorating soldiers of distinction who were now deceased. They went by a large kitchen and saw people busily cooking; women and men were working together, preparing food in pans and washing dishes, oblivious of those passing by. Did the soldiers eat well, Florence wondered, or did just the senior officers eat good food? She stopped to look in; those in the kitchen ignored her and carried on working. It was almost an unreal situation, as if the people were half in a trance. Those who were cooking moved about the kitchen in silence, not even noticing the team of nurses passing by. Florence drew herself away from the door and walked on with the group. She felt oddly remote, not knowing where she was, and wondering how she might begin to do something of value in the huge stone building amongst strangers and sick soldiers.

'They are cooking meat and vegetables,' she said to the officer escorting the team. 'It is good fresh food. Do they cook for the soldiers, or do they only cook for the staff?'

'Mainly the staff, Miss Nightingale,' the officer replied coolly. 'The soldiers cook from the rations they are given which are rather meagre I'm afraid. They must do their best with whatever stoves are available. A lot of them eat cold food.'

'Uncooked?'

'Sometimes there is no other way, and when you've been fighting on the battlefield, you don't make a fuss. It's a matter of staying alive.'

They walked in silence for a while.

'There has to be a better life than this, Miss Nightingale,' the officer said. 'Some of our wounded go crazy. They talk to invisible people and think they are back at home. It gives them comfort of a sort.'

'They will long for their families,' Florence said thoughtfully. 'War is abominable, and when you are injured you yearn for some comfort, any kind of comfort, if it is not available then the human mind will invent it.'

'There are many wounded men in this barracks,' the officer told her gravely. 'More than you could ever imagine. Can you not hear them moaning? You get used to it in time. And after the fighting at Inkerman you will see them coming through the door like a mighty flood. Miss Nightingale, I am talking *torrents*.' He touched her arm and bade her step aside. 'Take care where you walk, this floor needs cleaning; it is easy to slip on some detritus or other.' He straightened again solidly, remembering his duty. 'This way, Miss Nightingale, Doctor Menzies' office is just down the corridor there.'

Many more injured would arrive tomorrow, thought Florence, staring ahead, shocked and overwhelmed. Would her nurses cope? Would she? Many would need urgent attention, and the wards would be filled already with men from the battle of Balaclava ten days earlier. The officers who'd brought them up the cliffs had talked about the battle of Inkerman likely to happen tomorrow. "Inkerman next," one of them had said, shakily. "The men suffer terribly. I can't tell you how weary they are." Such matters must be documented, she reasoned. She would ask Major Menzies if he knew what they might expect. Would tomorrow's battle be worse? How long would the battles continue? There was quicker transmission of information now between Crimea and London through the advent of telegraph. Florence was more than glad of it! Wouldn't it make for better understanding between countries? Knowledge was vital. Was anyone taking account of the dead and wounded? It had to be documented so that matters might be dealt with more humanely. As she walked with her nurses down the cold stony corridor she heard the sound of women's laughter from a nearby room.

'Laughter, in here?' she said to the officer, looking surprised. She glanced at the doors along the walkway. It was strange to hear laughter in such a dismal, deathly place. She could also hear the voices of men chiming in. It sounded like a wild party.

'What?' said the officer, staring ahead oblivious.

'I heard people laughing in a room down there? Do women come visiting?'

He nodded. 'They do, but it shouldn't be happening. And it won't be happening much longer if Doctor Menzies finds out they are here, he will be furious. No, no, this isn't a place for women. We might have a few in the kitchens, wives and girlfriends of the soldiers perhaps to help with the cooking and washing, but . . .'

'But the others, who are not in the kitchens?' Florence persisted, 'the ones who are laughing?' There was a curious cutting off in the man just then, she thought. She could see there was suffering in his eyes. He was an officer from Doctor Menzies' team, a man who must oversee what happened with the wounded when they came in their masses from the war, an overwhelmingly painful task. Taking care of a contingent of nurses was no doubt elementary by comparison. But Florence thought they came as if bearing gifts, to take on some of the burden of treating the injured. They came, she thought, like a blessing. The late afternoon sun shone through the windows glistening on the hard stone floor.

'Entertainers,' said the officer finally. 'They're entertaining the injured soldiers, helping them feel more cheerful. They come from Constantinople.'

'*Prostitutes,*' muttered Mrs Clarke from behind her. 'That's what they are. And they're drunk.' The nurses murmured together. Mrs Clarke went silent.

'Doctor Menzies has asked the kitchen to prepare refreshments for you,' said the officer to Florence. 'A drink of tea and a sandwich. After that I shall take you to meet him.'

The man was becoming more nervous by the minute, thought Florence. It was odd to see an officer at Scutari so nervous. Is that what the hospital had done to him? 'The cups you will drink from will hardly be what you are used to,' he said, biting his lip and looking awkward. 'And we cannot wash them very well. We are short of water, you see. Everyone here is rationed to just a single pint each day. What's more, the water supply is poisonous. God knows what we are drinking. I think they throw dead animals into the drains.'

'You drink filthy water?' said Florence frowning. She saw that Mrs Clarke covered her face with her hands, hiding her despair. Good clean water was vital. Matters were very much worse than she'd ever imagined.

'What else can we do?' the officer said tensely. 'We had not expected such a vast number of wounded. I do think you ought to re-consider your mission, Miss Nightingale, it is most concerning to think of what you will suffer.' He coughed loudly; the sound echoed down the corridor and lost itself in its length. 'I have a chest infection,' he said, clapping his hand on his chest. 'It's the cold weather does it. We often get chest infections here. It's always so cold and damp. I doubt you will survive such wretchedness.'

'We are nurses,' Florence said quietly. 'We are ready.' She hoped she could believe it as she followed him into a room where a table was laid with plates of sandwiches for her team. The cups to drink from were chipped and unclean, but she knew that the nurses would be hungry, and because of the freezing weather and the arduous trek up the hill, they wouldn't be too particular. They would relax and gather their strength.

CHAPTER 12

The Strange Music Of Suffering

'I'm glad you had a safe journey,' said Doctor Menzies. He rose quickly from his chair as Florence entered his office. 'Though I have to say, Miss Nightingale, I cannot understand why you want to come to Scutari. It is an absolute pit of misery.'

'So everyone tells me,' she smiled.

'But we intend to alter all that,' Mrs Clarke said loudly, standing behind Florence and bracing herself.

Doctor Menzies shook his head and sighed. 'Ah, if only matters might be altered,' he murmured. 'The nightmare continues however.'

Florence turned to Mrs Clarke. 'Can you see that the nurses are happy in the dormitory, Mrs Clarke,' she said quietly. 'Thank you.'

'We have attempted to make the accommodation comfortable for you,' Menzies said, as Mrs Clarke turned towards the door. 'All things considered, that is. We have no flowers or any of the things that women like to have about, no ornaments and such, nothing like that.'

'The nuns are praying,' Mrs Clarke said to Florence. 'I'd rather not interrupt them just yet.' She spoke in a decided tone of voice. 'I'll stay in the corridor a while.'

'"*Praying?*"' said Menzies, with a laugh. 'There's no time for praying in here. We need action. Prayers get lost in the gunfire.'

'God will hear our prayers, Doctor Menzies and we must listen for his intervention,' said Florence. He looked rather listless, she thought, and his uniform was crumpled as if he might have worn it to sleep in. He was a strong looking man, though there was great tension in his features.

'Aye, that is the point,' Menzies said, wringing his hands. 'I've scarcely time to take a breath, let alone listen for what God requires me to do.' He called to Mrs Clarke as she made her way to the door. 'I am glad of the nuns, dear lady. I apologise. Do keep them praying!' He addressed Florence with a frown. 'This lady is one of your nurses?'

'Mrs Clarke was a housekeeper of ours back home, she wanted to join us. She is a very capable woman.'

'Hmmm,' murmured Menzies. 'Undoubtedly. She is quite a gritty piece of work. And you have nuns in the gathering, and other kinds of women, according to my officer here.' He turned to the man, still beside him.

The officer nodded. 'Oh yes, all kinds of women. And a fellow who walked at the back, a quiet sort of chap. Hasn't said a word. He has come with a trunk full of books. I believe he intends to teach the wounded how to read.' He chuckled beneath his breath.

Menzies looked at Florence with incredulous surprise. 'Do forgive me, Miss Nightingale,' he said. 'Most of the men are in pain or are dying. Reading will be far from their minds.'

'Not when they're feeling better!' Mrs Clarke exclaimed, from the doorway. 'And the nuns will lend a hand with the reading. I was amazed by their knowledge on our journey. They are full of stories and poetry. They're empowered by the Holy Spirit, you see, it gives them an added advantage.'

'The holy spirit is there to assist us all,' said Florence smiling. 'Now, Doctor Menzies, we must talk of less righteous matters.'

The accompanying officer stood firmly by the side of the doctor, but bent his head as Florence spoke. 'My nurses are here to nurse, Doctor Menzies, and once the patients are convalescing Mr Harrison will teach them how to read, if they wish. If they can read already, they might like to borrow a book from his library.'

'*Library?*' said Menzies loudly, looking confounded. 'Are we to have a library?'

'Yes, we would like you to have a library, Doctor Menzies. No, no, never fear, a small room is all that is needed at first. Mr Harrison will ask the men which books they wish him to acquire and I shall do my best to see they are sent from England. He has brought a number of his own to start with. But firstly, the men must be nursed back to health.'

The officer standing by blinked very hard.

'This nursing, Miss Nightingale,' said Menzies. 'How will you go about it?'

It was evident to Florence that the major hadn't read her letters, some of which detailed how she and her nurses would spend their time at Scutari. She had hoped he'd have read them carefully. 'Doctor Menzies,' she began. 'Have you read my communications?'

'Ah, your letters . . .' The major rummaged about among his papers. 'Letters, letters, I have so many letters, Miss Nightingale I never have time to read them, well not as thoroughly as I ought. But yes, I believe I read yours. Now where have I put them . . .'

He leant on his desk as if trying to stop himself falling; his long strong fingers sprawled across the chaos. She thought he might be overtired, or had perhaps partaken of some alcoholic beverage. 'My plans and expectations are listed quite categorically,' Florence continued.

Menzies braced himself and shook his head, bewildered. 'We do not have "expectations" here Miss Nightingale. Each day overwhelms us with surprises. We are constantly on our toes. Why, we can't even guarantee there isn't a Russian spy in this building somewhere, let alone an Irish reporter!'

'It is Mr Russell's reporting that has brought my nurses to your aid, Doctor Menzies, and me, of course. You are very much in need of help, that much is plain. It seems you are without the basic essentials at Scutari.' Florence waited, composed and watching him with interest.

Menzies stroked his chin and regarded her cautiously. 'Oh, we don't do so badly, considering there are thousands in here,' he said finally. 'These wards stretch a good four miles.'

It was apparent he did not trust her. But Florence had heard that Menzies trusted no-one. He was quite suspicious of strangers, and extremely awkward with women. She spoke again, eager to express her alarm at what the officer had so openly told her. 'Just one pint of water per day for each human being cannot cater for all their needs, Doctor Menzies. Your only toilets are chamber pots that are shared by lots of men. There is little food to be had and medicines are in short supply – you have only a few bandages and little in the way of lint. Soldiers are bringing their own blankets from the Crimea, filthy and covered with vermin. And it seems there is not a drop of hot water to be had.' She bent her head. 'I have documented it all.' She glanced at the officer who stood in silence by Menzies, looking nervous. Florence saw his look and decided not to detail the lengthy account of complaints he'd voiced as they'd approached. The officer had unburdened himself in a trusting and hopeful manner. He now looked embarrassed, but nodded courteously to Florence in the way of friendly involvement. Menzies scowled at him sideways, lowered his voice and sighed. 'You do not know the ways of hospitals, Miss Nightingale. Nothing is what you think, oh no, not at all. And this is a military hospital. We have very few doctors for a great many wounded men, and tomorrow there will be more from the battle of Inkerman.'

'And now they will have assistance,' said Florence, removing her bonnet determinedly and loosening her cape. We may be few in number, but we are mighty in spirit.'

'Do take a seat, Miss Nightingale,' Menzies said, indicating a chair. He continued. 'As I was saying, hospitals are . . .'

'I know how hospitals are, Doctor Menzies,' she said, taking on an admonitory tone. 'I have worked in a lot of hospitals. I have travelled around Europe and Egypt with friends. I have studied the ways in which successful hospitals work, and in different countries. I have worked at the Institute of St Vincent de Paul in Alexandria, Egypt, and I have undergone a three months course of training at Kaiserwerth in Germany at the Institution of Deaconesses. In England I was the superintendent of a women's hospital in London, and should you . . .'

'Yes, yes, Miss Nightingale,' Menzies said, scratching his head. 'You have qualified yourself admirably. You ought to have medals pinned on your clothes for all that. But let me tell you, this hospital will be a revelation. You are a babe in arms when it comes to injuries, my dear.'

'Do not patronize me,' Florence said flatly. 'It is all listed in my letters and in those of our War Minister too. Your wounded soldiers need immediate attention, as does the hospital. You suggest you know the administration of hospitals, but from all I hear and read, this one has lost its way.'

Menzies breathed in deeply and braced himself.

'And you know it,' Florence continued tenaciously. 'I would like to visit the wards as soon as I can, so that the soldiers might see me and get used to me. After that I hope my nurses will meet them also. I know there will be terrible injuries, but my nurses will hold their own whatever they encounter.'

'Oh, the soldiers don't always die of injuries, Miss Nightingale. Many of them die from diseases like typhus and cholera. Cholera spreads like wildfire.'

'And it will,' declared Florence, 'if there is poor sanitation on the wards. I do not know what the wards are like, but the yard I saw on the approach was well-nigh a cess pit.'

'Ah, that,' Menzies said quietly. He gritted his teeth. 'We must get it sorted.' He glanced at the officer beside him. 'Why did you take the nurses through there?' he asked him irritably. 'The other approach is better.'

'Sir!' the officer said, giving him a quick salute. 'They were all very cold and I thought it was quickest.'

Menzies sat silent for a moment. 'We have male orderlies to see to the men,' he said quietly. 'I cannot see your nurses attending to slop buckets, and worse. Oh no, I am not too happy about letting women on our wards. And I'm not too sure the doctors would like it, either. The male orderlies care for the personal needs of the men. They won't like women meddling. It would surely embarrass them. I assure you, Miss Nightingale, your nurses might faint at the sight of some of the injuries. I have almost fainted myself. There are injuries that can't be repaired where men are just waiting to die. Why, you wouldn't see a horse suffer like some of those men.' Menzies' face was becoming quite red with emotion. He waited for Florence to speak.

She was now seeing the enormity of her task, and the burden of knowing she had enlisted others to join her. What if it was all too difficult, what if one of her nurses was taken ill, or even died? They had all signed their contracts, but they did not know what the war would be like in reality. Let there be strength and cohesion amongst them, she thought, let them exude abundant love and kindness to the men and to each other. 'Yes, it is all quite clear, Doctor Menzies,' she murmured. 'Now when can I see the wards?'

Menzies bent his head and the officer beside him shuffled about nervously. 'I think you need to take some rest, Miss Nightingale. I can tell you straight, that whatever you foresee and feel, will be very different from the truth. That is how it works for us, and it is bound to be the same for you. You will be quite broken and fragmented, oh indeed you will, once you are in full knowledge of the true situation.' Menzies drew his handkerchief across his forehead. 'It works through body and mind in ways you would never expect. Not a scrap of imagination can ever match up to what you see. We might write about it in letters, terrible letters, but we do not always send them, for it is hard to believe our words. We have terrible deaths in here, wounds that torment their sufferer as if they were being tortured. And they are, oh, they are often in agony, but our soldiers must yield to their suffering in ways they would not dream of yielding to the enemy.' He rested his head in his hands.

Florence listened carefully. From what she'd been told, many more orderlies were needed, utensils were needed and knives and forks to eat with. Did the men have to eat with their fingers! She could supply them with cutlery, cans, towels, and such, she had plenty put by. It could be argued that men came to war with such things in a back pack, but was it reasonable to suppose they did not get lost during war? How ridiculous to suppose such things might be taken care of. She could also offer socks, shirts, tin baths, soap and towels and combs. She informed Menzies of her store, and she'd also brought bedpans to support their dignity, she added finally. 'The men must have some dignity!'

Menzies continued to release his deep frustrations in sighs and gestures. 'The way the body betrays us when we have wronged it is quite inconceivable,' he murmured. 'There is so much moaning and screaming, so much anger, so much sense of having failed. This hospital is an infernal place at night time.'

'I'm sure,' Florence murmured. 'Memories both comfort and torment us. Sickness is such a punishment I'm sure to a man who has just been in battle. *"Receive what cheer you may. The night is long that never finds the day,"* as Shakespeare says.'

'Too true, Miss Nightingale. But there is little comfort here, and far less cheer. Each day I wake with the nauseating feeling that tomorrow will only bring death.'

'I bring what cheer I can, but you say you are in need of nothing. Yet how can it be when you pour out such terrible truth?' She shook her head sadly.

'Do I? I'm sorry, Miss Nightingale. I am sometimes rather confused, but that is all. I have said all I can. I must think about Inkerman now, and see we make space for the wounded, for there are going to be hordes of them coming up the hill very soon.' He turned to the officer, still standing beside him. 'Are we prepared?' he asked him. 'Have the officers got things ready?'

'The wounded will begin to arrive when they are brought off the ship. We have released what stretchers we have. More are being made.' The man spoke nervously, uncertain.

'They will come with the most fiendish cries you ever heard, Miss Nightingale. Their wounds can be vicious; they sometimes ask what happened to a leg or an arm of theirs that has been thrown into the sea, as if we might stick it back on and they in turn might use it just as before.' Menzies threw up his arms. 'You do not flinch Miss Nightingale. A woman should never harden her heart in the way that is required of men. Where is a man to rest his head if women harden their hearts?'

The officer beside him coughed lightly and frowned.

'I do not wish to harden my heart or bury my womanhood, Doctor Menzies,' said Florence staring out of the window at the fading day. She nodded slowly at her words, annoyed that he considered women to be the custodians of higher sentiments. 'Women have powerful emotions, undoubtedly,' she continued. 'And their hearts are easily softened but one's feelings mustn't be wasted, they need to be distilled into actions that bring results.'

'Perhaps men have stronger characters,' said Menzies, emphasising the word "characters". It is men who get things done in the world, not women.'

'Well, we can see the results of that in this building, can we not?' she said boldly. She raised her shoulders and dropped them slowly, meeting his eyes, which she saw were fixed on her firmly. 'So many lives have been lost because of this war,' she said softly. 'I shall never understand why we fight so much.'

'Yes, it is quite a mystery,' said Menzies, looking perplexed. 'Doctor John Hall, Inspector General of Hospitals and Chief of the Medical Staff of the Army is to visit us tomorrow. It will be an inspection, so you will see things I hope at their best.

For a moment or two they were silent. Menzies looked downwards minding his own thoughts. He braced himself and sat up, then straightened some papers on his desk. 'You can see the wards tomorrow,' he said. 'Come to my office at lunch time. I cannot allow your nurses to accompany you however. There is plenty of work to be done, if work is what you are after.'

Florence took a breath and fastened up her cape. Progress, she thought triumphantly. At least it was a start!

'I can see you are a determined woman, Miss Nightingale,' Menzies condescended. 'This is a military establishment. You cannot come here bringing us meaningless abstractions and dictating how things ought to be; you must accept my authority, Miss Nightingale. Do you understand?'

'I shall now take leave of you, Major,' she said quietly, reaching for her bonnet. 'I shall come to your office tomorrow. And do expect me on time; for Florence Nightingale is always on time.'

CHAPTER 13

Awakenings

Florence's mind had been far too active for sleep, and the thin hard bed gave little by way of comfort. She had tossed and turned and finally rose at first light. The nurses too were up early, afraid of the rats scurrying about the dormitory. Florence had concluded rats had the run of the whole barracks hospital and would need to be dealt with urgently. Some of her nurses said their limbs were aching with weariness, but they must make an attempt to look sprightly Florence asserted, for the hospital would be visited some time that day by a Doctor John Hall, Inspector General of Hospitals, a very important person indeed, who was said to have a very loud voice.

The nurses were dressed and busily sewing blankets brought in for repair by an officer. But they were awaiting further instructions as to how they would spend there time at Scutari, for surely it wasn't in sewing, they said, they did plenty of that at home. Were they not there to nurse? Florence had noticed they had started to slip into gossip; she must talk with Menzies soon, and firmly. She didn't want to lose the ground she'd painstakingly gained.

Evie sat quietly by her sister and was trying hard not to grumble, though she was obviously bored and frustrated. Everywhere was cold, she said, and how horrible it had been to find soldiers in corridors, bloody and lying on straw. Scutari hospital was certainly a revelation, said Florence. And where was Benjamin Harrison?

Benjamin Harrison had been allotted a room by courtesy of Doctor Menzies, just a small one next to his own, with a bed, a table and two chairs, plus a good sized empty bookcase, the fact of which made him wonder what books had lodged there before on its shelves, and why the room should be empty, for there was little space at the hospital. He sat at the desk, wondering if the room had been somebody's office, possibly quickly vacated. He couldn't quite put his finger on it but he had the strangest feeling that someone had occupied it recently. He was deep in thought when Florence walked in to join him.

'You look worried, Mr Harrison,' she said. 'Is the room too small?' She glanced about smiling wryly. 'Or is it that you are not too pleased about being so close to Doctor Menzies?'

'You are quite right,' he said, looking a little dispirited. Florence took a seat by the window. 'I was told this morning,' he said, mindfully, 'by Mrs Clarke that is – she keeps her eye on me, you know, and wanted to see I had breakfast – that the officer who escorted us yesterday has been dismissed. He was obviously too forthcoming.'

'I have to say, he did speak a little frankly,' Florence replied. 'I could see Doctor Menzies was uncomfortable.'

'Hmmm,' murmured Benjamin. 'Come to think of it, I'm wondering if this was his office.'

'Possibly,' she frowned. 'It's sad, though, if the man's been dismissed all because of talking to me.' For a moment or two they were thoughtful. 'I am meeting Menzies at lunch time . . .' she said, her voice hardening. 'He has promised to show me round the wards. Oh, I had to beg him, of course. But I am very persuasive.' She narrowed her eyes, glad that the man of books understood her, and pleased by his self-possession. 'Just the two of us, not the nurses; it would probably be something of a shock for the injured soldiers to have all of us marching in. They might wonder what was happening, that and the fact that Doctor John Hall is visiting later in the day.'

'Yes, I heard about that. He is apparently an excellent surgeon and the main authority Menzies must answer to. I believe he is to make an inspection.'

'That's right,' said Florence, taking a deep breath. 'I hope to be introduced. Oh dear, I have set myself a formidable task, haven't I? They think I am interfering. Well, they must think whatever they like. I will not be stymied by the power of these men.'

'Relax, Miss Nightingale. You are strong and capable. You are able to achieve whatever you have set your mind to, I know it.'

She smiled. 'Do you? How strange you should say it. Richard has always said the same.' She saw he was looking at a card she held in her hand. 'He gave me this lovely card as I left. It is to wish me luck and I am keeping it in my pocket today.' She lowered her voice to a murmur. 'It's sentimental, of course, from another world, you might say.'

'Is Richard a relative?'

'No, no, he is the man I love. He is never far from my thoughts. He wanted to marry me, but I needed to consider my mission. I love him all the more for seeing how important it was that I came to Scutari.'

'And do you intend to marry him after the war?'

Florence composed herself and placed the card in her pocket. She must write to him soon. He would be eager to know how she was and what she was doing. And she must let him know how she missed him. 'No,' she said sighing. 'I shall never marry. We have talked about it a lot.'

'And he?' Benjamin Harrison looked incredulous. 'How hard he must find it, knowing that you reject him.' He spoke emotionally.

'But I do not,' she said quickly. 'He is here in my heart. I shall never reject him. He knows that I love him.'

'Even so,' Benjamin said awkwardly. 'It isn't enough . . .' His voice fell to a whisper. 'A man must have the living flesh of the woman he loves beside him, not letters or love that is only in the heart. It is too much pain.'

Florence looked at him anxiously. It was a great burden in her soul, this feeling she could never let go, she kept it close, like a prisoner. Was it cruel to keep Richard a prisoner like that? And yet she must. 'You speak as if from experience,' she said, feeling admonished.

'No,' he said sighing. 'I once had a wife, but she died. We didn't have children. I buried my sadness in the healing pleasure of reading.'

She glanced about at the shelves where he had placed a number of books. 'And so you came to Scutari.'

'Yes.'

'I'm sorry about your wife,' she said quietly.

'You have such a lot to consider, Miss Nightingale,' he said calmly. He leant back in his chair and folded his arms.

Florence felt a sudden sense of fear. She'd imagined how the hospital might be, but from what she'd been told and her experience so far, matters were very much worse than she'd thought. She had taken on the vigour of men over dinner back home with her family at table, but this was entirely different, to battle the power of senior army officers was something she had never experienced. Her friend, Sidney Herbert, the War Minister, had deep concerns over army health and was intent on reforming the War Office, he was used to administration and speaking in the Commons but did he have any idea what was really happening in this dungeon of misery? 'I always feel I should do things better,' she said softly.

'Everyone feels like that,' Benjamin said, looking at her kindly. 'It's impossible to fully succeed in anything. We live and we die and in between we try our best. I remember a poem from the *Illiad*, some words spoken by Hector. You will probably know them.' He took a breath and began to recite dramatically like a Greek philosopher on a stage;

'My time has come!
At last the gods have called me down to death.
I thought he was at my side, the hero Deiphobus—
he's safe inside the walls, Athena's tricked me blind.
And now death, grim death is looming up beside me,
no longer far away . . .'

Florence clapped and smiled. 'You are quite an actor Mr Harrison. Excellent,' she said admiringly. 'But best not recite that piece to a soldier who is longing for home. Those Greeks could be very depressing sometimes.' For a moment her eyes filled with tears. 'I had an owl once called Athena. I found her in Rome.'

'So I believe, and what an interesting story it is. Mrs Clarke has told me about it. I believe the poor bird died.'

'She did,' Florence said sadly.

'Here men die by the thousand,' Benjamin said finally. 'Every death leaves a silent space which makes us wonder at existence.' By way of changing the subject, he said, 'Mrs Clarke tells me you like collecting seashells.'

'Oh, I do!' she exclaimed, her eyes wide with interest. 'I have so many shells – shells of starfish, scallops, periwinkles, everything.

I keep them at home in a box. The little creatures that lived in them have long since gone, but what lovely homes they leave behind.' She glanced about. 'I see you've been sorting out your books.' She looked at the books on the shelves, others were piled on the table. There was a lot of noise in the corridor. One or two officers passed, talking loudly. 'I must find Doctor Menzies,' she said, getting up. 'It's almost lunch time. I must gird up my loins for work!' With that, she made her way out.

'Grab him, or I'll drop him!' the male orderly shouted. 'Whoa! Get hold of his legs! That's it. Now swing him to the next position.'

'Steady on!' screeched the soldier, as the two men lifted him up. 'There's a bullet in that arm. Ye canna be throwin' us about. Poor sod o'er there were alive last night, now look at him.'

'What?' said one of the orderlies, looking across. He nodded to his companion. 'Best get him shifted. There's lice all o'er him. The Doctor will have us for that.'

'There's allus summat,' said the other. If it isna vermin its maggots and rats as is eatin' 'em.'

There was a lot of calling and moaning as the wounded soldiers tried to summon the orderlies, who were laying fresh straw and trying to straighten up the men on the floor, some of them writhing in pain.

'Hall is a nasty piece of work,' one of the orderlies said as they moved the dead man to a corner. 'He'll have summat to say about this filth. But he won't give us any more help, and they'll all be comin' by the second this week, soldiers from Inkerman, beaten, damaged and dead. Soldiers from here, soldiers from there, even soldiers who are dead. Why do they bring us dead soldiers? What can we do with 'em? We canna dig the earth quick enough. Here, roll that fellah aside, will ye, he's not goin' to live much longer. I think he's suffered exposure.'

'Exposure, cholera, typhoid, this place is a pit of torment and it'll soon be infested with women!' said another of the orderlies. 'They came yesterday, a tribe of 'em. I heard they are here to help us.' He laughed very loud. 'They've sent women to Scutari to help us!'

The moans, shouts and cries for help continued.

'God has sent us his angels,' said one of the injured soldiers faintly. 'I prayed it might happen. Will the ladies help heal us?'

'Not likely,' laughed one of the orderlies. 'They're gentlewomen in bonnets, and nuns in habits. I don't know what they've come for. I saw a few sewing blankets this morning. Well, we're short o' blankets for sure and it's gettin' near winter.'

Two of the orderlies went to another of the soldiers and tried to move him further up the row. One of them got him by his arms and another got hold of his legs. But he fell with a thud to the ground. 'Yer too damned heavy!' one of the orderlies shouted, hearing him cry in pain. Just then they caught sight of Doctor Menzies striding towards them. 'It's the major, and he's come with a woman,' the orderly muttered. 'See that look on her face, she's well near faintin'.

Florence was silent with awe as she walked down the ward with Menzies. Here it was; the suffering exposed the absolute horror of what happened to men in war. The wounded were in so much pain and lying in so much squalor she could scarce take in what she saw. 'This man's wounds must be washed and dressed,' she said, bending to one of the soldiers. 'And he needs clean clothing; his shirt is covered in blood.'

'We have no fresh shirts,' said one of the orderlies defensively. 'And there's very little water for washing.'

'And fresh bandages?' asked Florence, frowning.

The orderlies bent their heads.

'My apologies, Miss Nightingale,' said Menzies. 'We have a great many wounded men in here. We do what we can. That will be all for now,' he said to the orderlies. 'Now go and help the others down there.'

Florence stood looking down the wards at the endless rows of soldiers lying on the straw covered floor.

'As you see, we have very few orderlies,' said Menzies.

'Men are lying in their excrement,' Florence murmured. 'I can send for more chamber pots from England. And you need more blankets and shirts.' For a moment or two she looked away, the fetid odour of urine and faeces made her gag.

'All requests must go through the Purveyor,' Menzies chanted ceremoniously. 'His office is in Constantinople. Though I doubt he will hear you out. He has a system.'

'Well, his system isn't working,' Florence said quietly. 'There is a need to improve the supply of drinking water here. Army engineers must come to mend the leaking drains, the stench is sickening and gases are escaping and making the soldiers ill. These men cannot lie on straw on cold floors like this. And the floors need cleaning; they are full of flies and lice. We need to have Turkish workmen to help us clean the wards and install new beds. It has to be done. I can help you, Doctor Menzies. We have funds raised by *The Times*, people have been very generous. We have plenty of brushes and mops. There has to be good hygiene on the wards or death and disease will prevail. The Purveyor cannot help but approve of things already in our possession. Please let us help you.'

'The Purveyor can be difficult,' said Menzies, stroking his chin. 'We have lots of problems.'

'Ah, I can see that the trick is to write to the War Office in England,' Florence said sharply. 'I must let them know of your "problems".'

Menzies narrowed his eyes and looked at her thoughtfully. 'These common men won't appreciate clean shirts, Miss Nightingale. The male orderlies have told me how they don't like their bodies being touched. Their shirts stick to their wounds and make them fester.'

'The wounds must be cleaned,' Florence persisted. 'These soldiers have been fighting for their country; they are only "common" in their allegiance. And are the staff here similarly faithful? The men need beds to lie on where it is harder for the rats to reach them. I can easily send for beds, a simple bed is easily knocked together and sheets and blankets can be readily acquired from England.'

Menzies pursed his lips and clasped his hands behind his back

'Do you understand, Doctor Menzies?'

He waved a finger in the air. 'Perhaps I know the truth, Miss Nightingale, while you, my dear, are simply possessed of wishful thinking. You could possibly obtain fresh shirts and bedding for the officers, but not, well, not for . . .' He lowered his voice to a whisper. 'Not for the *scum*, Miss Nightingale, as the Duke of Wellington called them.'

'And what about food?' asked Florence, ignoring his words, as she made her way between the men. 'I have been to look at the kitchens, the facilities are good. If the soldiers are given wholesome food, it will help them get better. And what if they cannot feed themselves? Do you simply leave them to starve?'

'A lot of them are dying, as you see.'

'And do you just let them die, next to each other like this?'

Menzies threw out his hands in a quick hopeless movement.

'And you say you are to have an inspection?' She shook her head in despair, then looked at him straight. The foul smell of the wards was sticking in her nostrils. She saw that many of the men were scarcely past boyhood. Some of the soldiers cried out to her as she passed, others lay dying, while others drank gin and sang songs of despair.

After another hour, Menzies said he could take her no further and would have to return to his office. 'You must eat Miss Nightingale,' he said. 'I shall send some food from the kitchens for you and your nurses.'

Florence looked downwards frowning.

'Well, I did warn you,' Menzies said, raising his heavy eyebrows. 'And so it has happened, just as I thought. I shall think no less of you for taking your team back to England. It was a question of seeing this place for yourself, I think . . . As I said, the wards are deeply disturbing. This war has got out of hand. We didn't expect it to continue so long . . .'

'These military men,' Florence said as they walked. 'Do they keep facts and figures? Politicians rely on their knowledge and experience. It is altogether nonsensical if the men who manage the army don't keep account of the way things are going, for who else is to understand it if not them?'

'Oh indeed,' said Menzies, drawing a deep breath. 'What went on with the Light Brigade was utterly beyond belief. And a lot of the men on those wards cannot for the life of them fathom why it happened. General Lord Raglan was at times delusional it seems, some of the wounded soldiers said he didn't know what he was doing since he hadn't seen service since Waterloo. Can you imagine? He did lose an arm at Waterloo however, poor fellow, but I do not recall he lost his mind. His cavalry Commander, Lucan, had long standing issues with Cardigan, no wonder the men were clueless, armies should have decent leadership not men who argue like boys. I speak like this because I glean that you see the truth. There is little point in giving you falsehoods and fantasies. You are a practical person, a woman who sees the straight line and knows where it leads.'

'If only I did,' murmured Florence, cool and detached. 'None of this solves the matter of thousands of soldiers lying wounded in this hospital, with all their desperate needs. Some of their wounds are horrific. And they've been hurriedly stitched, too. Horse hair and silk can infect the wounds if it is dirty.'

'Ah yes,' Menzies persisted. 'You are quite right, Miss Nightingale. And I should not speak of my annoyances so much. I am actually doing it more nowadays. I shall have to stop it. But such issues irritate me, you see. I am sometimes amazed by the nonsense that comes from my officers.'

'If there is something you would rather not discuss, Doctor Menzies, then do not let it enter your mind. We must take care of our minds as well as our bodies. Cast out those matters that irritate and weaken us. Only concentrate on things we can improve. Otherwise we are lost in a battle with the self.'

'I wonder why we bother about humanity at all,' Menzies said, sighing deeply. 'For we simply end up killing each other don't we?' He frowned, looking at the floor. 'A military man like me actually cares, you know. You might think we don't, but we do. We think we can make a difference, though I do wonder about that. It is somehow sort of beyond us.'

'Men will never stop fighting,' she said in a tone of finality. Menzies, she noted, was acting very gloomily that day. But Doctor John Hall was in the building. His presence could be felt in the air.

'Ah, there she is the petticoat imperieuse!' Doctor Hall cried out to one of his colleagues, seeing Menzies ahead with Florence. 'Just look at the minx, striding along with Menzies as if she is about to take charge!' Hall knew only too well about Florence's venture. 'She's devilish plucky, that woman,' he said. 'Oh, she is. She's been on those wards already and she's still on her feet. And I believe she is up to mischief. But she'll be gone by the end of the week. Oh, just you watch.'

'She's made of strong metal, Miss Nightingale,' said his colleague. 'I know a friend of the family. I believe she's been the same since child-hood. I fear we shall have her here for a long time yet.'

'We'll see about that,' said Hall. 'She and her nurses will get in the way. She'll expect impossible things. I believe she's one of those people who seek perfection. Well she won't find it here at Scutari and we don't want too much criticism sent back to England. I hear she likes writing letters. We'd better keep an eye on that; she'll be in cahoots with Russell I should think. He'll be knocking about somewhere.'

'And your sanitary inspection today, Doctor Hall, do you think it will be agreeable?' asked his colleague.

Hall strode easily and naturally with a certain indomitable power, a proud and confident man with a very grand title, who had also served in South Africa and India. 'Agreeable to whom?' he blustered.

'Well, to those who might want to criticise.'

'We shall always be held responsible for things beyond our control whatever we do,' said Hall. 'It is the lot of us medical men. To tell the truth I am quite sick and tired of it.' He gazed at his boots as he walked. 'And now we have this Florence Nightingale bringing us even more trouble. I must speak with Menzies, I need to know what that bossy boots woman is up to. I do not see why these women are here. It has reached me that Menzies has had a lot of opposition from divisional officers. The very idea of women on the wards is abominable to them.'

'Doctor Menzies!' called Hall from behind him. 'I am about to join you in your office, and I see you have a visitor.' Hall's companion gave a salute and left.

'Do you wish to speak with Miss Nightingale?' Menzies said, as Hall entered. He made a quick introduction. 'We have just visited the wards and are discussing one or two issues. Do sit down.'

John Hall frowned at Florence. 'No, no, I shall stand. I don't intend to be long.' He spoke very loudly, then bent towards Florence, seated by Menzies' desk. 'And you, Miss Nightingale, why do you look so forlorn?'

Hall looked tall and tyrannical standing in the doorway, whilst she herself felt fragile just then after her depressing experience touring the wards. She braced herself and tried to recover her composure. Emotion was very debilitating; she knew she would have to deal with her surging feelings. Well, at least she hadn't wept, though tears had been stinging her eyes.

'I saw you coming from the wards with Doctor Menzies, Miss Nightingale. Everything was in order, I take it?'

Florence lowered her voice. 'No,' she said boldly, 'it was not.'

'Am I hearing this right, Menzies?' boomed Hall. 'What is this woman trying to tell me?'

Florence spoke again, quietly. 'A soldier had his leg amputated this morning, without chloroform. He was in agony. That, Doctor Hall, is not in order.'

Hall looked at her straight. 'Hospitals under my command do not use chloroform for amputations, ma'am. The men must bear their pain in the manner of a true soldier. It is best if we tie them down, and let them shout the suffering out of their system. It makes them stronger. Some have chloroform, others do not. There are soldiers of different rank and nationality here, wounded and dying . . . Now the common soldiers . . . Your nurses would not want to be handling them.'

'I have explained all this to Miss Nightingale,' said Menzies quietly.

'But you haven't explained enough,' said Hall. 'That is apparent. You ought to have sent these ladies back to England yesterday, not given them accommodation. What on earth were you thinking of, Menzies? Are you insane?'

Menzies took two candles from his drawer and lit them. His office was gloomy though it was only early afternoon; he had just a small window for light. There was little light in the barracks hospital in November.

'Ah, it is a dark day. I hate dark days. I had better get on with that inspection,' said Hall, 'or I won't see a thing, and I shall have to abandon it half way.'

'And that wouldn't do,' sighed Menzies. 'For then I shall be seen as incompetent.'

'I would like you to consider what we've discussed,' Florence said to Menzies. 'When the wounded arrive from Inkerman we must come and help the orderlies take care of them. You cannot do it all alone.'

Hall frowned and looked by turns from Menzies to Florence. His words came slowly, with irritation. 'You must realise, Miss Nightingale that you are no way in charge at this hospital, and should you stay, you will answer to Doctor Menzies, and Doctor Menzies answers to me. I am the Inspector General. Now, I will not say this again . . .' He looked at Menzies with sharp piercing eyes. Menzies shook his head and sighed. Hall spoke loudly again. 'In British-occupied Russia, I am in *total* charge, you are not to come fussing in the hospitals over there. I hope you understand.'

Florence listened in silence, reflecting on all he said. Most of the battles were fought on the Crimean Peninsula in Russia. The British hospitals were mainly in Scutari across the Bosphorus from Constantinople. 'Do you fear me?' Florence asked quietly, looking at him straight. Her skin tightened with annoyance, why did Doctor Hall have to shout?

'Fear a woman?' he laughed. 'Your man from *The Times* would expect it, I suppose. The English suggest you are here to perform miracles, my dear. Do you walk on water, Miss Nightingale? Why, you are all but a slip of a girl, you might walk across water like a wolf spider I think.'

Florence saw that Hall's heavy jaw was jutting in anger as he spoke and his eyes were wild with frustration. Yes, he was afraid of something. She measured herself against him and found she was the stronger just then. 'I have been through some of the wards . . .' she said calmly. 'I have witnessed some terrible things.'

Menzies shuffled his papers; Hall stood waiting, livid with impatience. 'And best you don't see them tomorrow,' said Hall, 'when the wounded from Inkerman swarm in.' He lowered his voice and bent towards her again. 'My dear Miss Nightingale, I suggest you gather your nurses quickly and return to England. This isn't a place for women. Now do be sensible.'

Florence sat composed before him. 'We are not scared off by injuries Doctor Hall. We are nurses.' She stood slowly.

Hall gave a loud cough. 'You try me too hard, Miss Nightingale. How am I to address you if you intend always to oppose me? I see you like to be contentious. I do not wish to be rude or dictatorial but I insist you return to England.'

Florence gritted her teeth, and looked out of the window at fading light. Would the wounded men be arriving in darkness? Menzies had lit two candles already. Were candles used on the wards? Candles were costly. There had been a sort of lamp on one of the wards, with a small, wired hoop protecting the flame of a candle. She'd seen that the lamp could be set on a hook or else carried. Such a lamp could be very useful if a nurse was needed at night time on the ward, and when the nights drew in and she wanted to write she needed to have decent lighting. She wanted to make some urgently required listings – how many men were injured, how the injuries were acquired, how many men were dead, and how many men were missing . . . Her mind was set. She had much to do!

'Miss Nightingale?' thundered Hall. 'You are lost in a dream!'

'I am thinking,' she murmured. She put out her arm, as if to stop his words with the flat of her hand. She was thinking everything through, speculating on what she and her nurses must do. It was something she did, this drifting away into thought, she had done it since her earliest years, through it came her best ideas.

'I must tell you, Miss Nightingale, the British army cannot be seen to be weak,' Hall continued. 'Our men must be strong, they must suffer their injuries with a certain gravitas, harden themselves against sentimentality and pain.'

Florence replied softly but firmly. 'The British army consists of men, human beings, many of them young with hopes of a future. Do you not care about their futures? They have families back home.' She raised her voice, stronger because of her passion. 'No, you do not; you only care for power and victory. You have lost sight of what really matters, Doctor Hall. Let me remind you that lives matter too.'

Hall stamped about irritably, frowning. 'I know all this! You preach to the converted, Miss Nightingale. To have moral and ethical principles is all well and good, oh yes, undoubtedly. But the mind is subtly changed when men go to war. Such concepts are like rays of sun in a storm. We yearn for them, oh we do, but they are far away in the heavens. I do my best for the men. You can never know what it is like, never, never, never!' He shot his words at the floor as if they were bullets from a gun.

Florence went to the door. Both men watched her, disconcerted and curious.

'She will not leave,' said Menzies quietly, as they heard her footsteps receding. 'That, I fear, is unequivocal. Miss Nightingale will have her way.'

CHAPTER 14

Storms And Losses 1854

News had reached London that the Commissariat, the department arranging food supplies and transport for the army, was employing civilians. When Sidney Herbert heard that he was furious, and it caused him immense bother. Goods strangely disappeared, blankets and sheets intended for army hospitals never arrived, let alone food. It appeared the ships were being used for the transport of troops instead. The war, it seemed, was going its own way and the government could make neither head nor tail of where it was heading. The public heard that the allies had laid siege to the Russian port of Sebastopol, the Tsar's Black Sea base, but his armies had fought full blast. Then in early November 1854, under cover of morning fog, they had advanced on the British army at Inkerman. A great many lives were lost and the siege army had been left to suffer a ferocious Crimean winter. There had been atrocious storms and a lot of British ships were wrecked resulting in many casualties. Soldiers were left hungry and diseased. Even supplies of food arriving at Balaklava took ages to get to the troops outside Sebastopol. And the ever-darkening days of winter did little to help morale.

Such situations, however, were not unusual in wartime. But with the advent of telegraph, reports travelled as fast as lightning to London's Minister for War. There were days Sidney Herbert awoke with a start in the night, trying to work it all out, for news came thick and fast. And he'd shown his perfect teeth too many times in parliament of late being forced to smile at ministers he'd rather have frowned at. But a lot of people were angry. Women gossiped on the streets of London. Even dogs barked furiously at each other as if they too were dismayed. The business of Florence Nightingale and her nurses at Scutari wasn't looking good, and wasn't it Herbert's idea? Hadn't he written to her and invited her to go with those nurses? Doctors Hall and Menzies were finding her difficult to deal with; she had too much to say, far too many ridiculous unmanageable ideas, and she wanted impossible things, like hot water piped through the hospital, new shirts for the soldiers, beds, fresh linen and blankets, and particular types of food. Some of the soldiers had even requested special diets. "For pities sake, Herbert," Gladstone had laughed, "My Right Honourable friend that is ridiculous!"

But Sidney Herbert believed in Florence Nightingale whole-heartedly, and the quarrelsome voices in parliament were always quick to find fault whatever the matter. Herbert puzzled over how he could get more money for what Florence needed; for he believed her requirements were warranted and justifiable. The Military Commissariat would have to do things differently and help fulfil her requests. He knew that William Russell would always ferret out the truth one way or another, however gross the detail, and fingers would point at Sidney Herbert. And so they should, his wife had said, for wasn't he the Minister for War, and didn't he always do the best he could for the sons of the nation. And the country believed in Florence, just as he did himself. There were times he wasn't too well, and his heart would beat fast as a hare in his chest when matters got heated. His education at Harrow and Oxford had hardly prepared him for this, he had said to his wife. And Florence made heavy demands. He had recognised her ambition, her dream, only too well, but might it have turned into a nightmare, a nightmare which included him? He'd sent soldiers to fight against Russia; he'd sent Florence with her nurses. He by no means expected it all to go right; there were Generals, Majors, other authorities that could sometimes make things difficult, not to mention Lord Stratford, the Ambassador in Constantinople who Florence would also have to deal with. Would Menzies try to send her home? He would, he would, if he could!

Florence wandered about the nurses' dormitory that evening feeling intense. She had seen a lot since her arrival, and there was much she wanted to change. And she knew she had the full support of the War Office behind her, and also *The Times*, newspaper. William Russell, their correspondent, was now at Scutari hospital and they talked together a lot. But she somehow felt like a prisoner, as if her spirit were trapped. She felt useless and frustrated just like the men in the beds whose energies were trapped through their wounds. There was nothing to carry water in, no soap, no towels or hospital clothes. Many of the men lay in pain on the filthy floors, still in their uniforms stiff with blood and gore, many had left the battlefield wounded, only to be dragged up the cliff to the hospital or to crawl there on their hands and knees, many bringing cholera along with their wounds. Atrocious weather and hurricanes prevented the ships carrying vital medical supplies from ever reaching the hospital. And rats had freedom of the building.

Florence went to her desk. She needed to write a letter to Sidney Herbert. Once she'd done that, she knew she'd feel better, and trusted the letters to her family and Richard were always delivered. England now seemed very far away. She sat for a while, pondering. Would the wounded soldiers accept her and her nurses, would they understand that they were there to love and care for them? Or would Menzies and his men watch with gloating triumph as the soldiers refused their attention and pushed them away? She brought out her pen and ink and a clean sheet of paper and began;

'Dear Mr Herbert

Your orders shall be obeyed. I have got the Turkish washing-house belonging to these Barracks ceded to me, & the Commissariat chopped straw taken out. By the time the washing machines come out, I hope to be ready to furnish every man in Hospital with a clean shirt twice a week. If by that time I am superseded, I trust the Purveyor may be induced to carry it on.

I learn that, while our men come back to us ragged, naked & starved, there is an immense quantity of warm clothing lying at Balaclava, NOT sent up to camp from difficulty in transport. The French convey all our sick for us down to Balaclava, they carried 1100 in one day. I cannot too strongly reiterate what I said before about the necessity of warm clothing being actually in use by our troops. Otherwise we shall have an Army in Hospital . . .'

She went on to tell him of her urgent need for more nurses, warning him that the wretched Crimean winter was fast moving in, stressing how important it was to provide for the new situation, which was bound to be difficult. Then she ended her letter by saying she awaited his orders. She had plenty to do and consider. Just then a stranger strode into the dormitory and presented himself before her.

'Doctor Alexander McGregor,' the man said tiredly. He stood in front of her, an apron covered in blood tied roughly around his waist, his shoulders bent and a pained expression on his face. 'Miss Nightingale, allow me to introduce myself. I ought to have done so before, but you know how things are. I am a surgeon here at Scutari. It is good to meet you.' His voice came frail with exhaustion and he leant against the wall as he spoke. 'I have a lot of soldiers sick with the cholera and am in desperate need of assistance.' He had the ghastly look of a man who had lost much sleep.

Florence looked at him concerned. Frustration boiled within her. 'I can do nothing to help you, Doctor,' she told him irritably, 'nor can I help the infinite number of wounded coming through the doors of this hospital until I am granted the authority to do so by Doctor Menzies.' Her nurses sat silently sewing.

Doctor McGregor found a chair and sat down, resting his head in his hands. 'I too must answer to Doctor Menzies,' he moaned. 'He has made it plain how he feels about women on the wards but many of the male orderlies are old and weary and unfit for the work. I have wanted to bid you welcome, Miss Nightingale, but I've been busy with amputations as well as dealing with cholera, I haven't had a single second to call my own.' He glanced around at the nurses. 'We need more doctors, more nurses, more medicines, more everything!'

'Doctor Menzies is stubborn,' Florence said sharply. 'Or so it would seem. I make little in the way of progress.'

McGregor spoke again, urgently. 'I cannot tell you how important your presence is here, Miss Nightingale. My patients speak of you constantly, of your compassionate smile when you came to visit the wards, your kindness. You are very much needed at Scutari.'

Florence felt relieved, so the soldiers accepted her, well that was something at least. But whenever she'd encountered Menzies, he had always looked preoccupied and would walk right past without speaking. She looked down at her writing, so the soldiers liked her smile, ah, she was glad, but if only a smile were enough!

Doctor McGregor stood and gazed about at the nurses busily preparing bandages and sewing blankets, then he slowly turned and left. The great walls of the barracks hospital felt heavier and closer today, thought Florence. She could feel its horrific world closing in, its hideous, sickening purpose. Just now she despised it and was overcome with nostalgia for home. She wrestled with the feeling, and knew it would pass, for her calling was eager and strong.

Several minutes later, and almost as if by magic, Doctor Menzies arrived in the dormitory. – 'I am afraid I must ask for your help, Miss Nightingale!' he cried, breathless from running. The nurses stopped their work and listened. Menzies talked on quickly, hardly taking a breath. He was quite desperate, he said. 'We have too few orderlies to cope with the needs of the wounded from Inkerman. I never expected so many!' He glanced about anxiously. – 'Ah, Mr Russell, I did not see you arrive. Why are you hiding in a corner? Damn it, man, must you always report every detail of our struggles in that blasted paper of yours? It's a wicked combination of circumstances here, a dirty, grisly show to say the least, I know. But that is war, as you know only too well.'

Russell, a well made middle-sized man with long dark curls, a moustache and a beard, looked from Florence to Menzies and back, then carried on scribbling.

'You are a war correspondent, Mr Russell,' Menzies said with a cough. 'I cannot forbid you to wander wherever you will, but please understand how overwhelmed we are in this place. I am not responsible for the suffering you encounter here. I must visit Lord Stratford the Ambassador in Constantinople soon . . . Yes, yes, I have many issues to discuss with His Excellency and I wonder if he really understands the severity of our problems at Scutari. I rather doubt it. I am told he is far too busy giving balls and parties. A ball is a fine thing and I like a good dance myself, but there is little to dance about here.' Menzies drew himself up and bit on his lip. 'I think you would agree, Miss Nightingale?'

Florence stared at Menzies, divining his purpose. 'Mr Russell is a brave man, Doctor Menzies, he has seen many battles and understands what the soldiers are going through. I doubt he has attended any balls.'

'How right you are, Miss Nightingale,' Russell said with a laugh. 'I have two left feet, so I have.'

'Well,' said Menzies, pulling on his ear, which was something he was wont to do. 'I find your presence irksome, my man. Can you make yourself scarce?'

'Aye. I think they thought the same at Cambridge, which is why I didn't finish that degree.' He scratched his head. 'Difficult, I was, aye, difficult. Ah, I canna do wi' readin' and writin' other people's thoughts. I must write me own, so I must.'

'And so you do, frequently,' said Menzies with a sniff.

'And I shall keep on doing it,' said Russell. 'People need to know things. Those soldiers are enduring too much. This war is a load of nonsense, so it is.'

'And what war isn't,' murmured Florence. She straightened. 'Doctor Menzies,' she said quietly, rising from her chair. 'Have I not offered my assistance and that of my nurses, and have you not rejected it?' The nurses watched and listened. Florence continued. 'And now you are saying you *need* us. I am fully aware of the situation Doctor Menzies, and we are all prepared for duty. My nurses have been through the wards. We have medicines and bandages packed in the boxes over there.' She pointed to a quantity of large wooden boxes by the wall. 'And we have fresh clean shirts for the soldiers, for we shall have to remove their blood stained clothes before we treat them.' She frowned, thoughtful. 'Water, Doctor Menzies, we are going to need lots of water to wash their wounds. And Doctor

Menzies, as I have said before, we need more beds; the men cannot lie on straw on the floor like animals. Beds, Doctor Menzies, you must get us some beds. I shall go to see the Purveyor myself if I must. And I can send for supplies of other things we need from England. It will take a couple of weeks for them to come, but no matter, I shall see we get them.' The nurses and Menzies were silent, hearing her out. Florence continued. 'The Minister for War is deeply concerned that the soldiers are properly cared for. *The Times* fund raised by the readers has helped us buy many things. We intend to provide recreational facilities for convalescing soldiers, books and a canteen where they can eat and talk. A great deal can be done to help the wounded if you do not thwart our efforts.' She saw that Menzies could not escape her command just then. He must bend to her will. 'We shall attend to the wounded soldiers as is befitting.'

'Aye as well as the French attend to theirs!' said Russell, speaking up from his corner. 'The French can teach us a lesson or two, and they have better ways of corresponding.'

'Do you intend to follow Miss Nightingale about?' Menzies said to Russell, who was getting up from his seat.

'Oh, don't be worrying about that Doctor Menzies. I'm quiet as a shadow. Folks back home need to know the state of affairs, and I deliver it straight. I've put them on their toes about a lot of thieving going on with supplies that should be coming here. It's as well they know. We must be open about everything, so we must. Our soldiers don't even get a decent breakfast, they only get bread and water. Ah, they wake up to rubbish, so they do. And their dinners are nought but old ration beef, boiled and eaten with bread. Ah, it's rubbish! They're eating pig swill I tell ye.'

'Your *straight* correspondence Russell, is causing immense distress back in England,' said Menzies, heaving his chest. 'You exaggerate. Nothing is as bad as you say. The public don't see the efforts we make for our soldiers. They do not know the magnitude of our problems.'

Evie came in to join them, accompanied by Benjamin Harrison. 'It's a nice story, *The Winter's Tale*,' she said to Benjamin as they entered. 'I like how the statue comes to life with the music at the end. Shakespeare knew a lot about magic, didn't he? And jealousy, too. People can be very cruel when they're jealous.'

'Aye, there's a real winter's tale at Inkerman,' said Russell, nodding at Benjamin Harrison. 'And ye'll no doubt know about that, so ye will.'

Evie glanced around the dormitory and saw that the nurses were getting ready to depart. 'What's happened?' she asked, looking at Florence.

'We are about to go to the wards,' said Florence, looking at Evie darkly. 'You should have been here. How many times must I tell you to stay with the team?'

'My apologies Miss Nightingale,' said Benjamin. 'Evie came to my library. I am helping her with her reading. I gave her a couple of lessons and read her some chapters of *The Winter's Tale*. It's my favourite Shakespearean play and I thought she might like to hear it.'

'And it seems she did,' Florence said, sighing. 'And thank you Mr Harrison. But Evie, you didn't sew the sheet I asked you to repair and now we are short.' She turned to Evie once more. 'We have to keep pace with the washing and sewing. And now we must go to save lives. No, no, my dear, leave the sewing for now, we have more important things to do.'

Benjamin Harrison nodded at Evie and cocked his eyebrows. 'I'm sorry, Miss Nightingale. I just didn't think.' He glanced about, troubled.

'Thinking is very hard come by just now, Mr Harrison,' said Menzies. 'I haven't had a decent thought in my head for months.'

He put his hand to the back of his neck and frowned. 'Paperwork, more and more paperwork, I am forever sending off letters, and who is to read them anyway?'

'The Minister for War, I imagine,' said Florence. Poor Sidney Herbert, she thought, how she would love to talk with him now, and she thought of England and imagined him arguing in the Commons, or perhaps seated by the fire at her home, maybe enjoying a slice of cake and a good cup of tea. The warm flood of feeling caused her to smile at Benjamin and he smiled back in return. He was a tall, proud looking man and so far nothing had depressed him. He had a ready smile for everyone, and talked openly with William Russell about the ways of Crimea. She had seen how Benjamin had kept company with Menzies, falling into his way of conversing as far as he could. And he had done the same with Russell. And it seemed with Evie also, who was sometimes fretful and sulky.

The nurses were gathering together, eager to start the nursing they'd enlisted to do. They must ensure the soldiers were comfortable, that their wounds were washed and bandaged, remembering the skills they'd been taught. It was most important that the wounded were handled gently, Florence had told them, a man in pain could be greatly assisted if gently laid down and lifted at the back from his elbows if helped to sit up. The behaviour of some of the orderlies had caused her to cover her eyes, and it was almost as if those who were dying could just be forgotten. There was nothing worse, she'd told her nurses, than that a dying man, shocked and afraid, should be left neglected, and to hear him crying out when no more help could be given. But a nurse might still be tender, Florence had said, she could read him a favourite letter, sing him a song, hold his hand until the end, for a dying man could understand the soul's sensibilities readily and would die more peacefully knowing that somebody cared.

Menzies nodded at Florence. 'Listen,' he said quietly, cocking his ear to the door. 'Hear how they're all flooding in.' He gazed at the ceiling. 'More and more of them, but where am I to put them; there is so little room and our surgeons are in need of sleep.'

'I have things to do in my library,' said Benjamin. 'Do excuse me.' With that, he went out.

Menzies looked again at Florence. 'Are you sure you would rather be here than back in England, Miss Nightingale?' he asked quietly.

Florence gazed back at him boldly. He was a capable soldierly man, but she found his anxiety trying. He was nervous of inspectors, and recent letters had suggested they might arrive at the barracks without warning. He had told Benjamin Harrison that government were suggesting a commission to investigate the hospital, but he hadn't been given any dates as to when it would happen. He wanted things to go well, he'd said, but his efforts shattered about him time and again. He had too much to do.

'I think you know the answer to that, Doctor Menzies,' said Florence. 'No, I am not going home. Now Evie, are you sorted out?'

'For what?' said Evie, a little annoyed that her attempt to understand Shakespeare hadn't been acknowledged.

'For your role as a nurse,' Florence said, calmly. 'You are a nurse, Evie. I have informed you of what it takes and you know exactly what to do; now let me see you put it into practice. Gather your things and make yourself ready for duty. We must follow Doctor Menzies to the wards. Doctor Menzies, please lead the way!'

CHAPTER 15

After Inkerman

And so they came, their shrieks and moans echoing about the walls of the great barracks hospital. Florence Nightingale and her nurses received them, offering an arm to lean on and words of comfort, while deciding where they might be placed in the crowded wards. She wrote letters to her friends and her family, and also to Richard, always she wrote to Richard. And she wrote too, with immense sadness, to a Doctor William Bowman she knew from King's College Hospital, describing the "appalling horror" she had encountered;

". . . We have now four miles of beds – and not eighteen inches apart. We have our quarters in one tower of the barrack, and all this fresh influx has been laid down between us and the main guard in two corridors with a line of beds down each side, just room for one man to step between, and four wards.

. . . As I went my night rounds among the newly wounded that first night there was not one murmur, not one groan – the strictest

discipline, the most absolute silence and quiet prevailed – only the step of the sentry and I heard one man say, 'I was dreaming of my friends at home,' and another said, 'And I was thinking of . . .' These poor fellows beat pain and mutilation with unshrinking heroism, and die or are cut up without a complaint.

We have no room for corpses in the wards. The surgeons pass on to the next, an excision of the shoulder joint – beautifully performed and going on well – ball lodged just in the head of the joint, and the fracture stirred all round. The next poor fellow has two stumps for arms, and the next has lost an arm and leg . . . This is only the beginning of things . . . "

Now her work had started. The work she had been born to do. As the weeks went by the hospital received progressively more and more wounded. The lucky ones now had rudimentary beds to lie on instead of the cold floors, and the hospital had acquired more water for washing and to drink. Some days Florence got a note from Menzies to ask how she and her nurses were faring; otherwise he stayed in his office, talking with visitors and officers from elsewhere in the hospital, or he went on his rounds of the wards and tried to reduce the ever-increasing mountain of papers on his desk. Benjamin Harrison had happily received some excellent books from England and was ordering them into a sort of classification as well as creating a catalogue. It pleased Florence to have an organised library she said, and she'd encouraged recovering soldiers to make their way to his room. They could borrow a book if they wished, provided they returned it on time. Reading classes were held twice weekly, where Benjamin taught the convalescing soldiers. It was all working out very well. Evie was doing superbly, he'd said, she'd been learning to read when at home in England and had proceeded from where she'd left off, with boundless enthusiasm, too.

'She might well read books,' said Florence, looking round the shelves that morning, 'and I'm sure you encourage her,' she told Benjamin kindly, 'but she must always remember what she is here to do.'

'And I trust she does,' said Benjamin, eager to keep Florence assured. 'She grows in maturity and self-reliance by the day. The best thing to do with Evie is to trust in her good intentions. She shrinks away if she is criticised.'

'You are very perceptive, Benjamin,' Florence smiled. 'You have summed her up precisely.' She glanced outside down the corridor. 'I must find her; she is required on the ward very shortly. I have told her Doctor McGregor is in need of help. I hope she remembers. A young soldier who has just been admitted from Inkerman must lose an arm, the poor boy's arm has been shattered, and McGregor thinks it will help if Evie stays with him through the surgery. Amputation is a cruel business and the men have nothing to comfort them while they endure it.'

'And will she be able to do it?' Benjamin asked, with a worried look of surprise.

'I am certain,' Florence said decidedly. 'I have watched her sustain young soldiers before. She is very strong and capable. She can attend an amputation without the least revulsion, and shows immense compassion.'

'It's an awful business,' Benjamin said quietly, sitting down to think. 'You have taken on such a lot, Miss Nightingale . . .'

'Do call me Florence,' she said smiling. 'It's all so formal here. Authority has to be maintained of course in such an establishment, but short of giving a salute I am constantly made aware of the military status of the staff. I dislike military establishments. It's wrong to treat the body like a machine, dress it in military clothes, make humans obey commands that are sometimes not properly understood. Really, you know, it can't be forgiven, this business of fighting to the death without thought for the body, let alone the soul.'

'We've never quite sorted it out, have we,' Benjamin said thoughtfully. 'It's been going on forever, and I rather suspect it will continue.'

Back in the Commons in London, a different kind of war was in progress. There was enormous tension in the air at the cabinet meeting that morning.

Lord Aberdeen tapped his finger hard on the paper before him. 'Half of the men who are admitted to the hospital die!' he said censoriously. 'They die, Herbert, die! Miss Nightingale's efforts have proved to be quite unsatisfactory. Things are getting worse at Scutari.'

'I know, Prime Minister,' said Sidney Herbert quietly. 'Miss Nightingale needs time, there has just been an influx of wounded from Inkerman, far more than had been expected. Such a large number of casualties needs time and thought. It is true, I know, they were not prepared. But there are many reasons for that.' He leant sideways to his colleague. 'Chancellor Gladstone, might I have a page of your notepad please?'

The Chancellor tore out a page and passed it to Sidney Herbert who scribbled down some notes. Then Herbert glanced about at his colleagues, ensuring they were paying attention. 'The Commissariat is without adequate transport,' he began. 'The horses die from hunger and the bitter weather and the ground is a quagmire, the men have to carry their supplies on their backs.' The cabinet listened in silence. Herbert continued, he would say what had to be said, and they must all hear him out. 'I think we are much too mean with money! Miss Nightingale tells me there are many deficiencies at Scutari. I believe she has been at her wits end and has never received the support she feels she should have, which the soldiers need so badly.' Still the room was silent. 'There is a need for clean running water. We can send engineers to deal with that. And there's a need for more food, more beds, more linen, and of course, more surgeons; the weaponry out there is vicious and a man can lose a limb in minutes . . . And Miss Nightingale needs more nurses.'

Sighs came loud amongst the company. 'And where do you think you will find them?' said Lord Aberdeen, straightening his waistcoat.

Herbert, however, felt he might be winning. He talked on quickly. – 'I have sent out requests, and shall interview nurses who seem promising. Just as we did before. Miss Nightingale will refine their training at Scutari, and ...' He stopped, frustrated. 'I send no end of letters to Scutari, Prime Minister, to the Purveyor, to Stratford, but I wait for ever for replies. And how many times must I write to Doctor Menzies?' He picked up *The Times* from the table. 'But here you have it, William Russell, the voice of truth . . . or so he would have us believe. I have heard him described as "a vulgar low Irishman, who sings a good song, drinks anyone's brandy and water and smokes as many cigars as a Jolly Good Fellow," but he writes the truth of how it is. Lord Raglan wants no truck with him and has advised his officers to refuse to give him any time. Truth, you see. Oh, it's the truth alright, and the people would have me stretched on a rack for it too. Anyone would think I was indifferent to all this suffering. Ah, if only I were – *indifference*, a comfortable hideaway for sure. Russell is covering the siege of Sebastopol just now; heaven knows what he will make of it. It is quite a horrific business and I fear it will continue well into 1855.' He opened a file and passed a letter to Gladstone. 'There, take a look. It has come from a Sergeant Newman in the 97th Regiment. He has recently died, poor man, from a fever. Herbert gazed about at the ministers. They were all silent and thoughtful and he perceived they might be in sympathy with the impossible task before him. Gladstone bent his head and read through Newman's words;

"We are now about three miles from Sebastopol and under canvas tents, the rain pouring in torrents and all around miserable. Cholera has broke out amongst the poor fellows who are exposed in the trenches day and night with nothing but their big coats to shelter them from the rain or cold . . . We get biscuits salt port or beef and one gill of rum with some sugar rice and unroasted coffee. Just like our government the idea of sending coffee here not roasted. We manage it somehow, by grinding it in a broken bombshell with a round shot to crush it.

Water is very scarce and extremely muddy. I have not washed my face nor yet have since I landed here . . . being satisfied with enough to drink without washing my face and as for a clean shirt I think when I can find it convenient to wash one then I will put one on . . . This terrible cholera . . . has made fearful ravages here. I have just commenced to write again and there are now six poor fellows lying dead. I am rather loose in my bowels, but take as much care of myself as possible."

Gladstone blinked very hard. 'Well,' he said gravely. 'There has to be a Commission.'

'There has to be a railway at Balaclava,' said another.

'Of course,' said Sidney Herbert, sitting down with a thump.

Back at the hospital, Florence too was busy making decisions. 'I must visit Constantinople and request more beds from the Purveyor, she said, returning to the dormitory that day after talking with Doctor McGregor on the wards.

Mrs Clarke came forward. 'Do let me join you, Miss Florence,' she said, in the deeply serious voice she'd acquired in her time at Scutari. 'I shouldn't want you to meet that Purveyor on your own. He sounds tyrannical.'

'They are all pretty much the same,' smiled Florence. 'He can't be any worse than Doctor Menzies.'

'But Doctor McGregor is kind, is he not?' said Mrs Clarke. She liked McGregor and said he always worked too hard. She also had sympathy with Menzies and claimed he needed help with his paperwork and that if he could clear his desk he'd be a lot better tempered.

'Yes, McGregor is an excellent doctor too,' said Florence. 'And he is very supportive of the nurses. But you needn't worry about the Purveyor.' She smiled playfully. 'I won't be like Cleopatra coming down the Nile with attendants, no splendour or anything like that.'

Mrs Clarke gave a little laugh.

'But I'll be forceful and full of power, like Boadicea if anything, arriving in armour!'

'And I shall be your standard bearer!' Mrs Clarke added, nodding for certainty. 'That Purveyor needs to get it right; we require more beds, more bedding and more pillows. Those officers in Constantinople will be sleeping on feathers and dining on the geese they came from. – And we could do with more rice, lots of it, and vegetables and meat! The men need decent food. And we must ask for chickens, oh, lots of chickens, then the men can have good chicken soup and eggs. Now what else?' She screwed up her eyes, thoughtful.

'I really must speak with the Ambassador,' said Florence, bracing herself. 'We have much to discuss. Lord Stratford knows the purpose of our visit. I have sent many letters. I believe we are getting more nurses from England. It is vital. And I hope they are trained as well.

I do not have a lot of spare time to train them. I must go across the Bosphorus, I'm not looking forward to it either'

'I believe Lord Stratford can be frightening?' Evie said, raising her eyes from her sewing and watching them pull on their capes. 'I've heard some terrible stories from the soldiers about that Ambassador.'

'You won't be seeing him, Evie,' Florence said smiling. 'You have better things to do. You did well with the soldier yesterday. I was most impressed. It is no easy task to assist the surgeon like that. I'm sure the boy was glad to have you there.' Florence saw Evie shivered at the thought.

'I'm proud to have seen it through,' Evie said quietly. 'I'm going to see him again some time today. He was ever so brave.' She hesitated a moment, then said in a burst of emotion, 'Oh, Miss Nightingale, I could scarcely bear it! The doctor took off his arm.'

'But you did bear it, Evie,' Florence said quietly.

'It was worse for the soldier,' said Mrs Clarke, jealous that Florence should praise the girl so often. 'You're scarcely more than a child. You'll get stronger as you get older.'

'She is strong enough,' Florence said frowning. But she knew how much the work at Scutari meant to Mrs Clarke, the capable and considerate housekeeper from home, and how difficult it was for her not to try to take charge. Also, Mrs Clarke often wrote home to the family, everyone wanted to know how the venture was progressing, and Florence would have to say it was going well.

'She spends too much time in that book room,' Mrs Clarke said flatly. 'I needed someone to help me change the sheets this morning on that empty bed in the corner. The fellow in there gave up the ghost in the night. The beds down there are cursed, I tell you, they're cursed!'

'That's because the men who lie in them have cholera,' one of the nuns added, raising her head. 'It is a certain killer. I fear Doctor

McGregor may catch it himself, he is often working in that recess, the air is so fetid there.'

'That's true,' said Florence thoughtfully. 'There's not a single window in that area, and it is quite shut off.'

'The doctor doesn't want the other soldiers to hear screaming when he's doing his surgery,' the nun said, sighing deeply. 'It's very distressing to have someone having surgery right next to you.'

'They shriek so loudly you would hear them in Constantinople,' said another of the Sisters. 'That young soldier came from Inkerman. He also fought at Balaclava. He was trying to talk but his injuries were too severe. I'm always amazed by their bravery. *Balaclava* too!' She said the name with emphasis, her shoulders rising and falling. 'War after war after war.'

'It's a vile business, war is,' another of the nuns added. 'The Russians tried a surprise attack at Inkerman, apparently. But it didn't work out. They were fighting in fog.'

'But we won, we won!' cried another. 'Thanks to our infantry of course, who were supported by French reinforcements. We suffered a lot of casualties, but the Russians lost more.'

'Nobody wins in war,' another of the nuns murmured. Florence looked at the nuns, always so busy with their work, never complaining about their lot. There was a strange sense of fatality about them that gave them a sort of strength and their faces shimmered with hope, the elixir of life to Florence.

Finally, Florence and Mrs Clarke set out to cross the Bosphorus Strait, Mrs Clarke very straight backed as they got in the boat, her bonnet pulled on tight against the wind, and her checklist of needs held close to her chest. They would confront the Purveyor with the list, and then after that, Lord Stratford de Redcliffe, the Ambassador, and demand his attention. Stratford, supposedly in charge, could do with a good shaking up, Mrs Clarke had said flatly. If he didn't take notice of Miss Florence, he had better take notice of her! Soldiers had told her that the Bosphorus Strait, separating Scutari from Constantinople, contained corpses and amputated limbs carelessly flung from the ships into the river. 'A total disgrace,' Mrs Clarke whispered. Florence could see she was pale and tense despite her pretence of bravery. But they were intent on taking their grievances to the men at Constantinople who had power to fix them if they would. Florence had learned there was a lot of altercation and bickering in London and she knew Sidney Herbert would be blamed for the problems at Scutari. In her mind's eye she could see him studying his shoes as he sat in the Commons listening to a barrage of complaints. The British had lost Balaclava and had won Inkermann, but Sebastopol, the location of the Russian Black Sea fleet, was still under siege and the British army was suffering. The bitter weather meant more lost provisions through sunken ships and bad management and Sidney would be racking his brains to find a solution. The Prime Minister, Lord Aberdeen, had been warned that if he did not shake himself up, he was out and they'd vote in somebody else, while William Russell's truth found its audience all too quickly and stirred up a storm of its own.

'Never mind all that, Mrs Clarke,' said Florence, seeing her watching the water for amputated limbs rising up on the waves. 'We cannot take them back to their owners. Why distress yourself by looking?'

After they'd landed, they were escorted to a room at the top of a high flight of stairs. The Purveyor sat waiting in his office. He addressed them most impolitely and did not meet their eyes when he spoke, and merely returned to his writing after offering them somewhere to sit. Florence was courteous, for the list of what she required was long, and she'd determined to reserve the best of her strength for the Ambassador, who she'd been told was even more unbending. But first they must deal with the fellow seated before them.

This was a new situation, thought Florence, she was here in Constantinople, she had no military standing, she was a woman who had come to nurse and care for sick soldiers. Whatever she did, whatever she said would be noted and passed to Doctor Hall and also to London. She felt as tense as a tiger ready to spring. How dare the Purveyor ignore her? The room was small and claustrophobic, filled with cardboard boxes, a couple of which were open, the sleeves of army tunics falling over the sides as if the contents had been seized quickly. The war was moving rapidly, no-one wanted to suffer the misery of a winter war. All three sat silent for some moments. Then the Purveyor looked up from his work.

CHAPTER 16

Nursing Let Loose

Florence entered Benjamin's book-room deep in thought that day, thinking about her visit to Constantinople. She had gone across the water, landed, fought, and conquered! Or at least she hoped so. She was quite preoccupied, thinking it all through and had intended to inform Menzies about what had taken place, but arriving at his office and seeing he had visitors, she'd gone next door to see Benjamin instead.

He looked busy. She was feeling anxious and had letters to write to London. But where would she find the energy? Nothing could happen without energy. When she wandered tired around the wards and spoke to the soldiers, seeing how much they needed her, reaching out and asking her impossible questions, such as when could they see their families, or when would the war be over, she would try to draw energy from prayer. She might also read them psalms or wonderful verses from Wordsworth or Shakespeare or other poets she liked. There were poems she knew by heart which her father had taught her as a child and which lived in her imagination.

Benjamin was tidying his books. 'The officers here like to have the War Office think everything's in order at Scutari, but Mr Russell puts them right about that,' she said, sitting down while he put the last of his books in place 'The fact that battle areas can now communicate more quickly means soldiers might be treated much better. Nothing can be hidden, or at least not for long. Matters have to be documented properly, then there is no mistaking the truth of what is happening.'

Benjamin drew up a chair opposite and looked at her earnestly. 'Did you make notes?'

'Of course,' she said, shaking her head. 'I noted everything. And the purveyor knew he was dealing with someone who meant business. I wanted a result and I believe I got one.'

'Were they hard on you Florence?' he asked, clasping his hands and concentrating his gaze. 'They can be very tough over there, I know. The soldiers have told me all sorts. I thought about you all day. These officials have a lot of aggression in their souls; it is par for the course. You haven't to cross them.'

'Well, I did, you see. I crossed them. I had to. But it's going to get better at Scutari.' She spoke with certainty. 'I made out my case, loud and clear and they listened. Getting what you want is a sort of art and practise makes perfect. Papa said I learned very quickly. One thing I've learned in this hospital is not to be bullied.' She smiled with satisfaction. 'We shall soon have beds and bedding, more blankets, clean sheets and clean shirts for the men, all those things we have wanted and lots of other things too.'

'Doctor McGregor will be pleased,' Benjamin said. 'I saw him earlier on his way to the wards.'

'I am hoping to get more doctors to help him,' said Florence, sighing with relief. 'I intend to write to Sidney Herbert about it very soon.' She shook a finger in the air. 'I want doctors who are experienced in surgery. I mean serious surgery, Benjamin. Removing a shattered arm demands skill of the highest order, the surgery has to be precise, or the healing process will not be as it should. And we need more nurses. They too must be experienced. I made the Ambassador take notice.

'You saw him?'

'Oh yes, it was a very productive conversation. I believe he will do his level best to provide us with what we want. Mr Herbert will oversee the process once it's set in motion. It was a worthwhile trip, Benjamin. Oh yes, though something of a strain.' She sighed heavily.

'I'm sure it was,' said Benjamin, frowning at the thought. 'It was a windy day and the Bosphorus can be difficult to cross when the wind blows strongly from the west.'

'Menzies could be quite some time', he added, frowning and glancing sideways at the door. He laughed quietly. 'I can tell by the way he walks what mood he is in and how he is conducting his discourse. There are people in there who have come to carp I think. He will not be in very good humour.'

'His bad humour doesn't bother me, so long as it's reasonable,' Florence said straightening. 'I won't be diminished just because he's bad tempered. And I won't be a scapegoat either. There is much that needs addressing in this hospital and he cannot confine himself to sifting through pieces of paper. There are matters needing serious attention.' However the relief of having seen the Purveyor and the Ambassador, lightened her thoughts, and she hoped she could soon see Doctor McGregor and tell him how it had gone. She recalled in her mind how she'd alarmed the Purveyor by suggesting he might not be paying attention to his job, since important things were being missed. She smiled to herself as she related to Benjamin what she'd said. 'You didn't say something like that to the Purveyor did you!' she laughed. 'He became quite nervous and twitchy. "I shall write to London about that Purveyor," I informed Lord Stratford de Redliffe. "He practically dismissed me the minute I walked into his office. It seems my requests must be approved and authorised by him before anything can be sent to Scutari, which meant I must cross that terrible, deathly water! My letters go unanswered, Lord Stratford, so I have travelled here by boat to present myself before you so that . . . "'

'At that', she continued, 'Stratford invited me and Mrs Clarke to take a seat, saying that much was out of his control and wasn't his fault. And he'd assumed a calmer demeanour, nodding, as if in agreement with all that was said.'

'He knew he was dealing with a siren,' said Benjamin listening to the tale. He leant back and folded his arms.

'A Boadicea, Benjamin. A Boadicea! Siren indeed! I do not wish to seduce the Ambassador.'

Benjamin smiled. 'I doubt you could help it,' he said quietly. 'You are quite a siren to me. Your song is sweet and I find your perseverance and fortitude bewitching.'

'I will not bewitch you, Benjamin, I promise,' she answered softly. He had seen into her inner sanctuary, a place she thought she kept secret, and he knew who she was. She had revealed so much of herself to this man in his room, the two of them sitting alone by the light of a candle. Would it weaken her that he knew her, she wondered, and that she also found him attractive. She was roused by Benjamin Harrison in ways that were not welcome. Just then she was rescued from her thoughts.

The sound of people talking together in the corridor came to them loudly. 'It seems Menzies has finished,' Benjamin whispered. He smiled at Florence warmly. 'I can hear him shuffling his chair. It usually means he is back to sorting out his papers. The poor man

stares at them sometimes as if he doesn't know what to read first.'
He pointed to a book on a chair. 'That book over there is taken
from my father's library, it's all about Hagia Sophia, a magnificent
building in Constantinople. I've been wondering if Menzies has
ever gone to see it.'

'Miss Nightingale!' said Doctor Menzies, suddenly appearing in
the doorway. 'Good morning, Miss Nightingale. Do come and talk
with me.' He bade her walk into his office. 'I have been expecting
you.'

Florence followed him quietly.

'It's a bleak morning, Miss Nightingale,' he said, lighting a
couple of candles. 'And this room is such a dark little den. It is
getting darker by the minute.'

'Yes, I do hate the dark winter days,' she said, taking a seat.
'I long for the light of spring and summer, and I miss the bird songs
in England. The woods are an opera of birdsong at home in summer.
Do you see many birds at Scutari, Doctor Menzies?'

Menzies leant back and drew a breath. 'Well, not so many at
present but, I believe the shores of the Bosphorus are full of
migrating birds at this time of year, not that I have seen them
myself, of course, but I'm told there are all kinds of birds around
there just now. You obviously didn't spot them, but the weather was
bad yesterday, and . . . Now then Miss Nightingale, you have been
to the Embassy, though I doubt you got to see Stratford.'

'Ah, but I did,' said Florence, nodding assuredly. 'And my visit
was very productive.' She settled into her chair. 'Now let me tell
you how it went.'

For the next few minutes Menzies listened in awe. He wanted to
hear it all. There was something congenial about him just then, and
Florence felt he admired her tenacity and strength of purpose. She
delivered the tale of her mission in rich emotional tones, using

words she knew he would enjoy, criticising the Purveyor and suggesting Menzies knew better, and that the Ambassador himself needed to consider his priorities.

Then Menzies drew a deep breath, and with a sigh of satisfaction pulled out a sheet of paper from his drawer. 'I think this will move you,' he said, holding the piece of paper before her. 'It's a letter from Her Majesty, Queen Victoria. Well then, what about that? It was sent to the Minister for War, Sidney Herbert, and has found its way to my desk. It expresses the Queen's admiration for the wounded here at Scutari. I think the men will delight in it, it is just what they need!' He passed it across and Florence read through the words, quickly and eagerly with great satisfaction and pride;

> *"Let Mrs Herbert know that I wish Miss Nightingale and the ladies would tell these poor noble wounded and sick men that no one takes a warmer interest or feels more for their sufferings or admires their courage and heroism more than does the Queen. Day and night she thinks of her beloved troops. So does the Prince. Beg Mrs Herbert to communicate these my words to those ladies, as I know our sympathy is valued by these noble fellows."*

'It must be read by the chaplains in the wards,' said Menzies proudly. 'And we must post it on notice boards around the hospital. The Queen also sends gifts to be distributed by Miss Nightingale, and emphasises that Miss Nightingale's soothing attendance upon the wounded and sick soldiers has been observed by the Queen with sentiments of the highest approval and admiration.'

For a moment or two Florence sat in silence, gazing at the letter, a letter she knew would be valued like a precious jewel by the soldiers when she took it round the wards. The heavy blasts of cannon fire that tormented their minds, the cries of agony from those who were struck, would be soothed, at least for a time. She could hear the distant voices of officers somewhere in the building, going about their work. She felt far, far away from England, and in spite of her smile she felt like a mere drop of water in a great ocean and somehow estranged from her people. Her body had forced her on, her mind had been determined, and she'd achieved a great deal. 'How wonderful!' she whispered, lifting her head, and she looked at Menzies earnestly.

Menzies ran his hand through his untidy hair. 'Our men have paid a heavy price for those words, Miss Nightingale,' he said quietly. He stood there before her, a lost soul just then performing a dangerous job in a dangerous part of the world, so utterly different from London, where she knew her father would speak of her work at his elegant club, and Sidney Herbert would fight for their cause in parliament. But the machine of war was like a great wounded bird that could not fly. Could it ever be healed?

Back in the dormitory that evening, she took her supper with the nurses and they each read the letter. Next day they would read it to the soldiers in full daylight. The nurses told her the wards were filling up and wondered if the tribe of wounded would ever end. The siege of Sebastopol continued, and cholera was rampant, treatments like emetics, Florence insisted, were harmful and even deathly. They should never be used. It was bitterly cold and the hospital plumbing was bad, water was escaping through the pipes and there was little enough of it already. The nurses complained they had to clean the blood from the wounded before putting them in fresh shirts. But there was hardly enough water to drink, and the staff in the kitchens grumbled they couldn't boil rice for meals for the soldiers or cook them anything decent.

By the light of a candle, Florence wrote again to Sidney Herbert, telling him the death-rate at Scutari had fallen, which at its height had reached 52%, and she'd detailed again her requests, setting them out methodically, the most important coming first. She begged him to make the Commissariat work harder and organise a better form of management so that the ships came on time, bringing the requested goods, and didn't get plundered. She informed him also of her visit to Lord Stratford at the embassy and of the content of their talk. Sidney Herbert should anticipate a letter from him, she said, if not she would sail across the Bosphorus again and see what the Ambassador was up to. Her meeting with him, she said, had been excellent – well, after she had shown her mettle that was and hectored him. Men in high places liked to hector, she told Sidney Herbert, but she could hector herself if she must.

Putting aside her writing, she prepared to make her tour of the wards and reached for her lamp. The whole of her feeling just now seemed centred on getting what she needed from England. It was like an obsession. It annoyed her if people didn't do things right, and what's more, she said, it wasted time. She would reprimand her nurses for even putting on a bandage without thinking of how it was applied, for a bandage must be firm but not tight, she said, and had to be secured by folding it over and tying a knot in the end. It was only a simple procedure, but it had to be done correctly.

'I want to say goodnight, Miss Florence,' said Evie, suddenly beside her. Evie hesitated, looking abstracted, then found herself again and continued. The candlelight flickered on her face. How pretty she was, and she had such sensitive eyes, thought Florence. 'But first there is something I must tell you . . .' said Evie.

'Then tell me,' said Florence, holding out her hand for Evie to move in closer. The girl looked disturbed. 'Is the pain too much for you here?' she asked, softly. 'I can send you home if you like. This place isn't prison Evie. You can be safely escorted to England, if that is your wish.'

'I can tell that's the way it looks, but that isn't why I'm upset,' she said shakily. There were tears on her cheeks.

'Then do tell me,' Florence insisted. 'Pull up a chair and sit down.'

Evie did as she was asked, and began to unravel her thoughts. 'The boy who lost his arm,' she faltered. 'They took him to the graveyard this morning.'

'Ah, I see,' Florence said sighing. 'I'm sorry.' She clasped Evie's hand. 'You are young to suffer all this.'

'It isn't just that,' Evie said, her throat tightening with tears. 'You see, I talked with him, Miss Florence, after his amputation. He seemed quite well, but he wasn't. And we dressed his arm so carefully. I did it with one of the nuns. But . . .'

'But?' Florence waited.

'The life in him just gave up. Even Doctor McGregor was surprised. But he says it sometimes happens like that with young men, they can't bear the thought of losing one of their limbs. They just give up.'

'I know, I have seen it myself,' said Florence frowning, thoughtful. 'It's dreadful trying to comfort a soldier who is losing a limb; it's as if you are feeling it with them.'

For a few moments they were both lost in thought.

'But there are many other soldiers who need you, Evie,' Florence reasoned gently. 'And they don't intend giving up. They want to get better, write a letter to someone back home, read a book from Benjamin's library and . . .'

'But he *knew* you, Miss Florence,' Evie exclaimed. 'I have to tell you. He said he was one of your gardeners in Derbyshire, and that his sister is heavy with child. The father of the child is fighting at

Sebastopol. I fear for him, Miss Florence. They are coming in from the siege with frostbite as well as with wounds.'

Florence breathed in deeply, and recalled Amelia's brother, the one who could shoot up a tree in seconds to saw off diseased branches, the one who had poached a rabbit, a laughing, healthy young man sacrificed to war. Evie was staring at her now, but Florence looked away. She too had tears in her eyes. Poor, sweet Amelia, how would she feel on learning of her brother's death? 'What happened to his arm?' she asked Evie.

'It was a musket ball. There was so little left of it, Doctor McGregor found the amputation difficult. And the boy was in so much pain. People don't want to know about that, Miss Nightingale, do they? I was trying to help him write a letter, he wanted to tell them what had happened to his arm but he asked me not to mention pain. People don't like to hear about the pain, do they?'

'No,' Florence said quietly. 'And we can only imagine it; we can never feel it for another.' For a moment or two they were both silent with grief. 'Do you think you can get some sleep?' asked Florence.

Evie nodded and went across to her bed. 'And you?' she murmured.

'I must first go round the wards with the lamp,' Florence whispered, 'After that I shall take some rest.'

CHAPTER 17

The Interplay Of Emotions

Florence's letter to Richard on that grey wintry morning the following week had been slowly and carefully thought through. But it would not do. She began and discarded it three times. She was filled with emotion; memories of England, days out walking in spring and summer, Derbyshire woodland paths covered in forget-me-knots and other beautiful flowers. It was the spring she thought about most, when all new life began. Richard noticed everything and had always scribbled down notes for his poems, lovely verse which he read to her on their walks. She missed him, oh, how she missed him. She recalled how they'd danced at her mother's balls, the times they'd laughed together, the times she'd kissed his soft warm lips, so ready and urgent. And she'd held herself back, for she knew that the flood of his passion would have taken her with it. She had always held back, always. For this? For the life she had now? What had she done? But seeing the pain in the eyes of the wounded soldiers, and the way they reached for her hand in their times of terrible need, a different passion took over. How arresting they were in their suffering. They were powerful fighting men, struck off from their lives, some of them having lost limbs with the surgeon's knife in the most excruciating ways. There was a sort of treachery in their eyes, she thought, that was hard to understand. It had something to do with what men did to men, or what men did for power. Or perhaps not men at all, but nations instead when forces like greed, confusion and fear took over. She had certainly seen fear in their eyes when they were writhing in pain, a fear she could not share, for she had never known it in her life of safety and plenty. But this is what moved her, the awful need, the mystery of it all and the desire to help repair what human nature itself had tried to destroy with such reckless abandon.

She clasped her hands and stared at Sidney Herbert's last letter, lying before her on the table. She was being taken to task it seemed, by the administrative officers, for trying to take over at Scutari. Her work, wrote Sidney, was to officially act as Superintendent of the Female Nursing Establishment of the General Hospitals in Turkey; she had no authority over nurses in hospitals not in Turkey. Well, the system as a whole was in desperate need of reform, a fact that couldn't be kept hidden, she thought angrily. Why was there always a tussle? She could see there was much left to do and she would have to fight one or two demons.

She pondered on what she would say in her letter to Sidney and hoped it would reach the War Office without interception. She would say it again – she needed more nurses, and they had to be experienced and paid! The Crimean hospitals were badly in need of nurses. And because of their poor reputation, the government was not of a mind to hire more. Russell's reports however, relating the neglect of injured soldiers who must suffer such vile conditions in filthy, understaffed hospitals must surely make the Commons take notice, she thought, and she'd forwarded her case in earnest. She was leaning on Herbert heavily, and she'd had letters from home saying he was tired and overworked. But she knew she must shout out loud, or who was to hear? They weren't just grappling with wounded men at Scutari; cholera broke out in an instant when conditions were unhygienic – how many times must she write about it in her letters? She drew a breath and realised again that she wasn't breathing as she should; sometimes it seemed she would stop her breathing absolutely, her thoughts demanding all her strength.

Hall's inspection had reported that all was well at Scutari, except for a few readjustments. Hall could be kind and considerate, the orderlies said, but he did not like to rock the establishment who feared for their own positions. And he was deeply conflicted when it came to looking at the true situation of the hospitals. His voice was loud, and his orders were final. Or so it would seem. But she'd captured a look of dread and uncertainty in his eyes. It was quite unmistakeable. He was a man in uniform with a loud commanding voice. He was though a fighting man and she was a fighting woman.

She put aside her letter, it wasn't quite ready. She also had a half finished letter to her parents that needed attention. She must tell them about the death of Amelia's brother, and ask them if Parthe might visit the cottage. Amelia's mother would get a letter from Sidney Herbert in time, but Florence felt she should let the Nightingale's tell her what had happened first . . . And then she must write to Richard . . .

Her nurses were busy on the wards and she'd told them she needed an hour to herself that evening. She would keep to the time; it was important to keep to time. She wanted to write to Richard. But what would she say? How did he see the two of them now she had gone? Had she not given him the role of jilted lover? His mind was good and true, and his sensitivities were acute. But how she had hurt him. And she'd hurt herself in the bargain. What would he think of her *now*, she wondered. He would not care about the way

184

he was viewed by others, though everyone knew how he'd wanted her. And it was good to be wanted. But Benjamin was right; a man needed the woman he loved by his side. And she knew that Richard loved her. So much so that she had felt herself able to secure his love in her heart and keep it for a better time, in the way her mother did with favourite things. But love wasn't a thing, it was a feeling, and it either lived or died.

She got up and paced the dormitory, all was neat and tidy, but her mind was a chaos. She had not written her letter and her hour was up. She made her way to the door. 'What have I done?' she said loudly, her straying voice echoing down the empty corridor. She rubbed her face tiredly, her cheeks damp with tears. She wanted Richard, but she knew she must stay at Scutari. Another woman was taking over her mind, another Florence Nightingale, and she felt she must bend to her will.

'You say your mother makes good quince jelly,' said Benjamin, as he sat with Evie in his room. 'I can almost taste it as you speak. But I haven't had quince jelly since my childhood. And you found all those quinces by the hospital, did you? They're a very generous fruit to be so prolific. I believe they grow in abundance in Constantinople, they send them all over the world. Or at least they did. Who can tell what has happened to the little quince nowadays. You have gathered a lot, dear Evie. But what will you do with them?'

Evie looked down at the rich full fruits in her lap. 'I shall bake them,' she said decidedly. 'And I intend to collect more. I have baked them myself at home; they can be added to all kinds of meats. If we can get the kitchens to cook them, the smell will be delightful for the hospital, and when the fruit has been baked, the flesh of the quince is the colour of an autumn sunset. Ah, it is lovely.' She stared out through the window and closed her eyes. 'I do love the autumn sunset in England.'

'Indeed,' said Benjamin heartily. He took one of the fruits in his hand and rolled it about in his palm. 'They're very hard though Evie, I should think they need a lot of baking.' He handed it back to her thoughtfully.

'They do,' she nodded. 'But Mother leaves them in the oven by the fire and they are soft and ready to eat within a couple of hours. I shall tell the men in the kitchen how it is done, then the soldiers will experience a really delicious treat.'

He stood, then took some books from a box and placed them in order on his shelves. 'Did you know,' he said over his shoulder, 'that Constantinople was the richest place in the Eastern Mediterranean once, mostly due to the trade routes between the Aegean and the Black Sea. The Mediterranean is such a lucrative trade route, countries have always desired it. But it's been so violent of late, of course. November has been dreadful. I heard from one of the soldiers that the recent storm was the worst in living memory. Many of the ships bringing supplies were sunk. Even the horses at Sebastopol have been starving. Poor creatures, they don't know how to tell you when they're hungry, they just lie down and die.'

'You know many things,' Evie said, sighing. She glanced about at his books.

'I do,' he said turning to her, smiling. 'But unless I can learn from them and become a better person, I am simply a walking library. Would you not agree?'

'I think there are lots of thoughts in our heads which we don't have words for,' said Evie, giving him a curious look.

'That's it, Evie. Perhaps that is the reason for art. Art tries to articulate words that cannot be said. Music, for instance, is bigger than words I think. It is its own secret language and sometimes expresses all kinds of feelings we didn't know we had.'

'So feelings are more important than everything else then,' said Evie, nodding with satisfaction. 'Mother has always said so. She cannot read, but she knows things, and I can often tell what she's thinking just from the look in her eyes. It's the same with the sheep on the hillside near home, when you look in their eyes you feel sorry for them. It's as if they know their fate, the fact that we are going to eat them.'

'Very true, very true,' he said. 'Poor things.' He tidied more books, with precision and pride. 'Constantinople was renowned for its libraries,' he said. 'When books were being destroyed because of political instability, Constantinople squirrelled away its Greek and Latin manuscripts, and when the city fell to invaders, many wonderful books were taken to other countries for safety. I often wonder where they are. Such splendid Latin manuscripts . . .'

'Do you understand Latin?' she asked, wide-eyed and incredulous.

'I do,' said Benjamin, a little imperiously. 'I speak German, French and Russian too. It's enlightening to see the same words written and spoken in another language.' There was a strange mysterious lilt in his tone as he spoke. He stopped, thoughtful. 'It's as if there are different ways of being, which of course there are. Different words for different ways of living.'

'You mean like when people tell lies?' said Evie, listening intently.

Benjamin smiled. 'I'm not so sure about that. Anyway, Evie, won't Miss Nightingale wonder where you are?'

'She will,' said Evie, looking downwards and biting her lip. 'But she knows I'm upset.'

He looked at her curiously. 'Well, my dear, this place is hardly conducive to happiness.'

'The boy I comforted when Doctor McGregor took off his arm . . . Well, he died.'

'I'm really sorry. It is a sad litany here.'

'But Miss Florence knew him, you see. He lived in a cottage with his family near Lea Hurst. I believe he worked for her father.'

'Oh dear,' said Benjamin slowly shaking his head. There was a strange mournful note in his tone. 'When death comes close to home it is always worse of course.' He sat down beside her. 'Why don't we take those quinces to the cooks,' he said softly. Together they walked along the cold stone corridor and made their way to the kitchens.

CHAPTER 18

The Commission – Spring 1855

'Do take a seat, Doctor Sutherland. You have travelled a long
way and the sea is in a terrible mood just now. It is the wind,
of course, it is quite fierce today. Your colleagues are taking refreshments I hope. Have you had anything yourself?'

Sutherland waved away Menzies' words and was soon into more
important matters. 'Your officers have been very hospitable, Major.
They escorted us up the cliff and into the barracks. It appears they
are aware of my purpose. It is hardly the inconspicuous visit I had
hoped for however.' He raised his brows in surprise. 'And I believe
they have only recently suffered Doctor Hall.'

'Suffered, ah yes. But we are reported on constantly,' said Menzies,
shaking his head. 'My officers have been apprised of your visit, of
course, and as for the patients in our wards, word travels fast. There
are cruel rumours about this hospital, yet nothing is as bad as they say.
I challenge anyone to do better. I'll tell you now, you will find a lot
of the men on those wards speak well of me.' Menzies drew a breath
nervously. 'I am quite confident of that.'

'It seems that things are not quite as you think, Major,' said Sutherland sitting very straight in his chair and frowning. 'I see that your desk is drowning in papers, much like my own in London. Papers can attack us like enemies.' He took off his hat and scratched his head. 'This place is so grey and grim.' Sutherland scowled at the thought. 'And to tell the truth, I'm not sure where to begin, I hadn't realised how big it was. It will take some time to investigate . . .'

'Investigate?'

'Of course. This isn't just an inspection, it's an investigation. A Commission. I am here to investigate the issues *The Times* has reported. It seems your officers are better aware of my intentions than you yourself, Doctor Menzies. There are a great many deaths at Scutari. That is, compared to . . .'

'Do you think we are murdering people?' Menzies said of a sudden, staring at Sutherland angrily. 'It is a military hospital God damn it! There is a fair bit of murder out there though. They call it war. People are dying ...'

Sutherland's voice fell low. 'Yes, and far too many . . . I would have thought the wounded came here to get better, to *repair,* as Miss Nightingale says, not simply to lie waiting for the graveyard.' He glanced through the window. 'And what a massive graveyard it is. There are men digging the earth this very minute.'

'The dead must be buried,' Menzies said quietly.

For a moment or two they were silent.

'But so many?' said Sutherland thinly, in a curious tone of voice.

'Too many, yes, you are right,' Menzies said, irritably. 'I know these things better than anyone. The lady, Miss Nightingale, however, can be rather disruptive. She is so self-willed and it's as if my orders mean nothing. I do not believe it benefits the soldiers to have her wandering about finding fault. She disregards all the good we do here and only finds fault.' He clapped his palms on his desk three times. 'Fault! Fault! Fault! And she shouldn't be making me sack good orderlies simply because they are old, or because they are a little too rough with the wounded. Let me tell you, some of those orderlies are very capable and work with immense pride. This place goes on forever, Sutherland, it is three storeys high and the lines of beds stretch for miles. The orderlies are up and down the stairs day and night. It cannot be perfect. And it is really most curious that Miss Nightingale thinks miracles can happen in a military hospital.'

Sutherland sat quite silent peering at Menzies and listening carefully. 'Ah yes,' he murmured, nodding. 'I have it on good authority that Miss Nightingale expects perfection. But she will not get it, certainly not in wartime. Imagination is marvellously clever, but it cannot compete with reality.'

For a moment or two they were silent. Menzies spoke again. 'The orderlies, you see . . . We have hundreds of soldiers carried in here every day and you can't always handle them gently. And as if the place isn't cold enough already, Miss Nightingale opens every damned window there is. It is as cold as the poles in this barracks.'

'She makes you shiver, does she?' said Sutherland, glancing at the tightly shut window, 'foisting all her ideas upon you and trying to take the place over.'

'Not trying, oh, no not that, she *does* take the place over. She is quite a force to be reckoned with.'

'Indeed,' said Sutherland, stroking his chin, his eyes still on the window.

'Ah,' said Menzies, watching him carefully. 'The window? Oh, I know. I should open it. But the draught is bad for my neck.' He gave a sigh of hopelessness. 'The woman means well. And there are officers here who hang on her every word. Let us say she has a certain *je ne sais quoi*. And I have felt her power myself. But there is such a thing as practicality.'

'There certainly is,' Sutherland murmured, changing his position in the chair. 'But I have great admiration for her ideas.'

'You see . . .' Menzies continued. 'She offended John Hall by suggesting his Inspection was disappointing. I received quite a reckoning for that. The Doctor is fully aware of your visit, of course. It has caused him some disquiet. I thought it quite harsh myself, to demand a Commission. Oh dear, yes. Miss Nightingale is, I believe, a very good friend of Sidney Herbert.' He glanced at Sutherland as if expecting an answer. But none was forthcoming. 'It is all rather irregular,' Menzies said quietly.

Sutherland breathed in deeply and spoke again. 'Miss Nightingale wants to be taken seriously but it seems she is not. In fact, I am told you are rude to her time and again. I do not think you understand what she wants.'

'She wants too much. Her wishes are the stuff of fairy tales. They cannot be realised.'

'But can she not work towards a goal?' Sutherland asked, opening his eyes very wide and staring at Menzies with the full gravity of his office. A licentiate of the Royal College of Surgeons and a graduated M.D., he'd had extensive experience, and was proud to have been chosen for such a formidable task. 'Even an *impossible* goal, as you would see it. Though the reports we receive in London are quite unambiguous. Miss Nightingale lists her needs precisely and is intent on winning. No-one can doubt her dedication.'

'But we do not have the money for her needs and wants,' Menzies snapped, frowning. 'She has bought a lot of things herself with her own money, I am fully aware of that and the hospital is grateful. But . . .'

Sutherland interrupted him and leant forward slowly. His eyes flickered with intent. '*The Times* has set up a fund and people have been most generous. Much can be bought with that money.' He crossed his legs and folded his arms firmly as if ready for further opposition. 'Sheets and blankets and other things can be bought and sent to Scutari,' he said, looking at the ceiling. 'Our main problem is the shipping. The ships are not always used as Herbert would wish. Communications are sometimes bad.'

Menzies looked down at the papers on his desk. 'Is that so?' he said, throwing a couple of papers into the air. 'Who would have thought it?'

Sutherland went on. 'The Commissariat is looking into it however. Miss Nightingale is wilful indeed and has had people sacked for inefficiency. We are informed of these things.'

'So communications are sometimes *good*?' said Menzies, smiling wryly. 'Inefficiency is a moot point.' He swelled out his rather grand chest. 'I cannot see why Miss Nightingale's word should be more important than mine.'

'She is highly respected by the people in England, and also by parliament,' Sutherland said with emphasis. 'The care of our wounded soldiers is most important. You are being observed Doctor Menzies. I suggest you take care.'

'Spied upon, you mean!' said Menzies blowing out angrily. 'And not only by Russians. She is probably recording every single failing there is and none of the successes.'

Sutherland shrugged. 'I doubt it. She probably writes things down for herself. She likes to make lists and keep account of events, dates, deaths, that sort of thing. She is a good woman and searches for the best in people. Your best will be known Doctor Menzies. Miss Nightingale always means well. And by the way, has anything been done about the stench that issues from the wards? Do you know where it comes from? It is constantly reported, and even though the hospital is cold as the poles as you say, there is a smell of something rotten running through, it was quite apparent to me and my team.'

'I have no idea where it comes from,' said Menzies, shrugging awkwardly. 'Miss Nightingale's nurses clean what they can thoroughly. And that is all to the good. You have to consider however that there are a great many men entering this barracks each day, wounded or dying from cholera. It is hardly likely to exude the perfumes of Paris.'

For a moment or two they were thoughtful.

'I am told that the soldiers were walking in sewage before Miss Nightingale's arrival, ' said Sutherland, 'and that the floors were so broken and crawling with lice the nurses couldn't even scrub them.'

'The floors? Ah, the floors, I know. It's appalling. And you have to be careful where you tread or you might just fall through the boards, they are rotten. Did you know that? Right through to hell I suspect. Oh, and we have rats, rats, everywhere. Oh, don't forget the rats. Ah, such gross exaggerations.' Menzies bent to his desk and rested his head in his hands.

'You wasted valuable time with the nurses,' Sutherland said quietly. 'They were occupied for ages simply cutting bandages.' Sutherland looked at Menzies in disbelief and continued. 'You would not allow them on the wards. Miss Nightingale tells us everything.'

'I'm sure she does,' said Menzies, exasperated.

'Indeed,' said Sutherland quietly.

'It took time, Sutherland, *time!*' Menzies said, raising his voice. 'Miss Nightingale is adamant that people keep to time, you know, but she does not allow for the time it takes to get used to things. I was not used to a tribe of nurses walking into the hospital like that. It was sort of theatrical. And I hadn't prepared my officers.'

'And Miss Nightingale took *time* to visit Lord Stratford at the embassy. Hardly what you wanted Doctor Menzies. I am amazed she went across the strait to tackle the Ambassador. There has been a report . . .'

194

Menzies glanced about his office despairingly. 'What? Oh, I'm sure. I have one or two reports somewhere here. Do you not realise I am manacled to tradition, Sutherland? Of course, you do. I couldn't even contemplate the thought of those nurses on the wards at first. Those soldiers in there are used to male orderlies. Now however, with the influx of so many wounded arriving each day from Inkerman and Sebastopol, and the impossible task I have before me, it is all quite different. Much has changed, that is, and much has changed in my thinking.' He lifted his shoulders and let them fall slowly. 'Miss Nightingale and her nurses have been assisting us now. We have also created a sort of library next door. I must take you to see it. A bit of culture, you see. We have an excellent librarian in there who teaches convalescing soldiers how to read, or if they can read advises them on books, which they can take to their beds and return to him later. The man speaks several languages, and is a most agreeable fellow. Yes, I am pleased with all that.'

Sutherland coughed quietly. 'I'm sure. But there are still too many deaths, my man. That's what I have to investigate. I have not come to test the wounded on their knowledge of Shakespeare.'

There was the sound of footsteps on the corridor. Menzies straightened. It was the steady, regular tread of Florence Nightingale. Just for a moment Menzies and Sutherland were silent. Then they stood as Florence walked in. Sutherland gave a slight bow. Menzies introduced them, and showed Florence to a chair.

'You are quite a picture, Miss Nightingale,' said Sutherland smiling. 'Nobody told me.'

'Am I?' she said, surprised. 'Now what sort of a picture is that?' Florence straightened her dress. She saw that Sutherland looked her up and down with pleasure.

'You are strong as well as pretty, if I may say so,' Sutherland said, frowning at his words, as if he wished he had never said them. He looked at Menzies, who sat at his desk in silence. Sutherland fell into his homely Scottish accent. 'What man would believe that such a wee, bonny lass, could be so strong and determined?'

Florence smiled and knitted her brows. 'I have things to do, like you, Doctor Sutherland, so I mustn't be long, my nurses are waiting.' Sutherland remained silent. Florence continued. 'I am indeed a bonny lass, I think my father would agree, but I am not in the least delicate.' She braced herself and looked at him straight. 'Doctor Menzies says I can accompany you on your rounds. Are you ready? The daylight fades very fast, and the world is quite different seen by the light of a lamp, or even worse by a candle when the ghosts find freedom on the walls.'

'Yes, shadows might be something of a threat to delirious soldiers,' he said wryly. He turned to Menzies. 'Good to have talked with you Major,' he said, rising. 'I hope we understand each other.'

'Only too well,' Menzies said, shaking his head with annoyance.

Florence had seen that Menzies and Sutherland had found a sort of accord however. Well, at least for now. She knew that Menzies had dreaded the Commission, but one thing was clear, it was happening and whatever the team discovered would be reported to London and the hospital was bound to benefit. She intended to show Sutherland everything that bothered her; it was all written down.

In the first of the wards, without a second's hesitation she took him to a leaking pipe in a corner, brought to her attention by a wounded soldier in one of the beds nearby. The smell was nauseas. Sutherland got down on his knees and took tools to the pipe. After a couple of minutes, he looked at Florence with a mixture of concern and satisfaction. 'There is something rotting down there,' he frowned. 'Let us look further.' They made their way down the ward, and just as expected other pipes needed attention. 'There are putrid gases leaking from the pipes', he told her. 'Something is decomposing.' Four other men had joined him, and he instructed them to investigate the channels. 'Best not stand too near,' he told Florence, as the men lifted the floorboards to look at the plumbing, 'these gases can cause diseases, they are quite deadly. Menzies must hire some Turkish workmen to lay new pipes and set up some other beds. The funds raised by *The Times* will pay for improvements.'

They went along the wards, through the thin pathways between the beds, the wounded soldiers watching and observing as the doctor made notes on his pad.

'I think it's worse over there, Miss,' one of the soldiers said to Florence. He pointed. 'The bedding smells vile in no time at all over there.' The soldiers watched curiously from their beds. 'There's been something amiss with those pipes for ages,' said another. 'You get cholera down in this ward. Cholera spreads like hell.'

'Indeed it does,' said Sutherland. 'But it's going to be fixed, all of it.'

'Thanks to Miss Nightingale,' said another. 'She has special powers. Everyone says so. You're answering our prayers, Miss Nightingale. She comes fluttering in, she does, like a great moth in the night, gliding through the wards with her lamp. She brings us peace.'

'Isn't that wonderful,' Sutherland whispered as they went on their way.

'They dream,' she murmured. 'When I make my tour at night time, I hear them talk in their dreams. I think they somehow include me.'

'You comfort them,' said Sutherland quietly. 'You are like a sort of priestess to them. You are indeed a force for good Miss Nightingale. I am glad to be here today, it is quite a privilege to meet you.' There was a sort of elation in his tone, a kind of relief. 'Very good,' he said softly.

After they had finished their tour, Sutherland said he would need to return to Menzies and deliver his thoughts, which would then be sent by way of a report to London. 'There is a need for some big decisions,' he said as they walked down the corridor, returning to Menzies' office. 'Enormous changes must be made. Tomorrow I shall look at the kitchens.'

'And I hope you can see the Purveyor,' Florence added quickly. 'He should change his ways. You must sail across the Bosphorus and scare the Ambassador silly.'

'That is my intention,' said Sutherland, giving her a wry smile.

'Good,' said Florence. All in all it had been a productive day.

CHAPTER 19

Early Summer – Scutari 1855

At the start of summer that year, for some reason Florence thought of Athena, her owl. She heard no owl calls at Scutari, but whenever she thought of home, she heard them in her mind, and would think of the little creature who had lived with her so long, so warm and alive. She wrote to her family, telling them of a recent experience;

"Dear people
I saw Athena last night. She came to see me. I was walking home late from the Genl. Hospl. round the cliff, my favourite way, & looking, I really believe for the first time, at the view – the sea glassy calm & of the purest sapphire blue – the sky one dark deep blue – one solitary bright star rising above Constantinople – our whole fleet standing with sails idly spread to catch the breeze which was none – including a large fleet of Sardinians carrying Sardinian troops – the domes & minarets of Constantinople sharply standing out against the bright gold of the sunset, the transparent opal of the distant hills (a colour one never sees but in the East) which stretch below Olympus always

*snowy & on the other side the Sea of Marmora when Athena came
along the cliff quite to my feet, rose upon her tiptoes, bowed several
times, made her long melancholy cry, & fled away – like the shade of
Ajax – I assure you my tears followed her . . . "*

She thought it a strange letter to write to her family, and it had been
a strange experience. What did it mean, she wondered, if it meant
anything at all. And she wrote with news about the war. Sardinia
had joined them in January that year, she said, against the
encroachments of Russia and hoping to strengthen relations with
France and other western allies – more violence, more wounded,
more deaths. As she finished off her letter she wondered if it might
have been wrong to disclose the apparition of her owl. She didn't
want her family to think her unstable and hoped they knew the
way of her mind. Anyhow, the letter was written and sealed, and
she intended to post it the next day.

Now she must document the important matters of war, she told
herself firmly – the number of wounded arriving at the hospital, the
deaths, and where lives had been saved. Scutari hospital had now
changed much for the better, men were talking and laughing on the
wards, and they visited the library and learned how to read,
improved their writing and borrowed books. And they talked
together about issues other than war, all of which helped them heal.

Mrs Clarke had gone very quiet since they'd been to see the
Purveyor and Lord Stratford in Constantinople. It wasn't the fact
that she'd witnessed Florence raising her voice so loudly to such
awkward, hectoring men that bothered her, it was her own
preoccupations, she said. She would sit with Evie when troubled.
Evie liked helping troubled people and often sat with the soldiers
listening to their stories about people they loved, or hated, acting as
a consoling power on the wards, and Mrs Clarke had been glad of

her company. But Mrs Clarke had scarcely slept of late, and that morning had found herself lying in a heap on the floor, as if she had suffered a nightmare and fallen out of bed.

'No better?' asked Florence, as the nurses left for the wards.

'It won't go away,' Mrs Clarke said shakily, huddled in a blanket. 'The horrible images won't go. It's one thing tending the wounded here, but to see those limbs floating about in the water like that is different. It haunts me, Miss Florence, all the time.' She trembled as she spoke. 'Oh, it was all too much. And so many wounded coming in here every day, will it never be over?' She turned away, tearful.

Florence listened worriedly. It was hard, so hard, harder than she'd ever imagined.

'I'm sorry Miss Florence. I don't want to let you down, but I'm just not strong enough for this.'

For a moment or two they were silent as they sat alone in the dormitory.

'The poor Bosphorus,' Florence said sighing. 'I felt it too, that river suffers monstrosities. I am aware that bodies have sometimes been thrown overboard as well without names, it has bothered me. There is a lot of overcrowding on the ships and it means . . . Oh dear, Mrs Clarke, God looks on at such terrible things and hopes for better.' She shook her head despairingly. 'We mortals must do the same.'

It was a cold but sunny morning, and the light was bright in the room, shining through the windows. 'The sunshine is nice,' Mrs Clarke said, turning to her again and trying to smile. 'I like the early summer sunshine.'

'Of course you do,' said Florence, in sympathy just then with Mrs Clarke's wretchedness. The early summer sunshine was most welcome. She could not justify having brought her, not really, nor could she apologise for it either for Mrs Clarke had been determined.

Each nurse must find her own way, or return to England, she'd thought, and so it must be. 'I'd love to be back in England,' Florence offered, watching her middle-aged housekeeper's face as she spoke. Mrs Clarke had taken on an aged look of late. She frowned more than usual and often screwed up her face when soldiers came through the hospital doors in pain. It was best to greet them with warmth, Florence had told her nurses, never with shock or fear.

Florence continued, 'It's early summer in England and it's wonderful to think of it. Here it's very different, to have so much sea all about us strangely makes death seem closer, for the sea itself owns the earth and you sense it is eager to take us back as its own. It is a strong and inviolable force.' She rubbed her arms at the thought. 'When I hear it roar, I think, no, not yet, not yet!' She admired the tenacity of her nurses, and had expected to see occasional tears, and the weeping she'd heard from some of their beds at night and she'd known that a few would go home.

'The sea rages worst at night time,' Mrs Clarke said shakily as if reading her thoughts. 'I feel so frightened. Everywhere is so rocky and hard at Scutari. I think of the gardens at home, their loveliness right through the seasons, and there was always the friendly robin that would look through the kitchen window. Do you remember the robin?' Mrs Clarke talked on with a little sob in her throat.

'Yes, of course,' said Florence. Her own spirit often fell victim to depression, but she forced herself out of it, like a breathless swimmer who had hit upon violent waters. For a moment or two she was rapturous. 'I remember *everything* – crystal chandeliers, dancing, champagne . . .' The pull of home was strong. She could see she would need to have a serious talk with Mrs Clarke. William Russell from *The Times* intended to return to England that week, would Mrs Clarke like to accompany him, she wondered. He would see she was taken care of. It would be hard to lose her, but Florence had seen that other nurses were also weakening and might need to go home. Sidney Herbert had sent more nurses, and they were trained, well, at least on paper, but she'd had to check up on them daily. They must always follow her instructions, she told them, they could not go their own way, nursing in England was a very different matter from nursing at Scutari hospital.

'Some of the nurses don't like me,' Mrs Clarke ventured, as Florence turned to leave. Her voice rose with emotion. 'They say I try to overpower them. One of them called me a harridan. Called me a harridan, they did. But I am only following your rules, Miss Florence.' The relief of unloading her feelings made her talk louder, so loud that Florence glanced about to see there was no-one listening. The nuns objected to her own authority, she was fully aware of that, some called her cold and indifferent, and they whispered about her behind their hands on the wards, it was a stumbling block she was trying hard to overcome for it wasted valuable time. But were they taking it out on Mrs Clarke?

But everything was going quite well, on the whole. They were now into 1855. Many improvements had been made at Scutari. The wounded no longer lay cold in the corridors, but were at once taken to a bed. The improved sanitation and better food had increased their general wellbeing, lessened the spread of diseases, and made for faster healing. The writer Charles Dickens had helped pay for laundry equipment and the hospital now had a machine for drying the washing. The soldiers could have crisp clean shirts and clean beds. Leaking pipes had been repaired, and there seemed to be a curious new energy in the air and a firm hope for the future.

'We'll talk later on,' Florence said tenderly. 'You stay here and rest, dreams can be very unsettling, I know. And you are right, Mrs Clarke, it was traumatic crossing the Bosphorus and you shouldn't have come. But you did beg me, you know. You are very persuasive.'

Mrs Clarke sat looking confused, working her hands together slowly. 'It's just that . . .' she began. But she couldn't find the words. 'You see I . . .' she continued. 'You see, so many of the wounded are young. They have had no life. I can't seem to . . .' She stopped in the middle of her talk. Florence knew how hard it was for the older woman to speak of her deepest feelings to someone she had known so long and to whom she had been a confidante and guide. And as Florence gazed at her now, she saw that the woman she'd known so well was lost, not just lost at Scutari, but lost in herself. 'Later,' Florence said, touching her arm. 'There is plenty of time. Think about Lea Hurst and how it is in the summer, its beauty and glory. Don't think about Scutari. Not now. I must talk with Mr Russell, he is returning to England shortly. I can sort out passage and soon you will be back home.'

There was a lot she needed to talk about with Russell, the single-minded, hawk-eyed reporter, who was everywhere all at once and seemed to have the wings of an eagle. He was a powerful force wherever he went and ruthless with his pen. Poor communications, little in the way of keeping accounts of deaths and losses, bad food, poor clothing, everything was noted by his pen. There was an urgent need for regulation and Russell missed nothing. Even if goods found their way to Constantinople, there were insufficient storage facilities to keep them safe before they were redistributed. There was also trouble over medical supplies, for those sent from England sometimes didn't tally with those that arrived in Crimea, leading to suspicions of pilfering. And Florence knew from letters that there was constant mental pressure on the ministers in parliament. There had been nasty, almost insane arguments where failures were always somebody else's fault, for who could be held responsible when everything was running amok.

'And you, Miss Florence?' said Mrs Clarke, her eyes round and concerned. 'Must you always think about Scutari? – How long will you stay?'

Somewhere, far away down the corridor they heard the clicking of heels. Florence started. She ought to be on the wards by now, the nurses would miss her. The sound of the footsteps receded and stopped. She breathed deeply for a moment and felt strangely alone. Yes, she would have to continue to think about Scutari, she must. But she did not know how long she would be there. She reflected for a moment on the improvements she'd made, and the love she'd received from the soldiers. The putrid smells on the wards had gone, and she'd insisted on cleanliness everywhere. Men still wept in the night however, crying for home, crying for their loved ones, crying for the loss of their friends and crying in pain. But summer was arriving and her heart hurt with memories. 'Yes,' she said solemnly. 'I must always think of Scutari. And the other hospitals too, that are part of this terrible conflict, not just the hospitals in Turkey but those in Crimea too. I must battle Doctor Hall. The other hospitals need change Mrs Clarke, and I shall work towards that fiercely. Mr Russell has told me such stories. But you know how it is; I have no authority over Crimean hospitals, only the hospitals in Turkey.' She bit her lip intently. 'As yet, that is, as yet, but I have plans.' She waved a finger in the air. 'I shall fly in the face of this ridiculous system where the good of the wounded is the last thing considered.'

'You are frustrated with it all,' said Mrs Clarke. 'We are all so tired.' For a moment or two they were silent. 'Mr Monckton Milnes,' Mrs Clarke whispered finally. 'Do you ever think of him?'

'Oh I do, I do,' said Florence. 'Constantly.' She laughed and threw out her arms. 'I *dream* of Richard.'

'He was a wonderful horseman,' said Mrs Clarke abstractedly. 'One of the best I ever saw. I would watch through the window and see him galloping away, cantering across the hills.'

'Galloping away.' smiled Florence.

'Yes, he has gone,' the older woman added softly.

'I know,' said Florence, her eyes glistening with tears. 'Come to think of it,' she murmured, 'you often sent him away with cakes from the larder. I saw you. I saw those looks you gave him too. He is quite a flirt, you know.'

'He did flirt with me, Miss Florence. But I was old. Had I been you, Miss Florence, I would have married him in an instant.'

'Oh, well,' Florence said sighing. 'I didn't. But I might one day, you know, some time in the future.' She fell thoughtful then straightened. 'Now I must go to the wards. The nurses will wonder where I am.' She stood for a moment, contemplating her much loved friend so tired and unhappy. 'But we must talk again soon. You are going home, Mrs Clarke. I think it's the best idea.'

Later that day, Florence went to see Benjamin in his library. He was reading and looked up at her in surprise. 'Florence, how good to see you. You have no doubt heard that Doctor Menzies has left us.'

'Yes,' she said quietly. 'The inspection wasn't in his favour. I am hardly a friend, though I wasn't unfair to him, Benjamin. You know I must always speak my mind. Oh that I could think before-hand sometimes. I speak too freely.'

'So long as what you say is honest, Florence, that is what matters, surely, and I'm sure you are not the only source of opinion. Matters here are too big for the officers to handle. Ah, let them come in here and read poetry.'

'Poor man,' she murmured. 'My experience of Menzies has varied. He often seemed weary of it all. He has a wife and family to consider. Perhaps he had wanted to leave for some time. And who could blame him. I don't know if he's been stationed elsewhere, but I shall learn in time. McGregor has taken his place.'

'Yes, Doctor McGregor is softer footed and has a different spirit altogether. I hear the language of his tread next door quite differently.'

'McGregor has been good to me,' said Florence. 'He has a warm disposition and I have seen him perform operations in terrible conditions, sometimes with only candles to light his way. The flames of the candles waver but never his hand, oh, not for a moment. I must write to Sidney Herbert. I disapprove of the way Mr Herbert is being seen in parliament just now. It is wrong that fingers are pointing his way when he cannot be blamed for other people's incompetence.'

'Yes,' said Benjamin, shaking his head in disbelief. 'I believe he's been voted out.'

'He has,' said Florence dismally, slumping down in a chair. 'My parents wrote to me about it. I must write to Mr Herbert soon. But he is sure to know my feelings. He'll think he has let me down, which he hasn't of course. He hasn't been appreciated and the others don't know the immensity of his efforts. Let them try to get another Minister for War who is half as good as Sidney Herbert.'

'And Lord Aberdeen,' said Benjamin drawing a breath. 'He has gone too.'

Florence nodded. 'Yes, Palmerston is the new Prime Minister. Aberdeen has resigned. He had no choice. He and Stratford have been blamed for so many things. It is all changing in London. Herbert will still have some influence though and I suppose he will be needed for advice for quite some time. Palmerston will keep him close I'm sure. These matters are complex.'

Benjamin sat thinking for a moment, turning the pages of a book. 'You are quite amazing, Florence,' he murmured. 'Not once have I seen you weaken.'

She bent her head, smiling. 'But it doesn't mean I haven't,' she said softly. 'I never let people see it, but I do cry Benjamin, often. I fall into terrible depression sometimes, but I never let anyone see it. And I know I'll recover once I have straightened out my thoughts. And I must, for I have to show strength for my nurses and also for the soldiers. We cannot always be strong.'

He looked at her and listened, nodding thoughtfully at her words.

Florence continued, as if needing to speak her mind. 'I do not see depression as a weakness though. It is more a way of seeing truth, I think. For how can anyone be happy, the world being how it is? All we can do is enjoy the sunshine of our thoughts as they come. And they do, you know, they sweep in sometimes, like when a soldier is suddenly healed and has finished with pain. And when they smile it is absolute joy.'

'I'm glad you feel joy,' he said, his fine features wrinkling with warmth. He leant towards her. 'This Crimean war must be the war to end all wars,' he said plaintively. 'And you have dealt with it all admirably.' He met her gaze with a serious look. 'Yes, I am full of admiration.'

'I think Mrs Clarke is going home,' she said. 'I am sad about that, but I fear she cannot stand it any longer. She is a lot more nervous than I thought.'

'I shall miss her,' sighed Benjamin.

'And Evie,' she said, looking away. 'You like her?'

'I do, she is often here in this room and I have taught her a lot.'

'And I'm glad about that,' Florence said with a little hesitation. 'She is often on the wards too, though not doing quite what she came for.'

'What do you mean?' he asked curiously, looking at her and waiting.

'She is far too easily distracted from her work when the young men call her across, to laugh with her, tell her a joke, or have her read them something from a book.'

She saw that Benjamin frowned. 'She is needed, you see,' Florence said, quickly. 'We are so short of nurses, every one of them matters, every single minute. Evie is young and romantic and needs a man in her life.' Benjamin did not speak, though he looked concerned. She knew he was fond of Evie. But important things were left undone and she answered to her emotions more than her duties.

'Will you dismiss her?' Benjamin asked concernedly.

'You make me sound cold,' Florence said frowning. 'If I must send her home, it is only for her own good. You see, the other nurses get annoyed when she doesn't make up the beds when she should. I have told her time and again that she is here to work. Her sister gets angry about it too and they argue. Evie hates doing chores, but the beds must be made and the floors must be cleaned.'

'Ah, the chores. I know. Her sister has come to my room sometimes searching her out. I can see that Evie is difficult. But . . .' He broke off and went silently to his bookcase straightening books, which was something he did when emotion got the better of him.

Florence rose from her chair, making to leave. 'She will have to leave us, Benjamin. She can't just do as she wishes, and she takes no notice of my words. The other nurses see it.' It seemed Evie would have to return to England with Mrs Clarke and Mr Russell, though she would rather have let her stay on. She would write the necessary letters that evening.

Benjamin spoke over his shoulder. 'That's a pity,' he said quietly. 'Oh well.' He turned to her slowly. 'I shall see her before she goes, I hope. You will send her down to me, won't you, after you've told her what is happening.' He bent his head and sighed. 'I expect there'll be floods of tears. But you're right. She is not fitted to this place. The girl has too much heart.'

Florence went to the door. She was surprised to find that Benjamin and Evie had formed such a strong attachment. She was also jealous.

CHAPTER 20

Embley Park – Approaching Winter 1855

Time moved on quickly. Life opened new vistas, new pains, new amusements, new loves. Much was declared marvellous, much was declared disappointing and disgraceful, horrifying even fearful. It was the reign of Queen Victoria in England and Napoleon III in France. One of Emperor Napoleon's aims was to reconcile his country with England, and Queen Victoria had visited the Palace of Versailles in August that year hoping to improve relations. News travelled fast and people sat down to read newspapers together and gossip. A lot had happened in the year 1855. Everyone knew about the work of Florence Nightingale at Scutari and it was something they liked to talk about. Alfred Tennyson, the much admired poet, who had written *The Charge of the Light Brigade*, had published *Maud and Other Poems*, a new book of poetry, and had attended a social gathering in London at the home of the poets Robert and Elizabeth Browning. Those who thought themselves refined would quote the odd verse of poetry at parties. *Maud* though, was rather more argued over than enjoyed, for it was hard to understand the story. Tennyson, the Poet Laureate, was the leading poet in England and his poetry was loved for its imagery and melodic sound and the fact that it helped with the trials and tribulations of life when a time of scientific progress took issue with religious beliefs. It helped people feel less afraid of the future and what might happen after death. *Maud*, however, was an enigma, for some said her character was ambiguous; others simply turned the page for there were always treasures to be found in Tennyson's lines.

The ever restless reaper had now taken Nicholas I, the Tsar, who in his time had taken many lands and had also led Russia into the wretched Crimean War, a fatal error it seemed to many a Russian soul. Nicholas I, the Emperor, had been someone men might spend a whole afternoon discussing, for his reign had certainly been 'detailed'. He'd been known for geographical expansion, single-mindedness and wilful determination, and it had to be said he'd had a will of iron and had made a happy marriage, siring seven healthy children. He had died from pneumonia on March 2 that year, at the Winter Palace, St Petersburg, during the siege of Sebastopol in which thousands of soldiers commanded by the English Field Marshall Raglan, and French Marshall Canrobert, had besieged the naval maritime base of the Black Sea fleet. For Raglan and Emperor Nicholas however, all that was over and done with; they were lost to the land of the living. The press and the government blamed Raglan for the way the poor British soldiers suffered, living as they did in terrible conditions with inadequate food and clothing, and little, if any, medication for their injuries, though the blame in truth lay elsewhere. Bad communications, poor transport, theft and atrocious weather all played their part in the dark and weary war.

Mismanagement of the Crimean War was an endless topic of discussion at William Nightingale's club, and also privately in the parlour of his houses at Lea Hurst and Embley Park. Lord Aberdeen, Britain's Prime Minister had now resigned and Lord Palmerston had taken his place. Sydney Herbert, Minister for War, had exchanged a plethora of letters with Florence Nightingale that year and would sit by his fire reading them again and again, puzzling over how he could satisfy Florence's demands, talking to people, writing letters, and short of touring London with a begging bowl doing everything he could to get money for what she needed at Scutari, and trusting that what he sent would arrive at the right address. But there were days he could not function and must take to his bed, hiding his painful grimaces from his wife and claiming he was just overtired. His constitution was weak, though he wouldn't admit it; Herbert wanted no part of weakness and stiffened himself against it as far as he could. Inwardly though, he feared it, for life itself could attack you, and could even kill you. He was deeply concerned about the welfare of soldiers and both he and Florence had discussed how officers could purchase commissions when promotion should really be based on ability and merit. It annoyed her, and rightly so. But what could he do? He'd said in the Commons there ought to be more military instruction, a more professional approach in the ways of soldiery and had shared a lot of ideas with his colleagues, but then came the Crimean war, and what a disaster! He felt an affinity with Florence, he'd said to his wife, it was like a kind of enchantment, as if the whole of his purpose in life depended on something they both understood and which the two of them might work at together.

And he'd said such things to William Nightingale too, who now sat in his parlour at Embley Park thinking it over. He'd had lunch, and coffee had been served. The maid came in to clear away. William watched through the window as Sir Harry Verney rode away. Nothing unusual in that, except that he came more frequently now. It looked certain he would marry Parthe and Parthe was quite content. Mrs Clarke had stayed mostly in her room after her return from Scutari. Frances said Scutari had made Mrs Clarke a bit crazy; she acted like someone possessed, walking the gardens in the night, murmuring and weeping. The doctor had said it was a natural reaction and they should let her alone to get over her gross preoccupations, no questions whatsoever, not the least hint of chastisement for leaving, nothing like that must be said, for she murmured Florence's name constantly and obviously felt she'd defected. 'She is truly ill', Frances Nightingale said, 'and she looks so terribly pale.' It didn't surprise her at all, Parthe had added sadly, for she'd known Mrs Clarke would come back, and it hurt to think of what she'd suffered.

Parthe stood by the window, watching Sir Harry as he rode off into the country. 'I shall marry him, Mama,' she said, smiling. 'I find him very attractive, and I can't marry Monckton Milnes. Oh dear Mama, it's going to be hard, but we have to tell Florence about the lovely new lady in his life.'

'Well, it won't come from me,' Frances declared emphatically.

Parthe said nothing in reply, and carried on watching Harry Verney cantering towards the hills.

'I thought it quite wonderful, you know,' said Frances, 'that Queen Victoria should write a letter for Florence to read to the soldiers at Scutari. Florence has got things organised there and the Queen is grateful.'

'Everyone is getting married,' said Parthe sighing. 'I shall marry Harry Verney, and Richard will marry that woman . . . I can't remember her name.'

'I hope he writes to tell Florence,' William Nightingale said quietly, returning to his chair and picking up his book. 'I shall be most annoyed if he doesn't.'

'But Parthe is happy, my dear,' said Frances. 'At least there is that.'

William Nightingale turned the pages of his book.

'You want me to marry Harry, Father, you have often said so,' said Parthe, always in need of approval.

William coughed, but said nothing.

'But do you like him?' her mother asked softly, breaking the sudden silence. 'Your father and I would be happy to think you *liked* him.' She was finishing embroidering a rose in the corner of a piece of linen. 'You mustn't just marry him for the sake of it, Parthe.'

'For the sake of what?' said Parthe. 'Show me a better man I might marry. There is no-one as charming as Harry. And Mama, he is rich. I shall want for nothing.'

'But do you *like* him?' her father said, reiterating her mother's question. 'I mean really? He has seven children already, my dear, and he is very much older than you. I shouldn't want you to . . .'

'But of course I like him, Papa. You insult me to think I would simply marry him for money. I have not found anyone I like so well, apart from . . .'

'Oh dear Parthe, do stop it,' said her father. 'You can't have Richard, he is taken.'

'But not by Flo,' Parthe said quietly. 'Flo is far away in that horrible military hospital. Fancy wanting a life like that, when she could have had Richard.'

'That's how it is,' said William. 'Could have, perhaps, but not any more. The man gave up. And so he should. Flo made her choice.' He turned to his wife. 'Do write and tell her, Fanny. I suspect Richard will leave it until the last minute. He has courted her long and hard through many summers and winters to no avail.' He shook his head. 'It is quite extraordinary isn't it? I presume you warned her, my dear. I hope so. You will have told her to expect him to find someone else to care for. It is an age old adage that a broken heart can sometimes only be mended by finding someone else to love.'

'That is what has happened with Harry, I think,' said Parthe thoughtfully. 'The death of his wife has broken his heart and I am to mend it.' She drew a breath of satisfaction. 'And I'll do it, Mama,' she said smiling. 'I shall make him an excellent wife. He is very sweet and kind.'

'You are a good woman, Parthenope,' her father nodded. 'We are blessed to have you for a daughter.'

'I always do my best, Papa, and will continue to do so. I like to please you.'

'And you must please yourself also,' said her mother quietly.

William Nightingale sat silently staring at the fire. His face was warm from the heat. He thought about Florence cold in Crimea, the winds and the sea roaring about the rocky cliffs and he hoped she was sensible and didn't neglect herself. Just then there were tears in his eyes, but nobody saw them.

CHAPTER 21

Scutari – Winter 1855

Hearing Florence's footsteps, Benjamin came to the door of his library to greet her and made a soft startled gasp as she entered, for he'd never seen her so disturbed.

'I have received a letter,' she said, pronouncing the word *letter* very distinctly.

He saw that she held it in her hand. Unknowingly she needed him immensely. Benjamin Harrison, the man of books, knew he was a valued friend.

'A letter I ought to have expected,' she told him shakily. She sat down slowly. 'It has come as a shock. I wasn't ready, you see. I never imagined it would happen.'

He closed the door and turned the key in the lock so that no-one would interrupt them. 'Do you want to tell me about it?' he asked cautiously.

She smiled thinly, tears forming in her eyes. It was strange that she didn't mind crying in front of Benjamin. She dried her eyes with her hanky, while he drew up a chair and sat opposite.

'Why are you so unhappy? he asked searchingly. 'Is the letter about one of your family?'

'No,' she whispered. 'He never got to be my family. He wanted to marry me. He proposed to me twice, but ...'

'But you rejected him,' Benjamin said, bending his head.

'I did,' she murmured. 'I had to.'

For a moment or two they were silent. He braced himself and spoke to her straight. 'So tell me about this letter,' he said. 'I think you want to, since you have it with you, and what's more, you are crying.'

She felt comfortable with Benjamin, she was sure of him. 'He is marrying someone else. I am sorry for his sake and mine. Something beautiful has gone.'

Benjamin gazed at her fixedly. 'And do you *know* her?'

Florence shook her head. She was wondering how to defend herself against what she had done. Having rejected Richard's offer of marriage, she felt guilty. 'I feel so empty,' she said, miserably. 'But I knew I could never be married. I've seen how women get married and turn into inanimate objects, as if the very life has drained out of them.'

'Only women?' Benjamin said, sighing loudly. He screwed up his eyes with thought.

'Oh, it happens to men as well,' she murmured. 'But men are much freer to find their place in the world, whilst women serve husbands and children.'

'Oh dear Florence, you have lived a privileged existence. A lot of those women you feel sorry for will be perfectly happy playing nice tunes on their pianos and sewing. They read, they draw, they do things, you know, oh all sorts. They support their husbands too.'

'The men are supported while doing interesting work. It is never the other way round. I have always had a longing to do something valuable and special, just for myself.'

'And you have,' he said nodding. 'You have done it.'

'Have I? Have I really helped at Scutari? I hope so.'

'But of course. Do I need to tell you? Have faith in yourself, dear Florence.'

She nodded slowly and straightened.

'You have been fortunate enough to have support from the government. Your father has influential friends. Others are not so fortunate. It has helped you achieve your potential.'

'Yes, it is true,' she said, acknowledging his reproach. 'The poor must live like the beasts of the field sometimes.' She drew a breath and continued. 'Life is always a struggle. If you ask the soldiers why they have lost an arm or a leg, they do not know. They just say they fight for their country.'

Benjamin stood and paced the room. 'Damned country, they are all fighting for their country out there and those who are injured end up in the hospital, and you dear Florence and McGregor and others do the best you can to help them, if it's possible that is, and they don't finish up in the graveyard.'

'Ah yes!' she said sadly. 'I loath it when they must die. I feel I have failed them. But they are proud to fight for their country are they not? We must always value them for that. Richard is a politician. Politics will be a part of his considerations. You see, he *needs* a wife. Most people want to be part of a society, just part of anything; they do not like to be alone.'

Benjamin returned to his chair. 'They get a job and get a life.' He swept his arm towards the window where men were digging out the earth to make room for more of the dead. 'What is it this thing called "life?"'

'I believe it is a sort of suffering,' she murmured, 'a suffering that has to be endured.' She held his gaze, clinging to the warmth she had come to enjoy from his strength. 'One way or another, we suffer.'

'And now you are suffering in turn,' he said, glancing at the letter she was holding in her hand.

'Yes, it is quite absurd, isn't it.' She shrugged. 'What did I expect? Someone was bound to steal him away from me finally.' She glanced through the window and saw that a man was wandering about in the sunlight. It was Doctor McGregor looking at the graves. He moved slowly, not knowing he was watched.

Benjamin sighed, exasperated, almost annoyed. 'Dear Florence, how can you lose what isn't yours?'

'But he *was* mine, he was. He totally was!'

'Only while you held him captive. You talk about captivity. You captured his heart and hurt him; now he has torn it away and you are hurting in turn. But that is the price you must pay for having treated love so casually. Love won't be treated like that. It has to be a sort of pledge or it is nothing.'

'So my love for Richard is nothing?' she said. He rose again, restless, and went to stand by the window looking out.

'So what will you say in reply?' he asked, over his shoulder.

'I'm thinking about it,' she said hesitantly. 'Though does it really matter what I say? He no longer loves me, he loves someone else.'

'Well then,' he said, turning. 'You have said it yourself and must accept it, pain and all. Will you congratulate him?' He came forward, close to her again.

'How can I?'

'But Florence, like you say, people want to be a part of something rather than float about in the ether like an earthbound spirit.'

She listened to him carefully, just as she always did when she came to his room. She watched him straighten his waistcoat. Even here at Scutari, he was always smart and smiling, always thoughtful and caring. He had been a friend to Menzies and the soldiers who came for books, and he had been a friend to her. 'You must think me pathetic,' she said, taking a deep breath, and putting the letter in her pocket. 'Pathetic and selfish!' She had thought to let him read the letter, but realised he had read it already in her face.

'Come now, Florence, that's nonsense?' He leant forward and dared take her hands. He spoke softly. 'You are the finest woman I have ever known.

'Goodness, Benjamin, you applaud me too loudly I think. I am no angel. I have wronged Richard. I did not even release him before I left.'

'Release him?'

'Yes, I told him I loved him. I ought to have lied and released him.'

'But did you . . . Did you *love* him? I mean, really.' He faltered slightly as he spoke.

'I did,' she said softly. 'Very much.'

'Then why should you lie? We should never lie about love.'

'Because lies can sometimes bring peace,' she said quickly. 'Though I have never thought lying the least bit acceptable or appropriate.'

He drew a breath, thoughtful. 'I do wonder about that,' he said quietly. 'I might have escaped a lot of scrapes had I lied. But it's sort of like opening a door on to something unfathomable. Love relationships are often very hard work. Those who love very deeply are worst affected I think. Literature is full of such stories.'

'What are you reading?' she asked, bracing herself and trying to change the subject. She noted a wad of papers on his desk. 'It looks like a manuscript. Is it in French?'

'Ah yes,' he said, looking. 'It's a book that is not yet published. It was a stroke of luck I got to see it. I've been asked to review it. It is a splendid story called *Madame Bovary*, the debut novel of a French novelist by the name of Gustave Flaubert. I must write to tell them my thoughts before they are lost.' He frowned and bit on his lip. 'Now, what do I think? Oh, a great many things. It is wonderful writing and I'm certain it's going to be popular. It tells of a woman with a rich imagination who has found herself stuck in a dull, unsatisfying marriage where she feels her spirit is confined. It's as if she can't even breathe. It is an empty provincial existence. And in order to pass the lonely excruciating hours she takes lovers.' He watched her face as he spoke, his words did not embarrass her. 'You understand?' he ventured.

'Indeed,' she answered. 'It is bound to happen.' He still held on to her hands and she did not move them.

'Now there's a woman who ought never to have married!' he said, smiling. It will be serialized in the *Revue de Paris* next year. It is such a heart-rending tale. She ought to have married for love, then that misery would never have happened. Loveless marriages leave a trail of disaster behind them.'

'But she will hurt so many people by taking lovers,' said Florence with a questioning look.

'She will, and she does,' said Benjamin, sighing. 'It all leads to disaster. But she felt like a prisoner, you see. And would a prisoner not want to escape? She cannot pretend to love her husband, for she cannot lie.'

'No, she cannot,' said Florence. Benjamin lifted her hands to his mouth and kissed the tips of her fingers

CHAPTER 22

An Unbroken Will – May 1855

Opposite the window of Benjamin's room was the lonely Scutari graveyard where Turkish soldiers were constantly digging and preparing the ground for the dead. Benjamin's library was on the first floor of the great three storey barracks, a huge stone edifice, formally an army barracks, now a place to house wounded and dying soldiers. It had a miserable haunted history thought Benjamin, looking out on the cold still day. And there seemed to be a curious silence about it of late, the familiar moans that normally echoed down the corridors had lessened, as if the building itself was in mourning.

It was half past ten in the morning and he was waiting for Florence. They were about to make a journey to the Crimean hospitals across the Black Sea. There they would meet with John Hall, the Inspector General and see what those places were really like. Florence was eager to see if they were as good as Hall had reported. Truth and facts were what mattered when it came to the needs of sick soldiers, she'd reasoned. Judging from what she'd heard, they were certainly in need of improvement. Scutari hospital had been transformed into a place to live in, not simply a place to die in; the money raised by *The Times* had helped enormously as well as the assistance of a team of new nurses sent by Sidney Herbert.

Benjamin glanced about his room. The library, too, had been successful, and the soldiers liked visiting to practise their reading and writing and borrow books. Florence would sit of an evening helping them write to their families and ensured that their letters were posted; their domestic lives back home were forever in their minds and they talked a lot about their families.

The great white sky he looked on just then seemed devoid of even a hint of the storms that had ravaged the area throughout winter. The soldiers said the spirit of the hospital had magically improved since Florence had arrived with her nurses last year in early November. The death rate had reduced dramatically. It was an absolute miracle. During her first winter, thousands of soldiers had died at Scutari, but more had died from diseases like cholera and typhoid than battle wounds. Cleanliness, she'd told her nurses was vital, that and fresh air and exercise. And if a soldier was in possession of some strength then he ought to use it and exercise his limbs so that the blood flowed faster round the body and could carry out its healing powers. Doctor Sutherland's Commission had been of great value; broken pipes had been repaired so that poisonous gases no longer escaped into the wards, the sewers had been flushed and hospital ventilation had been checked and overhauled. Florence wanted to see how it was in Crimean hospitals now. From what she'd heard from the soldiers there was still a lot to be done to make their suffering more tolerable and to give them earnestness for life.

The thought of Florence coming to look around his hospitals, however, must surely have been daunting for Doctor Hall, thought Benjamin, and her letter asking to visit him would have put him on edge. As a doctor he liked to think his hospitals were in excellent order and said so, but it was hardly what the officers who visited Scutari reported. Dear, tender Florence would need to put on her armour when she visited Hall's hospitals, which he had stated emphatically were none of her business!

Benjamin and Florence had both agreed that Doctor John Hall had an excellent military history and his work commanded much respect. He'd been sent from Bombay straight to the Crimean War in 1854 as Inspector General of Hospitals and was idolised by some and hated by others. But he hadn't expected to have problems with this chimera called Florence Nightingale and her stern platoon of nurses. Benjamin smiled to himself. He had seen how Hall had tried to knock Florence off balance with his height and power of position, though it hadn't been easy to look down on Florence Nightingale. No wonder he'd called her a "petticoat imperieuse"! She certainly was. But Florence didn't weaken, and intended to make the journey. She'd been told by officers at Scutari that Hall would be difficult and might even have her recalled for causing him bother. But she was a woman of immense courage and valour when it came to what she wanted, and bother him she would! Florence was no ordinary woman and the major had a lot to learn.

Hall annoyed Evie too, Benjamin reflected, and she often expressed her anger in the library over the way he cautioned his staff about the use of chloroform, claiming that men with serious gun shot wounds wouldn't survive such a powerful compound during their surgery and the quick and steady application of a good well sharpened knife was a better alternative. Let a man bawl for his life was his mantra, rather than have him sink into a silent death with chloroform. Well, that was how it went for the ordinary soldier, not so for the officers. Benjamin couldn't imagine having a limb removed from his body without anaesthetic, but it was part of the common way, and the soldiers were often in a terrible state when they entered the hospital and simply surrendered to the surgeons as a matter of course. Chloroform however, he reflected, was known to be toxic, and its use in battle hadn't been properly researched, whether or not a doctor used it was a difficult choice. But there wasn't time for debate when soldiers arrived at the hospital shrieking with pain, vultures circling the cliffs, their rasping, hissing cries firing the hearts of the men with even more terror. Benjamin had heard though that Hall had been known to turn a blind eye on surgeons who liked to use chloroform. There were those who claimed he had a heart, though he did not like to show it. Benjamin heard a lot from the soldiers who came to his room. Hearsay had it that hospitals in the Crimea were reputedly poor and inadequate and that a lot of the sick and wounded were sent to Scutari, but the ships were overloaded and many soldiers died in transit often resulting in reckless, nasty evictions. A number of officers however said Doctor John Hall was an upright servant of the Queen, a strict disciplinarian and a hard working man of action which the medical profession could be proud of. Well, reports and opinions varied, the man had his followers. Benjamin decided Hall, poor fellow, must yield himself up to whatever despair confronted him, and war was indeed desperate.

He glanced at his clock. Florence was late, it was unusual. But she was bringing Evie, and Evie might be anywhere; it was sometimes hard to find her, and what's more, she didn't keep to time. She had begged Florence not to send her home and Benjamin was glad, for he enjoyed her company and a lot of the convalescing soldiers liked her, she brought her own special skills, her youthful beauty and kindness.

Doctor McGregor was busy in his room and Florence's nurses were on the wards. Half an hour earlier the corridor had been busy with voices, now it was silent, that was the way of the hospital.

There was a certain rhythm in the way the wounded behaved on the wards, they would talk for a while, read for a while, wait for the nurses in silence, then settle to tell each other stories. The place had developed a life of its own, had its own heartbeat and history. Just then he heard footsteps.

'I have quite an entourage outside,' said Florence, entering hastily. 'A number of Turkish soldiers will attend us on our journey, they will organise the food and horses and pitch our tents.'

'And Evie?' said Benjamin, seeing she stood by Florence, bending her head and looking guilty.

'Evie, as you know, is to join us,' said Florence. 'Well then, Evie, I take it you are ready?' she said tentatively.

'Certainly,' said Evie, nodding and straightening her shoulders. She looked smart and elegant in her fresh nurse's outfit, fitted at the middle and showing off her tiny waist. 'I intend to take care of Miss Florence,' she said, her face serious and beaming. 'Now that Mrs Clarke has left us, I need to be with her when she sails the Black Sea. I am told it is a place of death, just like the Bosphorus.'

Benjamin breathed in deeply. 'I daresay you're right, Evie. No mermaids out there for sure.'

'Evie comes at her own request, of course,' said Florence, looking at her thoughtfully. Evie looked strong and beautiful just then with her soft blonde curls peeping out beneath her cap. 'She is a little lax in her timing, however, which will have to improve, but as a nurse she is second to none.' She met her eyes and smiled.

'Where were you?' Benjamin asked Evie.

'Oh dear,' the girl said, embarrassed. 'I apologise for making you late, but there was something I needed to do. I don't know what would have happened if I hadn't done it.'

'So what did you do?' he asked curiously, watching and waiting. Her shoulders rose and fell. 'Well,' she said slowly. 'Strange things happen at Scutari. I mean really strange things, Benjamin. The men see ghosts sometimes. They hear the voices of their families back home. And they act as if they really are there. We have to go find them.'

Benjamin folded his arms and frowned. 'So you go along with their fantasies?'

Evie continued. 'Yes. But I usually make sure they get back in their beds after. This morning though, it was different.'

'How was it different?' he asked.

Florence listened carefully. There was a certain understanding between Evie and Benjamin, a sort of togetherness she envied. Did Evie see him as a brother, she wondered, or maybe even a father. She hoped it was nothing more.

'I followed a soldier who'd climbed out of bed and wandered out to the cliffs,' said Evie, frowning at the thought. 'He does it a lot.'

'You mean Silas,' said Florence. She smiled at Benjamin. 'He is named after the Roman god of trees. I think his father is a carpenter, he needs to be watched. He's very young, and the war has made him half mad.'

'Early this morning I found him at the edge of the cliffs,' said Evie. 'I called him back and told him he couldn't leave the hospital, and must always let someone know if he wanted to walk outside. He stared at me with such cold strange eyes, as if he didn't know where he was.'

'Silas, ah yes, Silas,' said Benjamin shaking his head sadly. 'I have read him some simple tales about Roman gods and goddesses. He likes to dream.'

'He is suffering from shock,' Florence said quietly. 'He constantly imagines he is hearing the sound of battle. All he can say is, "I must save my family. Help me to save my family!" So sad.'

'Well,' said Benjamin quietly. 'I suppose he thinks he might reach home by way of the cliffs. He might have fallen in the Bosphorus though, and no-one would have known where he was.'

'And will he always be the same?' said Evie miserably.

Benjamin spoke quickly, assuming a lighter tone of voice. 'He hasn't been here very long. Once he can relax, he can be helped by the other soldiers to heal what it is torments him. The men help each other. I've seen it.'

'On the battlefield too apparently,' said Florence assuredly. 'They risk their lives for each other.'

'It's all so horrible,' said Evie. 'Don't you think so, Benjamin?'

'I do indeed,' said Benjamin. 'I do indeed.' With that he took a long last look around his library, picked up his things then they all three went through the doors of the hospital and joined the waiting company to sail to Crimea.

'I'm glad you weren't queasy, Miss Florence,' Evie said, as they arrived at their destination. 'You didn't need any of the medicine we brought either.'

'Yes, it was quite an achievement,' said Florence, though her voice was a little tremulous. She would now meet Doctor Hall in his own territory. She braced herself and looked about.

'The sea wasn't quite so unruly today,' said Benjamin, as they walked along the beach, glancing around for the horses while the men moved the tents and essential things from the boat. 'The Black Sea has a dreadful reputation. But you can't be too careful. We were ready for anything, weren't we?'

'It was a good crossing,' Florence said nodding. 'But yes, that glorious sea, where if you are lucky, you might catch a glimpse of porpoises and dolphins, is full of human remains. We are in the Crimea, Evie, but heaven knows how it will greet us. To my way of thinking, it won't be with gladness.' They were waiting for assistance when they saw John Hall come striding across the beach to meet them with a retinue of soldiers and aides.

'I am glad you had a safe passage, Miss Nightingale,' he said, advancing towards her. He gave a slight bow. 'The Black Sea has delivered you with grace, but that is only a part of it. I fear there is far less safety to be had on land.' He glanced about concernedly. 'Women in these parts are always vulnerable, you know.' He looked her over sideways. 'Would you not agree?'

'I have heard it said,' Florence replied quietly, exchanging greetings. Benjamin, Evie and their Turkish assistants walked cautiously behind. Soldiers in the Crimea were always cautious and suspicious, there were spies everywhere, and just as Benjamin had said, many spoke very good French, which disturbed French soldiers and made them whisper. Hall and his men eyed Benjamin guardedly. Evie kept her head bent low. 'Yes, there is much to be feared in these parts,' said Florence, thinking about Sebastopol and the vast number of wounded entering Scutari hospital. 'So many men are dying, not from battle wounds, Doctor, but from fevers. Thorough cleanliness is a big part of the answer, as well as good food and fresh air. Men will heal quite naturally if well taken care of. They do not need to die.'

'Yes, yes, as you have said before Miss Nightingale.' Hall straightened and frowned at the soldiers listening close by. 'But I do not need your advice on such matters.' He regarded her closely. 'I have been doing this job a long time, Miss Nightingale. What is it you are here for, exactly?'

'Did you not read my letter?' she asked, speaking loudly and precisely.

'Well, a letter is just a letter,' Hall said shrugging. 'I do not have time to read them all; I receive them in their hundreds constantly.' He ran his hand across his brow. 'Do please tell me your purpose. I feel it is somehow sinister. I believe you are here to find fault. But you do not know the ways of the army, my dear. You might learn a thing or two to turn your stomach while you're here, but let me tell you this business has to be stomached. Oh yes, for that is the way of war.'

'I see' she said quietly, her skin tightening with annoyance. She turned to look at Evie, walking with Benjamin and gave her a smile of assurance. Their Turkish assistants were pulling on the reins of their horses. There would be quite a ride to the encampment. Hall claimed he didn't have any spare tents and was glad they had brought their own. 'We cannot rely on things reaching us,' he said, throwing out his hands. 'Ships get sunk. Things get stolen. Matters become more difficult by the day.'

'Too many soldiers are dying,' said Florence. 'We are quite overwhelmed at Scutari. Doctor McGregor is becoming exhausted, but he does what he can. We need more doctors, more nurses, deaths from diseases like cholera however have lessened and that is a blessing.'

'Yes, I heard,' Hall said thoughtfully, walking beside her, tall and strong, his hands clasped behind his back. He turned to look at her, and gave her a nod of admiration, 'You have done very well at that hospital, oh, without doubt. But you will not change my perspective on these matters.'

'Perspective?' she said, frowning.

'Yes. I am able to view things in relation to each other more clearly than you, Miss Nightingale. That is what I mean. I have much experience, you see. Whereas you . . .'

'I do not need experience to have compassion,' she interrupted, looking at him quickly. 'And I learned many things at Kaiserwerth hospital in Germany, and hospitals in England as well, and also, of course, Scutari.'

'I am a senior officer in the British army, Miss Nightingale,' he said imperiously, looking at her straight. 'But I am not without compassion. Oh no, I am by no means heartless. Though where is compassion on the battlefield when swords and gunfire are coming from every direction? Then there is a complexity of emotion, Miss Nightingale. Ah yes, human emotion is confused when a man is faced with a bayonet coming at his breast. In the dark horror of warfare, men will fight to the death or be seriously wounded, that is the way it goes. Some may survive without as much as a headache, those are the lucky ones. What do you hope to find in my hospitals here?' He glanced at Benjamin and Evie as he spoke and looked them up and down.

'Evie is one of my nurses. If ever there was a need for compassion, Evie has it in abundance.'

'And the man?'

'He is Benjamin Harrison, a librarian. He came to Scutari with books and has created a library for the soldiers.'

'A library? And do they use it?'

'They do indeed, while convalescing. He also helps with their reading. He is a great believer in knowledge. Knowledge is power, Doctor. Is it not? *Scientia potentia est.*' She looked at him and smiled wryly. 'Benjamin is also a very good friend and asked to come with me. Evie will also help me converse with the soldiers. She will talk to your wounded men and offer them succour.'

'Will she?' he said, though in a slightly mocking tone of voice. 'You seem to have it all worked out, Miss Nightingale. Are you in contact with London?'

'But of course. They know of my every move.'

'I'm sure they do,' he said heatedly.

'You need not fear me Doctor Hall. I mean you no harm. I only want to help. The soldiers know of me and you will no doubt hear them calling my name from their beds. It is testimony to how they value my nurses. Do you not see it?'

'I've got more to do than listen for them crying for nurses.' He said with a sniff. 'You are all the time looking for fault, Miss

Nightingale, and you will certainly find it. And you'll not be content until you do. Oh, how easy it must be to find fault in a time of war.'

'You have it all wrong,' she said quietly, turning to him as they walked. 'I seek to repair and improve. You'll have letters from London of course, apprising you of my visit. I have been given authority, you see, to find out how things are.'

Hall straightened quickly. 'Ah, have you. But you do not have authority to do anything in my hospitals here,' he snapped. 'How many times must I tell you? Only at Scutari.'

'Perhaps I do not,' she said flatly. 'But let me see if I can help you make improvements.'

Hall shook his head then looked at the sky.

'You are a surgeon, Doctor Hall, and I am a nurse. I can help you if you will let me.'

All this time, Benjamin and Evie had been silent, walking along with the Turkish soldiers bringing their horses and carrying their things. Florence, Benjamin and Evie mounted their horses to traverse the rocky terrain. Hall remained hostile, his back very straight, an excellent horseman she decided, and a highly skilled army officer, but how he scowled. 'Improvements!', he called to the sky.

'Improvements,' said Florence.

'You think we need improvements do you?' he said, looking at her straight.

'I am sure of it,' Florence replied. 'Hospitals always need improvements.'

'I know how to manage hospitals!' boomed Hall, so loud that his horse reared up and he needed to pull on the reins and with infinite skill caused it to relax.

An unfortunate start, thought Florence. They were most

unwelcome. It would have to go in the report she sent to London, though on second thoughts perhaps not, she would put it in her letter to Sidney Herbert. She had much to tell him. And she needed to speak with William Russell *The Times* reporter. She glanced about as they went. She wondered where he was, she hadn't seen him since he'd taken Mrs Clarke back to England. He might be anywhere.

'What is to happen when we get to the encampment?' asked Benjamin, riding up close. The doctor was riding ahead.

'I'll see how it goes,' Florence said cautiously. 'A lot depends on his mood. I suspect he will see we are settled first before he leaves us.'

'You look tired Miss Florence,' said Evie.

'And rather too pale,' Benjamin murmured, thoughtfully.

Florence's horse was unsteady and Evie leant across and took hold of the reins. She was used to horses from her life on the farm in Dorset, and the animal responded quickly. But she glanced worriedly at Benjamin. 'I think Miss Florence is unwell,' she said quietly.

'Yes,' said Benjamin seeing Florence had started to sway. A quarter of a mile before them they could see the large encampment. 'Florence, are you sick?' he asked softly. 'Shall we stop?'

'What?' Florence said faintly. 'Oh, I daren't be unwell. Where is the major, can you see him?'

'Yes, do you want me to fetch him?' said Benjamin. He reached across and touched her hand. 'How cold you are,' he said worriedly. 'I shall send a soldier for Hall.'

'Yes,' she said shuddering. 'I'm feeling strange.' She lurched forward suddenly, struggling to keep her balance. 'I need to sleep . . . Ah, Benjamin, let me lie on my comfortable bed. Let me have the sun on my face. Look, it is shining through the window . . .'

'She was as well as could be when we came off the boat,' said Evie, afraid and concerned. 'Now she is white and cold. Best bring the doctor. Cold then hot, cold then hot, and nauseas, that is the way of a fever.'

CHAPTER 23

Lea Hurst – Early Summer 1855

Parthe had brought her drawing down from her bedroom, so that others might evaluate her work. The house was silent that day, her parents had gone to see Sidney Herbert in London to enquire about passage to Scutari to visit Florence, it had been a terrible strain on them all to have Florence suffer Crimean fever on her own in that dreadful place.

The two Nightingale maids and the cook had taken a chaise into town. The gardener had come into the house, and he and his wife had been invited to comment on the drawing. The gardener's wife had been amused. 'I'm sure that owl could fly off the page!' she remarked. Both she and her husband had agreed that the drawing was beautiful, and that no-one could ever have drawn an owl any better. Their words had cheered Parthe no end, for the gardener was sure to have encountered owls at dusk and he liked to draw pictures of animals and flowers himself. Making the drawing of Florence's owl and creating the story had been a sort of distraction from the family's fears, for Florence was so far away and had suffered her illness alone. She'd been back in Scutari several weeks and was rapidly recovering, but they were all concerned for her strength. Her letters home however, were written as if nothing had happened. Florence never complained. But that was Florence; she would work herself to a shadow, and they could tell from her writing that her hand must have been trembling for a few of the words were illegible. She was quite unwell. But who could they enquire of? Mrs Clarke was back home and they didn't want to write to the officers about her health. There was nothing else for it; someone would have to make the journey.

'Flowers are magical,' said the gardener. 'I remember the day I tried to draw a daisy. A daisy is two flowers in one, you see and not so easily captured on a piece of paper.' He made a shape with his fingers. 'The large outer petals make up one of the flowers, and the cluster of tiny petals at the centre make up another.' He laughed. 'You can actually eat the leaves of daisies you know, they taste like artichokes.'

The gardener's wife, seated at the kitchen table, looked at her husband curiously and claimed they had never eaten daisy leaves in their lives. Amelia, the maid, looked at her child and frowned. 'I shouldn't like him to try them,' she said, adjusting the child's sun hat. She had just returned from a walk across the fields. Her long fair hair fell soft down her shoulders and Parthe said she looked beautiful.

'You must let me draw you sometime,' said Parthe. 'Your hair has captured the sunshine.' Parthe looked about abstractedly. 'Florence used to make daisy chains for Richard Monckton Milnes and put them around his neck,' she said, smiling at the thought. 'Flo could be so romantic. But she didn't even marry him in the end. He is marrying somebody else. And he doesn't know a thing about her illness. He'll be devastated when we tell him.' She sat down at the table and rested her head in her hands. 'Richard might be there at the Herbert's with our parents. I believe he visits. If he's there, they will tell him.'

The smell of baking bread came from the oven. Mrs Clarke would be down shortly to see how it was going. She'd prepared three loaves for baking that morning and had then disappeared to her room. She didn't talk a lot nowadays and often went about her chores with a strained expression.

'Try not to worry, Miss Parthe,' said Amelia. 'Miss Florence has a strong constitution, but I know how you feel. I constantly fear for my man at Sebastopol. Yet worrying does us no good. I would like to marry him, and pray he'll come home to me safely. So many men are dying at Sebastopol. I can only live in hope, and Mother has never been the same since the death of my brother at Inkerman. We expect him to walk across the fields every day, but we know that he won't.' Her voice trembled as she spoke. 'Death is so horribly final.'

'And your man has never seen his child,' said Parthe in a thin and sorrowful voice. 'It's a terrible thing when loved ones are so far away. I wish Florence hadn't been taken ill in Crimea. At Scutari, she would have had Doctor McGregor to take care of her. I doubt Doctor Hall would have cared for her like Doctor McGregor.'

'Oh don't say that, Miss Parthe,' Amelia exclaimed, frowning. 'I should be very sorry if that is how he is. Doctor Hall has a mixed reputation, but I feel he will give Miss Florence the best of his care. It's a wicked state of affairs over there.'

Parthe continued. 'Each day we wait for a letter. And that girl, Evie, has cut off my sister's hair! Can you believe it?'

'She has cut it shorter, Miss Parthe, that's all,' Amelia urged. 'Mrs Clarke says it helps break the fever. My mother believes in it.'

'It will break my sister's heart when she finds she has had a haircut while she was ill,' said Parthe, adding the final pencil lines to her owl.

'The thing about hair, Miss Parthe, is it grows,' Amelia said gladly.

'Our parents are to talk with Mr Herbert about visiting Crimea,' Parthe said worriedly. 'They want to go all that way . . .'

Amelia looked at her astonished. She was beating up eggs to scramble in the pan for her baby, who also enjoyed a piece of Mrs Clarke's fresh bread. The baby sat quietly waiting in a small wooden chair, beautifully made by the gardener who was a fine carpenter. Mrs Clarke rarely came down, and was often heard sobbing in her room. 'The Crimean war is a curse,' said Amelia, 'the Nightingale parents would be wise to stay out of its way.'

'I have almost finished writing the book,' said Parthe, glancing at the papers on the table. There lay her story, the "Life and Death of Athena, an Owlet from the Parthenon." She wanted to send it to Florence to help cheer her up in her illness.

'The drawings are lovely,' said Amelia. 'That owl looks realer than real!'

'I have told the tale, exactly as it happened,' said Parthe, with satisfaction. 'The owl was discovered lost and alone in Athens. Listen, while I say how it was.' She held the page before her and read it out loud like an actor;

"'This distinguished individual was born, (as nearly as can be ascertained) on the fifth of June 1850. Her (future) Mistress was returning from a visit to Pittacus, the learned Conservator of the Parthenon, and his wife, the sister of the Maid of Athens, when passing under the walls of the Acropolis she perceived a little ball of fluff tormented by a group of children. Athena had fallen from her nest . . .'"

'Well, there it is,' she said, finally ending the tale. 'That's what happened. 'And now the poor creature is dead. But she had many happy times, you know, while she lived.'

'And she was just "a little ball of fluff"', Amelia said sadly. 'What horrible children they were to torment a defenceless little owl.' She found a saucepan to scramble eggs in, smiling at her baby, sitting very quietly in his chair.

'Yes, it was hard to manage Athena at first,' Parthe reflected. 'She would peck at everything in sight. Very unpleasant if she bit your finger! But she soon learned some manners and finally took her meals right from her mistress's palm. It was a very sad day when she died. It was Athena's fault in the end though because she wouldn't take food from anyone other than Florence.' She gazed about the kitchen, biting her lip worriedly. 'I do hope Florence likes the drawing.'

'She will love it,' said Amelia. She finished scrambling the eggs then spooned them into a bowl to feed to the baby. The child clapped his hands with pleasure. 'Oh, that terrible Crimean fever,' Amelia whispered with a shiver. She had never heard of it before. And Mrs Clarke rarely spoke of the illnesses she'd witnessed at Scutari; she fulfilled her duties in the house and organised the maids and the cook but had little to say about the war, and if she chanced to speak of it she cringed. "To think I went with her," she would murmur. "To think I gave strength to her purpose. The Crimea is a place of terror." She'd believed Doctor Hall would look after Florence, however, for though he had a booming voice and was known to be belligerent, she believed he always meant well and that many of the problems they'd spoken of were beyond his control. But she'd also said that dear Miss Florence would know she was in danger for she'd witnessed so many deaths from that awful disease and was bound to be fearful, and recovery could often be slow.

Parthe rose from the table and picked up her drawing, then made her way to the door. The baby ate his food contentedly, his mother searching his features all the time looking for the face of her lover at Sebastopol. She heard the screech of a jackdaw on a tree by the window and chilled at the sound. Then she laughed at her child and remembered her lover's arms holding her close and imagined how it would be when at last he came home.

'But I cannot keep *feeling* this overwhelming emotion,' said Frances Nightingale, as she sat with her husband in Sidney Herbert's very grand house that day. 'Day and night I think of her. I need to see her, Elizabeth. I need to touch her, to hold her hand and tell her how much I love her. I did not say it enough, you see.' Elizabeth Herbert understood, and Frances handed her a letter. 'Do read it my dear; it's to the mother of one of the soldiers at Scutari. Florence wrote it in April, it is only one of many, but it moved her so much to write it she wanted to send me a copy.

Elizabeth Herbert took the letter, murmuring as she read it. That the boy should speak of his mother like that brought tears to her eyes.

"Barracks Hospital, Scutari
12 April 1855

I am very sorry to have to communicate to you the illness of your poor son, Private John Cope, 95th Regiment, No. 2884. He was admitted here about ten days ago suffering from diarrhoea. He was immediately attended to by surgeons, by one of my nurses and myself. He was fed in small quantities and frequently with port wine and arrowroot.

He often murmured, "dear, dear mother!" and tried to say many things to you—that he was well cared for and wanted for nothing— that he had no wish for anything. I sent for the chaplain, who came twice, and both times he was quite sensible and prayed fervently, and said he was quite happy in mind and could follow all that was said.

*He spoke little after this, and sank rapidly and died at 2 o'clock on
the morning of Easter Sunday, quite quietly and without pain, in the
full hope of a resurrection with Him who rose again on that day.
I remain with true sympathy for your grief,*

P.S. I would have sent you something of his, but he left nothing."

Sidney Herbert's wife, mother of seven, shook her head sadly.
As wife of the Minister for War, she must constantly comfort her
husband when he grew sombre. He received multitudes of letters
often filled with pain and anger. It was sometimes as if he had killed
those men himself, she said, he would slump in his chair motionless,
still in his frock coat, his top hat forward on his face. He didn't
know where the war was going, he said, and read through William
Russell's reports time and again breathing over them nervously like
a hounded animal. She feared for his health she said, for he could
do no more than he did.

William Nightingale glanced at his wife sideways as Elizabeth
Herbert handed back the letter, and he saw that his wife hadn't
properly pinned up her hair and she wasn't wearing her gloves.
Even in summer, Frances liked to wear her lace gloves. It was
strange to see her without them. She kept on reaching for his hand
and stroking his long fingers, something she did when upset. 'We
both want to see her, my dear,' he said softly. 'We must hear what
Sidney has to say. Oh, what is to be done about anything? Everyone
aches for a solution. That war was a mistake from the first. Now
poor Sidney bears the burden of trying to solve it.'

'He is quite trapped,' said Elizabeth. 'Officials want different
things. And they often oppose each other. I hate it when they all
come at Sidney like an army of arrows. For they do, you know,

there are so many differing opinions.' Elizabeth Herbert pulled out her handkerchief and blew her nose. Frances thought she looked frail that day, not at all her robust self. And she could hear a slight hostility in her tone, as if Florence's demands were getting too much for Sidney Herbert. Florence's energy was itself a battle ground, for she would always demand to be heard. And things must be done, she said, *done*, not written and talked about, but done. The War Office though couldn't always meet her demands, even when they were valid. But Florence would rouse the ministers to the highest pitch of their power and she asked no more of them, she said, than she asked of herself.

Sidney Herbert suddenly entered. One of the servants had gone to find him. He'd been out on his horse, thinking, which he often did if he needed to calm his nerves. He was very much disturbed that day. 'You poor people!' he gasped. 'You did not say you were coming. You should always tell me.' He threw his hat on a chair and took a seat, leaning forward to listen, curious and worried.

'It was sort of spontaneous,' said William. 'I apologise. A letter would have taken far too long to reach you, and Frances was eager to see you. My dear wife doesn't know what to do with herself just now. She can think of nothing but our daughter sick in Crimea, trying to recover her strength. Oh, that we might be with her to offer some cheer!' William Nightingale spoke in a rush. 'My dear Sidney, I think you understand our errand. We need to visit her; we cannot have her simply abandoned out there. How can we get to see her? Do not worry about money, I can deal with all that, just arrange passage as soon as you can.'

Sidney Herbert was flushed from riding. 'I had to get out,' he said, rubbing his face. 'It's sort of escaping.' He looked at his wife, who sat quietly close by. 'Ah yes. We must talk, my friends. You will stay overnight, I hope.'

'We'd be delighted,' said Frances. 'I am weary of wandering the rooms at Lea Hurst. My spirit goes ahead of me, it is somewhere in that war zone looking for Florence. I am quite lost from myself.'

'Yes, we must talk,' said Sidney. 'And we will, we will.' The maid came in with another pot of tea and poured him a drink. 'You see, I am doing so much talking and writing, I can scarce keep up with it. Will you have another cup of tea? Please do. Let us go outside on the lawn.'

The maid gave a slight curtsey and looked outside. It was such a beautiful day. And it was always easier to talk outside, said Herbert. They made their way to the large table on the lawn, and sat on the comfortable wicker chairs looking out on the flowers in the garden.

'Everything looks so lovely,' said Frances. 'Summer makes every-thing so beautiful.' For a moment or two they were silent, the maid coming and going, Elizabeth Herbert giving her quiet instructions. Frances Nightingale continued. 'Everything except the Crimea.'

'There are wars going on everywhere,' said Herbert leaning back in his chair and sighing. 'Some mother's son, some woman's husband, some woman's lover, they are dying somewhere all in the name of war. And somehow, it seems it is my lot to try to set things right. I tell you my friends, it is quite an ordeal.'

Frances gazed at him, hanging on to his words, as if he might offer answers to her own despair. 'Poor Sidney,' she murmured. 'Of course.'

'Florence appears to be busy,' Sidney Herbert continued. 'Her letters would suggest she is fine. I suspect she has fully recovered, you know. It's difficult to know what to say . . . And you set me a difficult task.' He smiled at her warmly. 'I do not think Florence would appreciate it even if I sent you on the wings of Hermes, wearing his magic sandals. I know Florence very well, and it would cause her great distress to have you turn up in such a place. And I cannot ensure your safety either. If only I could. It is all very difficult with Sebastopol still under siege; the doctors are moved to tears and exhausted. Yes, Raglan has quite a job on over there. And it doesn't help when you have lost an arm in war. He will recall Waterloo very darkly.'

'I'm sure he does,' said William. 'I can't begin to imagine what it's like to have an arm amputated in war.'

'He is a brave man,' said Herbert sagaciously. 'Not always wise, but brave. But what is wisdom when you have so many balls in the air. A General is not a juggler. You know, he wouldn't let the orderly take away his arm until they'd taken his wife's ring away from that finger.' Herbert looked at his wife and frowned, then turned again to William. – 'You might go if I can get you passage, but I cannot vouch for your safety at Scutari, there are spies everywhere and heaven knows what's going on. I am unable to stop you doing what you want however, I can only warn you. There are men shrieking like banshees out there and their boots are soaked in blood. Thousands of our bravest men have been killed and maimed in that war. I am arguing with Palmerston, I am arguing with Gladstone, I am arguing with everyone, even myself. Let me not argue with you.'

'You are right,' said Frances, quietly. 'It is good to be with you here at your home. It is so much better than a letter, you see.'

'Of course,' he said, nodding for certainty. 'We can think about this again after dinner. But you know how I feel. I do not believe that gems of wisdom will fall from the sky to help us. If only it were so.'

'No, no, wisdom must come from the self,' said William, shaking his head despondently. 'But how we are to find it I do not know. And it seems you too are at a loss, dear Sidney.'

'Quite right,' said Sidney Herbert abstractedly, frowning at the ceiling. 'Now, how would you like some caviar? Let us enjoy ourselves a while. I have a bottle of excellent wine we can open too.'

Elizabeth went to find the maid.

CHAPTER 24

Scutari, Late Summer 1855

Several weeks passed by. The Nightingales were living at Lea Hurst for the end of summer. None of them felt like moving to Embley Park for winter. It had been an exhausting year and everything was so uncertain. Thoughts of visiting Crimea had been abandoned. But they all lay in their beds at night, wondering and worrying, and walked about in a dream in the daytime hours. They vigorously wrote letter after letter and sought out news from Sidney Herbert who was confronted by the general public both at home and in his parliamentary office. Florence Nightingale was loved and admired. How was she? Had she recovered? They hadn't heard a lot from Russell about how she was doing. Herbert had been to visit the Nightingales once or twice, though he rarely stayed long, for he must keep a watchful eye on his colleagues, some of whom might try to discredit him if he wasn't there to fight back, for there were many differing opinions regarding the war in Crimea and whether or not the British should even be in it. But in it they were, and matters could always be criticised in retrospect, said Herbert. There were leaders, there were stirrers, and there were fighters. Then came the government, who while constantly saying there had to be an answer to the pain and suffering, did not offer resolutions. And even if they did, their ideas didn't work and led only to more frustration. The Crimean war was condemned by an angry public. Some of the military officers said it should just be abandoned. "Do you think we need a new Prime Minister?" people would argue. "Or a new minister at the War Office?" Though it was often hot air according to Sidney Herbert and he went on his way dependable as ever. *"Things done well and with a care, exempt themselves from fear,"* he told himself. Well, it would do for now. There was always a quote from Shakespeare somewhere to help a Minister for War through his day.

★ ★ ★

Florence, back at Scutari, had joined her nurses on the wards, and Benjamin was back in his library, and Doctor McGregor, who'd been informed throughout Florence's ordeal, was glad to have her back and was deeply interested in the state of Doctor Hall's hospitals, for hearsay was one thing, experience was quite another. Having been stricken with Crimean fever, Florence hadn't had chance to discover as much as she'd hoped for over there, but she'd got to know Doctor Hall much better, she said, and felt it would be easier to discuss things with him in future. Hall still protested that everything was fine, but that was John Hall, and she was Florence Nightingale who believed she knew better, for was she not a petticoat imperieuse? She knew he was nervous of her influence and his eyes flashed if she dared to interfere with his affairs, but as she'd returned to her healthier self he'd seemed more sensitive of her cause and in many small ways had been kind.

But she'd had to return to Scutari. A deep love for the wounded there filled her heart and she had come to know them well. She seemed now to see a whole world of wounded soldiers, doomed, fated and reaching for mercy. Would there ever be a world fit to live in, she wondered as she went through the wards that day, a world where people didn't kill each other and could overcome cruelty and greed. Her burning zeal had been lost to illness for a while, but now it was back, and what a glowing charger it rode on!

Doctor McGregor was delighted to see she was well. 'You fair shook the doctor up from the sound of it,' McGregor said one morning, standing in the doorway of the library. But he talked exhaustedly and needed to lean on the doorpost. She thought he looked frail and tired. 'Several of the nuns have gone home,' he said weakly. 'They have found things difficult here and should never have come; they left during your illness. And you know about those you discharged yourself, of course. I believe you have notes . . . I don't know why these women volunteer without first finding out about what it is like at Scutari . . . It is a serious business and some of the nurses faint with weariness and dread . . . Herbert has sent us more, they are better trained, he says.'

'Miss Florence! Miss Florence!' Evie's voice came fast with her footsteps on the corridor. 'Someone has been stealing the sheets! They were all laundered and folded in the cupboard by the door and a whole pile of them have gone. Someone is stealing, Miss Florence. I try to keep my eye on the bedding before it takes a trip across the river, sheets and blankets disappear, you see, and I am not as quick as Mrs Clarke when it comes to catching the culprit.'

'You mean it has happened before?' said Florence, surprised.

'Yes,' Evie said, uneasy and cross. 'The sheets might have gone in the time we were away, I've only just noticed. Other things might have gone too. I must check.' She clasped her hands tensely and bit on her lip. 'We have to be careful; some of the nurses want their eighteen shillings a week and anything else they can get.'

'Perhaps it wasn't a nurse,' said Florence. 'It might have been anyone. The cupboard needs a lock and key.' She scribbled down some notes.

McGregor looked at Florence and Benjamin by turns. They were both thoughtful. Things had got a bit slack during Florence's absence. 'We had best lock up the silver!' said McGregor, seeing their concern. There were far more important things to think about than bedding.

Florence gazed at McGregor worriedly; he looked like a deer from the woods at Lea Hurst, a deer that had forgotten to eat, lost from the herd and losing its coat. His features were thin and haggard and he was badly in need of sleep. She noticed his greying hair hanging untidily down his neck and it didn't look very clean.

Evie glanced at Benjamin. 'Well', she said, sighing, 'I don't want to think the nurses are stealing. It doesn't rest well with me to think we have thieves amongst us. I only know that as many as twenty sheets have gone, and that is a lot to carry.' She stood for a moment, frowning then quickly went off down the corridor.

Florence rose and went to the door. 'I'm sure there's a simple explanation,' she said. 'But we have to keep matters in check. They are dull, household issues, for sure, but a well managed household is vital, and we have a rather big household here.'

'Well, they'll not be stealing from me,' sighed McGregor. 'My cupboards are filled with instruments I use for surgery, and my desk is filled with letters.' He frowned deeply. 'But we don't want that Russell fellow reporting to London that things have been stolen that the public have generously paid for, do we?'

Florence looked at him curiously. His face was thin and bony, his eyes had sunk and there were dark circles beneath them. But his skin shone with a sort of luminosity she had seen on the skin of the dying. For a moment it stopped her breath.

'I'm writing a letter just now to the War Office,' McGregor continued. 'They want to know Miss Nightingale is well and I can now reply with pleasure that you are.' He gave her a serious look. 'Do come and find me, won't you, should you be feeling faint.' He faltered as he spoke. 'You have done very well. Cholera can kill within hours. It can take five days for the infection to seize you, we have to watch out. I think you must have caught something here at Scutari before you left. Our water still needs attention. Ah yes, there is still a lot to be done. The thing is to boil it before it is drunk, you see. Yes, boil it.' He put his palm to his forehead. 'I am not always careful myself.' He moved towards the door and stumbled.

Florence rushed forward quickly. The thought of a sick Doctor McGregor was more than alarming. He was a vital force at Scutari, and they were short of doctors. He would freely give 24 hours of his time, but time often short changed him. 'Let me help you to your office Doctor,' urged Florence. You need to sit down and rest. You neglect yourself I think.'

'I am having some very strange dreams,' he murmured. 'Yes, they are quite disturbing. My body is trying to tell me something.'

'Your body can't talk, but your health can,' Florence said softly. 'Now come, let us go to your room and for the next few hours you will rest and mustn't be disturbed.'

A peculiar lost expression came over his face. 'I dare not die. You do understand, don't you?' He gave her a terrified look. 'You came and cried to me once,' he said as they went to his room. 'You brought me your tears. But that was at first. Now they have gone. Have you cried them all away, Miss Nightingale. Has your spirit hardened?'

She smiled at him warmly. 'Not at all, but perhaps I have created another self to assist me.' She frowned at her words, thoughtful.

McGregor continued. 'The army you know, we have always been proud of our army, but pride can turn into evil if the devil takes hold.'

'Too true,' she said quietly, settling a cushion on his chair. 'Is there somewhere you might lie down in here?' she asked, looking about.

'I rarely lie down,' he faltered. 'Much of the time I doze in my chair when I'm tired. I fear if I sleep there are men who might need me urgently, for death can happen in seconds. I must catch it before it takes over!'

'And just now you must catch some rest,' she said, settling him into his chair. 'You ought to have a bed in here,' she murmured. Looking around, she wondered where they might put it. 'I intend to lock the door behind me and I'll return in an hour. During that time you will do nothing but take some respite. Is that clear?'

He rested his head on his arms on his desk and within minutes was sound asleep.

'He doesn't have the least idea how hard he is working,' she said, returning to Benjamin in his room. 'But he's sleeping now. I have sort of demanded it. I have put his key in my pocket so no-one can bother him. There are other doctors here, perhaps they are not as skilled, but McGregor must restore his strength.'

'And you?' said Benjamin coming forward. 'What about you, dear Florence? Do you know of your own hard work, or does it just drag you along like a victim? We haven't to fall victim to our feelings.' He bent his head.

Florence lifted her face, but still his head was bent, as if his words had embarrassed him. He lifted his head and moved in closer towards her. 'How long is it since a man has kissed your cheek?' he asked tenderly. He waited. She did not speak. He continued. 'Or a pair of strong arms embraced you? You are a beautiful woman, Florence, with earnest emotions and passions. You have cut yourself off from your family . . . and you have cut yourself off from *love* . . .'

'No, no,' she said, turning away. 'I love the soldiers on the wards . . . I see them as . . .'

'They are not *lovers,* Florence. You say they are your children, your spiritual children, whom you have saved. And so they are. But the love a woman has for children, even her own flesh and blood, is different from the love she has for a man.'

'I can never have a lover,' she exclaimed. 'Not now, not ever.'

'*Never?*' he asked, his eyes dark and questioning. He moved closer and brushed her cheek with his lips.

She did not move, but began to breathe quickly and tremble slightly as she felt his breath on her face. 'I am quite vulnerable just now,' she told him shakily.

'Vulnerable to what?' he said, holding her tightly against him. 'To *love?*'

She bent her head.

'To be vulnerable to love can be good,' he said.

'No, no,' she faltered. 'Because of my passion it would drain me of the love I need for others.'

'Wrong! Wrong!' he protested. 'Love expands in the heart, and its heat warms all who come close. Florence, I wish to come closer . . .' He drew her into his arms and kissed her.

'Nothing is more wonderful than love,' she whispered.

'Nothing,' he murmured. 'Nothing at all.'

CHAPTER 25

The Confused Language Of Love

Two young soldiers had been admitted to Scutari hospital in the dead of night. Florence found them in the morning while touring the wards. Both had been injured at Sebastopol and neither looked more than eighteen. How many others were left at the siege to die, she wondered, when the doctors could do no more, and constant fighting and bombardment of the city brought increasing death and destruction?

'Cold poultices must be applied to the eye three times daily to bring down the swelling,' she said, watching carefully as the nurse tied a bandage around the head of one of the two young arrivals. 'Do it when you change the dressing. He is lucky he didn't lose the eye. Doctor McGregor is a highly skilled surgeon but it's as well this soldier was almost unconscious. I believe it was a complex procedure, but the eye is safe and sound and the tissues will heal very quickly.' The nurse acknowledged the instructions then went on her way down the ward. Florence saw that the soldier was moaning and in shock. She stroked his hair gently. 'Now you must sleep,' she said softly. 'You have lost much blood.' He was restless and afraid and trembled as she spoke. He'd been brought from the siege with others, terribly wounded. And he looked so young! She adjusted the sheets on his bed and straightened the sleeves of his nightshirt. '*Cruel, cruel war,*' she murmured. '*Why must it happen?*'

'Thank goodness he didn't die, Miss Nightingale,' said the young English soldier lying in the bed beside him. 'Blood was pouring from that eye like a fountain. We were both brought in together. We'd been together on the boat, right from the start . . .' His voice trailed off, as if he had more to say, but would rather not say it.

'Officers helped you on the boat, I take it,' said Florence, seeing he had a bandaged arm.

'Yes, I was lucky I could walk, but they carried him on a stretcher, poor fellah. I thought he was a goner. He was only in a hospital gown. It was covered in blood and he was falling senseless by the minute.'

'In a gown, you say. So he had been in a hospital somewhere?'

The English soldier did not answer He touched his arm and winced. 'Nice clean job,' he said triumphantly. 'That doctor is one of the best. I heard Lord Raglan lost an arm at Waterloo. It's the right one as does all the work, this is, the thought that I might have lost it gives me the shivers. It hurts real bad, but that surgeon's a winner.'

'Yes, he is,' she said giving him a gentle smile. 'It's been well taken care of like you say, and carefully bandaged.'

'We English are fighting for Queen Victoria,' said another of the men, lying in an opposite bed. 'But Miss Nightingale, why do we have a Russian on the ward at Scutari?'

Florence straightened, surprised. '*A Russian?*' She frowned, concerned.

'Yes, the one with the injured eye.' He lowered his voice to a whisper. 'He's *Russian.*'

Florence glanced about worriedly.

'That's right,' the English soldier said, guiltily. 'I suppose I ought to have told you . . . I heard that one of the POW hospital huts was attacked and the men had tried to escape.' He frowned as he gazed at the Russian, lying silent in his bed, totally drained of energy, white as a ghost and still. 'He'd found his way to the shore and collapsed and they carried him on to the ship. No-one would have known who he was. He had no pack, no uniform, no identity at all and was bleeding like hell. He fell unconscious on the boat. I thought he might die, but he made it here to Scutari.'

'And he's Russian?' Florence said incredulous, regarding the English soldier curiously. 'Are you sure?'

'He's been in a delirium, Miss Nightingale,' the Englishman said, still whispering. 'He speaks in Russian. He rambles in Russian. I have no idea what he says, but I know the Russian language when I hear it. Russians can sometimes speak French, but they're not so good with English, he didn't understand a word I said when I spoke to him early this morning.'

Florence looked at the pale young soldier, fast asleep and out of uniform, he was just a man, and at Scutari hospital he was a man in dire need. 'There are several different nationalities on these wards,' she said quietly, 'and from various ranks. Do not say a word about this to anyone. Mr Harrison can come to speak with him. Our librarian speaks excellent Russian and can find out where he has come from and what has happened. This man must be moved to Kululi hospital as soon as possible. Prisoners of war are taken there, they do not come to Scutari.'

'That's right, Miss Nightingale,' said another young soldier. 'POWs go to Kululi.' He looked around the ward and frowned. 'Best get him out of here fast, Miss. There's bound to be trouble if you don't.'

'Be kind and allow him to rest,' urged Florence, speaking softly and calmly 'Doctor McGregor will be down very shortly. Then we can make some decisions. There is still a lot of fighting at Sebastopol just now, it is chaotic. November will soon be upon us, then December, then comes the frostbite and gangrene.' She stood for a moment gazing downwards, then went to the Russian soldier and straightened the sheets on his bed. 'He is here by accident,' she said. 'It is right that he receives our care.' She pulled out her notepad and scribbled down some notes.

The young Russian's bed was soon empty, though the soldiers didn't enquire about him next day when Florence made her rounds and were silent just as she'd requested. She'd spoken with Benjamin who'd told her the soldier was fearful of what might happen now he was captured. He had spoken of his family, saying they'd be relieved he was still alive, but he didn't reveal any more. And he hoped his eye would repair, he said, as the doctor had promised. He'd not been able to remember much, other than the sound of the hospital hut exploding and everyone running away.

'I listened to it all intently,' Benjamin said to Florence later that day. 'He was very concerned about his friend. Someone he'd had to leave when an officer had taken him prisoner. The man had been his companion during the siege.'

'I wonder if he'll see him again,' sighed Florence. How often it happened in war, this loss of a cherished companion, even a brother.

Benjamin nodded sadly. 'I hope so. He even asked people to search for him.' He reached for one of his books. 'Now let me look . . .' He found a piece of paper in the pages. 'Here, I have it.

His name was "Leo Tolstoy". He apparently wrote stories about Sebastopol, excellent tales.'

Florence made notes in her notepad. Tolstoy's name would be listed somewhere, she said, along with his details. A man must heal in both body and mind, she thought. And a friend in wartime was just like a celestial being.

They sat once more, talking together about the hospital, about the wounded soldiers and the officers, about the fact that Lord Aberdeen had been voted out of office as well as Sidney Herbert. They did not talk about their kiss the other day, and both averted their eyes as Florence rose from her seat making to leave.

'Miss Nightingale!' called Doctor McGregor, as he saw her passing his office.

She turned and saw he waved a letter. 'I have received an important epistle and I believe it is to your advantage!' He was smiling widely.

She took it quickly, feeling suddenly lighter of heart.

Benjamin Harrison rushed out of his room, wondering at all the excitement. For some minutes there was silence. Doctor McGregor and Benjamin waited.

'It's a letter from Queen Victoria,' said Florence curiously. 'And it's signed by Lord Raglan.' She looked by turns from Benjamin to McGregor, filled with mounting pleasure as she read it. How she had longed for this moment, how she had prayed for it! – 'I am now to be recognised as the General Superintendent of *all* the military hospitals, and the principal medical officer will therefore communicate with me on all matters, and is to give and receive orders only through *me!*' She smiled. 'I finally got my way!'

For a moment or two all three were thoughtful. 'It's wonderful,' laughed McGregor. 'It gave me such joy to read it. I congratulate you wholeheartedly, Florence. Well done.'

She closed her eyes and allowed the moment to absorb her.

'And now John Hall must salute you,' said Benjamin, laughing. The doctor nodded in agreement.

'Oh, let me think,' Florence said excitedly. 'There is much to improve. Hall cannot obstruct me from improving those hospitals and teaching the nurses better practice. The major should let people know what the hospitals are really like. He needn't fear telling the truth of how things are, for I do believe he tries his best. And he had best not oppose those nurses who support me either. Oh, a lot comes back from the soldiers. They have many grievances, but I think they are often right in what they say. I have experienced Doctor Hall's tyranny myself, have I not? He is quite averse to women.' She read through the letter again and smiled.

'Congratulations,' said Benjamin quietly. 'There is so much good in that zealous heart of yours.'

'Indeed,' said Doctor McGregor, his voice suddenly faint. The smile faded from his features as he leant against the wall and closed his eyes.

'You are very tired,' said Florence. 'My first order will be that you, dear doctor get more sleep. Dedication becomes annihilation if we don't watch out. A human being is not a machine, though the military would seem to think so.'

She smiled at both men. 'This is a special day, oh yes,' she said. 'Now I must go to my dormitory and think. I have a lot of ideas, and now I can put them into practice.'

'I believe the siege is ending,' murmured McGregor. 'The April and June bombardments of the city have proved successful. The Russians are defeated.'

'I think they are,' said Florence. 'And the siege must stop. The blind fighting leads nowhere.'

'The poor major,' said Doctor McGregor. He braced himself and tried to rub the tiredness from his face. 'He isn't going to know what has hit him when he learns of your letter. But he does have supporters. There are men who see him as a skilful and learned surgeon who is fiercely concerned about cleanliness; they mock the idea of him traipsing around in squalor. He mustn't be judged too harshly. It's a difficult life for a doctor in places like this.'

'It is,' Florence said quietly.

'Well, Florence knows right from wrong quite clearly,' said Benjamin. 'It can be hard to know the difference in wartime.'

'You are right,' said Doctor McGregor turning towards his office, though a little unsteady on his feet.

'". . . I think she loves me, but she chooses to deny it,"' Benjamin murmured as McGregor and Florence left him. '"She has resolved to tame herself into a thing of rule and measure . . . But some hour, some hour yet, will seal the compact between us and I shall have her yet!"' Oh, such words the Greeks delivered with their wonderful mythologies. But they were words, just words. He sat for a while, immobile, ruminating all that had passed in the last few days. He knew, for his own part, that Florence longed for love, but did he, Benjamin Harrison, a mere man of books, have it in sufficient measure for Florence Nightingale? For she needed love without boundaries; love that encompassed the world. It was a much bigger love than anything he'd known before and he wondered if it might break him. She'd rejected the man at home and left him torn and bleeding with a sickness from which there was no recovery. The spirit didn't forgive a wounding like that, and she herself had been wounded. Would he be wounded too?

CHAPTER 26

Endings 1855

"'On a dark lonely night on Crimea's dread shores
There'd been bloodshed and strife on the morning before;
The dead and the dying lay bleeding around,
Some crying for help—there was none to be found
Now God in His mercy He pitied their cries,
And the soldiers so cheerful in the morning do rise.

So, forward my lads, may your hearts never fail
You are cheered by the presence of a sweet Nightingale.
Her heart it means good for no bounty she'll take,
She'd lay down her life for the poor soldier's sake;
She prays for the dying, she gives peace to the brave,
She feels that a soldier has a soul to be saved.

The wounded they love her as it has been seen,
She's the soldier's preserver, they call her their Queen
May heaven give her strength and her heart never fail.
One of Heaven's best gifts is Miss Nightingale.'"

Evie's soft sweet singing floated through the air as Florence approached the dormitory. The other nurses were out working on the wards, but there was something the matter with Evie; they needed to talk. As she entered the dormitory, Florence saw Evie was bent towards her sewing. Never doing what she'd been asked to do, always doing something else, that was Evie. Today she had her hair pinned up and the smooth whiteness of her neck shone in the morning sunlight. 'There you are,' said Florence. Her voice sounded hollow as she entered the large empty quarters. 'I was looking for you, Evie,' she said. 'I knew you weren't in the library, Benjamin was reading with one of the soldiers on the ward and his room was empty.'

'Sometimes I go to the library when Benjamin isn't there,' she said petulantly. She did not lift her head. 'What are you trying to say Miss Florence? Do speak plainly.'

'Then I will, my dear,' said Florence, with a deep sigh of frustration. 'Though I doubt what I say will be of value, you will always do just as you wish.'

Evie lifted her head as Florence approached her. She put down her work and waited. For all the world, thought Florence, it was hard to chastise Evie, who was kind and thoughtful and lost in a world of her own, she might be anyone from one day to the next; Joan of Arc, Boadicea, Helen of Troy, anyone from Benjamin's books. 'I was mending one of the sheets,' she said quietly. 'And I was thinking.'

'And you were singing a very lovely song.' Florence smiled knowingly. 'I heard my name. Was it a song about me?'

'It was,' said Evie. 'It's a ballad. I learned it from one of the soldiers. I think it came in a letter from home. They are singing songs about *you*, Miss Florence, and making up poems. You are famous. The soldiers are rejoicing that the siege is finally over and they want some laughter and music. They speak of your gentleness too.'

'Do they?' laughed Florence, in a tone of disbelief. She gazed through the window. She wasn't quite sure what to say but Evie's words were moving.

'Why did they have this war?' Evie said unhappily, 'The siege is over, but the war continues. Will it ever end?'

'Of course, but men are constantly being wounded and they bring them here, hoping we can heal them. But we are not miracle workers, Evie, we are nurses, we cannot work miracles. The Royal Scots Greys, The Grenadier Guards, The Royal Fusiliers and many others, wonderful brave men, fall like autumn leaves on the battle fields, gone on the wind. They are often fatally injured or maimed. The government thought the war would be over and done with swiftly, but war has other ideas.'

'And it just goes on,' murmured Evie.

'What is the matter?' Florence asked softly. 'This is a good time to talk if there's something you want to tell me.'

'It isn't important. I'm not in the least bothered,' Evie said quickly. 'Really, it doesn't matter.'

'I think it does,' said Florence standing before her and waiting. Evie sat on her bed, her hands clasped in her lap. Whatever it was it obviously mattered a lot.

'I went to see Benjamin, this morning,' Evie began, talking in a hushed tone of voice. 'He helps me, you see. He's always so kind and good.' For a moment or two they were silent. Evie's face flushed with feeling. She bent her head and worked her fingers nervously together. 'Benjamin knows things, you see.'

'What did you want to ask him about? Please tell me. I get worried when you're unhappy. I am here for you, too.'

Evie threw out her hands and shrugged. 'I shouldn't have come to Crimea with you; I ought to have stayed at Scutari. But I wanted to be with you, both of you. I thought I'd be helpful. And the soldiers had told me such terrible things about the Bosphorous. Silly things really. I feared for you, Miss Florence. They told me tales of monsters rising from the water ready to devour you, that sort of thing.' She lifted her eyes, meeting Florence's gaze. 'But there were worse things than that, Miss Florence. There were limbs floating about, bones and blood. I could scarcely bear it. But I tried to be strong.'

'You did, and thank you,' said Florence, seeing that Evie's eyes were fearful at the thought of the dreadful crossing. 'You are a very strong woman, Evie. But we have to renew our strength each day for this work. You must never think you have failed.'

'But I do. I always think I do things wrong. When you were ill,' she stammered as she spoke, 'it was terrible when you were ill. Mrs Clarke wouldn't talk to me. We were both distressed, and . . .'

'It's alright,' Florence murmured. 'Do go on. Whatever you say is just between you and me. Is there something I should know?'

'It's like drowning,' Evie said shakily. 'Some days it's hard to breathe, but I try very hard. I have to, you see, or I'll die. I feel like Mrs Clarke did before she went home. I have nightmares about the war.' She looked at Florence pleadingly. 'And I'm sorry for cutting your hair. I didn't want to do it, but I heard it brought down the fever and Doctor Hall said so, too. He brought me the scissors.'

'Did he now,' Florence said, smiling. 'Well, it's nice to know that he didn't want me to die. Benjamin told me you cut my hair. It was a good idea. I wrote home to tell them about it. It isn't a secret, Evie. Don't worry. It's quite okay. And the shorter style is very easy to manage. No harm has been done.'

Evie looked at her straight, a sense of relief in her features. 'My sister says I'm a nuisance and I ought to return to England.' Her eyes filled with tears as she spoke.

'*Go home?* But the soldiers love you and . . .'

'But Benjamin doesn't,' she cried, imploringly, starting to weep. 'He didn't even know I loved him. I thought he knew, but he didn't. He had no idea. When you love somebody you sort of think they know.'

Florence looked at her surprised. 'Yes, I suppose you do,' she murmured.

'Love is a curse, I think,' Evie continued. 'You can't think of anything else once it gets you. And it tires you out. It takes away your strength.' She gazed at the ceiling, suddenly strangely exultant. 'But it's such a wonderful feeling!'

'It is,' Florence said softly.

'Have *you* ever been in love, Miss Florence?' Evie asked, looking at her boldly.

Florence laughed lightly. 'Oh yes. It's a feeling that wants its own way. It can be quite destructive. Yes, I have loved very deeply, and he loved me as well, but it did not take him long to find someone else when I came to Scutari.'

'But you did not answer to his love?' said Evie, frowning. 'Not if you came to Scutari instead.'

Florence shook her head. 'It's true,' she said sighing. She touched the necklace beneath her collar. Each day she wore it, each day she thought of him. 'But you, my dear, have been bold, very bold indeed, and I'm sure Benjamin was thrilled he had earned your love.'

'And he did *earn* it, Miss Florence. He really did. He helped me with my reading, told me what to read, explained things over and over. He has so much patience. I told him early this morning that I loved him. It was really hard. But he doesn't love me back, not at all. He thinks I'm just a girl. But I'm not you see, I'm a grown up woman with a grown up woman's feelings.'

'I'm sure,' said Florence.

'It's a terrible thing to let love get lost in the great wild forests of life,' Evie said tearfully. 'I am in mourning. Will I never get over it? She quoted a passage from Shakespeare; *"And when love speaks, the voice of all the gods, Make heaven drowsy with the harmony."*

'It's true,' said Florence. She smiled to herself. Evie had certainly enjoyed her literary studies. 'We have to pray about these things.'

'I don't like praying,' Evie said flatly.

'The love of God will never desert us,' Florence said. 'And through it we have eternal life.'

'But I don't want eternal life,' said Evie. 'Why would I? Wouldn't it be just like this one, fighting over and over?'

'I don't know,' Florence said thoughtfully.

'But why doesn't anyone know?' Evie said, brooding on the thought. 'Why should we waste our time in praying if people just die so horribly and nothing ever gets better?'

'It *will* get better,' said Florence. 'It must. The love we seek is beyond our reach. We must pray and remember our creator.' She gazed at the floor silently.

'You say Miss Parthe is getting married,' Evie said quickly. 'You say he is very much older than she is. Age doesn't matter to love, does it?'

'Men are often much older than their wives,' said Florence, thinking of her life back home.

'I am seventeen and Benjamin is thirty four,' said Evie, a little self-consciously. 'He was troubled by my words. I should never have said them. I've made a fool of myself.' She spoke dejectedly.

'Not at all,' said Florence sympathetically. 'It's good to speak from our souls, if we can dare to do it.'

'I was crying like a child.'

Florence thought about Richard and she thought about her love for Benjamin. She remembered Richard, at this time of year in particular; their walks in the woods, their long intense conversations on so many subjects. And she thought of Benjamin and why she had grown to care. He was rather like Richard in a way. But she knew she could never love him as he'd have wanted. She wondered about her emotions. Were they in truth cold and calculating, just like her thoughts on mathematics, did love itself have a sort of geometric shape, mathematical inclinations that could be organised and structured, and somehow measured for approval? The thought disturbed her.

Evie was talking about the siege, saying how glad the soldiers were that it was over. They were bound to be relieved, she said, now that the city had fallen.

Florence reflected on her time at Scutari. It had been a bitter eleven months. Once the summer had died and the leaves went from the trees, so the men had grown weak and weary. The Russians had shown great courage and resolve trying to save their Black Sea port. But they had been defeated. The allied navy had undertaken six bombardments of the capital since October 1854 and on the 5th September 1855, that year, came the last. Could it really be over? She wondered hopefully. Oh, the dead, the dead, so many dead! A surge of sadness went through her. Lord Raglan too had died. He'd been courageous until the last despite his damaged reputation at Balaclava and the loss of an arm at Waterloo, and now in the end he had died from dysentery and depression. And something else was disturbing her. Doctor McGregor had taken to his bed. He had caught the cholera.

CHAPTER 27

More Endings

The siege was over, but Florence still thought of Sebastopol and the soldiers who had died or were maimed, their wives and families. The sounds of war still lived in her mind as the fighting continued. And the moon continued to shine in the same old way on the confused and wretched cycle of life and death, slinking off as the morning sun looked in on the hills, the beautiful lines of ravines, the woodlands covered with a profusion of summer flowers, their innocent perfumes dancing on a gentle breeze. So it had been for Sebastopol, now in flames with men fleeing for their lives. The terrible tragedy of war was borne by the living, so many, so very many, hurting in every fibre, for that is what war did, and it would breathe its sour breath over the land for years to come claiming its place in history. People shuddered and wept at its power, it was impossible to turn back the clock; what was done, was done.

Florence in her lonely hours wondered if anything was learned from such brutal experience, for it seemed that even the sharpest eyes and ears in parliament saw and heard nothing productive. When she went out walking in the evenings at Scutari, the moon shone on the Bosphorus as if in sympathy, as if the very water itself might be the tears of all mankind. She couldn't understand why brother killed brother; for the two young soldiers she'd treated of late were only eighteen years old, and while one of them was English and the other Russian, were they not simply brothers in the eyes of God? And was it not just an accident that they came from different countries and different families? Did they not look at the same moon at night and share the warmth of the same sun?

It had been a long siege, a siege of bloody battles and enormous losses, plundered villas and beautiful buildings destroyed. Apart from being killed by the armies, many had fallen sick with cholera and died. She had witnessed men on the wards who, whilst they had lived, because of the sound of the siege guns blasting in their ears would never hear the voices of their families ever again, nor the sound of music and birdsong. Others might never walk again, or having been blinded, see the faces of their loved ones. As she walked along the cliffs that evening, she wondered what to write to her family. No words could describe her feelings. Only the tears that fell down her cheeks could say how it was.

'The Russians have left Sebastopol, but I believe it has been heavily mined,' said Benjamin next day in the library. 'The officers tell me the city is ruined. Images of saints have been broken and scattered, doors have been forced to the ground, and beloved, silk covered furniture has been hacked to pieces in many of the grand houses. I ask you, Florence, what is the use of that?'

Florence was sitting in a chair by the window. She gazed outside. In her mind she could hear her parents calling her home. She could hear Parthenope weeping. She was exhausted. The new railroad had taken food and clothing to the siege, and also five hundred guns and plentiful supplies of ammunition, enough to kill many more men. 'Admiral Nakhimov, Commander of the naval and land forces at the siege, has died from a head wound,' she murmured. 'I heard about it this morning. A sniper apparently, and further bombardments killed thousands of others. It seems the railway did its job, the weapons did theirs, and we in turn did ours. We have all done our duty, haven't we?' For a moment or two they were silent.

'Well, the Tsar's fleet has gone from the Black Sea,' Benjamin offered tentatively. 'Isn't that what the allies were after?'

'*Destroyed*,' she said tiredly. 'Death. Destruction. I cannot praise anyone for that.' Again they were silent. Florence spoke again. 'When I was in Balaclava and recovering from cholera an officer begged me to ascend the stone rampart next to a wooden gun carriage. I was to sit upon the centre mortar, just to show I was brave.' She shrugged her shoulders. 'Oh, indeed I was brave! That's what they wanted, Florence Nightingale to show she was brave! A Frenchman shouted "Gentlemen! I behold this amiable lady sitting fearlessly upon that terrible instrument of war! Behold the heroic daughter of England – friend!" Everyone shouted "Bravo! Hurrah! Hurrah! Long live the daughter of England!" The sentry was amazed I should do it.' Florence leant forward and narrowed her eyes. 'But I cut him short, and said, "My good young man, more dead and wounded have passed through my hands than I hope you will ever see during the whole of your military career. Believe me, I have no fear of death." And I tell you, Benjamin, it's true. I do not fear passing over. But I thought of my work, for even as I said those words to the sentry, I felt ill and thought I might collapse.'

'But you did not die,' he whispered. 'You fought it. You are indeed a warrior, Florence. Your purpose provides your strength.'

She smiled. 'Does it? But I hate the whole thing.'

'We must bear it, Florence. War is in the system. Death is in the system of life.' Benjamin spoke quietly. 'We do our best to live when we can, but the need to fight is always there in the shadows. To tell the truth, it is a great mystery to me, why we build beautiful cities then wreck them.' He sighed and threw out his arms in a hopeless gesture.

'And so Sebastopol is in ruins,' she murmured. 'A soldier told me they could almost hear the city weeping.'

'It wouldn't surprise me,' he said gravely. 'I wonder if stones have feelings?' He frowned and glanced through the window. 'I mean, in the silences that follow the shrieks and screams of suffering, does the wind send condolences through the blasted and ruined buildings, the fallen and collapsed walls. Does it look around in the darkness and wonder at humankind?'

They sat for some minutes, gazing through the window in silence. The sky was practically still, not a cloud in sight. But men were still fighting far away, battling on, though many of them didn't know why.

'Have you heard anything from London?' Benjamin asked her. He was curious as to what was happening now that Herbert was no longer in power. 'I mean recently.'

'I hear from my family, and others, but I haven't heard a thing from the War Office. I must send them a letter tomorrow. They will want to know what is happening now that the siege is over. Russell will have written about it, I'm sure. Who knows what will happen to Sebastopol now. There were many bombardments but the Russian defences were untenable.'

'They were forced to get out,' said Benjamin. 'They had to go home.' For a moment or two he looked lost, for he too must go home.

She met his eyes and smiled softly, avoiding her real feelings, knowing it could never happen, the love she'd hoped they might share. He looked away and escaped into one of his books, turning the pages quickly. She enquired if he'd slept.

'Not so well,' he said. 'And you?'

'Hardly at all.' All her worries had descended on her, she said, she felt shaken by what had happened at Sebastopol, and even though the siege had ended it had exacted a fearful toll. Just now she had little energy and there was still much to do.

'Evie is on her way to England,' she said. 'I thought it best to let her go.'

He nodded, frowning at the thought. 'What can I say? The girl is deeply unhappy.'

'She told me,' said Florence, drawing away from his gaze. 'She told me she loves you.'

He smiled, embarrassed. 'I see. She would. There is little she does not say that she feels. I am fond of her Florence. I would lie if I said any different, but it isn't, it isn't . . .'

'I know,' she said, stopping the flow of his words. 'She is far too young for nursing in this place, but she has learned a great deal. She gave such an excellent interview when I enlisted her. And she said she was in her twenties.'

'Did she,' he said, biting his lip, thoughtful.

'Benjamin,' she said quietly, embracing him with her eyes. 'You have done no harm in letting her love you. Some beautiful thoughts will stay with her all the way home and once she is with her family, they will help her cope with the terror she has witnessed in Crimea. I know she's enjoyed the times you have spent together. She will never forget them.'

'It was a joy to teach her,' he reflected, smiling.

'You have given succour to each other.'

For several moments he stared at the floor then looked up. 'And *us*?' He gazed at her meekly. 'What about us?'

'I must do my important work . . .'

He sighed. 'Do you know what I think, Miss Nightingale?' He fixed his eyes on her firmly and straightened. 'I think you are afraid of love. You see it as a sort of enemy. I mean the love between a man and a woman. You think you must push it away or something will be stolen from your strength. It will not. Real love gives. It does not take. I have said it before.'

She could not bear the hopeless look in his eyes and turned away quickly.

'Tell me, Florence. Are you trying to punish yourself for something? Why not wear a hair shirt like Francis of Assisi? Is the horror of this place not enough?'

Her eyes hardened. 'When I was in Crimea, I thought I would die from the fever, but I didn't, I lived, so what you are saying is nonsense.' She straightened her clothes and frowned. 'We have needed each other here.' She glanced at a bag he was busily packing with books. 'Will you leave? The war is still with us, even though the siege is over.'

'But I do not fight,' he said, lifting his shoulders and dropping them slowly. 'I think it is time for me to go. And the cholera is so prevalent. I always think the books might carry some disease or other.' He sighed. 'I do not think it will be long before this fighting is over, then we can all return to our lives back home, that is, those of us who are able. My mother and sister have missed me. And the soldiers here miss their families. I learn a lot from the soldiers, reading loosens their minds and their voices.'

She watched him take books from the shelves. 'Please don't leave,' she said shakily. It disturbed her to think she might lose both Doctor McGregor and Benjamin together. 'Pack away the books, if you must, but please don't leave. Let us spend Christmas together, at least. The patients love your stories; you know so many by heart.'

'And you, Florence, you have done so much for the soldiers,' he said, standing very still and looking at her deep in thought. 'And for the hospitals here in Crimea. You have seen how illness is passed from person to person through bacteria and viruses and you have seen how the filth in this place, when you first arrived, was killing the patients, how the water they drank, the air they breathed, the food they ate could kill them, wonderful observations so simple when realised. But you saw them, Florence, you voiced them, and you fought for your beliefs. You have saved many lives. And you've seen that the clothes are washed and the lice destroyed, and that nothing is pilfered from the linen cupboard! Ah, that wretched linen cupboard!' He laughed loudly.

'Yes,' she murmured. 'We need to keep a check on things don't we.' She smiled and found her notepad deep in her pocket and her pencil. She recorded as much as she could. 'The three main things that have helped destroy the army in Crimea,' she said, 'are ignorance, incapacity, and useless rules! What is the point of rules that defeat their objectives?' She straightened and hardened her voice. 'I can't stop you leaving, of course,' she said finally. 'But I am not too strong just now. McGregor is very sick and I feel his weakening spirit strongly as the soldiers do on the wards. They fear he will die. He has said himself that the cholera can kill very quickly. He has been looking thin and gaunt for a long time now. I suspected some illness would befall him. He has worked too hard, you see. It isn't just the skills of surgery that are needed with the patients; it is the actual consideration and caring that McGregor can give that is priceless. He gives of his essence.'

'I agree,' said Benjamin. He stared down at the floor. 'Everything is changing.'

'I've made lots of notes,' she said, quickly turning the pages of her notepad. 'They will serve me well when I petition the Queen for monies to improve the hospitals. I've even made diagrams and graphs so that all is made clear. I want to see better living conditions for the army and there is need for a Royal Commission. I intend to see it is done. I am determined.'

'Always determined,' he murmured.

Their talk continued. It was political and sociological, not at all romantic. She didn't dare indulge in romance, though the urgency to do so was always on the edge of her thought. Oh, the warmth, the warmth of love! She touched the necklace on her neck. Richard. Dear Richard. He would soon be married. But not to her, not to Florence Nightingale. Who was she, this Florence Nightingale, she asked herself. Was she some sort of weird priestess, some curious pretender who wanted applause? She shook her head. No, she was not! She had heard her voices. She could not deny them. And she'd served God most loyally, saved lives and given love with beautiful extravagance to the soldiers, the best kind of love she could give and they'd received it gratefully.

'Your necklace?' he said. 'I have seen it glistening when the sun finds it on your neck.'

'Yes, it is precious.'

'Was it a gift?' He looked downwards as he spoke.

'Yes,' she said tenderly. 'It was a present from Richard, given to me just before I left.'

'And you always wear it?'

'I always shall,' she said, touching it gently. 'I promised.'

'Will you *never* let him go?' Benjamin said flatly, knitting his brows.

She shook her head. 'I can't.'

'But why do you cling to the memory of something that hurts you? This man will marry someone else.' He drew a breath exasperated and looked at her straight.

'I'm sorry,' she murmured. There was much pain in his eyes, it made her look away.

'And you never break promises,' he said quietly, again leafing through a book. 'I'm beginning to feel like a fool. My mind is full of you, Florence, even when I sleep.'

'But nothing can come of it,' she said, bracing herself and smiling. Her emotions were hard to manage, they could never be shown on a graph, couldn't be captured in words or numbers, but they took control of her blood. 'You will have to forget me,' she told him, in as calm a voice as she could.

'Ah well,' he said, meekly. 'I shall say no more. But I shall leave Scutari very shortly. I must. I shall say my goodbyes to the patients I have come to know, and then I shall return to England.'

'Doctor McGregor is dying,' she said sadly.

'I know,' he replied softly. 'He will be buried here at Scutari. I have seen them digging his grave.'

'They waste no time,' she said, suddenly feeling cold. She rubbed her arms. They looked together through the window to the graveyard. It was a bright clear day. But Doctor McGregor lay sick on the bed in his room, two new doctors attending him.

'Have you talked with the doctors?' he asked her.

'Of course,' she murmured. 'One of them will have to take over. She trembled slightly as she spoke. Everything was moving so quickly. She saw as he watched her, the very same look she had seen in the eyes of Richard. Now, because Benjamin loved her, he would fear for her welfare. But she could not love him as he wanted. Oh, that look! Was the Greek mythological god Anteros taking revenge? Anteros punished anyone who dared reject love; there was a price to be paid for abnegation of something so precious. Now she had sacrificed it twice. But only for a better good! Didn't that somehow make it right? And it hurt each time she had done it. And it hurt her now. Benjamin looked as if there were more he wanted to say. But it seemed he had done with love talk now. His head was bent as he packed the last of his things. 'We must go to see Doctor McGregor,' she said. They left the room together.

CHAPTER 28

Finding A Path To Peace

Now that Sebastopol had fallen, no-one could deny that Russia had been defeated. But the Russians had continued to fight with fortitude and all negotiations for a settlement with the Turks had failed. Benjamin and Florence sitting in the library, read through all the reports arriving at Scutari, trying to see where a path to peace might be possible between the countries. Austria had given Russia an ultimatum, warning them to capitulate and accept the terms on offer. What mattered most was an acceptable agreement between the Tsar and the Sultan about demilitarisation of Russia's Black Sea port and its coastlines, which would then weaken the power base of the Russian navy. Russia had been unnerved by the loss of Sebastopol, and other important bases had fallen that winter. It would also, in the agreement, be forced to return Ottoman territories it had taken and to abandon its claim as protector of Christians in the Ottoman Empire. Benjamin sighed at that. It had all worked out quite stupidly, he said, since Russia's claim to be protector of Christians in the Ottoman Empire had been one of the reasons for conflict. 'What have the soldiers fought for?' he said despairingly. 'So many deaths, for what?'

'Death from disease and malnutrition mainly,' said Florence, 'and exposure too. Bitterly cold weather is a killer. And the Russian economy is ruined now. War leaves so much ruin.'

'But men will never stop fighting,' said Benjamin. 'If they do not fight over one thing then they'll fight over something else.'

Florence gazed downwards. It was all so complex. She'd heard so many conversations over dinner back home, private conversations between military men and her father, and they rarely agreed on anything. Sidney Herbert had often left the house with his head bent low, riding through the darkness on his horse, deep in thought, and she'd wondered sometimes how his horse had found its way home.

Benjamin leant back in his chair and sank his chin on his chest. 'It's like a bad dream,' he murmured. 'If I hadn't loved you Florence, I doubt I could have survived in here.'

For a moment or two they were silent.

'It's a strange atmosphere on the wards just now,' she said finally, 'now the men know they're soon going home.' She smiled at him warmly. How right he was. Love kept you warm, it gave you energy, it helped you cope with the strains and stresses of life.

'Still so many to bury,' he murmured, looking outside. It was early afternoon and the sun was yellow on the gravestones.

'It makes me ashamed . . .' she murmured. 'It's important the soldiers think they've fought for something of value. To lose so much for nothing would be unbearable.'

'Well, let's hope there'll be a peaceful passage now through the Black Sea in the future since the Tsar is removing his fleet. – I hear that Palmerston is to launch an inquiry into how it has all gone down. I have to say, I'm glad I didn't have a role in it myself. I wouldn't know where to begin. All I have done is keep the soldiers entertained.'

'Far, far more than that,' she said keenly. 'And what's more, you haven't been paid.'

'It doesn't matter. I have money enough from my mother to keep me going for years. She eagerly awaits my letters and often asks about the wonderful Florence Nightingale. I have much to write about once I return to Edinburgh.'

'We are both busy with our pens,' she said. 'I have often wondered what you're writing when I've seen you working by your candle.'

'I've been working on a book,' he said, proudly. 'And it's almost finished; I'll send you a copy when it's published. I suppose you would say it's about the sheer futility of war.'

'I didn't know,' she said frowning and curious. 'I thought you were writing letters.'

'Oh, I've been writing letters as well. My mother shares my letters with my brother. My father died a long time ago. Mother raised us by herself.'

For a moment or two they were thoughtful.

'But you did not mention your book?' she persisted, looking at him straight. 'Why did you never speak of it?'

'Ah well, I too have secrets, you see. But I never talk about my writing. These files here . . .' He picked up several files from his desk and stared at them for a moment. 'All my notes are in here. I must pack them safely. Will you write about Scutari?'

'I shall write about nursing,' she said determinedly. 'And I shall do my best to explain what it is and the way it should be done.'

'Poor McGregor,' Benjamin said, sighing. 'He cannot go home now, can he. He talked about home so often. How hard he worked in this hospital. I fear he wore himself out.'

'You are right,' Florence said, annoyed at the thought. 'We needed more doctors. I have always said it. But he died very bravely, not on the battlefield perhaps, but a sort of battlefield. It was over quite quickly in the end and now he is buried in the cold earth of Scutari. Dear Doctor McGregor. We could not save him. He was just a man afflicted with cholera like the others. He knew he would die. He had known it would happen at Scutari, but he didn't know how. I could tell from the look in his eyes sometimes that he feared it. He looked baffled, even terrified when he sat by himself in his room, his hands still bloody from surgery. I would help him wash them and treat him like a child, sponging his arms, and combing through his hair. He was often lonely. But he's gone. And the living must go on living.'

'And when you return, will you live with your family?' Benjamin asked tentatively.

'I will. We have two fine homes, we are lucky. But Parthenope is to be married soon and will live at Sir Harry's Claydon House on the Claydon Estate, the ancestral home of the Verney family since 1620. It's a very beautiful place.'

'Sir Harry is a wealthy man,' sighed Benjamin.

'Yes, it's a grand home for Parthenope to live in and raise a family. Sir Harry has a family of seven children already, which Parthenope will help him care for.'

'She will never want for anything,' said Benjamin. Having had his love rejected he spoke grudgingly, conscious of the fact that while he came from a learned family, they were not like wealthy aristocrats. Having money was important. And money had been vital to Florence, the handsome allowance from her father was sufficient for herself, and she could also buy shirts for the soldiers, linen, beds, provisions and medicines. Yes, money undoubtedly mattered. And there he sat a relatively poor librarian, who had found himself in a military hospital in the midst of the Crimean war, trying to engender a love of books in the patients at Scutari. How he had got there, he wasn't sure. He had read an article somewhere and made a sudden decision. Did he regret it? No, he did not. He had met and fallen in love with a wonderful woman. Unrequited yes, but he had never felt love since the death of his wife and for that he was grateful. 'Soon you will see your family,' he said, trying hard to sound casual.

'I hope so,' she murmured. But what was to happen to Scutari hospital when the war was over? What was to happen to her and Benjamin? Would they part for ever? Sebastopol had fallen but the war wasn't finished. There was still much to be done. Wounded men who'd recovered must now return to their homes. Transport would have to be arranged. Letters had to be written. She would write to Sidney Herbert for help, he was no longer War Minister, but offered his assistance where he could, as did Gladstone, the new Prime Minister, who'd always been sympathetic to what she'd been trying to achieve. And both were family friends. How she longed to see her family. After she'd suffered the cholera she'd felt as if her strength were departing. But she would not yield to death; she would fight it, she had seen death occur too often and cholera could suck the lifeblood from a body within days. Her body felt weak, though her soul was strong and she had much to offer by way of improvements in nursing. Perhaps she must close the door on nursing herself, but she could still offer her ideas. She could always write. And she had made profuse notes that she had built into charts and graphs for better understanding. She was faint with weariness, but she would not be defeated; she could still be of service to God. She thought of how she'd penned letters for soldiers to their families, how she'd organised screens for privacy when the men had suffered amputations, and how the soldiers had loved her for her efforts. That was important. She'd written to the families of those who had died and had sent their wages to their widows. Dead men had wages due to them and she resolved their families would get them.

So she and Benjamin found their way through Christmas, drank brandy, ate cake and laughed with the soldiers who shared out their gifts, sang songs and tried to be merry.

And very soon it was January. New Year snow fell on the crags of Scutari and the Bosphorus was covered in ice, which the winter sun could not thaw. February came and the war mercifully ended. The Treaty of Paris was signed on the 30th March 1856, between Russia on the one side and France, Great Britain, Sardinia and Turkey on the other. The Ottoman and Russian Empires agreed to bring a halt to all military operations in the Black Sea and the treaty guaranteed the independence of Turkey and made the Black Sea neutral territory, closing it to all warships and prohibiting firearms on its shores.

Florence thought a lot about home. Spring was arriving. In England spring was rarely cold. Benjamin showed her an article in *The Times*. 'They're calling you a "ministering angel" he said with a quiet tender laugh, '"*The Lady with the Lamp*".' He saw her features light up with his words. 'You are certainly a singular spirit,' he added quietly.

She leant forward to look. 'That will be Russell,' she smiled. 'Well, at least he has something good to write about now. Mama tells me people are sending her poems about me and songs.'

'The soldiers on the wards are singing again, can you hear them?' said Benjamin. 'They are happy. No more fighting, no more killing. Well, at least not here.'

She put her hand in her pocket and pulled out a folded piece of paper. 'It's a letter from Queen Victoria,' she said. 'A good one too. How I wish my family could see it. I must write a reply straight away. I've been thinking about it.'

'May I see it?' he asked. 'But only if you don't mind.'

'Of course, I brought it to show you.' Her eyes glistened with pleasure as she handed it over.

'A letter from Queen Victoria!' he laughed. 'How incredible.'

"DEAR MISS NIGHTINGALE, – You are, I know, well aware of the high sense I entertain of the Christian devotion which you have displayed during this great and bloody war, and I need hardly repeat to you how warm my admiration is for your services, which are fully equal to those of my dear and brave soldiers, whose sufferings you have had the privilege of relieving in so merciful a manner. I am, however, anxious of marking my feelings in a manner which I trust will be agreeable to you, and therefore send you with this letter a brooch, the form and emblem of which commemorate your great and blessed work, and which I hope you will wear as a mark of the high approbation of your Sovereign!

It will be a very great satisfaction to me, when you return at last to these shores, to make the acquaintance of one who has set so bright an example to our sex. And with every prayer for the preservation of your valuable health, believe me, always yours sincerely, VICTORIA R. 1855"

Benjamin stared at the words. 'Well, I am in awe,' he said catching his breath.

'And so am I,' she smiled. 'I have read it several times over.'

'And the brooch?' He looked at her searchingly.

'I have hidden it away, but you can see it later on. The letter and the brooch arrived together with an escort. I was alone when they entered the dormitory. It is such a beautiful brooch and it's engraved with the words: *"To Miss Florence Nightingale, as a mark of esteem and gratitude for her devotion towards the Queen's brave soldiers, from Victoria R. 1855"'*.

'A very important brooch I'm sure,' said Benjamin, admiringly. 'And it is well deserved. I long to see it.'

'And you will,' she said smiling, returning the letter to her pocket. 'Now, come, let us walk out and breathe the New Year air. I think we need to reflect on what has been achieved in our time at Scutari. And they passed by limitless graves, the dead silent in the earth, men who had lived and striven with their military forces, fighting for their countries, memories, hopes, passions surrendered to the timeless dark of infinity.

CHAPTER 29

Hearth And Home

The last of Florence's nurses were leaving Scutari and the last of
the patients. Benjamin Harrison had packed up his books and
was returning to his home in Edinburgh. Evie had returned to Dorset,
and Florence was preparing to return to Lea Hurst in Derbyshire, the
Nightingale summer residence. It was August, a glorious month in
England, especially Derbyshire with its wooded natural beauty,
streams and wild flowers, crumbling stone ruins and waterfalls.

Everyone was out and about talking about Miss Florence coming
home and wondering how they should greet this extraordinary
woman who the country had become so proud of. When would she
arrive? Ought they to organise gatherings and cheer? Nothing was
known precisely about her movements. But everyone knew that
Miss Nightingale would return very shortly. The Angel of Mercy
would once again walk their land. People talked wildly with each
other about what she had done, how it must have been, how
thankful they were that she'd survived, for it was quite a miracle,
her being slender and delicate, and so gracious too, it was hard to
believe that she'd walked amongst those wounded soldiers at

night-time with her lamp, fighting men damaged in body and soul from that terrible war, and she had calmed their spirits. And if anyone hadn't heard before, they had certainly heard now how Queen Victoria had sent Florence letters of gratitude and a beautiful brooch inscribed with wonderful words.

From where he sat in the parlour at Lea Hurst, Sidney Herbert looked out on the garden. It was a seat William enjoyed, but Sidney liked to sit there on his visits, and they'd all expected him that day. It was a day of rejoicing, and summer was evident all about them, in the grounds of the house and in the countryside. Sidney Herbert had enjoyed the ride to Lea Hurst, the wind whispering in his ears and the sun on his face. There was a lot going on at the War Office, tying up loose ends and all that but he was no longer War Minister and didn't intend involving himself in matters no longer his business. But as regards Florence, she would always be part his business and he was concerned to hear any news. The table by the door was heaped with letters and cards awaiting her return. The maid said she'd never stopped answering the door to messengers. It was all a bit hysterical, said Frances, and she hoped it would quieten down. Someone had even knocked to ask if Queen Victoria was in residence.

Inside the parlour sat William Nightingale, Frances Nightingale, Parthenope Nightingale and Sidney Herbert. Frances kept taking her shawl on and off nervously, Parthenope fiddled with the bows on her slippers, William stirred the fire and Sidney Herbert as usual stared out-side at the garden. It was a large room, but the chaise longue and the chairs were drawn close together, as was the way for afternoon tea. The atmosphere was charged with thought. What would happen to Florence once she was home, what would she do back in England? Her last let-ter to her father said she intended to visit the Queen to ask for a Royal

Commission into the disasters of the Crimean war, for much had to change. And there were stirrings in India against the rule of the British East India Company, which functioned as a sovereign power on behalf of the British Crown. Florence had said in a letter that from what she had heard and read there was a need to look into their hospital sanitization. Would that be her next project? The East India Company was in control of a large part of India now and had been trading as a private company since the 17th century. It was a diplomatic and military operation nowadays with soldiers called sepoys defending its trading centres. The sepoys were Muslims and Hindus, who'd been loyal to the British officers but there were those who suspected the British would prefer they were Christians, since a lot of Christian missionaries were arriving amongst them. Tensions were emerging due to all sorts of issues not least was the matter of a new type of rifle cartridge, wrapped in grease coated paper and said to be easier to load into the barrels of rifles, but rumours had spread that the grease came from cows and pigs which was deeply offensive to Muslims and Hindus. Issue followed issue and the noise was becoming a cacophony.

'The East India Company is having one or two problems,' Herbert said, frowning at the thought. 'There are sounds of rebellion.' Sidney Herbert turned to William Nightingale and reached for his whisky. 'It's not my problem now thank goodness!'

'And you haven't been well,' said Frances, searching his face worriedly. 'I heard you had . . .'

Herbert put out his hand as if he would stop her words. 'I am quite alright, dear Frances. Don't believe everything you hear. I've been rather overworked, that's all, as I imagine Florence has too. Together we have reached for the moon.'

There was a long pause, then William gazed at Herbert with a look of sincere admiration. 'No-one could have done more,' he said. 'You are both remarkable people.'

Herbert smiled and took a drink of his whisky. 'Florence is a sort of conqueror, you know, people are organising parties to celebrate her coming back home. What she has done at Scutari is amazing.'

'She doesn't like fuss,' said Frances, sitting on the chaise longue with Parthenope. 'She has saved many lives and given wounded soldiers hope for the future, we are all very proud, but she won't want applause. It isn't her way.'

'She has been the perfect nurse,' said Parthenope, 'and has reformed nursing completely. She has made it into highly respectable work. Remember before Mama, how people raised their eyebrows when we said that Flo was nursing?'

Frances Nightingale nodded in agreement. 'Oh, talk about raised eyebrows, and oh, what looks. How did we ever endure it? Now Florence has made nursing into something women might aspire to, a sort of *exalted* work. Oh yes, you would only get a brooch from the Queen for something outstanding.'

'No-one else has ever had a brooch like that from the Queen,' said her husband. 'Not ever. Flo has really done us proud.' He glanced at Sidney Herbert, who was staring down at the carpet. 'Indeed Sidney, I am a very proud father. And thank you for all you have done for her too.'

Parthenope sniffed. 'I can't imagine why she should want to take herself off and suffer like that though in that horrible Scutari hospital when she might have had a comfortable life with a husband and children, she preferred that war and that harsh rocky land to our lovely soft hills and flowers.' She gazed out on the Lea Hurst gardens. 'There is so much beauty in England just now. I just couldn't bear to be without it.' She shook her head confounded. '*All that horror,*' she whispered.

'Horror indeed Parthenope,' sighed Sidney Herbert. 'But it's over, and Florence has triumphed. I call it wonderful!'

Parthenope shrugged. 'Well I don't agree. She might have died.

You have no idea how we've worried about her, especially when she had the cholera. And poor Mrs Clarke is half deranged from it all. She has terrible dreams.'

'Florence has witnessed some dreadful things,' said William quietly, changing his position in his chair and gazing at the fire. 'I hope she can clear her mind of the worst, these horrors linger, you know. She will have to pick up her life in England now, which will not be easy. She told us in her letters how disturbed she was by what she discovered when she first arrived at Scutari, the lack of even elementary care in our army, the lack of true leadership. It was all quite a shock.' He glanced at Herbert again. 'There is a need for places of training where our military can be taught to be first class officers and commanders; we can't just let any old Tom, Dick and Harry manage the battlefield like that.' He laughed quietly. 'Fighting the French indeed. How ridiculous. I can't believe Raglan thought we were fighting the French.'

Herbert smiled and nodded. 'Yes, poor Raglan, what if he never said it? The soldiers only need a hint of something like that and the word spreads hell for leather. Dangerous stuff.'

'I'm glad Amelia's man is back home safe and sound,' said Frances. 'I thought he would never return when I heard he was fighting at Sebastopol. Her brother was killed, you know. I think the girl was expecting another bad letter.'

'I wonder what is happening in Constantinople now?' said William. 'So much devastation. Stratford, I suspect, will be on his way home.'

'I can't say I know what Stratford is up to,' said Herbert. 'We haven't corresponded of late, but I'm sure he'll be glad to see the back of that place. Who'd be Ambassador over there in the midst of that war?' For a moment or two they were thoughtful. Herbert continued. 'Constantinople was enormously rich once. Cities rise and fall. It's a strange old business.'

'And there are so many beautiful drawings and paintings of it,' Parthenope added spiritedly. 'I've seen quite a lot in the books in our library.'

'Yes, a very prosperous city,' Herbert continued, 'located, of course, by the Mediterranean Sea.'

'Those waterways are very much prized,' said William. 'But it appears the Tsar's fleet has had its day. We didn't want Russia getting into India, did we?'

'But so many men had to die,' said Parthenope.

'Florence saved a lot of lives,' Frances said straightening. 'And she says she intends to write books about what she had learned. Instruction books on nursing, that sort of thing, oh all kinds of writings. She'll probably make diagrams too, like those she draws on her letters. Wherever did she get her ideas?'

'She's a genius,' said William. 'Flo is very astute and discerning. Yes, she is quite remarkable.'

'I wonder if she will ever finish her novel,' Parthenope said thoughtfully. '*Cassandra*, I think she called it. I know she wanted to finish it. All that anger about the rights of women. I suspect a lot of women won't like it. She is on her hobby horse in that book, about how she is against marriage, how women become the slaves of men and children, all things like that.'

'She has always seen herself as having a life of service,' William said emphatically. 'Service to a cause is important.'

'And is not service to a family important?' said Parthe. 'I love Flo dearly, but I have to say there are times I don't understand her. And it's such a relief to know she is coming home and can be normal with us. Not long now and we'll have her back here safe and sound.'

'She is right in what she says though, Parthe,' her mother said thoughtfully, 'in that women can't even have a half of an hour to themselves for fear they are taking time they should give to others.'

'Is that what she says?' William looked at her straight.

'Well, words to that effect,' his wife said awkwardly. 'She is very much against the domestic life and thinks it limits our intelligence.'

'So has living with me limited your intelligence, my dear?' he asked, looking hurt and confused. Frances worked faster with her needle, trying to finish embroidering a flower on a napkin. 'Tell me my dear, what would you rather be doing now, this minute, instead of embroidering that flower on there?'

'I have no wish to be difficult, my dear,' she said embarrassed. She turned to Sidney Herbert. 'Do forgive me Sidney. You are only too aware of what Flo is like; we don't need to tell you. She is very much her own person and thinks that families *use* people, not for what they are, but for how they might be used. She says it means women can't learn about the world in the way that men do. She writes about it a lot in her letters. She often got angry at the way the officers tried to boss her.'

'But that is the nature of the military, my dear,' said William. 'They are in the business of bossing.'

'I believe it will be in that novel,' said Parthe. 'Oh, all will be revealed in there.'

Sidney Herbert was quiet, listening. They were all feeling tense, but were animated too by the thought of Florence returning. It was difficult to know what to do by way of celebration, for she had said to keep things calm, she didn't want a party or anything like that.

'She'll just want to greet us quietly, I suppose,' said William. 'Her mind will no doubt be very different from what we remember after what she's experienced. We must give her time to settle down. Best not ask too many questions. Just let the house absorb her for a while, and the environs, you know.'

They all looked around. It seemed the house understood.

CHAPTER 30

Becoming Florence Nightingale

Florence went through the woods towards Lea Hurst, her family's summer home. She crossed the little stream she knew so well, stopping a while to remember. It was such a glorious day. Best not remember it all, she thought, hearing the song of the stream flying across the stones, same song, same place, same feeling. Too much to recall, sometimes the heart couldn't cope. It was the very same sky, and there they were, the very same forget-me-knots covering the banks. She touched the necklace beneath her collar; she had worn it always, whatever her spirit. She stared at the glistening water, hearing its eternal memories. She had lost herself at Scutari. It was less than two years yet she scarcely knew herself now.

She moved away from the bank, turning her eyes to the slope she now had to climb. She had an odd sense of something in her deepest self leaving her. '*Come back!*' she whispered to the trees and the hillside. '*Do not desert me!*' For a moment or two she felt as if she couldn't move. A light breeze crept across her face, and she imbibed the scent of the grass, the beautiful scent of the countryside she knew so well. 'I must rest,' she murmured, looking for somewhere to sit. They would know she was on her way; she had sent her things on ahead and had instructed the man to tell them she wanted to walk through the August woods and would be with them mid afternoon. She'd declined wholeheartedly the government's suggestion she travel on a British man-of-war and be greeted in the way they felt befitting. She laughed to herself. A British man-of-war! She'd written to Sidney Herbert to say she would travel in private. She didn't want anything sensational, she was simply Florence Nightingale, a nurse, in her regular grey dress with the white lace collar. What could be better than to travel by train incognito and take in everything she saw without anyone interrupting her pleasure?

After some minutes, she stood and walked on. But climbing the hill felt harder than before when she'd run to the top like a mountain goat in times gone by. She stopped again to catch her breath. She had gone to Scutari and had done what needed to be done. Now she intended to write about what she'd learned. Again, she walked on. Pain shot down her limbs. She stopped again. But she wasn't afraid. She needed to take more exercise and resolved to take a walk each day, just a couple of miles at first, then more later on. She'd get better. Yes, that is how she would do it. She would eat good food and take walks in the Derbyshire air. And she would ride her horse across the hills. Her father had said the horse was waiting and knew she was coming. It was hardly likely, but she knew he could invent on the truth if he thought it of good purpose.

She stopped to look at the little cottages on her way, wondering how the families were faring who lived there and what they would think of her now, how they would greet her. But she would not visit them today. There would be plenty of time later on. She passed the orchards, the trees heavy with fruit, the farmyards with the barking dogs and clucking hens that people kept for their livelihoods. Her feet sank in wildflowers, how she loved the velvety grass of the hills! She wanted to take off her shoes and feel the grass beneath her feet, but she must walk a bit further and quicken her pace. There were a few more streams to negotiate before she could see Lea Hurst. She walked on slowly, enjoying the landscape, which seemed strangely empty just then. She touched familiar boulders, familiar trees, as if she were renewing her acquaintance with them.

Holloway village in Derbyshire, where she'd lived for much of her life, was as lovely as ever. She gazed all about her. Nothing seemed to have changed. It was scarcely two years she thought again, but two years at Scutari felt like a lifetime; it was almost as if time had stopped while she'd been there. Here time seemed eternal. She thought of what she might do to create the improvements in nursing she knew must happen, how she might help the ordinary people care for their sick families. She imagined the drawings, the graphs she would make, the way she would present her knowledge. Only the rich could pay for healthcare, it didn't seem fair, there had to be a better system. There was also a need for trained nurses to be present in the workhouses, where people often fell sick. She'd made notes of her ideas and plans. And she must try to visit the Queen, who she hoped could persuade the government to arrange a Commission to investigate the healthcare of the army and analyze the data she'd meticulously gathered together. Sidney had informed her that the Nightingale Fund, created by the general public, had now raised £44,000; it was a vast sum of money and would help to educate nurses and midwives, buy paper, pens and ink.

She stopped on the bank of the Derwent river and leant against a tree, her heart pounding with effort. Only another two miles and she'd be home. The thought brought tears to her eyes. Her trunk would be there in the hall, along with her precious writings and the clothes she had worn at Scutari. She had so much to read and write about. She'd heard that the health system in India needed improvement too, the British ran the hospitals in the Raj and they were in need of a different structure. There was important work to be done in the hospitals there for she'd heard some awful stories and must ask to speak with the Viceroys. She was learning now to see the value of what she'd achieved, rather than feeling deflated by what wasn't possible. Life would always take a shape of its own, she'd decided. However carefully it was managed, it was trying, exasperating, and yet it was also quite beautiful. She was lighter of heart, and things that had perplexed her deeply bothered her less than before as she came to the top of the hill. Life without war was wonderful. Joy suffused through her blood, the joy of being alive!

Further ahead in the sunlight, she saw that a familiar figure came walking towards her quickly. It was her father.

'And so you come home Florence Nightingale!' he cried, his arms wide open in welcome. 'I knew the path you would take and I knew where to meet you!'

'Father!' she cried, running towards him, 'I must breathe you in! I've missed you so much!' She fell into his warm embrace. 'Ah, the scent of your hair, the shine in those pale blue eyes. My dear Papa, I am in Holloway and I'm alive!' Her heart was full of Holloway, for its people, its birdsong, its river, and her family.

'My precious Florence, you look strong, but I fear you are far too pale. He looked her over carefully. 'Your mother is bound to notice. You need to partake of some better food than you've been having. Some of your favourite dishes are waiting in the larder. I'm relieved you have arrived home safely. You are wise to have dodged the crowds. You are quite an astonishing woman, my dear.' He put his arm around her shoulder and drew her close. 'I am completely overwhelmed by your achievements. It's hard to believe you are here and are not some sort of eidolon trying to trick me! Come let us hurry, they are all waiting back home. Oh, Flo, was there ever a day like this?' His laughter rang about the hills. It was one of those glorious summer afternoons the two of them knew so well.

ACKNOWLEDGEMENTS

I've enjoyed writing this book immensely. It grew within the time of the Covid-19 epidemic when the streets were still and silent and everyone was staying at home. Much of my life was lived through my phone and my computer, which meant I could delve freely into Florence's history, books dropping in my porch like autumn leaves, my browser forever busy on the Internet, and information coming down the email from communicators who had time to share ideas.

I would like to thank friends who have spurred me on with their enthusiasm and interest; they know who they are. Doctor Robert Duckett, in particular, as a literary editor and librarian has been most inspiring, reading my chapters as they emerged and making valuable comments.

Florence Nightingale was a complex woman with a profound certainty of purpose. She had a singular kind of intelligence and the story might have been longer, but I've attempted to add as much as I can about her life and times without making the book too heavy. I like to imagine my readers slipping it into their bags to read when they feel inclined, something easy to carry, easy to open and easy to read.

I am thankful to my son, John, for always enhancing my knowledge in so many areas of life. We talked about Lady Elizabeth Butler and her marvellous paintings of military action and I imagined her visiting Florence to talk about war. Then I eerily discovered that the scene I was about to create had actually occurred in reality and the story began to unfold like a strange materialization. I hope you can feel her presence as you read, and imbibe some of this woman's extraordinary essence as I did myself.

Wendy Bardsley